Other Books by Sherrie Hansen

Night and Day
Daybreak

Maple Valley Trilogy:
Book 1: Stormy Weather
Book 2: Water Lily
Book 3: Merry Go Round

Love Notes

Wildflowers of Scotland Novels:
Thistle Down *(Prequel Novella)*
Book 1: Wild Rose
Book 2: Blue Belle
Book 3: Shy Violet
Book 4: Sweet William
Book 5: Golden Rod

Wildflowers of Ireland Mystery:
Seaside Daisy

Wildflowers of Bohemia Mystery:
Plum Tart Iris

Wildflowers of Scotland Mystery:
Ragged Robin

Highland Heather
A Wildflowers of Scotland Mystery

By
Sherrie Hansen

Published by Blue Belle Books
St. Ansgar, IA

Blue Belle Books

www.BlueBelleBooks.com

PO Box 205, St. Ansgar, Iowa 50472

This book is a work of fiction. Names, characters, locations and events are either a product of the author's imagination, fictitious or used fictitiously. Any resemblance to any event, locale or person, living or dead, is purely coincidental.

Copyright © 2022 by Sherrie Hansen

All rights reserved, including the right of reproduction in whole or part in any format.

Cover Design: Sherrie Hansen
Cover Photo: Sherrie Hansen

Manufactured in the United States of America
ISBN: 979-8-4386-7392-7

Dedication:

To the doctors, nurses, aids, and physical therapists in Florida and Iowa who patched me back together after I broke my back and helped me get my strength back so I could return to my life at the Blue Belle Inn and travel to Scotland once more.

To my husband, Mark Decker, who not only shares my love of travel, but encourages me and cheers me on through thick and thin, good times and bad. I love you.

Inspiration for Highland Heather:

*Staying at a B&B on a farm in the Scottish Highlands that makes the most delicious meat pies and has a perfectly wonderful, most-comfortable-bed-ever (even when you have a broken back.)

*Seeing the heather bloom in the Highlands while on a trip to Scotland.

In a stony field in Minnesota
A blushing bluebell stood alone.
Now you'll find her in the Highlands,
Where her heart has found its home.

Glossary of Scottish terms:

Some of the older generation of Scots in Highland Heather speak with a heavier Scottish accent than their younger counterparts. No worries. Ye'll catch on fast.

ken = know

bairn = baby

ye = you (pronounced with a soft e, more like yeh)

awright = all right

nae = no, not

dinnae, cannae, wouldnae, etc. = don't or didn't, can't, wouldn't, etc – the Scottish equivalents of our contractions

Chapter 1

"You're sure this is really what you want to do?" Heather McPhearson took one last look around Rabbit Hill Lodge and hugged her mum goodbye. "I'm only going to be a few hours away."

"But with everything that's going on, and all the stress you're under..."

"The Highlands is where I want to be. I promised William and Lyndsie. Running the farm is a dream come true. All those cute little lambs and hairy coo – it's perfect for me."

"Oh, Nathan," her mum whispered, looking at Heather's da. "This is so hard."

"It'll be fine, Violet." Her da turned to Heather and snuggled her into a hug that enveloped her like lamb's wool, spun to a sheen and soft as a sweater. His eyes were shining when he said, "I always hoped you'd find your life's work here in Scotland, dear daughter. Every year when you set off to spend your summer vacation with William and Lyndsie in Blue River, I worried that you'd fall in love with some All-American, Minnesota-born-and-bred farm boy and never come back."

"Uncle William tried his best, but Aunt Lyndsie was quick to foil his every attempt." She gave her da a final squeeze and pulled away. "Nobody good enough for me. I think Mum paid her off." She pushed the worry that she was too Scottish for American men and too American for the Scots out of her mind. But it would be back. Even with all the uncertainties about her health, and the variables that lay ahead of her at McKnight Farms, that much she knew for sure.

"I know William trusts you implicitly, but the farm is so far from everywhere, and winter will be here before you know it." Her mother didn't appear all that doubtful, just concerned.

"Uncle William and Aunt Lyndsie have taught me well." It was odd, seeing as she was related to neither of them by blood, that she could almost swear she had inherited the McKnight's business acumen, William's knack for husbandry, Lyndsie's gourmet cooking abilities, and both of their love for the Highlands and the coos and sheep bred to thrive in the harsh climate.

One more quick round of hugs and kisses and she was tucked into her tiny car and on the road to Aberdeenshire. A furnished country house awaited her, so she had only to bring her clothes, shoes, jewelry, and a few personal affects. And of course, a few of her mother's paintings to brighten up the place.

She was about an hour east of Dornie and Eilean Donan Castle when she heard sirens dead ahead. She hadn't been paying attention to the road signs or her exact location, but she couldn't be that far from Fort William. At least if there were injuries, they wouldn't be far from help.

She came to a stop at the end of a long line of autos about a quarter mile – maybe a half mile from the scene of the accident.

She tuned in to Radio Scotland, but nothing good was on. She looked for a CD but didn't find anything that interested her. She wasn't in the mood for the Red

Hot Chili Pipers. The emotion of saying goodbye and leaving home had given her a slight headache. She sat quietly for a few minutes, but gave up. Doing nothing was one thing she was terrible at. She had no patience.

She started to catalog the things she needed to do when she got to the farm. She'd already familiarized herself with the sheep she'd be tending – a 300 head flock containing Highland Mules, Scottish Blackface, and North Country Cheviots. They were perfect for the natural pasture and heather moorland they grazed, producing an excellent tasting lamb.

She was already familiar with the Highlanders, Belted Gallways, and Aberdeen Angus cattle from working on William's farm in Minnesota, but she felt sure she still had much to learn.

Sometime before Christmas, she planned to add a small flock of bronze and white turkeys to be reared free range to sell to local customers. And of course, she would work toward her main contribution, which was to update and expand their butchery and larder to increase the volume and quality of products on the farm. She already had several ideas and had been practicing on some great new meat pie recipes they could produce and market with McKnight beef, lamb, poultry, and hopefully pork. She'd miss the kitchen at Rabbit Hill Lodge, and working with her mum and Lyndsie. But she couldn't have everything.

She could almost hear her mum saying, "You'd have a much better chance of meeting someone if you stayed around Dornie. McKnight Farms is so remote. How are you ever going to..."

"All it takes is one." Heather knew full well what her doctors had said – if she was going to have a baby, she needed to do it now. Heather still couldn't wrap her head around being given a deadline for meeting and marrying someone so she could make a baby while her womb was still viable. What a crazy situation.

She pushed the improbability of being able to make it happen on a timeline from her mind and tried to think happy thoughts. She was sure she would make new friends and even find a new family of sorts to surround herself in Aberdeenshire. William had already met several of the neighbours and assured her that they were eager to welcome her to the neighbourhood.

She looked up and saw a policeman waving her to the far left shoulder adjacent to the scene of the accident. A policewoman was using a handheld blower to move glass and metal debris from the pavement. They would use the woman to do the clean-up, and the man to direct traffic, eh? So typical.

She moved slowly ahead as the trickle of autos they were allowing to proceed crept along, finally reaching a normal speed. On her way again.

Her heart was singing as she hugged the hills and valleys along Old Military Road. Her car slowed down as the road grew steeper. She climbed higher and higher in elevation as she neared the crest of Cairn O'Mounth. The intense, unfiltered sunlight at the higher elevations would bring out heather blossoms earlier than they bloomed in the valleys and the islands, where the hills were surrounded by mist and shaded by the mountains on three sides.

Her breath caught in her throat as she crested the hill. Before her lay a carpet of rosy purple heather in shades from deep to pale, dusty to brilliant. The blossoms glistened in the sunlight. Bumblebees dipped their wicks, scattering pollen into showers of fairy dust that rained down in the sunlight. She could see a deep river cutting through the valley, tall peaks in shades of blue layered against the horizon. She'd always wanted to see the hills in the Highlands purple with heather, but she'd spent her Augusts in Minnesota, or tied to Rabbit Hill Lodge. The heather peaked during their busiest time of year, when children were on break, families were traveling, and buses filled with pensioners were rolling in from Glasgow and Edinburgh to see Skye and Eilean Donan Castle and enjoy a made-from-scratch, traditional Scottish meal.

She stopped and took a few photos of the shifting rays of sunlight floating over the hills. In contrast to her talented mother, Heather was all thumbs with a paintbrush and artistically challenged by the mere thought of putting colors on canvas. But her photos had their own form of artistry. She knew instinctively what to focus on, and how to crop and tweak and make them beautiful.

She kept driving, closer and closer to William's newly purchased farm, glancing at her GPS periodically to make sure she stayed on track. She knew the general way to the ranch, and William had given her verbal directions, complete with landmarks to watch for.

She glanced down one more time as she approached an intersection to see which way she should turn and discovered an error message. Connection lost. She slowed and started to fumble through the papers on the passenger seat. She knew she'd jotted down the basics somewhere. Where were they? She had to be close. She could see some wee lambs and Belted Gallway cattle and all the breeds she knew William raised.

That was when she heard a pop. Her auto careened out of control and ground to a sickening stop.

She remembered hitting a bump in the road, a deep

pothole just on the edge of a passing place as she'd come over the ridge. But that alone shouldn't have popped the tyre. She had a quick vision of the smashed glass at the scene of the accident on her way to Fort William.

She looked around and tried to figure out what to do. She was going to have to move the car out of the center of the single track road or no one would be able to get by. Knowing how most Scots drove, she'd likely be crashed head on because of course they would assume she was going to move out of the way at the last minute by pulling into a passing place. Driving on single track roads in Scotland was like one big game of chicken.

The thought had just left her mind when she saw a lorry barreling down the road at her. By the look of it, they either didn't know there was no place for her to get out of the way, or didn't care.

She was just ready to jump into the field at the side of the road when she heard brakes screeching and cusses emitting from the open window and the clatter of whatever was in the back end of the truck shifting and slamming into the walls of the lorry. What a mess! She leaped to the side, fully expecting her car and all her belongings to be pulverized on impact; then, to burst into flames.

"Stop!" She screamed. She held her breath. She prayed. She sweated off a good pound or two. She made promises to God that even she knew she wouldn't keep if only He would spare her auto.

Miracle of miracles, the lorry roared to a stop just millimeters from her front bumper.

That was where the good news stopped.

"What in tarnation are ye doing stopped in the middle of the road?" The man leaped out from the lorry and came charging in her direction, his face furious and his teeth bared.

"I have a flat tyre."

"That's what happens when ye dinnae do regular maintenance checks on yer auto."

"They're brand new. I came upon the scene of an accident earlier."

"Never EVER drive o'er broken glass."

"I know that! I drove exactly where the police directed me. This is not my fault."

"Well, it certainly is nae mine!" The man yelled. "Yet it's my road that's blocked, and me late getting to my chores. If I dinnae get home soon, I'll nae get dinner, and if ye think I be mad now, ye've nae seen nothing."

What reason did he have to be so mad? So he'd had to brake his vehicle and stop. She was the one with a perfectly awful flat tyre, the one who'd almost lost everything she owned on the whole earth, the one who'd very nearly had a heart attack, the one who'd broken the heel on her favorite pair of shoes jumping into a hedgerow. What was wrong with this man? She'd never met anyone so rude.

"I dinnae have time for this," he stewed. "Is there nae someone you can call?"

She hadn't grabbed her mobile when she got out of the car.

"My Uncle William might be at the farm."

"William McKnight?" The man thunked himself on the forehead and groaned. "Nay. It cannae be. Lord and saints preserve us."

Great. The man was obviously not a fan of McKnight Farms.

"Ye dinnae know how to change yer own flat tyre?"

"I think I helped change one once when I was..."

"Saints preserve us. Ye've got nae business even

driving around the Highlands if ye dinnae ken—"

She finally found her voice. "Will you please stop? Throwing a hissy fit over something that is completely accidental is not helping anything. I am not trying to ruin your day and I would appreciate it if you would help me find a solution instead of yelling at me!"

The man seemed to be shocked beyond words,

She heard applause coming from behind the lorry. What?

"I could hear you screaming all the way from the lower pasture, Da. You're scaring the ewes, ye old crabbit! Besides, getting so worked up is bad for your heart." A younger, more handsome version of the old crabbit turned to her and extended his hand. "Brodie McBryde. Much as I hate to admit it, this is my da, Munro McBryde."

She smiled politely and tried not to roll her eyes. She ignored her better instincts and took his hand. "Heather McPhearson, niece of William McKnight. Your father seems to know him."

"Ah. Our new American neighbour."

"I may have American parents, but I'm Scottish born and raised."

"Really."

"Really."

Their eyes locked like two rams intent on having the same ewe. What was going on, she didn't quite understand, but she let him look her over without breaking her gaze.

"On your way to the farm then?"

At second glance, the man looked nothing like the old crabbit. His features were less craggy, and his hair was much thicker – a rich, wavy auburn. His eyes were the color of bluebells, and he was well over six feet tall, with the broadest shoulders she'd ever seen.

She tried to regain her composure. "I'm going to be managing things once my Uncle William leaves."

"Really."

"Really."

Brodie continued to stare at her. His gaze wasn't hostile like his father's, but it wasn't exactly welcoming either. He was sizing her up awright, and it made her more uncomfortable than she wanted to admit. The old man looked like he was enjoying the show, but kept his mouth shut. Probably trying not to laugh at her and her fine showing in her new neighbourhood.

What did it matter what either of them thought of her?

Brodie looked her straight in the eyes. "You need some help?"

There it was. Much as she hated to admit it, she did need help.

She stood tall and tried to keep her pride about her as best she could. "I can manage just fine if ye're in nae hurry. If ye want the lane unblocked sooner rather than later, ye might want to lend a hand." Her Scottish brogue was as thick, and true, and spot on as the best of them if and when she wanted to speak like an old coffin dodger. They didn't like Americans? Well, she had dual citizenship, as much Scot as American. Now, if they didn't like women. There wasn't much she could do to change that, and most certainly didn't want to.

Brodie lifted the hatch of her car. "We're going to have to unload the boot to get at the spare tyre."

Oh, no. She hadn't thought of that. Lord, give me strength. She'd spent hours cramming every nook and cranny of her car with everything she needed to set up her household in the high country. This was not the first impression she'd wanted to make, not the introduction to the neighbourhood she'd hoped for. From now on, she'd be perceived as the needy, incompetent, clueless woman down the road. Exactly the kind of reputation she did not need.

Brodie reached for the biggest of her three suitcases and lifted it from the boot. She watched as the Victoria's Secret bag she'd used to pack her lingerie toppled from its perch at the top of the pile. She tried to catch it, but she was about two seconds too late. Brodie turned just as she was outstretching her arm and bopped her in the pelvis with the suitcase. The Victoria's Secret bag fluttered over their heads and tipped. Her panties and bras rained down on them in shades of lavender, rose, and sage green. All of her favorites. The bag was full of the things she'd worn her last few days at home and washed at the very last minute so she would start out with all of her clothes fresh and clean. By that time, the suitcases had not only been too full, but carefully packed in the boot. The bag had made perfect sense. She always saved bags for reuse – a pretty bag from a lingerie store for her pretty lingerie. Why oh why couldn't she have chosen one from Runnings or Fleet Farm or Menards? Not that anyone with a brain and an eye for the finer things in life wouldn't have figured out that her lingerie was from a place like Victoria's Secret even without the telltale bag.

When she looked up, her cheeks were flaming and Brodie was grabbing handfuls of underwear from the hedgerow and cramming them into the bag. The smile on his face might have been priceless in a different time and place, but as it was, she was mortified. She couldn't even force herself to look at Mungo. Or Magnus or Mason or Mango or whatever the heck the father's name was.

"Thank you," she was finally able to whisper through a throat clumped with badly crumpled pride.

"Don't worry about it," Brodie said, his voice as smooth and gentle as hers was thick and globby. "Anything else not zipped up tight that I should watch out for?"

Her mind flew to a few other personal items she'd tucked away at the last minute. Thank God – she grabbed her Betsy-Tacy bag from its place by the left side window even though the tote had a zipper on top and wouldn't have spilled her secrets anyway. She didn't want either of them anywhere near it.

Brodie removed another suitcase and an old trunk while she tucked her treasures in the front seat with her purse. It must appear to them as though she was a stereotypical female basket case with no useful purpose on earth except to cause trouble. She could only hope Brodie had a handful of smart, sassy sisters, or a strong, independent mother and aunts to grant him a little understanding and shed a little grace on her feminine proclivities – which did not mean she was not extremely qualified and perfectly capable of overseeing a farm operation.

That was when she became aware of the stress sweat pouring from her upper body. The sun was high overhead and hot as blazes. It was still August after all. She'd worn a long-sleeved shirt made from some sort of light thermal fabric, no doubt because her always-too-cold mother had convinced her it would be chilly beyond her endurance in the mountaintop climes of the highlands. Her mother had reminded her that Heather was used to living in a valley lined by lochs that kept the temperature moderate. It was so like her mother to chide her about things that she didn't need to be reminded about at all. And why was she mad at her mother now of all times? It was Brodie and Mango that she should be railing against. But they were helping her – Brodie quite willingly and with growing enthusiasm by the looks of it. Maybe his battery had gotten charged by her underthings. Who knew? Mungo was acting just as disgruntled as ever.

Almost everything had been removed from her auto, the flap lifted and the spare tire removed. They were using the jack to take off the flat tyre.

Brodie looked over his shoulder. "A wee spare tyre like this one won't last long on the roads around here. It may not even make it down the lane that leads to the farm."

"I was going to say I hope ye're good at dodging potholes," Magnus said. "But ye're obviously not."

"Like you're one to talk, Da. You're not even supposed to be driving."

She sighed.

"I can fix the tyre in my shop if you'd like."

Right. She wanted to be indebted to Brodie McBryde for fixing her tyre in addition to changing the tyre and helping her unload and reload her auto.

"Is there a garage in town I can take it to tomorrow? I don't want to impose on you."

"Town is ten miles away over bumpy, single track roads. You can try, but you'll likely end up broken down again, blocking the road."

"Fine. Take the tyre." She sighed. Could she be any more humiliated? For all she knew, William had a shop or a staff member who knew how to patch a tyre. But the last thing she wanted to do was to have to call Brodie tomorrow and tell him she needed to have him fix the tyre after all. Better to admit defeat, get the inevitable over with, and try to move on.

Brodie seemed to sense her defeatist attitude. "It'll be fine once you get settled in. The Highlands are much more than a string of bad roads. You'll love it here once you're over the hard part of learning about what to do and not do."

"I'm sure you're right."

"William will see to it, make sure you're comfortable with everything before he leaves you alone."

Munro – Was that his name? – snorted.

Fine. A vote of no confidence. But it was only one vote. The other neighbours would undoubtedly be very supportive, encouraging, and happy to have her in their midst. And certainly the staff members who had agreed to stay on were there because they were looking forward to progress, to seeing what she was going to do to make the farm grow and thrive. With their support and confidence, they could accomplish anything. Her confidence began to creep up incrementally as she surveyed the hills and valleys surrounding the single track road. There had to be one bad apple in every bushel. Just because Munro had a bad attitude didn't mean the rest of Aberdeenshire would.

She'd already pledged to find a good church in nearby Alford, check out the area restaurants and cafes, attend art shows and craft fairs, and maybe join a garden club. There were all kinds of ways to meet people in the neighbourhood, to win friends and meet influencers. She could do this. She would do this.

Brodie's well-muscled back rippled as he tightened the lug nuts on the spare tyre. "That should do it."

"Thank you."

"Now to get everything back in its place so the hatch

will close."

"Good luck." She felt herself slipping back down into pessimistic mode. "I mean, quite honestly, it took me hours. Hopefully I can kind of remember how things were stacked."

Brodie stood and squeezed her shoulder after looking at his father to make sure the older man wasn't looking. "It'll all work out. I promise."

"Thanks." Maybe she'd found her first friend, or an ally at least.

A half hour later, she was driving down the lane to the newly christened McKnight Farms very, very slowly. The potholes were as deep as shallow wells.

It's going to be fine, she tried to convince herself. A golden eagle soared overhead. She could hear the plaintive moos of the hairy coos and the baaing of new lambs and their protective mothers, the trickling of a stream, the sound of the wind whistling over the moors.

It was gong to be fine.

#

Brodie knelt down and hefted Heather's tyre to his work table. He would visually inspect the tyre first since she seemed convinced that she had picked up a shard of glass at the scene of an accident back near Fort William. If he didn't find anything, he would spray the tire with water diluted with dishwashing soap and see if a bubble led him to the leak.

"Dinnae waste yer time," his father griped. "We've got more important things to tend to. The black face ewe could be delivering right now. Have ye even been out to the pasture since that American woman took up our whole afternoon with her fancy underwear? She deserves everything she got for driving a car that's completely unsuitable for highland country living."

"We're her closest neighbours. What alternative do I have? Ignoring her wouldn't be a good way to welcome her to Alford."

"Well, if ye fix her tyre, at least she'll be able to leave when the time comes. Shouldnae take long if ye ask me. The woman has nae clue what it's like to live in the mountains. Her fancy underwear attested to that fact straight away."

"So now you're judging people on how sturdy their underwear is?"

"She'll freeze to death if that's all she has in her fancy suitcases."

"I'm sure she'll buy some thermal underwear if she needs to, or layer some warm woolens over the top. Probably already has some packed away in one of those big suitcases so she has them handy come winter."

Brodie ran his fingers over the tyre, slowly in case he ran into a shard of glass like she'd claimed he would. "Maybe she's just hot-blooded. Maybe she doesn't get cold like you do."

"Dinnae be getting ideas, if ye ken what's good for ye, lad. If I see her broken down on the road again, I'm going to keep driving."

Brodie pulled out a sliver of tempered windshield glass from the tread of the tyre and put in a jar. "What? Right through her? Good grief, Da. She seemed nice enough."

"Dinnae let her suck ye into her drama. William McKnight stole the Morris' farm out from under me with his fancy talk and grand American money. Dashed yer dreams and mine in one fell swoop. Ye'll do nothing to encourage her. The sooner she fails and runs home to

America, the sooner we can swoop in and get back what we lost."

Brodie's dream was to use his degree to work as a bridge building engineer like he'd planned, but it didn't seem like a good time to bring it up.

"Good grief, Da. She said she grew up near Dornie. She was born in Inverness. Is American blood a different color than Scottish?"

"Nay, but if her blood is the color of those underthings, she's nae more capable of running a farm than the man in the moon."

"I guess we'll soon find out."

"Just dinnae do anything to encourage her. We'll nae be helping her solve any more problems. I forbid it." His da rocked back on his heels with his legs locked.

Brodie wanted to remind his da that if Brodie wasn't the kind of person who was inclined to help people, he'd be in Edinburgh working at the engineering firm he had loved, earning big bucks and still dating Barbara. But he didn't. Family was family, and his da's heart attack had warranted giving up his dreams and coming home. Temporarily anyway. When a person set his mind to being helpful, it extended to everyone and every situation. He couldn't turn the helpful switch off and on at will.

Conversely, he hoped Heather wasn't the needy, constantly-getting-into-trouble-sort-of-woman he feared she might be. He didn't want to be like his da and leap to a negative conclusion about her based on one brief meeting, but on the other hand, he was already busier than anyone deserved to be, and he really didn't have time to be getting her out of messes.

Chapter 2

Heather watched as William cleared his throat to indicate it was time to stop the chit-chat and bring the meeting to order.

"Gentlemen, I'd like to introduce my niece, Heather McPhearson. She's spent every summer working at my ranch in Minnesota since she was ten years old and I must say, she's actually more like my daughter, since I don't have one of my own. I taught her everything I know, and I have complete confidence that, with your help, she has the ability to bring McKnight Farms to a new level of excellence.

She looked around the room. Bless William's heart, but he might be laying it on a little thick. She would rather he'd led with her degree in Farm Management, and the culinary and food production experience she'd had at Rabbit Hill Lodge instead of the family ties he and she shared. But what was done was done. She'd have to prove her worthiness to the men of McKnight Farms the old-fashioned way.

"Heather, why don't you say a few words?"

She caught one of the herdsman giving the slaughter man – Hank, wasn't it? – a look. That didn't bode well.

She stood. She wasn't always happy about being 5 foot 11 inches tall with broad shoulders and long, slender legs, but she did pose a commanding presence, and today, she needed all the help she could get.

"Hi, guys. Thanks for welcoming me on board. You've done a great job of laying the stepping stones and paving the way for success. I believe that together, we can make this farm even better than it already is, grow our offerings and maximize our revenues, which will help all of us achieve our professional goals – maybe even win a few awards. I'm counting on your support. With your knowledge of the farm, I'm confident we can raise the best cattle and sheep in Scotland right here at McKnight Farms."

There was a long silence and finally, just as she was taking her seat, a smattering of polite, maybe even half-hearted applause worked its way around the room. She grimaced a little – on the inside. Maybe the purple and green streaks she's put in her hair hadn't been a good idea after all.

She tried to ignore the hostility emanating from one or two of the men. It was palpable. They certainly weren't the majority, but hard feelings spread like cancer, and she couldn't afford to let bitterness or jealousy take root.

"What exactly are ye proposing we change?"

She hadn't said anything specific about doing things differently than they'd been doing for who knows how many years, but the men weren't stupid. They knew if her aim was to make things better, and grow the business in new directions, there were bound to be changes.

"What's wrong with the way we been doing it? No sense fixing something unless it's broke."

"The way you've been doing things is very admirable, and it worked well for you for many years." She didn't go into the numbers, or the fact that the farm had been hemorrhaging money for almost a decade. "But the world is a different place, and if we want to remain viable, we have to change with it."

"What if we dinnae want to change?" Hank asked.

"Aye. We're a pretty content lot. We ken what we're doing and we give it our all. No need to mess with success when ye've already got a good thing going."

She could see William shifting in his seat, looking as uncomfortable as she felt.

"We don't necessarily want things to change – although I think I have some really good ideas that I hope you can get behind. It's more that people – our customers – the consumers – have a different set of expectations than they had a few years ago. If we don't please them, we'll have no business. People are eating differently, shying away from beef and pork, eating more poultry and seafood. They're trying to be healthier, and the overly fat beef that's been marketed in the past has gotten a bad reputation.

"That's where the Highland Coo's modern beef carcass comes in. We all know that the Highland's lean, well-marbled, flesh ensures tenderness and succulence with a very distinctive flavour. But what most people don't know is that slow-maturing Highland beef is extremely healthy and nutritious with lower levels of fat and cholesterol and a higher protein and iron content than other beef. Studies in the US have verified that Highland Beef is 38% lower in fat content and 4% lower in cholesterol than steaks from local supermarkets, criteria increasingly demanded by today's market."

She stole a glance at William, who looked more comfortable, even proud. A wee bit of warmth stole into her shoulders. She started to relax.

One of the men actually smiled. "If ye want things to

change, ye have to do something different."

"Kiss ass." The grumbling came from the very back of the room. There was a moment of dead silence before the room erupted into whispering and cynical sounding comments, some spoken under their breath, and others as complaints loud enough to be heard throughout the room.

"Like it or not, Heather knows what she's talking about." William stood, projecting a blustery, upbeat attitude. But even he seemed nervous. "She knows the younger generation, what they want, how they think, not only in Scotland, but across the UK, on the mainland, and in America. How many of you know what today's young people think about anything, especially why they eat what they eat?"

His comments brought on a round of laughter. She smiled and sat back and let William work his magic. She hadn't really expected the men at the farm to welcome her with open arms and hang on her every suggestion, especially after getting a taste of Munro McBryde. But Uncle William had been so sure they were excited to welcome a new manager. She should have known better than to believe his wishful musings.

A voice cut through the clatter. "So why dinnae ye tell us aboot one of these ideas of yers. I mean specifics."

She stood. "I'd like to introduce a herd of Red Duroc grunters. Pork producers in the United States have done an excellent job of promoting a new, lean, healthy generation of pork. They call it the new white meat. Pork products are selling better than ever before, in part because the price is lower than what people are paying for beef. Why lose out on the latest trend when we can capitalize on it instead?"

"And what are we going to do with pork?"

"I'd like to add a Pork and Bleu Cheese option to our line of meat pies using our own, home-grown grunters. Add a little garlic, mushrooms, black pepper, cream, and of course, the Stilton cheese, and you've got a pie that's pure gold. The flavors marry well with the pork. People will see it as unique and give it a try."

"Why Red Durocs?" Another cynical-sounding voice asked.

"Durocs do well both indoors and outdoors. Since we don't have a hog barn, I want a breed that will do well in a pasture. Durocs excel in both warm and cool weather, and have been successfully raised in northern climates. Durocs have excellent feed efficiency. They can take a small amount of feed and turn it into a large amount of muscle mass. They're prolific breeders, good mothers, and easy to handle. The calm personality and fast growth that Durocs are known for are sought-after traits and exactly what I'm looking for at McKnight Farms. Any other questions?"

"Something wrong with good old-fashioned Scottish grunters?"

"White-haired, pink-skinned pigs are very sensitive, sunburn easily, and need to be raised indoors in a commercial setting. In keeping with our traditions and goals here at McKnight Farms, I want a breed that will thrive in our pastures. Duroc pigs are a solid choice."

"Who's going to take care of them?" A man in the back whose name was Angus, spoke up. By the way the other men where nodding and egging him on, he appeared to be a ringleader.

He went on. "I ken cattle and sheep, Harold kens poultry, but nae one on staff kens anything aboot grunters. At this stage of my life, I dinnae intend on taking on a new task that I care nothing aboot."

It was a test. If she backed down and let the men dictate what they would and would not do, she might as well give up and go home right now.

"I'm sorry to hear that you won't be joining us in our new ventures, Angus. I've heard great things about your work and I was hoping you'd jump onboard." She was taking a huge risk. What if they all quit? What if they all stayed but refused to do what she asked? Doubt washed over her in waves.

She looked directly at the man. "Angus?" He looked surprised that she was singling him out. "I really think the new business opportunities we'll be exploring in combination with the things we already do well will make for a very exciting time of growth for each of you personally and the company, too. I hope you'll reconsider and lend us a hand in getting the new phases of the operation underway."

"Sure. Well." Angus sputtered. "When ye put it that way. I guess I could give it a go and see what happens."

She gave him a big smile. "My attitude exactly. We'll try a smattering of new things and see how they go. If they don't work after they've been given a fair trial, then we'll move on and try something different."

The rest of the men looked at each other like they were unsure what had just happened, but she knew full well. She had scored a victory.

William beamed at her from the sidelines. A few minutes later, when the men had left, he joined her and patted her hand.

"Well-played, Heather."

"Thanks for backing me up."

"No worries. Let me know what kind of hog shelters you need for the Durocs."

"I will." She pushed back her chair and wondered

how and where she was going to find a litter of Red Durocs and a good breeding boar in Scotland.

#

Brodie thought about calling before he dropped off Heather's repaired tyre, but he hadn't asked for her mobile number and he didn't want to advertise the fact that he'd rescued a damsel in distress to the whole kit and caboodle at McKnight Farms. If she wasn't around, he would simply drop it off and head home. One of their men should be able to put it on, an easy feat now that her car was not full to the brim with everything she owned. If Heather was there, he'd show a little neighbourly concern before taking his leave. Either outcome was fine with him. He wasn't picky. It wasn't as if he was looking for an excuse to see more of her.

The road to the buildings was full of potholes and narrow enough in some places that the hedgerow scraped against the sides of his truck. He hoped now that Heather was running things, she'd see fit to put down a load or two of crushed rock and trim the bushes where they hung over the road. Walter Morris, the previous owner, either hadn't had the funds to keep the place up the way he wanted to, or hadn't cared. He'd heard that William had already done a major overhaul on the loft over the production facility and freezer storage rooms where he assumed Heather would be living, and the main house, too. He assumed the barns would be upgraded before winter set in as well. They'd needed it for at least three decades.

He drove up one final hill, took a second to enjoy the views from the top –first McKnight land, and then his da's in the distance. The hills were dotted with several breeds of sheep, cattle, and some random ducks. The sun filtered down through the layers of the hillside and the colors glowed with light. It was a sight he would never tire of. Not that the views weren't just as striking in Edinburgh, probably even more so along the Firth of Forth where he was supposed to be. He pushed aside a flicker of bitterness. The situation was what it was. No sense ruminating over what could have been.

He pulled into the yard and surveyed the buildings surrounding it on three sides. The shrubbery and gardens had been trimmed back and spruced up. Fresh mulch and new cobblestone walkways set off freshly painted blue doors against classic stone walls. What looked to be a new lamppost was designed to mimic Victorian street lights in Edinburgh. The place had gone from looking like a dumpy, long-neglected farm to a Broadway set readied for a scene from Peter Pan.

He knew the Morrises had loved the place, but the fresh look William had brought to the farm was inspiring and forward looking. The organized, precision-oriented side of his engineer's brain sprang to life just looking at it. He was very impressed. And if his da had not still been at the helm of McBryde Enterprises, he would have gone home and started scrubbing, painting, and landscaping the second he got back. If he had time, maybe he would anyway.

"Brodie?" Heather walked up to his truck. She was dressed in a more practical look, bib overalls in faded denim with a blue, gingham scarf to tie back her long curls.

"I brought your tyre." He opened the door and stepped out of his truck.

"Oh, good." Heather's face lit up. "I've been hoping I would be here when you dropped by so you can show me how to change the tyre. I tried to watch when you were putting on the spare, but with the stress of having to unload my entire boot with your father looking on and heckling from the sidelines, I can't say I remember much of what you did."

Awright. He hadn't planned on doing the job, but he respected the fact that she wanted to help put the tyre back on, to learn how to do it herself.

"Sure. I have a few minutes." He rolled the wheel out of the back end of his truck and over to her car.

"Thank you! I really appreciate it." She knelt down beside him and reached her hand to steady the tyre.

His heart did a flip flop. What it meant, he had no idea. He'd have to mull on it later.

Heather smiled and there it was again, like a summersault on soft grass.

"I suppose I could ask one of the guys to show me, but I really don't want them to know I can't change a tyre." She looked chagrinned.

"No worries. Let's start with the jack. The tricky part is that each one is a little different. The thing they all have in common is that you need to place it under the sturdiest part of the car and then use the handle to raise the car high enough to slip the tyre into place."

He reached over to place the handle in the slot of the jack.

"No. I'll do it. Learning by doing. It's the only way that works for me."

He watched and gave a few directions as she struggled though the process. They were almost done when a truck drove into the yard.

A man who looked to be about his age stepped out of the truck. He couldn't see his face, but there was something familiar about the way he stood.

"Knox?"

"Hey, Brodie. Fancy meeting ye here." Knox walked over to him with a huge smile, grabbed his hand, and started pumping it. His brogue was thick. He sounded just like Walter.

"So ye got the farm after all! I heard some shark from America swooped in and stole the farm from under Munro's feet." Knox looked in Heather's direction.

She was crouched low to the ground, tightening lug nuts.

Brodie's eyes followed Knox's just in time to see the look that passed over her face.

"Nice to meet you, Knox..."

"Knox Morris. Knox, I'd like you to meet..."

His voice and Heather's rang out at the same time. Knox looked confused.

"So ye found yerself a wife down in Edinburgh." Knox reached for Heather's hand. "Are ye an engineer, too?"

Now Heather looked confused. "No, and definitely no. I mean, I have no idea if Brodie has a wife. He's just helping me change a tyre. I'm Heather McPhearson, the new manager of McKnight Farms, and niece of the American man who reputably stole the farm from the McBrydes, although this is the first I've heard of it."

Brodie shrugged. "No wife in Edinburgh or anywhere." He could have added that his girlfriend dumped him when he gave up his job working on the Firth of Forth Bridge, but he figured that was a conversation for another place and time. If ever. Now that he knew what Barbara was really about, he preferred to forget about her altogether. "I'm just being neighbourly."

Knox raised his eyebrows, looked at Heather, looked

back at him, and winked knowingly. But he didn't know anything. Same cocky, always-making-assumptions-about-things-he-knew-nothing-about, Knox. He'd been a schoolmate when they were younger and growing up on adjacent farms, but Brodie certainly hadn't kept in touch with him over the years. Two minutes with the man and he remembered why.

Brodie looked at Heather. He could see William exiting the main house and walking toward them, but it changed nothing about what he was about to say by way of introduction. "Knox is the son of Walter Morris, the previous owner of the farm." He looked at Knox. "So what brings you back to the farm if you know it's been sold?" He hoped it wasn't to cause trouble. If he remembered correctly, Knox had left home at 18 after a huge row with his father, and since, had wanted nothing to do with the farm or his da.

"I thought maybe I could offer a helping hand to whomever bought the place. I mean, who kens the farm better than someone who lived and worked with the land, the animals, and the equipment for 18 years?" Knox seemed to put two and two together – he'd set his sights on William approaching them from the house. "The construction contractor I was working for in Falkirk dinnae need me right now, at least until they finish framing a few more houses. My crew does the finish work, and the schedule got off kilter because of the shutdowns during the pandemic."

William had obviously heard his spiel, although Knox was working hard at making it appear that he hadn't even seen William,

William joined the group and introduced himself. "Knox, I'd be happy to put you on the payroll for the next few months if you're of a mind to stay and let

Heather pick your brain while she's getting acclimated."

NO! Brodie wanted to scream. *You don't know this man. He's bad news. Big time trouble. It's the last thing that Heather needs.* He stole a glance at Heather. Her face seemed to echo Brodie's thoughts. But what could be done or said now that the offer had been given?

"I'd love to come on board and help however I can." Knox winked at Heather, who looked like she was about to crumple, or explode, or both.

Brodie could see the determination on Heather's face, the reticence to go against William. He could tell she was mortified that William had offered the position to Knox without consulting her.

Heather's voice quavered a bit but he was proud of her for having the courage to say what she did.

"Thanks for the offer, Knox, but I've got a whole crew of experienced helpers who chose to keep working at the farm when it sold. I'm sure their advice will be all the help I need. And really, we've already made so many changes in the way things will operate from now on that we'll be looking more to the future than to the past."

"Typical American thinking," Knox said. "Cancel the past – pretend it dinnae happen – tear down the statues of the great men who built the land whose freedoms ye enjoy today. I've read all aboot it in the papers. Here in Scotland, we value the past and the things we can learn from it. I feel sure William here will receive great benefit from my wisdom because of the job he just offered me, which I am happy to accept."

Brodie groaned to himself. What now? William had offered. Heather had declined. Knox had deferred to William and accepted. There was no good ending to this scenario as far as he could see.

William cleared his throat. "It's just a few months,

Heather. I'm sure Knox will be a big help."

Brodie stifled another groan. So Heather had been put in her place. William had just stripped her of her authority over a man he knew nothing about. He looked at Heather and waited to see what she would say. He wished he could come to her defense, but who was he to say anything?

"I'll need a place to stay," Knox said, ignoring anything Heather might have to say in advance of her even saying it.

"Is the Loft still open or have you accepted any bookings on Airbnb?" William looked at Heather with guilt dripping from his bearing.

"I'll have to check. I haven't had time to look at my email with everything that's been going on." Heather sounded like she was slowly being strangled.

William looked increasingly uncomfortable. "Knox, I'll be heading back to Minnesota tomorrow morning, so you will be answering to Heather. But she's only just arrived, so she won't have time for handholding. You are to make yourself useful and support her in every venture, giving advice only when asked for and doing whatever she asks of you. Is that understood?"

This William was too nice for his own good, and certainly for Heather's. Heather had indicated that William was a real sweetheart, but this time, Brodie thought he'd gone too far. William should have told Knox to hit the road as soon as Heather made her feelings known.

And Knox. What a user. Knox wasn't taking the hint, but then, knowing what he knew of the man, he wouldn't have expected him to. If Brodie had to guess, he'd bet money that Knox had no job to return to and nowhere else to go, and that a few months would turn into however long he could mooch off the McKnights. They'd probably have to evict him if they ever wanted their loft back. He just hoped Knox could be trusted around Heather. The hairs on the back of his neck bristled just thinking about it.

"I know Knox well." Brodie surprised himself by speaking his thoughts aloud. "I'll make sure he behaves himself."

Heather smiled and looked a little less panicked at his words. He was glad his short little speech was able to set her mind at ease, and even cheer her up a bit, but he feared it was probably going to take more than a little rhetoric from him to keep Knox from doing more damage than good.

Chapter 3

Heather pawed through the laundry basket where her clean underwear was supposed to be, hoping for a glimpse of lavender buried somewhere beneath the other panties and bras that she'd washed after they'd ended up flung over the hedgerow. It was the third time she'd looked and the fact that she still hadn't found them was not encouraging. Not only was the lavender lingerie set one of her favorites, it was the perfect match with the T shirt she had planned on wearing. She'd bought it at a tiny lingerie shop in the heart of Paris, and she not only loved the color, she adored the memories of her trip to France. The set was beautiful, and sexy and sweet. And, it had cost her a small fortune! She had the bra, but that was little comfort if she'd lost the panties that went with it. She finally gave up and found a pale pink set to wear, thus solving the immediate problem.

Her day was filled with meetings, a business lunch, and tours of the actual land, some of which was scattered on different parts of the hill where the main farm was located. Later that afternoon, if she could find a free minute or two, she'd try to make time to go back to the scene of the flat tyre debacle and search the roadside vegetation. Who knew where they could be by now after the stiff winds they'd had last night.

It was probably a good thing William was leaving for

Minnesota. She was furious with him for giving Knox Morris a job without so much as asking her if she thought it was a good idea. She did not. She didn't want Knox's advice and she didn't want to feel like she was walking on eggshells for fear of making a remark that would hurt his feelings or imply that his family hadn't run the farm properly. She didn't want to be looking over her shoulder and wondering if he was rallying the staff against her and mounting a revolt to retake the farm. It was hard enough already, having the mostly old, jaded, somewhat cynical, resistant-to-change staff that she'd inherited rather than the upbeat, young, enthusiastic crew she'd hoped to hire herself.

She stepped into her panties, hooked her bra and slipped it over her head, found her T-shirt and pulled on a pair of blue jeans. Better Uncle William left before she slipped and told him what she really thought of his decision. She put on socks and a pair of shoes that would stand up to the terrain she'd likely encounter on the farm tour.

The worst thing was, she had no one to talk to about what was bothering her. She couldn't confide in any of the staff. They all knew Knox. Besides, she didn't want to make William look like a buffoon in front of any of them, even if a sweet, loveable one. It wouldn't inspire confidence in their management team. William and her da were close as brothers and Lyndsie was her mum's bestie, so going to them for a wee bit of support, righteous indignation, or even sympathy, was not an option. Her doofus brother was so clueless that he wouldn't begin to understand why she was upset. She had friends in America, but they were all friends of William's or his family. Her Scottish school friends had scattered and she'd never really bonded socially with them anyway since she'd been gone all summer, every year, when she'd been with William and Lyndsie in Minnesota. She'd hoped to make new friends when she arrived in the Highlands, but griping about her boss slash uncle to someone she'd never met before was hardly the right footing on which to start a friendship.

Her mind flitted to Brodie, who was sadly the closest thing she had to a friend in her new home. But he was a friend of Knox's as well, so big help he was.

She kept her cool while she said goodbye to William. He planned to return about once a month, probably every two months in the wintertime. One of the guys had offered to drive William to the airport in Aberdeen, which was fine with her.

She was organizing her thoughts and jotting down a few questions she wanted to ask the suppliers she had appointments with later that day. Her first meeting was with the supplier from whom they got their Highland Coos and Aberdeen Angus cattle. They'd already beefed up their herd a bit, so to speak, and would likely be acquiring more of one or both breeds in the days to come. The Belted Gallways they'd already introduced to the mix came from a different supplier and were getting on famously. They seemed to be thriving in the McKnight Farm pastures even more so than the Aberdeen Angus. Since it would be her job in future days to make decisions regarding what breeds to buy and in which fields to pasture them, she wanted to find out all she could about the unique Scottish varieties, all of which were slightly different than their American-bred counterparts.

When she heard the knock on the office door, which was tucked under the Loft, next to their kitchen and production facility, she assumed it was the cattleman she was scheduled to meet with. But when she opened the door, she found a distinguished man who looked like an older version of Knox. Could it be his father? Had he come to visit Knox, and if so, would it be a frequent occurrence? Or did the elder Morris have buyer's remorse? Her happiness to see William depart morphed into regret. Perfect timing. Not.

"Heather McPhearson," she said briskly. "What can I help you with?"

"I'm here to serve ye papers."

"Papers about what? I have no idea who you are or what this has to do with me."

"I am Duncan Morris, brother of Walter Morris, and half of this farm is mine."

Heather took a deep breath. "Let me get this straight. You're the brother of the previous owner? I'm not sure why you're here now. Your brother was paid in full for this land. My Uncle William—"

"I've been gone because I served in the military. The Cyprus conflict. I was injured. Took me awhile to get home but I'm here now and I'm owed my half of the inheritance."

Heather searched her brain for a time frame that would make sense of his claim. As far as she knew, the Cyprus event had occurred in the mid-seventies. She waited for a minute or two before she spoke. Her first thought was, had he injured a body part, or his brain? Because none of this made sense. "I sympathize with your situation, and I appreciate your service, but it seems that it's your brother that you need to speak to, not me."

"I just want my share. Buying something isn't legal if ye buy it from someone who has no right to sell it. That's why I'm notifying ye. Ye were ripped off. Ye bought something that weren't Walter's to sell. Now, I'm home, and I want my share. I've hired an attorney and he says the sale was invalid since I dinnae approve it."

By this time, a crowd had started to gather.

"Will someone find Knox, please?" She turned to the old vet. "I'm sorry, Duncan, but you're going to have to leave. I'm not sure if your brother and the rest of your family believed you were MIA or presumed to be dead, or what happened. But whatever needs to happen to make sure things are straightened out is going to have to be discussed with your family and their attorneys. Hopefully Walter will give you half of the proceeds of the sale. But I am not an attorney, and I can't help you."

Duncan started to curse under his breath. She tried to be patient, but Duncan's outbursts were eroding her morale and what little confidence her staff had in her management skills.

She pointed at two of her brawnier staff members. "Please escort Duncan to the edge of McKnight land and make sure he doesn't come back down the lane."

What else could go wrong?

By that afternoon, word that Duncan Morris was back home had spread all over the neighbourhood, to Alford and beyond. Knox claimed he was at the grocery fending off curious onlookers for over an hour, with everyone wanting to know what he knew about his Uncle Duncan coming home for the first time in years. Knox told her, "They all remember him and think he should have gotten half of the income from the farm sale. Everyone seems to agree that the sale needs to be redone so he can be part of the decision making."

"But William went through all the proper legal channels to purchase the property. Walter has his money. You can't just go back, pretend it never happened and start over. What about all the improvements William has already made?"

Heather was so upset that she cut her last two appointments short. Tomorrow was a new day. Things certainly couldn't get any worse. She hoped they might be better.

#

The next day, Heather woke up early with the goal of making the stone house look like home. Things had been a little too crazy for her taste, with first Knox and then Duncan's homecoming to haunt her. Her Uncle William had promised neighbours who would be happy and welcoming. He'd also guaranteed her opened-ended decision making so she could take the business in the direction she wanted. Instead, she'd faced one stressful situation after another.

She carefully unwrapped the first of her mum's paintings that she'd brought from home. One would never guess by looking at her mum's colorful paintings that Violet was always cold and chilled to the bone, or even painfully shy. Her mum's artwork glowed with vibrant pastels just like Rabbit Hill Lodge, as though each painting could suddenly form a rainbow.

Growing up at Rabbit Hill Lodge was probably the reason she'd felt comfortable living and working at McKnight Farms. The McPhearsons had not only worked together as a family at the teahouse and B&B, they'd created and lived and loved. Her mum always said her creative muse was fed by Nathan's music, Heather's warmth and intensity, and her brother, Frasier's, mysterious aura. She remembered the way her brother had said good-bye – with a quick and perfunctory hug followed by, "I'd like to say I'll miss you, but I won't."

"What will you do with no big sister to boss you around?" Heather had spoken the words in a teasing way, but she was seriously worried about what would become of her brother once left to his own devices. Frasier had inherited their mother's artistic temperament and her father's musical genius, but not a whit of common sense. He'd no doubt paint a gallery full of amazing landscapes, and compose a plethora of haunting melodies that he could play on any one of six different instruments, but fail to organize a single paying gig. Her brother was as spacey and left-brained as could be. What he needed going forward was a wealthy benefactor, or at the very least, a skilled agent, but who knew how that would come about when he was too shy and reluctant to put himself forward – a problem she'd never faced.

She hung the first of her mother's paintings, the one with a violet sky reflected in the watery loch around Eilean Donan Castle at the end of the entry hall so it would be the first thing she saw every night when she walked in the door. The second, Dornie from the Bridge, she hung on the wall at the end of her bed so she could look at it while she was falling asleep. The last, which remained nameless, went over her sofa. It was a contemporary fusion of colors, and each time she looked at it she saw something different. It reminded her of her mum's many facets.

Oh, how she wished she could talk to her mum about everything that was going on.

When she'd broken down the box the paintings had been packed in, she decided to walk across the west pasture and see if she could find her missing panties. The lavender butterfly bikini bottoms were so skimpy that they could have easily gotten caught in the hedgerow and gone unnoticed. If the lingerie hadn't been part of a matching set, she might not have been so determined to find it. She at least wanted to try.

A half hour later, she'd checked on all the sheep that were grazing between the farm buildings and the place where she'd had her flat tyre. Petting the sheepdogs that herded the flocks, she watched the Highland Coos chewing their cuds. It hadn't rained since her incident so she could see the marks on the road where she'd careened to a stop. She'd worn her sturdy shoes and jeans so she would be safe from any brambles or raspberry cane that might have thorns. With any luck, her panties might be snagged in a sticky spot – hopefully not so sharp that they'd been snagged or torn, but just enough so they hadn't blown away in the wind.

She was just finishing doing a thorough visual search of the area when Brodie appeared over the ridge, a dog at his side, waving a wisp of lavender in his hands.

"Looking for these?"

Her heart jumped with joy and clenched in a grimace all at the same time. "You found them!"

"Ginger brought them home early this morning. As soon as I saw the color – well, and the style – I figured they were yours."

His fingers brushed against hers as he handed them over, and she felt her cheeks blushing red.

The dog sat patiently at Brodie's side, as though waiting for her reward.

She reached down to pet Ginger's head. "I didn't bring a treat."

"Don't—" Ginger danced on her hind legs in a flurry of happiness. "Don't say that word. She knows what a t-r-e-a-t is and once the word is said, there's no taking it back."

"Oh! So sorry I got her hopes up only to let her down."

"You didn't know what would happen. But we should probably walk in the direction of the shepherd's hut down the lane. I keep a secret stash hidden away for occasions such as this."

She smiled. "So rewarding your dog for retrieving women's underwear is a routine thing at McBryde Enterprises?"

"It used to be my job. When I was but a wee lad, I'd sit with my da on the back steps every night when the sun got too low to work, and show him the dainties I'd found over the course of the day."

He had to be kidding. She raised her eyebrows and laughed at the picture he painted.

"You think I'm teasing you, aye? Well, I'm here to tell you that here in the Highlands, the wind brings in bits and bobs from round the world. They sail right o'er the ocean and land here in our fields."

Ginger rubbed against her side and wagged her head as if to concur.

"You mentioned wanting to be an engineer." She changed the subject. "What made you give up your dream and come back home?"

"I am an engineer, and I have not given up on my dreams." The lilting tone of Brodie's voice was replaced with an edgy quality that she'd not heard before. She waited for him to explain, but he remained silent.

So be it. She looked down at her mobile to catch the time. "I should probably get back to the farm. I have a meeting with a dairy producer in a little over an hour."

"And what about you?" Brodie was still looking down, whether in defeat or respect, she didn't know. "Is this what you've always dreamed of doing with your life? Is McKnight Farms your future, or a brief stopover on the journey?"

"I think it's my calling, and I think I'll love it all the more once I work my way through these glitches and get people onboard who share my enthusiasm and vision for the farm."

"Good for you." Brodie reached over and patted her on the back. It was something her da would have done and a gesture she desperately needed after the last 48 hours. "May your troubles be few and your blessings be many as you embark upon your new endeavors. And yes, it's probably an old Irish blessing instead of a Scots one, but then, we all come from near the same place, don't we?"

Thank you, Brodie." She was just starting back across the pasture when Ginger started barking furiously.

Brodie charged off after her. "Stay back. It could be a wounded animal or a poisonous snake. I don't want you coming to harm."

She ran after him as fast as she could. "Well, I don't want you coming to harm."

"Sweet Jesus. Help us, Lord." Brodie ground to a halt. His back was to her, so she couldn't see his face, but his back tensed and heaved with the makings of a crisis.

"What's wrong?"

"It's a dead body. For a second, I thought it was Knox."

Her mind flashed to Duncan. The two, uncle and nephew, looked so much alike. Her heart sank. It couldn't be. Not now, when everything was supposed to be looking up, and William gone, and everyone already suspicious of her ability to manage things.

She caught her breath and said, "Older gent? Camo shirt?"

She heard Brodie's sharp intake of breath. "Yes. Friend of yours?"

She reached his side and looked down at her worst nightmare. "Duncan Morris." Bloated and blue. "Older brother to Walter. Left home to join the army in the early seventies, worked in the Army Corp of Engineers for a couple of years, participated in the event in Cyprus and was rarely seen or heard from again in these parts until yesterday, at least from what I gathered when he stopped by to inform me that William's takeover of his family's land was invalid because he was still alive and owns half the farm."

"I know him. We always called him Uncle Dunk." Brodie moved to the door of the shepherd's hut. "Looks like he's been living here. We always leave a few provisions in the hut in case a bad storm sets in or we have to spend the night caring for a ewe or a heifer that's in labor. Our pasture is close to your house, but fairly far from our buildings. Further than you'd want to be in a heavy snowstorm."

She grabbed her mobile. The reception was terrible in the pastures with few exceptions.

"I'll ring the police." Brodie took out his mobile and punched in 999. "Better me since I'm known to the police, and haven't seen the man since I was a child." He paused. "Assuming the two of you had words."

"A few. Mostly kind. There were a lot of witnesses."

"That could come in handy."

Her heart plummeted. Was Brodie implying that she'd be viewed as a suspect?

She resisted the urge to reach for her mobile and

bring up the camera. "How do you think he died?"

"All I know is that he's dead."

"Maybe it was natural causes." A girl could dream.

"Maybe. Or it could have been intentional if he ruffled the wrong people's feathers."

"Now what do we do?"

"Wait."

So that's what they did. Ginger the dog had far more patience than she did, but eventually, the police arrived, asked them a million questions, and finally, took the body away. But not before mentioning that Heather shouldn't go anywhere until they finished their investigation.

Chapter 4

"Knox?" Heather tried not to yell – the last thing she needed was to be labeled as the woman boss who screamed her head off. But Knox hadn't been coming to work, and hadn't even spoken to her since his uncle was murdered, and she needed to put an end to it. He wasn't going to drain funds from her payroll unless he was on her side, working just as hard as she was to make a success of the farm.

Knox sauntered into the courtyard and slowly made his way toward her office. "Something I can help you with?"

"Something?" Heather challenged him. "You're supposed to be helping me with everything. That's your whole purpose in being here – to give me advice and share what you know about the farm operation. Instead, you sleep until noon and complain when the people who staff the production facility under your loft make too much noise. They're doing their jobs!"

Knox shrugged and rolled his eyes. "How am I supposed to help ye when all I ken aboot is how my da used to do things, and all ye're interested in is doing new and different things?"

"There are plenty of ways we can build upon Morris traditions to make the future of the farm better. But you don't seem to be interested in either then or now. So tell me why you're here. And I want the truth."

"Respectfully speaking, Ms. McPhearson, I plan on taking over management of the farm when ye give up and go home." Knox laughed.

Pretend all you want, she thought. At least she knew what his game was. Brodie had told her that Knox had never wanted to take over the farm – or even work there – when his da was in charge. Heather guessed now that his da was out of the way, he'd changed his mind. While it might be admirable that Knox really did care about the land that could have been his legacy, it was too little, too late. He'd missed his chance. Period.

She returned Knox's insolent stare with one of her own. "I understand that you're grieving the loss of your family's history and your own heritage. But the fact is, your da's farm was hemorrhaging money when he sold the place. We're going to make a profit this year."

"Over my dead body." Knox was mad now. But at least he was revealing his hand.

"I understand this is hard on your ego," she fired back. "But you have two choices. One, stay and help rebuild your legacy so one day, you can bring your sons and daughters to the farm for a tour and say, 'Your grandda and his da before him planted the seeds that helped birth this farm. What you're seeing today, I helped create.' Choice number two, you can pack your bags, get the hell out of my loft, and never set foot on this property again."

Knox appeared to be thinking. He thought she was a royal bitch. She understood that. But his choices were still the same.

"You don't have to like me," Heather said. "But as long as you're here, you need to treat me with respect. I'll not pay someone who's working against me or undermining me to the rest of the staff."

Knox looked at her like she was the insane one. "I guess I'll be on my way then."

"Just give her a chance." Brodie walked into her office. His voice cut through the tension in the room like a knife just out from the hot water tap.

Where had Brodie come from?

Brodie dug his heels into the ground and faced Knox. "Heather's determined to make a success of the place, and once she sinks her teeth into something, she's not going to let go. You can be a part of it, or you can wash your hands of the whole kit and caboodle and move on, but I'll not stand by and watch you try to take her down."

She decided to hold her tongue, at least where Knox was concerned. She'd said all she had to say and given him more than a fair chance. It was up to him now. As for her, she hoped Knox would leave. She didn't trust him, and she wouldn't put anything past him. He was lazy and arrogant. If it weren't for the fact that William was a lot sweeter than she was, Knox would have been gone before he even started.

"Fine," Knox was saying. "I'll give it a try."

Heather tried to manage a sincere smile. "So will I. Fresh start then?"

"Sure."

Brodie spoke again. "Why don't you take a shower and get ready to report to work in a half hour. From now on, Heather wants you here by eight every morning."

Knox didn't look happy, and she wasn't sure how she felt about Brodie stepping in. If Knox shaped up, she'd thank him. If Knox continued to be underfoot while serving no good purpose, they'd have to talk, she and Brodie.

"Knox, I want a report on the three kinds of sheep your da raised when he had the farm. I want to know which ewes are the best mothers, which have the biggest lambs, and which have the greatest longevity and the best overall lambing record. I want to know which breed produces the most pounds of saleable meat, and which meat is most tender and brings the highest price. Any questions?"

"No, Ma'am."

She watched as one of the older men offered to help him, which kind of defeated the purpose. The important part was, she'd let Knox know what was expected of him. With Brodie's help.

Brodie approached her when the rest of the crowd had dispersed. "Sorry to interfere. I think it's better to have Knox where we can keep an eye on him until our murderer is found."

Her breath caught in her throat and she almost choked. "You think he may have killed his own uncle?"

"I think the Morris family is hiding something. Anything is possible. You shouldn't let down your guard even for a moment until we know what we're dealing with."

A shiver ran down her spine.

Brodie stepped closer. "I stopped by to tell you I'm going to shear my sheep sometime in the next day or two. I thought perhaps you'd like to see how it's done."

"That would be great. I've been reading up the subject, but it's always best to learn by doing." She'd known she would have challenges when she agreed to run McKnight Farms – like figuring out how exactly to sheer sheep – but it had never occurred to her that she would have a dead body and a murderer to contend with.

#

"Brodie McBryde?"

Brodie moved downwind of the flock of bleating sheep he was attempting to herd into the pens so he could shear them. He couldn't hear who was calling over the clatter. The sheep should have been sheared a month or two ago, but his da's heart hadn't asked if it was a convenient time to go on strike.

"Would you please say again who's calling? I've moved to a slightly quieter place so I can hear you."

"This is Douglas from McSween, Braden and Harris Engineering. I'm calling to inquire about your availability for a position on the Kilchoan Mull Bridge project."

His heart leaped in his chest. "It's been approved?"

"Pending final design modifications from our firm."

Wow. He laughed aloud. "Trying to put another ferry out of business, are you? It sounds like quite a project."

"The main ferry from Oban to Craignure will still get plenty of use, but we're thrilled to have the opportunity to work with the Bridge Commission to link the remote peninsulas with Tobermory. It's amazing how many people live on the Ardnamurchan peninsula and work on the island. I think the project will be very well-received."

"It must be very exciting to have the contract on a job that will positively impact so many people's everyday lives."

"Exactly. We're looking for a few more good people to head up the design phase, and then, the actual construction."

"I'm honored that you thought of me." Someone must have recommended him. He was good at what he did, but obviously, his name hadn't popped into their heads from thin air.

"You come highly recommended from your supervisor at McClintock and Sons. Your work on the Firth of Forth Bridge and your summer internship in Denmark both lead us to believe that you're the perfect man for the job."

Well, at least Barbara thought he was good for something. Or perhaps she was going to be working on the same project and this was her way of manipulating them back into the same time and space so they could resume their relationship. Which left him to wonder if McSween, Braden and Harris knew anything about him or if this was all part of a plot by Barbara to get him away from the farm.

He listened as Douglas put the offer on the table, salary, expectations, time frame, commitment... ah, commitment. How could he make a commitment to living on a remote peninsula or island for three or four years when it was several hours from home? What if his da had more problems with his heart? Even if he didn't, his existing problems kept him from doing much of anything by himself. Would his da be able to hire someone to do the jobs Brodie had been handling?

"When do you need my answer? I'd like some time to mull things over – no pun intended."

Douglas hesitated – disappointed that Brodie hadn't jumped at the opportunity? "I need to have a firm commitment as soon as possible, but if you need the time, a week from today at the latest. If you pass, we'll need some time to make an offer to the next person being considered for the position."

So he had 7 days to figure out what he wanted to do with the rest of his life – and whether or not he was interested in Heather in any other way than the girl next door.

Douglas was busy extolling the benefits of coming on board at McSween, Braden and Harris. It was a handsome offer.

But his mind had already flown back to Heather. Maybe one of her crew would come over for a few hours once or twice a week after their shift ended to help out his da. Or maybe he should stay in the Highlands, forge a partnership with McKnight Farms, and build both farms to a new level of excellence.

Which brought him to the real problem. Did he even want to return to work? He missed working as an engineer from the very depths of his heart. Farming was farming. He loved his da's land, and the Highlands, and their herds. He found great satisfaction in doing farm work, but it didn't challenge him or stimulate his brain in the same way that designing and building viaducts and suspension bridges did. Especially when they spanned seawater. He could see moving back to the farm one day, when he'd fulfilled his destiny in the engineering field. He could envision retiring and spending his golden years on the farm, entertaining grandchildren and providing his family a place to come home to. But to give up everything he'd worked so hard to accomplish? Abandon his passion, the thing that brought him the greatest joy?

As soon as he thought the words 'greatest joy,' Heather popped into his brain again. He barely knew her, and he didn't have a clue if she was interested in him, but he found himself thinking about her more and more. One thing was for sure – he would love to get to know her better, and that would be unlikely if he moved to the Ardnamurchan Peninsula or even the Isle of Mull. She certainly wouldn't have time to run down to see him with everything she had on her plate. And he wouldn't want her to. She'd made a commitment to life in the Highlands. She'd made sacrifices of her own when she accepted the job of managing and expanding McKnight Farms. The last thing he wanted to do was to deter her from her goals.

Maybe his da should see if William was interested in purchasing his da's land. It could be McKnight, McBryde and Son.

No. That wasn't what he wanted – at least not now.

He should probably talk to Barbara and find out what was going on with her – if she'd already accepted an offer from Douglas, or if she'd recommended Brodie because she wasn't interested in leaving Edinburgh. He preferred not to speak to her at all. He certainly had no intention of climbing into bed with her, either literally or figuratively.

He was walking back to the pens to start shearing sheep when he saw an unfamiliar lorry exiting Heather's back pasture. It was separated from her other land by a grove of Frasier Pines and two stone fences. The only way to get to it was to climb the stiles over the fences and navigate his way through the dense forest between. The pasture wasn't even visible from most of his farm. If he'd been working in any other place, he never would have noticed.

The pasture was where they kept their black Aberdeen Angus cattle. He went to the edge of the road and tried to see whose lorry it was, but it was fast disappearing into the distance. It appeared to be unmarked. He took his mobile and snapped a photo that might prove handy, assuming it was clear enough to enlarge.

That was when he noticed that Beauty, the big black bull, was no longer in his pen. He ran for his pick-up, jumped in and fishtailed around the pens and outbuildings to get on the road. Heather hadn't mentioned any plans to sell the bull, and Beauty was prime breeding stock – worth thousands of pounds. Had Heather – or William – agreed to rent out the bull to another farmer to breed his heifers? It was possible, but these days, with farmers all vying for the best in their class, it was unlikely.

He rushed to the end of the drive and out onto the road, where his view was still partially blocked by the lay of the land, hills and curves alike. The lorry had disappeared right along with Heather's bull.

He thought about his not-so-patiently-waiting sheep and Heather's farm. He needed to get to work. It was hard enough sheering with only one strong man to do the job. He hoped the harness he'd designed would hold the sheep still long enough to take their wool, but he wouldn't know for sure until he got started. He would have liked to speak to Heather about the call he'd just gotten, but now was not the time. He would ring her up the second he got back to the pens and let her know about her bull. She would probably be able to clear the matter up awright.

Or, if the contraption he'd built was a fail, maybe she would come over and hold his sheep still while he sheared.

Chapter 5

"Who in heaven's name would do such a thing?" Beauty the bull being stolen made Heather feel like she was in the Wild West, reliving America's frontier days instead of the Highlands of Scotland in the 21st century. The whole thing didn't make sense. "What did the police say?"

No one said a word. She looked at Charles, one of her beef experts, and tried to hide her anger. The whole thing was infuriating! "Can one of you please help me understand why someone would want to steal a bull from us? And in broad daylight! Pretty brash move."

"Everybody kens Beauty is a complete sweetheart." Charles scratched his beard. "If I were going to steal a bull to add to my herd, it would be a gentle one like Beauty that wouldnae give me any grief when I came to load him up."

Charles crinkled up his forehead. "The mystery is, nobody but our neighbours and friends ken how well-behaved Beauty is. And what purpose would it serve any of them to pinch him? A well-known bull like Beauty would be noticed and discovered straight away, before they could get any use out of him."

Another of the men said, "The police are already scouring the area and checking all the auction barns. Whoever stole him would have to drive miles and miles before it would be safe to pasture him or try to sell him."

Charles frowned. "Poor Beauty. Beauty was born and raised in an open pasture. He will nae like being kept in a shed. Crooked old crabbits. I wouldnae be surprised if Beauty cannae even perform under those circumstances after going aboot it the natural way in the grand outdoors for his whole life. Unless they hook him up to a machine to get what he wouldnae do willingly."

Heather sighed. "I have no idea what really happened here, but it feels like someone either wanted to hurt us, or subject us to a financial hit." First a murder, and now this. What was going on?

"I agree. It's going to take a lot to replace a bull like Beauty. Yer herd will suffer in quality and diminish in quantity until ye find another like him." Charles frowned. "It seems more and more like an intentional act of malice. A loss like this will carry on for breeding season after breeding season."

"I'm not sure we will ever find another Beauty." Heather tried not to let her discomfort – okay, her out and out fear – show. Who hated her or McKnight Farms enough to do such a thing? She didn't want to overlook any possibility. "And you're absolutely sure that Walter Morris agreed to leave Beauty behind? Could William have misunderstood his intentions?"

"Ye can check the contract yerself, but I ken for certain that Beauty was specifically named as an asset, and that he was to be included in the sale. The purchase included 100 percent of the farm's livestock including our breeding stock. That bull is worth thousands of pounds. Anything that valuable, whether a piece of equipment or livestock, was listed or excluded on the bill of sale. And Beauty was included. I'm sure of it. The main reason so many of us wanted to stay on and work for Mr. McKnight when the sale went through is because we ken and love our herds."

"Thanks for your input, Charles. I appreciate all you're trying to do."

"If I were ye, I would check every piece of livestock on the farm, make sure nothing else has been taken. If they absconded with anything else, we should let the police know straightaway."

She nodded. "I already asked Randy to do a complete inventory."

"I also want to mention that the new sheep ye bought were delivered two days ago, and were going to be marked in our colors today. If someone wanted an opportunity to make off with them, yesterday would have been a perfect time, before they were branded so to speak."

Her heart sank. She personally hated seeing the smears of red, blue, or green paint marring the wool of the lambs that grazed in the highlands, especially those that foraged the open pastures. But it was the established way to mark which lambs came from which farms so they could be sorted if the sheep wandered off or got mixed up. If their new batch of sheep hadn't been officially processed or marked, it would be almost impossible to retrieve any that might have disappeared along with Beauty.

"Thanks, Charles. Please let me know when the inventory is complete." She rubbed her temples and tried to make her headache go away. She'd already had to ring up William to tell him about Duncan Morris' dead body being found. Now, she had the unenviable task of calling him and letting him know what else was going on. A prize Aberdeen Angus breeding bull disappearing wasn't exactly her fault, but it had happened on her watch. She was so thankful Brodie noticed and reported it when he did. What would she do without him?

#

Brodie took the clippers and ran it down the length of the first sheep in line, repeating the motion until the sheep was clipped clear of its coat. The thick wool fell to the floor in waves. He flashed Heather a satisfied smile. "I wasn't serious about you having to help me shear my sheep."

Heather scooped the wool from the floor before the next sheep came down the chute and placed it into a bin. "I wanted to help. I need to learn how to do this. William didn't have sheep on his farm in Minnesota so I have no experience to fall back on." She used her legs to steady the next sheep in line just the way Brodie had shown her. "Besides, I can't even begin to list all the things you've done to help me. I owe you."

Ginger was a pro at herding the sheep through the chute. They continued to pass through as Brodie sheared them one by one. "Thanks, but it's been my pleasure. I never meant for you to feel like you needed to pay me back."

"I'm not trying to pay you back. I'm just a friend, helping out a friend. One good turn deserves another, right?"

Brodie was glad Heather thought of him as a friend, but he hoped it didn't end there, and that one day it might go a little further. He stripped another sheep while Heather held the animal in place so he could reach in to capture the wool.

He looked up while they switched sheep. "Any word

on Beauty?"

"Nothing." Heather grabbed another sheep.

"Have the police been in touch with you about the autopsy on Duncan Morris' body?"

"Yes. Just before I came over to help." She straightened up until the next sheep was in place. "I'm sorry to say that it appears to be murder. Duncan was hit in the head with a rock and died of an internal hemorrhage a short while later."

Brodie sighed. Not the news he wanted to hear. "I thought I saw a bruise forming over his left eye." He paused. "Have they said anything about suspects?"

"Well, besides telling me not to leave town, they mentioned needing to interview all the neighbours and my entire staff to see if anyone saw anything suspicious. I don't know if that means I'm a suspect, but it wouldn't surprise me. As far as they know, I'm the last person who saw him alive except for whoever clunked him on the head with a rock."

"Maybe he tripped and fell on a rock, got up and repositioned himself, and then died of a brain bleed? Isn't that possible?" His mind was whirling in a thousand directions. Had it been too much to hope that they would rule it death due to natural causes?

"I don't know how they can figure out exactly what happened, but they must think they have enough forensic proof to say someone hit him."

Brodie's mind continued to summersault with dreadful possibilities. He hated seeing Heather put in this position, and worse yet, everyone knew his da and Duncan were sworn enemies. And who knew what his mother was up to and how she figured into the situation? He'd always sensed that something was off with her and the Morrises. In all the years they'd owned adjoining land, they'd never been neighbourly. Quite the opposite. His mum and da would likely be among the first to be questioned.

He was just thinking that he should find a time to go into town to visit his mum when Heather asked, "How long before the wool grows out enough to clip again?"

He tried to put his parents and their quibbles with the Morrises out of his mind. "Most breeds get shorn once a year. We usually do it earlier in the summer so the sheep stay cool in the hotter months, then grow their wool out enough to stay warm in the winter. But it was this spring when Da had his heart attack and it just didn't get done."

"It must have been a shock when he – it must have been a hard time for both of you."

He ignored the opportunity to talk about his da's health. "I think the sheep will be fine by the time winter sets in. This type of sheep produces a lot of wool. Several of the varieties could easily get shorn twice a year and often have." He paused and watched as Heather struggled to get control of the next sheep to enter the chute. This one looked a little anxious.

She gave the ewe a gentle pat and scratched behind her ears. "Settle down, sweetheart. We're not going to hurt you. Just giving you a summer haircut. You'll be so cool and pretty when we're done." Her voice grew soft and smooth. "It's all good. That's right, lassie. Slow and easy."

Brodie smiled. Heather was a natural. Although taking his time with the jittery sheep was slowing him down. "I can usually do one every two or three minutes."

"Well, this one needs to be pampered a bit."

He'd like to pamper someone a little bit awright, and it wasn't the sheep. "I just want to get them done so they're more comfortable for the rest of the summer, and not too cold this winter."

"I can see you're trying not to trim them too close."

"It's just one of many things I need to do before I go back to the city."

He could see Heather's body tensing. Did that mean she wanted him to stay?

"I suppose that makes sense." Her voice was stiff and wounded sounding. "Do you have a time table for going back to your job?"

"If I accept the job offer I just received, I'll have to relocate to Tobermory or somewhere else on the Isle of Mull, or the Ardnamurchan Peninsula, in a little under two months. The design phase for the new bridge needs to be finished this winter so construction can start first thing next spring."

"Oh." Heather refused to meet his glance. "Do you have a plan for the farm? Who will help your da? Or is he fully recovered?"

"No." Was he imagining it, or did she sound sad? He grabbed another sheep. "That will all have to be worked out."

He looked up at her. The sheep bleated and he got back to work. But the image of her disheveled clothes and curly locks, covered in flecks of raw wool, her skin hot and glistening in the sun, her hair tangled and her lips curved into a wary smile...

He didn't want to leave her.

But he loved what he did. He was good at it. As his da would say, he had a knack fer it.

He waited, perhaps to see if she would admit that she didn't want him to go. He wasn't surprised when she wouldn't say it. She might be thinking it, or maybe not. But she wasn't going to admit it out loud.

Conversation was as sparse as the coat of fluff left on the sheep when he was done with his shearing. His heart was torn, and by the looks of it, hers was, too. There was no easy solution. There was no road project, no bridge construction slated for the Highlands. And there was no McKnight Farms in the lowlands.

Chapter 6

When Lyndsie's voice rang clearly over Heather's mobile's speaker, Heather had never been so happy to hear anyone as she was at that moment.

"I hear ye've had some troubles of late, sweet friend," Lyndsie said.

"Where are you?" Heather asked. "Still at Rabbit Hill Lodge or back in Minnesota?"

"Right here in Scotland where I belong. I'm thinking of coming to visit ye before returning to America. It's almost the end of the season and yer mum says she can get by without me. Sounds like ye could use a little support, and I also think I need to have a talk with my cousin and find out what on earth is going on with the Morrises this time."

"Your cousin?"

"Knox is my second cousin. Remember, I'm a Morris by birth. Walter and Duncan are – were – my da's first cousins."

No! "Seriously?" The Morrises were relatives of Lyndsie's? She had met Lyndsie's da on more than one occasion, most of which were not all that pleasant. Based on what she knew of Lyndsie's family, a lot of things suddenly started to make sense. "How did I miss this?"

"William claims he told ye. My connection to the Morrises is how he found out aboot the farm being for sale in the first place."

"I have no memory of it, but that doesn't mean he didn't mention it. I probably just didn't make the connection. Morris is a fairly common last name."

"Well, it's none of yer doing and shouldnae be yer problem to deal with either. I have a few loose ends to tie up here before I head yer way, but I'll be there soon. We can try to figure out what happened to Duncan and do some fun things, too."

"Sounds wonderful. I've been working on the new meat pies I want to start making. I'd love it if you'd do some brainstorming with me and weigh in on the final menu."

They said good-bye and Heather was left to think about the Morrises. The fact that they were relatives of Lyndsie's – even if a bit distant – explained why William had given Knox a job.

Talking with Lyndsie had helped. She had goals and dreams for what she could make of McKnight Farms. She wanted to focus on those rather than dwelling on the negative aspects of her new situation. She needed to try to solve the problems that were occurring and move past them.

Despite her best efforts, her first couple of weeks in the Highlands had definitely not been unfolding the way she'd imagined when William had first offered her the job.

She'd envisioned having a staff that was committed to trying new things and revamping the farm under her capable leadership. Why else would they have stayed on? She'd assumed that she would have a warm, supportive environment to work in. She'd been raised in that kind of family. She'd gone to a great university where she had wonderful professors. She'd been surrounded by and cheered on by a system of extended friends and family all of her life. She'd known the task before her would be a challenge, daunting in some ways, but she'd never guessed that she'd be dealing with people who resented her or didn't believe William should own the farm in the first place, or that she wasn't capable of doing the job she'd been tasked to do.

What a mess.

#

Brodie tried to work the tension out of his shoulders. Something was very wrong. First, Duncan's death, and now, an unheard of incident of American Old West style cattle rustling. What was going on could be an attempt to take William down. Or, it could have nothing to do with McKnight Farms. Working on the premise that the crimes were unrelated to William or Heather, who were they after?

Unfortunately, when his mind played Spin-the-Bottle, the neck always seemed to stop at the gate to his own family's land.

He wondered who owned the lorry that had transported Beauty? His da certainly had no such vehicle, or even access to one. Or did he? His da's physical strength had been greatly diminished by his heart attack, but his mind was as sharp, his mood as obstinate, and his game plan as intent on causing trouble as always.

His father hated Duncan Morris. He'd never been quite sure why. But now that Duncan was dead, he had to find the answers. If his da wouldn't talk, maybe his mum would. He was just looking for her number on his mobile – definitely not a frequently dialed one – when a call rang through.

"Hey. What's up?"

"Barbara?" Her saying 'What's up?' was the equivalent of asking him if he was in the mood for sex.

He was not. At least not with her.

He didn't know what to say. She was no longer his girlfriend. That much he knew for certain. The question that remained was, would they be working together again if he accepted the job he'd been offered? If so, he needed to be polite and forge a new, professional working relationship with her.

"I stopped by your place in Fife on my way back from a repair job at the Firth of Forth Bridge. I hope you don't mind, but I stayed the night. That bed is so comfortable, and I always have the sweetest dreams when I sleep there."

Again with the suggestive tones. He made a mental note to schedule a trip to Fife and clean out his flat ASAP.

"I really wish you wouldn't..." Telling her what he thought had never stopped her from doing exactly what she wanted. The only thing that would curtail her behavior was to change the locks, get rid of the furniture, and turn off the electric.

There's always a silver lining, he told himself. His da's heart attack and having to move back home had essentially ruined his well-planned life, forced him to rearrange his goals, and adjust his dreams. But at least now, he saw Barbara for what she really was. And, his current situation was only temporary, he reminded himself.

Barbara spoke again. Was she even trying to figure out why he was saying so little? "So I hear you got a call from the hiring manager who's putting together the team for the Kilchoan Mull Bridge."

"Aye. Are you going to be working on the project, too?" He didn't want her to think it made a difference as to his decision, but he did want to know. And in a way, it did make a difference. He was less inclined to go if Barbara was going to be in charge of the project. It wasn't out of the question, but it might deter him or at the very least, lessen the chances of him accepting the position.

"I'll be there for the first six months while we're finishing the design phase, which should make for a nice cozy winter." She laughed in that deep, throaty tone she used when she wanted – or maybe he should say expected – something. "After I go back to Edinburgh, the construction phase will be headed up by whichever of you has proved yourself most indispensible and committed to the project."

He sighed, and it must have been loud enough to be heard over the airwaves.

"Really, Brodie. Edinburgh isn't that far from Mull. A short ferry ride to Oban and a hop, skip and a jump to my place. Or, we could meet someplace romantic in between like Loch Awe."

"Um. Gotta go. Other line." He disconnected and took a deep breath. He tried to imagine Heather being so forward and couldn't. Heather was a strong woman, and clearly knew her mind – although he had no clue if she was interested in him as anything other than a friend. His point was that if she was, she wouldn't go about showing her interest in such an oily way.

He re-conjured the image of Heather helping him in the shearing shed and tried to imagine Barbara lending a hand with anything to do with the farm. It would never happen.

He looked down and checked his text messages, hoping he'd find a note from Heather. The only message he found was from a number he didn't recognize, which turned out to be a blast from the past – an old friend, Teresa, that he hadn't spoken to in years. Why on earth would she contact him now? He hadn't spoken to her or seen her since he'd left home to attend University.

He had women coming out of the woodwork all of the sudden. A few months ago, he might have enjoyed having a little variety in his life, but as things stood now, he only cared about one.

Chapter 7

Heather opened the door to the courtyard and held it for Lyndsie while she went through, then walked down the steps of the old Morris House. Heather hated thinking of it that way, but with everything that was going on, there was no denying it or pretending it wasn't true.

"Listen," Lyndsie said. "I know the Morrises aren't the best branches on the old family tree, but it's the family I was born with. And I'll tell ye something else. If I'd had a perfect family situation when I was growing up, I wouldnae be the woman I am today. My da, with all his faults and foibles, loved me into being. And having to deal with him pretty much every day of my life since then has molded and shaped me into the strong, smart, sassy woman ye all love."

Heather tried not to smile. She admired Lyndsie more than words could say, as she'd told her on many occasions. A little humor to put things in perspective was good – the whole topic was a little too fresh and raw.

A few seconds of silence later, when they heard Knox's voice speaking in hushed tones, she was thankful she'd not shared any more thoughts. The voices were coming from behind the shed, or maybe through the open skylight in the loft.

"Fancy pants and her grand ideas," Knox said. "I'm

so sick of her haughty opinions. She acts like my da dinnae ken a thing aboot farming."

A second voice answered him. "It's like everything he did has to be changed just so she can prove her ways are better than his. Snooty bitch."

It was probably good Heather didn't recognize whose voice it was. She didn't even want to know. Or maybe she did, so she could let them see how snooty she was when she was firing someone's butt.

The men went on griping for a few minutes. That's when she noticed Lyndsie hoofing it to the stairway that led to the loft.

"Knox Morris! Ye get down here right now and explain to me what the dickens is going on!"

"May I say who's calling?" Knox answered in an insolent tone.

"It's yer second cousin, Lyndsie Morris McKnight, and ye'd best get yer butt down here lickety-split if ye know what's good for ye. And ye best bring whomever ye're talking to along with ye."

Heather shrank into the background. It appeared Lyndsie was going take the lead on this one. As maybe she should. It was her husband who had hired Knox. Knox was her cousin. Perhaps Lyndsie's words would carry more weight than Heather's would.

Knox more or less tumbled down the stairway, his shoes in his hand, his hair disheveled, and his shirt tucked in on one side and hanging out the other.

"Knox Morris, I'm ashamed of ye. William hired ye to be helpful to Heather, and here ye are, bashing her behind her back with lies and unfair accusations. I've known Heather since she was born, and worked with her since she was old enough to hold a whisk in her hand, and she dinnae have one arrogant bone in her body. If ye cannae be helpful like William thought ye would be, then it's time to pack yer bags and go."

In the course of a minute, Knox looked angry, and then sad, and then pitiful and scared. "Lyndsie, ye ken what it was like for me, growing up. Nothing I ever did was good enough to please my da. Nothing I did lived up to his expectations. Aye, I have a bad attitude, but this is my chance for redemption. Please dinnae take that away from me."

"I understand ye have issues, Knox." Lyndsie's voice softened. "But ye cannae take them out on Heather."

"I couldnae wait to get away from the farm." Knox looked contrite. "I dinnae want anything to do with it. But when I heard it was sold, I felt all kinds of regret. I ken the farm will ne'er be mine, but there's nae way I can just walk away."

"Then tell me why we should keep you on the payroll." Heather decided to jump in. "Because you've been warned several times that I'll not keep you on the books to have you talking about me and undermining my efforts to make this place a success."

"May I answer yer question?" Lyndsie snapped. "Because I think Knox is going to take on the job of being caretaker for yer new pigs. The truth is, he knows nothing aboot this farm or the livestock, or anything else, because he never lifted a finger to help his da or do anything on the farm. Whatever he does, it will be new to him, so may as well let him take on the grunters."

"Um, that would be fine," Knox said.

Lyndsie stared at him. "Which means there is some reason – some very important reason – that ye want to be here, even if it means ye have to tend the hogs."

Heather looked Knox in the eyes. "I don't know what your plans are, Knox, but..." She thought about Brodie's theory that they should keep Knox around so they could keep an eye on him. "I don't plan on having another discussion like this – ever. One more strike and you're out."

#

Fifteen minutes later, Lyndsie was back at work like there had been no words, and everything in the world was completely wonderful. "So tell me, Heather. Are ye planning on manufacturing any traditional pies? Beef and Ale, Chicken and Leek, Chicken and Ham, or Mince Pies?"

"No. Everyone makes them. They're too overdone. We already have the most flaky, moist, delicious, made-from-scratch pie crust ever. If we can come up with some different and unique varieties that no one else is doing, we'll have it made."

"Ye said ye'd come up with a few ideas already. Which ones are ye most excited aboot?" Lyndsie looked genuinely interested.

Heather's spirits soared for the first time in days. The men tried – some of them were actually very good cooks – but it was so nice to have another woman with whom she could bounce ideas around. Especially one that Heather already knew and trusted.

For a minute, she considered telling Lyndsie about her health concerns, but she was worried how she might react if she knew Heather was putting her career at McKnight Farms ahead of the need to have a baby – like yesterday – if she was going to be able to have one at all. It was such a complicated decision. If Lyndsie knew how critical the timing was, she'd probably get William to fire her so Heather could concentrate on getting pregnant.

She lifted her head and tried to put dire pap smear results and precancerous cells and major life disappointments out of her mind. "How about this one? Pork and Blue Cheese Pie. The filling ingredients will be pork, mushrooms, cream, Stilton cheese, butter, onion, and black pepper. I've already made several prototypes and it tastes heavenly."

"You go girl. It would be the first thing I'd order." Lyndsie tapped the end of her pen against the table. "How aboot a Greek pie made with McKnight lamb? I have a Greek meatball recipe – Keftedes – that could be adapted to a pie filling. I think the seasonings include eggs, onion, black pepper, cinnamon, maybe some nutmeg, and I'm nae sure what else, but I'll check when I get back to Minnesota. If I remember right, the gravy is unique – egg yolks, beef broth, and lemon juice, which we could use or replace with something more traditional. A good taste tester could help us decide. The recipe is in a cookbook that I got as a wedding gift from one of William's relatives who lives in St. Louis. I'm sure it would be easy to adapt."

"Sounds wonderful. At least one company that I know of is already doing a Moroccan pie with lamb, but Greek would be unique." Heather said, "My mum has a brown gravy recipe that has a dash of lemon juice in it. That might be a compromise, and we wouldn't have to worry about tempering eggs."

"Sounds like a good idea. Nae sense making things more complicated than they need to be."

"Isn't that the truth." Heather paused. "I'd also like to do a Chicken Balmoral Pie. The base would be chicken, but the pie would include a layer of haggis, so we would use our own lamb and beef, along with oats, stock, onion, and spices, and then, bacon and leeks, as well as butter, cream, whisky, and black peppercorns to make the sauce."

"I know ye've been experimenting with a new peppercorn whisky sauce. The taste I had a few weeks ago was divine."

"I think it will be a big hit. Another pie I want to try with the same peppercorn whisky sauce is a Mince and Mash Pie with ground beef, mashed potatoes, garlic, cream cheese, leeks, and onions. I know it sounds similar to a shepherd's pie or our cottage pie, but the sauce and the seasonings give it a completely different appeal."

"Ye're a natural, Heather. Great instincts." Lyndsie smiled and gave her a wink. "Ye should ask yer friend, Brodie, if he would be a taste tester. He probably has a well-rounded palate after growing up in the Highlands, going off to school in the lowlands, and then living in Edinburgh and Fife."

"Do you know Brodie?" Heather tried to act casual. She was eager to find out what Lyndsie thought of him – without being too obvious. Lyndsie was such a good judge of character.

"We were here finalizing the sale of the farm when his da had his heart attack. Brodie and I get along famously. I'm very impressed by him."

"Okay. Good. I like him, too."

Lyndsie acted cool as a cucumber. "Have ye ever talked to him aboot his time in Fife? There are some amazing restaurants in that area. If he's eaten at any of them, he'd have a good yardstick by which to compare yer menu. Have ye ever eaten at the Peat Inn?"

"No. But I've heard their food is top notch."

"Their presentation is amazing." Lyndsie smiled. "So, back to meatballs. William's mother gave me an idea for a Swedish Meatball and Mash Pie. Again, ye'd have to adapt the meatball recipe and experiment with the gravy, but I think it would be a hit."

Heather picked up her notebook. So the filling would be what? Beef? Pork?"

"Both. Mince, pork sausage, eggs, nutmeg, cloves, allspice, onion, milk, and bread crumbs. The gravy's made with beef stock, sour cream, and light cream. And of course, the standard potatoes we use on our cottage pies with cream cheese, garlic, light cream, butter and garlic salt and pepper."

"Thanks for all the great ideas." Heather jotted a few more notes and kept looking down even after she finished writing. "I wish I could count on Brodie to be a taste tester, but he'll probably be gone by then."

"No! Where's he off to?"

She told Lyndsie about his new job opportunity. She tried to sound happy about it, but Lyndsie knew her better than most people.

"So it's breaking yer heart."

"Well, I'm not happy about it, but what can I do? We barely know each other. It's just disappointing that my first friend is about to leave just when we're starting to get close."

Lyndsie smiled knowingly. "Too bad it's nae Knox who's leaving and Brodie who's staying."

"My feeling exactly. So any more thoughts on our expanded offerings?"

"Aye. One more." Lyndsie shuffled though her notes. "How does this sound? A Seasoned Pork, Parmesan and Pumpkin Pie? I ken it's a bit out there, but imagine a filling made with pork mince, celery, mushrooms, onion, pumpkin puree, sour cream, Parmesan cheese, eggs, spices, and black pepper with toasted pumpkin seeds on top."

Heather used her instincts to envision how it would taste. "It sounds perfect for autumn. But when they see the words pumpkin and pie together, won't they think it's sweet instead of savory?"

"I dinnae think they'll jump to dessert pie with the both pork and Parmesan in the title, but we could switch it to Seasoned Pork, Pumpkin and Parmesan Pie if ye think it would help."

"That sounds better to me." Heather loved the way she and Lyndsie could bat around possibilities and come up with the sort of grand ideas that neither of them would likely think of on their own.

Lyndsie's face took on a faraway look. "I hear Mac and Cheese pies are the latest hot seller. Sounds like carb overload to me, but if they can make Mac and Cheese pies, why not a Bavarian Hunter Schnitzel Pie with homemade spaetzle noodles and mushrooms tucked in a wonderful cream gravy like the Germans use for their rahm schnitzel?"

"Now that sounds pure dead brilliant. You're making me hungry!"

Lyndsie smiled. "Here's another thought. I know other companies make Christmas themed pies that include bread stuffing. Again, this might not be my favorite due to the high carb content and the fruits I'm aboot to suggest, but remember that teahouse I took ye to in Iowa? The Blue Belle Inn? They make something called Herb-Scented Chicken with Apple Cranberry Stuffing and Sauvignon Blanc Sauce. I think it would be wonderful in a pie if the proportions were right. I'm guessing the filling ingredients would include chicken, chicken broth, tarragon, cream, butter, apples, both fresh and dried cranberries, raisins, celery, green onion, and herbed bread stuffing. Ye'd need a good sauvignon blanc for the sauce along with light cream, white pepper, more tarragon and maybe some garlic. I know of a local winery on Skye that makes a good varietal with undertones of apples and fruitiness that is nae too terribly sweet."

"It sounds delicious, and perfect for what I'm trying to accomplish – pies that are tantalizing and unique, or at least unique to Scotland."

Lyndsie's face lit up. "I love dissecting flavors and trying to recreate recipes for things I've eaten at my favorite restaurants. I would never use a recipe idea from the Midwest at home in the US, but in Scotland, what could be the harm? If we set a new trend and make whoever inspired the recipe famous, we can always split our millions with them."

"I like the way you think."

Lyndsie had a pleased look on her face – and a slightly devious expression, as though she was about to go rogue. Heather had learned to recognize the look. Man, was she glad she hadn't told Lyndsie about her probably-never-mother-to-be woes.

"So," Lyndsie began. "Ye ken full well that I've always thought nae one was good enough for my little Heather, but I am totally sweet on Brodie. And the thought of the two of ye together – well, I think the world hangs on him."

Heather smiled. Lyndsie was nothing if not honest and direct. "But Brodie is leaving." Even if he wasn't, she didn't know him well enough to ask him to father a child with her.

The whole thing was ridiculous. Besides, that's what sperm banks were for. She just had to find the time to do some searching online. She'd probably have a gazillion choices and there would be no awkwardness, no rushing into something before she was ready, no hasty, ill-gotten decisions.

"Brodie will come home for holidays and special occasions, won't he?"

"Maybe," Heather answered. "Probably. I don't know."

"Well, I am offering to stay at the farm and keep an eye on things so the two of ye can go off on an adventure together, just have some privacy without all the farm hands around to watch ye. How does that sound?"

"It sounds heavenly. But I have no idea if he's even interested in..."

"Trust me," Lyndsie said. "Ye could go to Crail. Have ye been? I love it there. Or take him home to meet Violet and Nathan, give him a taste of Rabbit Hill Lodge and then go on to Portree. I ken of a wonderful excursion boat owned by a friend of mine – Captain Robin – that gives great tours of the Isles. His wife, Becca, has an amazing restaurant called Café Fish that's right on the harbor. Her Fisherman's Pies are to die for."

Heather smiled. "I love the idea, but it's probably a bit soon to be—"

"Hello?" Heather and Lyndsie both turned and looked toward the door.

A beautiful, buxom blond stood just outside in the courtyard. Her legs were long and her hair was perfect. She looked like a Barbie doll come to life.

"I'm looking for Brodie McBryde. His da thought he might be over here."

"No." Heather's heart went into high gear. "Um, sorry. I haven't seen him since yesterday morning." She thought back to the time they'd spent shearing sheep and bagging wool and... "I don't know where he might be."

"Do ye mind if I wait for a wee bit before I head back to the farm? Brodie's da never did like me much. I'd feel more comfortable here if ye dinnae mind."

"So how do ye know Brodie then?" Lyndsie smiled politely but got right to the point.

Heather wanted to cry – and laugh. It wasn't the first time she'd noticed it, but Lyndsie had lived in the U.S. for so long that she was starting to sound like she was half Minnesotan.

"Oh, Brodie and I go way back. We were high school sweethearts years ago, and then he went off to University, and I got married, and then he moved to Edinburgh. So I got divorced and moved to Edinburgh aboot the time he moved home, so I thought I'd stop by while I was home visiting my family – ye know, see if the old spark is still there."

They never did ask the woman's name. But when she was ready to leave, she asked them to tell Brodie hello from Teresa. When she finally departed, they had learned all kinds of interesting bits and bobs about Brodie.

Heather sighed. "Well, I guess that's that."

Lyndsie bristled. "What is wrong with ye, girl? She had her chance. Brodie is clearly nae interested in her or he would have already—"

"Let's talk about recipes, please. I really appreciate being able to pick your brain and I love the new ideas we're coming up with."

Lyndsie sighed.

Heather knew her well enough to know that they'd be back on the subject of Brodie McBryde soon enough. But for the time being, she didn't seem too intent on pursuing it. Or so she thought for about two seconds.

"Listen to me well, Heather," Lyndsie said. "I'm still as young as I want to be, but I'm getting to the point that I'm stuck in my own personal ruts, making the same favorite dishes o'er and o'er again. And of course, I'll never look at anyone other than my own sweet William. But ye – ye're young and energetic and very creative. Ye can accomplish – ye can have – anything ye set yer mind to, Heather. With food and with men."

Heather ignored the second part of the comment. "Only because I had such good teachers. And you're not getting old. It's hard to change up a menu like the one at Rabbit Hill Lodge when you have so many customers coming back and back and back again because they love a certain entrée on the menu."

"Aye, and bus tour guides who make the same requests year after year because they've gotten such good feedback on previous tours."

She'd had such fun brainstorming with Lyndsie. And because William owned the farm, as his wife, Lyndsie not only cared about Heather's success, she had a vested interest in what she made of the place. More importantly, Heather felt like Lyndsie was one of those rare people who really got her. These days, the only other human being she felt that way about was Brodie, who was no doubt off getting reacquainted with his old flame by now.

"Heather?" Lyndsie looked up from the menu.

"Yes?"

"Dinnae give up. Yer mum and da went through some troubled times when they first met. If they had given up, ye'd nae be here today."

"I understand what you're saying." But she didn't. Not really. Her mum and da's love story may have turned out the way it was meant to despite multiple obstacles to their happiness along the way, but they weren't those people now. Besides, the problems Heather was facing with her reproductive system went way deeper. How could she get serious with a man knowing she might never be able to have a baby?

She had the greatest respect for Lyndsie and William's relationship and the life they'd built together despite the fact that William spent most of the year in Minnesota and Lyndsie, in Scotland.

Her mum and da, and several of the other role models in her life, had definitely gone to great lengths to be with the ones they loved. Whether intentionally or not, they'd installed high expectations and a sense of perfectionism in her. Her mum was somewhat of a free spirit, but her da's music was always pitch perfect and carefully rehearsed. She'd grown up working in a tea house where recipes were followed to the letter, precisely made and religiously executed for consistency's sake, an essential ingredient in the restaurant business. Was it any surprise that Heather liked life to be sane, predictable, and well-planned? Dashed dreams, random dead bodies, missing bulls, murders, and ex-girlfriends showing up unannounced were just not her cup of tea.

Chapter 8

"Da? It's time we had a talk." Brodie stormed into the house he'd grown up in and wondered how many times he'd had it out with his father over the years. Their clashes were legendary. No big surprise there – they were as different as night and day. For years, he'd thought he must be adopted – he was nothing like his father. And his mother was, well, unlike anyone he'd ever known – very probably unlike anyone in the world.

But his mum wasn't here. His da was, and he was the one Brodie was about to confront.

"What is all the ruckus aboot now?" His da stumbled through the door between his bedroom and the kitchen.

Right, like Brodie made a stink about every last thing. He'd not yelled at his da since he left for university, and definitely not since his heart attack. Not that his da hadn't deserved it at least a dozen times. Much as Brodie would have liked telling his da what was what, he didn't want to be the one to put the final nail in his coffin.

Brodie finally got his da to look at him. "Here's what's up. You've always hated Duncan Morris, and I want to know why."

"Why pick on me? Why dinnae ye ask yer mum? It's her business with the man that left us enemies."

"What are you talking about?"

"Ask yer mum."

"Did you kill Duncan?"

"Now why would I do that? I've lived with what the two of them did for almost three decades. If I'd been planning to kill the man I would have done it back then, when the pain was fresh."

What was his da talking about?

"Yer mum and I made the best of the whole mess, and I've continued to deal with it all these years. Nothing has changed."

"Except that Uncle Dunk came back."

His da said nothing. He went to the refrigerator, opened the door and took out some leftovers from the night before. He started to eat from the container.

"What happened between you?"

His da continued to eat. Brodie waited and waited. What an infuriating man!

His da finished off whatever had been in the bowl and dropped it in the sink. He couldn't be bothered to put it soaking. No. That would be too much to ask.

"What happened?"

"Ye're the engineer."

"Is that supposed to be a clue?" Duncan had worked for the Corp of Engineers. Was his da saying there was some connection?

"All I'm saying is that ye're supposed to be good at math." His da took a bite of something else from the refrigerator. He hadn't been paying attention to what it was. "So ye want to ken what the problem was between me and Duncan? Do the math."

What was the old man trying to say? Of course Brodie was good at math – geometry, trigonometry, the whole kit and caboodle. He never would have graduated from engineering school if he hadn't had a gift for numbers. What on earth was his da getting at?

Then it hit him. His da had said something had happened almost three decades ago. Whatever came between his da and his Uncle Dunk had happened in the 1990s. Brodie was born in the 1990s. He was 29 years old.

He turned away from his da and left him chewing on whatever it was that he was eating. It was not quite a twenty minute drive to his mum's house.

Numbers. He could do the math awright.

#

"Miss Heather?"

Heather turned and saw the new, kinder, sweeter Knox motioning to her from the corner of the barn. She had to admit that ever since Lyndsie had confronted him, Knox had really appeared to be trying. The new leaf he'd turned over included being very helpful and polite.

She said, "What can I help you with?"

"I just wondered if I could speak to ye for a minute."

"I guess I have a few minutes. It's been a long day."

Knox looked chagrinned. "I wanted to mention a few things that might help ye understand a little more of what went into building the farm, and what may have gone wrong in the latter years, right before I left home."

Her interest was piqued.

"One thing I've been thinking aboot a lot is that when I was young, my Uncle Duncan – I used to call him Uncle Dunk – always came home for Christmas. It was a merry time, like textbook holidays should be, but the older I got, the more was made of the fact that I was the spitting image of Duncan. For reasons I didn't understand, the subject seemed to make every one extremely tense. Especially my da."

Heather nodded. "I noticed the resemblance almost immediately. But it's not that surprising knowing Duncan was your uncle. Genes skip around like that on a regular basis from what I know. I don't think it's a bit unusual for a child to resemble their grandparents or great-grandparents and certainly their cousins, aunts or uncles."

Knox grew silent, then said. "I wouldnae have thought anything aboot it except that whenever it was mentioned, my mum would get all upset and agitated, and then take to her bed. My da would go storming out of the house and nae come back for an hour or two. Uncle Dunk never seemed to be bothered by any of it, but my parents sure were."

"So you're thinking there may be more to the story than they let on." She pondered what he'd said. "Do you think the cause of whatever tension was there between them might somehow factor into what happened to your uncle?"

"Aye." Knox hesitated. "My da is a very complex man, and we dinnae get along all that well, but if the past can shed some light on the present, I thought I should share it."

"Thanks, Knox. Maybe you should mention what you told me to the police, see if they can make anything of it."

"My da would be very unhappy if I said anything. Of course, it wouldnae be the first time he's been upset with me."

"So is your da still around, or did he retire somewhere in a tropical zone like he said he was going to?"

"Well, that's the funny thing. For all the angst between them, he told me he was going to retire down in Cyprus to be closer to Uncle Dunk."

Heather smiled. "Well, I've known plenty of siblings who fight all the time, but still truly love one another when it comes down to it."

No one said anything for a few uncomfortable minutes.

Heather looked up at the stars just in time to see a shooting star streak across the Milky Way.

"I was just wondering," Knox began. "If I could see the house I grew up in, look at my old bedroom, see the rooms where we celebrated Christmas and Easter and had birthday parties and family gatherings, I might be able to remember more, piece a few more things together."

Her mind screamed no, but she could think of no good reason not to. "Maybe another time. Not tonight."

"I hear yer Uncle William has done some upgrades to the interior. I'd sure like to see what it looks like now that it's all gussied up."

"Well, like I said, maybe another time."

"Sure. I'll look forward to it." Knox tipped his hat and stood watching as she went into the house. His old house. She felt horribly uncomfortable. When she finally put her back to him and went inside, she had the feeling that he was still watching. She locked the knob lock, and then the deadbolt, pulled the curtains closed and walked to her room, hoping against hope that it wasn't Knox's old bedroom.

Chapter 9

Brodie navigated a curve in the single track road with long-practiced ease. He was not fond of narrow roads and passing places in other parts of Scotland, especially not the ones on the Isle of Mull and the Ardnamurchan Peninsula. But the roads around Alford were so familiar that it wasn't a problem.

He hoped his mum would be at home so he could talk to her and get his suspicions out in the open. A part of him also hoped she'd be gone so he didn't have to face the possibility of what she might say.

The roads widened to a firm two lanes and the houses lining the roadways got closer and closer together until you could not see between them. He'd gotten used to living in the city when he was at University in Edinburgh, but it wasn't his favorite. The Kingdom of Fife had been a little less densely populated, but he'd still been in a flat surrounded by other flats in a built-up area. If there was one thing he loved about the Highlands, it was being surrounded by wide-open spaces, with views stretching out to the end of the horizon. It was the main reason he'd opted to stay on the farm with his da when his mum and da had split and she'd moved to town.

Their relationship had deteriorated from that point on. As an adult, he could understand that his mum had felt betrayed, rejected, and alone when Brodie had decided to stay with his da. It was as if she'd counted on him taking her side, recognizing his da's deficiencies, and confirming her decision to get out of the marriage. In a way, he had, but he'd loved living on the farm and he'd liked the way his life was. Enough had changed – he didn't want the place he lived and the house he slept in to change, too. Life with his da had not been easy without the soft, feminine influence of his mum's presence. Brodie had taken over most of the household duties – cooking, cleaning, doing laundry, and tending the vegetable garden. They were skills that had come in handy once he'd moved out on his own, but he'd missed growing up in a normal household with both a mum and a da present.

    He thought about his mum. She hadn't found another boyfriend, or gotten remarried, or had a new batch of children with some other man, or done anything else that would have made Brodie's life more complicated. Nor had she invited him to visit or spend winters with her, or come to his soccer games, or science fairs, or done anything to make sure she remained a valued, constant presence in his life. She'd sulked, and withdrawn, and bought a one bedroom house with no guest room for him to stay in, even if he'd wanted to come for a visit. She'd never called him, although she'd always seemed happy to hear his voice when he'd called her.

    He wound through the streets of the tidy residential neighbourhood where his mum had lived since the day she left home. Many of the cottages had more garden than square footage. It was a well-kept neighbourhood and fit his mum's personality, not his. He thought she was happy, but he had no way of knowing for sure. She wasn't one to say much or even to express her emotions non-verbally. She'd hugged him the day he went off to University.

He pulled to the side of the road and eased his left tyres onto the sidewalk so other cars could still get through. He locked his truck and walked up the drive to his mother's front door. Her house was not a second home to him, even after almost twenty years. It was her house. That was it. She'd structured her life the way she'd wanted, and from his perspective, it had been fine. He did hope she was happy. More than that, he hoped she would still be happy when he went inside and wondered aloud if she was guilty of murdering Duncan Morris.

"Brodie!" Her face lit up, making him feel guilty as sin.

"Hi, Mum." He went through the door she held open for him and sat down on the sofa in the lounge. The rooms were all small and closed off from each other. The sofa faced the window and had a single painting of a tropical beach hanging over it. He turned around and took another look at the artist's inscription in the right hand corner. Had he been dreaming, or was it signed Duncan Morris? Why had he never noticed?

He stifled a moan and looked at his mum. Her face was frozen. He'd never been able to read her. His da blurted out his every thought, no matter how rude or inappropriate, farting out criticisms and opinions like they were stink bombs. He didn't like anything about the way his da communicated, but at least he did it.

"What brings ye here?" His mum's voice was stilted.

"I need to talk to you about a few things."

She said nothing. She took a seat opposite him and looked over his head at the painting.

"So, I'm sure you've heard that Uncle Dunk is dead." He used the term his mother had always used when referring to Duncan.

"Aye."

"You don't seem too sad."

She shrugged. "He lived a good life."

"Did he?"

"He lived where he wanted to live and did what he wanted to do. Nae everyone can say that at the end of their lives."

"Had you seen him any time recently?"

"Nae really."

That told him a lot. "What does that mean, Mum? Had you talked?"

Her face went all stony like it was prone to doing even when the conversation wasn't about a dead man she had known for decades. Still, she didn't answer. He waited, thinking she might eke out a comment eventually, but she did not.

"Mum, the man was killed. Murdered. I don't know the cause of the tension between you and he and da, but it's been there for years. There's got to be more to the story than I know about."

"What are ye getting at, son?"

"You're plenty strong enough to pick up a rock and bash a man in the head. I've seen you do worse when you're angry." He glanced to his right at a place in the wall that had been plastered over twice that he knew of where his mum had smashed something in the heat of anger. It didn't come out very often, but she had it in her.

She laughed – a cackling, wounded kind of laugh, shook her head and rolled her eyes. Was she hurt because he would suggest such a thing of her, or miffed that he was confronting her about something from her past? What was going through her mind?

He had no way of knowing.

They sat in silence for several minutes.

Brodie stood and strode the short distance to the door. He opened it, and looked out in the street. Knox's pick-up truck was stopped in the middle of the street in front of his mum's house, just a little off-center of his.

What was he doing here? Spying on him? Or had Knox come to see his mother? He watched as Knox sped off. His mother still didn't say a word.

#

Brodie put his hand on top of his head to make sure it didn't hit the ceiling when he hit the string of deep bumps and ruts that lined the track to McKnight Farms. It drove him crazy. He'd already thought about the way it needed to be reengineered to avoid problems in the future. He hated the bumps so much that he was tempted to offer Heather his services for free.

He leaped out of his pick-up and strode to the loft. He figured Knox was up there. Ah. What a stroke of luck. Knox was just coming down the stairs.

"What were you doing at my mum's house?" Brodie stared Knox down. He hadn't meant to come across as accusatory. He'd intended to strike up a casual conversation and try to get at the truth without backing Knox into a corner.

"I wasnae at yer mum's house. Ye were."

"You were stopped in front of her house. You were scoping the place out." So what was his problem? Why did the mere sight of Knox Morris put him on edge? What was it about the man that made him want to punch the guy in the mouth?

Knox bristled. "Yer eejit truck is so big that I had to slow down to make sure I could squeeze by."

"If you weren't coming to see her, then you must have been spying on me."

"I could care less what ye do or dinnae do." Knox slugged his right fist into his left hand with so much force that his wrist snapped back.

Was it because Knox looked so much like his Uncle Duncan? From the moment Brodie was old enough to be cognizant of his surroundings, he'd associated Uncle Dunk's presence with tension, anxiety, hard feelings, and an extreme sense of negativity from both his da and mum. Knox's looks were so similar to Duncan's that his mere presence brought it all back.

"What's this really aboot?" Knox was practically in his face. "Are ye afraid I'm going to be the one who gets to shag Heather instead of ye?"

Brodie's fist hit Knox in the jaw before either of them knew what was happening. It was like his arm had a mind of its own.

"Tell me what your business is with my mum." Brodie demanded.

Knox stroked his jaw. "If ye're so convinced the two of us are up to something, why not ask her?"

"I did!"

Knox laughed. "I was going to see a friend of mine. I saw yer truck and wondered what ye were doing. I forgot yer mum lived there. I was putting things together in my head when ye walked out."

"What friend? It's a neighbourhood of pensioners. My mum is one of the youngest there."

"Ye look just like her, ye ken." Knox laughed again.

Brodie grabbed his arm lest it lurch out and smash

Knox again. Why, he didn't know. He did look just like his mum, and it was a compliment to say so. His mother was a beautiful woman.

Knox sneered at him. "Ye probably will be the one to shag Heather. The pretty boy always gets the girl. How could I possibly compete with features so fair as yers?"

His fist connected with Knox's shoulder this time. He twisted Knox's arm behind his back and was ready to pommel him when Heather walked out of her house.

"I heard a commotion." She looked at Knox. "Should have known." She turned and looked at him. "Brodie? What's going on?"

A crowd was starting to form. The crew from pie production lined up just outside the door to their facility. Brodie felt completely discombobulated. Knox, on the other hand, looked calm and totally in control.

"Can I speak to you privately?" Brodie asked Heather.

Knox swore under his breath. "Can I speak to ye privately?"

Heather rolled her eyes. "Brodie, I'll start with you."

He followed her through a sliding door framed in wisteria vines and roses. They entered her office. He felt weak, sheepish, like a lamb with its tail between its legs. He'd wanted to swagger, to be as confident as he had when he'd hit Knox, but his heartfelt reaction was more shameful than cocky.

Heather slid the door closed, went to her desk and sat down. "Please tell me what's going on."

"Knox was being rude and insulting to you and me both."

"Did you do anything to egg him on?" She looked apologetic.

"No. Not really." Even as the words left his mouth,

he realized he had. And he'd basically admitted it.

Heather sat back in her chair. "Is there a reason you're here? Is there a reason Knox wasn't working? Or was he?"

"He wasn't a half hour ago." He didn't know what time Knox's shift ended, so he couldn't say for sure that Knox had been skipping out on his duties, but he strongly suspected Knox had been about to pay his mum a visit during work hours.

"So where was he a half hour ago?" Heather asked patiently.

"He was in his truck, in front of my mum's house. Something odd is going on with my da and my mum, and evidently Knox, and who knows who else. It's connected to Duncan and his death. I just don't know how."

Heather sighed. "The police were by to question me again this morning. I didn't know Duncan, nor did he pose any threat to me, but I suppose they have to follow through on every lead. One of the men in pie production told me that Knox told the police they should check into my background, and that I was at the top of his list of who might be guilty."

"I don't know what Knox's game is, but he's trying to make you look guilty – maybe me, too. And for what? Uncle Dunk wasn't around that much when I was growing up. When he was, he was nice and brought expensive presents and always seemed interested in me. I had no reason to want him dead."

Heather looked thoughtful. "You and Knox are close to the same age, aren't you? You were neighbours growing up, maybe in the same class at school. You must have been each other's nearest friend to play with and hang around with when you were kids. Why aren't you friends? Or did something come between you at some point? Why the antagonism?"

"I don't know. My father always said we were too much alike, but he was wrong."

Heather just looked at him. "If it helps, I don't think you're anything alike."

"First good news I've had all day."

"Would you like to be here when I speak to Knox?"

"He specifically asked if he could speak to you alone."

Heather squirmed in her chair. "Maybe I don't want to be alone with him."

Brodie raised his eyebrows. "Awright."

Heather shrugged. "No one said I have to do what he asks."

"True." He thought about what he wanted to say. "Knox is bad news. I don't know how I know it, but I do. But then, I've always thought all the Morrises were bad news. No offense to your friend, Lyndsie."

"None taken. Lyndsie's dad is also quite – well – shall we say unique? Not in a murderous way, but certainly always making trouble, even for his family. Especially for his family."

"My mum and da were always polite to Uncle Dunk – which is what he instructed me to call him – but there was an underlying tension, except that's not a strong enough word. It was extremely blatant whenever Uncle Dunk stopped by. More like hatred, smoldering just beneath the surface. I've questioned both my mum and da about it, but neither one of them will talk – at least not to me."

"Well, I guess I should go out and ask Knox to come through." Heather looked reluctant.

"I'll do it." Brodie eased off the seat of the chair,

stood, and walked outside. He looked around. Knox' truck was gone.

He went back inside to tell Heather, who didn't seem surprised.

"Be careful," he said before he left. His next step?

A sudden thought popped into his mind when he was halfway down the rutted lane and hit a bump so deep that he lurched up in his seat and hit his head on the ceiling of the cab.

He recalled signing up for an ancestry tracing service a few months back. He'd paid the yearly fee and sent in his saliva sample as requested. When his da had taken ill, the whole thing had been forgotten. More important things to tend to.

What had made him think of it now? Barbara had talked him into starting the process, curious to know if he had some illustrious relative in his lineage generations back. Wasn't that the trend?

He could care less about such things. He'd done it to make her happy. He might never have looked at the results, but something about the way Knox had taunted him about looking just like his mother had made him think. He did look a lot like her, and nothing like his da. He'd always thought he didn't favor either one of them when it came to personality traits, temperament, skill sets, or anything else that he could think of. He would have sworn he was adopted except for the fact that he looked so much like his mum. He'd already paid for the service – why not check out the results. What could it hurt to check out his genetic profile and see if he had any surprise matches?

Chapter 10

Heather double checked her figures and turned off her calculator when all the numbers agreed. She'd been working on the books for so long that she could barely focus her eyes. She was totally ready to take a hot bath and spend the rest of the evening in her bathrobe and slippers with her feet up and her favorite songs playing softly in the background.

She had just stood and was reaching to turn off the light when Knox appeared in the doorway. She jumped and then tried to pretend she'd tripped to cover up the fact that he'd scared her half to death. The last thing she wanted was for Knox to know she was afraid of him. And rightly so.

"Can I speak to ye?"

He'd had his chance earlier, but she truly didn't want to make anything worse, especially since everyone else had gone home for the night.

She turned and sat down again, motioning for him to take a seat across from her. "Sure. I have a few minutes."

Knox smiled. It was probably the most sincere looking facial expression she'd seen him display. "I'd like to start over – assuming ye'll give me one more chance."

Heather sighed. "Tell me why you believe you should be here – why you want to be here. This has to be difficult for you. Why do you want to keep putting yourself through this kind of torture?"

"I want to be here for ye. To help ye and William make a success of the place. It's the only way my family's legacy will continue, and that means a lot to me."

"I understand." And she did. But Knox's feelings about growing up on the farm seemed to be very conflicted. She'd sensed that from the beginning.

Knox seemed to understand something, too – that she didn't trust him.

"Life with my da was kind of rough. He wasnae the best parent, and my mum died when I was young. I think my da thought the only thing I was good for was providing farm labor when he needed help. Which was all the time."

"Sorry to hear things were less than ideal." She thought of her own childhood. She'd been expected to help around Rabbit Hill Lodge, especially over the holidays when they were busy and she wasn't in school. But she'd also been free to be a kid and pursue her own passions. Her mum and da were proud and supportive of her and always had been. It was hard for her to image a family being any different.

Knox looked far away. "The best part of living on the farm was being here when Uncle Dunk came to visit. He came a lot when I was younger and my mom was still alive. Every holiday – plus, if my da ever had to be gone to a cattle show or livestock exhibit or anything like that. Uncle Dunk would always come and stay while da was gone to help on the farm and make sure the chores got done, and make sure my mum and I had everything we needed."

"So you must have been pretty broken up when his body was found."

"I hadnae seen much of him since my mum died. It seemed like something came between him and my da after that. He came once or twice after she was gone, but it wasnae the same."

"Well, two brothers..." Heather tried to put her thoughts into words. "Not to generalize, but women have a way about them that unites people, brings them together. They often have the gift of hospitality. Not that men can't have it, too, but women..."

"Uncle Dunk had it." Knox looked far away again. "Funny, since he was the visitor, but I felt more at home when he was around."

"But if he grew up on this farm, in the house, it was as much his as it was your da's."

"Right. Uncle Dunk really should have gotten half of the proceeds of the sale when William bought the farm. My da was kind of a shyster. By the time he sold, Uncle Dunk hadnae come around for over a decade. I think my da was hoping he'd ne'er come back or find out that the farm sold – so my da could keep all the money."

"Doesn't sound fair to me, but these kinds of things happen in families from what I understand."

They sat in silence for a minute or two.

Heather finally said, "None of this explains why your uncle ended up dead. Do you think your da was involved in some way? Is that why you want to stay around?"

"To the best of my knowledge, my da is down in Cyprus living on a beach somewhere. But of everyone I ken, he had the most obvious motive. I mean, if he dinnae want to share proceeds from the farm with his only sibling, kill him off and that would be the end of it."

"Uncle Dunk didn't have any children?"

"Nay." Knox stood and paced around the perimeter of the room. "I need to get going."

"Sure," Heather said. "It's getting late anyway." She looked down and paused and thought about what she should do about solving the problems she was having with Knox. "I'll see you tomorrow then."

But when she looked up, Knox was gone.

#

Brodie couldn't get Heather out of his head. He hated the fact that Knox lived just a few meters from her, and that she herself was in a house that Knox felt proprietary about. He didn't know which of the bedrooms Heather was sleeping in at the old Morris house, but for all he knew, it was Knox's childhood bedroom.

The situation with Knox could explode at any moment. He felt it in his bones. Knox was unstable – maybe even dangerous. He might even be a murderer, although he hadn't figured out exactly why Knox would want to kill Duncan. He supposed the logical reason was that Walter's money would go to Knox one day, and if Walter only got half as much as he had now, Knox wouldn't get as much either – unless Knox ultimately got Duncan's half, too. Duncan didn't have any children. A favorite nephew would be a likely prospect for an heir. Unless Duncan had a girlfriend in Cyprus that no one knew about.

All this speculating was making his head hurt. If his mum or da would open up and tell him what was going on, he could at least start making some hypothesis based on legitimate facts.

And, if he could stop thinking about Heather, maybe he could concentrate on figuring things out and moving on.

So why wouldn't the woman leave him alone? Heather was one of the most capable women he'd ever met, yet he felt an irresistible urge to protect her. He wasn't ready to settle down and he had no desire to stay in the Highlands once his da had bounced back from his heart attack, yet the idea of being with her held so much appeal he couldn't stop considering the possibilities.

Possibilities. He compared the way he felt when he was with Heather with the way he felt when he thought about Barbara. The two women were exact opposites in their approach to life, their attitudes, and their physical auras.

Concentrate, he reminded himself. Heather was meant to be in the Highlands. It was where she could use her gifts. It was where she could pursue her passions. The farm was a perfect fit for her, but not for him. He was one of only a handful of people in the country, maybe the world, who had the ability to build bridges of a large magnitude. He belonged in the Islands, near the Firth of Forth, or on a peninsula. His gift was to bring worlds together, link remote areas and bring them to life, invite the sharing that occurred when people could go easily from one place to another. It was a task he took very seriously. The thought of it brought vigor and life to his existence. He didn't want to be stuck in the Highlands where everyone already knew everything about everyone else and nothing ever changed – where no one wanted anything to change – which was exactly why Heather was going to have a hard time making her plans to change things up work, at least with her existing crew. Their only motivation to make things bigger and better at McKnight Farms was that they would still have a job. They certainly didn't share Heather's vision or passion for new, creative ideas.

The more he thought about Heather, the more he realized that he needed to forget about her and move on. His da was right – if Munro McBryde was even his da.

How could he and Heather be happy if being together meant one of them giving up their dreams and not being able to use their gifts? It would never work. The sooner he got her out of his head, the better. It wasn't what he wanted, but it had to be.

He felt like he was in a daze – still thinking about Heather with every breath he breathed, trying not to, exhausted from wanting the one thing he couldn't have. Then he logged on to his email and noticed a letter from the ancestry company he'd signed up for. It had taken them long enough. He was tired and his head was still aching. He was overloaded already. But he had waited a long time. Might as well take a look see.

Despite his reservations, he logged on and pulled up his family tree to see his results. He knew his da didn't have his DNA on file, and he assumed neither did his mother.

A few clues started to filter in as the database began to populate his page.

What? Knox must have had his DNA tested, too. But there was no way they should be connected.

What? Knox Morris. Very closely related. Possible half-brother.

No! His mind grappled with what he'd seen. The only options he could think of were mortifying. No. He could not accept it. No. It couldn't be. There was no way in hell.

He went to his profile and changed his settings from public to private. He prayed that Knox hadn't seen what he'd seen. There. Assuming he wasn't already too late, Knox might be able to see he had a close match, but he wouldn't be able to see that it was Brodie.

If what was there was true – and how could it not be – DNA didn't lie – Knox and he shared the same father. The thought made him sick. Again, he tried to concentrate, to get past the emotions and look at things logically. The options were first, that Brodie's da had engaged in sex with Knox's mother, who had conceived a son. Or, that Knox's da had engaged in sex with Brodie's mum, who had conceived him. Or... his mind flew to the bloated body he'd found in the field. Or... Uncle Dunk was his real father. And Knox's, too.

Chapter 11

Heather spread out the colorful plaid she'd chosen to decorate her lounge and dining room. The blue, purple, and fuchsia looked beautiful against the backdrop of the stone wall and exposed beams, and tiny lines of bright green added a note of cheer.

She had just finished measuring and was starting to cut – she loved cutting on a plaid fabric where all you had to do was follow the lines – when her mobile chirped out the ringtone she'd assigned her mum.

"Mum!" It was so good to hear a familiar voice.

"I miss you so much, Heather. How are things going on top of the world?"

"You always put such a positive spin on things, Mum."

"I try, but that doesn't mean I'm not worried about you, dear daughter."

Her mum's endearment was something she had heard countless times from both her mum and da. Today, it made her want to cry. It broke Heather's heart to think she might never have a child to speak those words to.

But as always, she soldiered on and got down to more immediate problems.

"Did Lyndsie tell you about Walter Morris' son, Knox, coming home and hanging around? William invited him to be on staff but he makes me nervous, so there's that. And I'm assuming you know we found a dead body, which turned out to be Duncan Morris, Walter's brother, who was in the process of starting legal proceedings against William, claiming he should have been given half of the proceeds from the sale. The police think it was murder, so they're investigating half the neighbourhood."

"That sounds stressful."

"I'm trying to focus on the farm, and putting my ideas into practice, but I'm meeting with more resistance than I thought I would."

"Is this Knox making trouble or just being a nuisance?"

"Both. But it's not just him. The work crew is polite enough, but they generally treat me like I'm an invasive species."

Her mum laughed. "You have such a creative way of putting things."

"The only bright spot has been one of the neighbours, Brodie McBryde. He's been so supportive and encouraging – I really don't know what I would do without him."

"I'm so glad you have someone you can count on to be there for you."

"Me, too. And the reason he's even here is just a complete God thing." Heather loved the little catch phrase Lyndsie used to refer to things that worked out as they were meant to because God had a hand in the timing. "He came home shortly before I arrived in the Highlands to help his da on the farm after his da had a heart attack."

Violet was silent for a moment. "Does that mean that he'll be going back to wherever he came home from?"

Now it was Heather's turn to be silent as she considered how she would feel when Brodie left. "I suppose so. I'm not wishing any sort of trouble on his da, but I hope he won't be leaving anytime soon."

"I hope so, too." Her mum hesitated again. "And what about your other situation? Have you spoken to the doctor again?"

"No. I'm still waiting to hear the results of the latest tests." Heather sighed. She didn't like talking about her fertility issues, but she supposed she should be grateful her mum didn't lecture her on the unlikelihood that Heather was going to meet someone to father her child in the Highlands.

She went back to making her plaid into pillows and valances and whatever else might come to mind after her mum had filled her in one what was going on at Rabbit Hill Lodge, Eilean Donan Castle and Dornie. She threaded her sewing machine with a deep purple bobbin and started turning under edges and sewing seams. She was doing what she always did, and did best – staying busy.

But for the first time since she'd moved to the Highlands and taken charge of the McKnight Farms operation, she felt dread, apprehension and discouragement. What if Brodie moved away in the near future? What if she never made any friends? What if she didn't find someone to have a child with until it was too late? What if the staff and hired hands never came to respect her? What if she failed?

She chased her fears from her mind and bucked up on the inside, where it mattered. She didn't need Brodie's help to succeed in her mission. But she wanted him to be a part of her life. She didn't know much about him – his favorite foods, his favorite color, or what he liked to do in his free time. They'd never had a date, or gone on an outing. But she liked what she did know of him, and he had become so dear to her in the short time she'd known him that she couldn't imagine life without him.

#

Brodie watched as his da struggled to get up off the sofa and navigate his way to the loo. His natural inclination would be to give his da a hand to make sure he didn't fall. But the fact was, his da needed to get stronger and learn to take care of himself. Not for the first time, he felt a surge of pity for his da. Most older folks had a spouse to take care of them when they were in need. Until recently, he'd always thought his da was the reason his mother had left home and moved into town. And maybe his da had been to blame. But based on what he'd recently learned about his mother and the twists and turns in his family tree, maybe she had been at fault.

A few minutes later, his da came out of the loo and snorted. "So what were ye up to all day? Lazing around? Or were ye off flirting with that woman from McKnight Farms again?"

"Her name is Heather, and I am not flirting with her."

"Fine. Ye keep on helping her out – if that's what ye want to call it."

"She's new to the area. And Knox is over there, stirring up trouble. She needs someone to help her."

"Seemed pretty independent to me."

Brodie tried to downplay his feelings. "She is. But

she's also—"

"A woman." His da opened a jar of peanut butter, stuck a knife in, licked it clean, and stuck it back in the jar for a second round. "That's how they worm their way in. And once they're in yer gut, there's nae getting rid of them. I should ken."

In your gut? Brodie had always thought when you let a woman in, it was into your heart. "Da? I wish you would tell me what mum did to you. I have my suspicions but no way to confirm them if neither of you will talk."

"Ye best watch yerself, lad."

Brodie took a deep breath. "You'll still be my da – always will be – no matter what."

His da sat down at the kitchen table with his jar of peanut butter. "I'm nae a bloody tattle tale."

"That's not what this is about, Da. I'm a grown man, and if whatever happened concerns me, I have a right to know."

"Ye'll have to ask yer mum."

Brodie rolled his eyes. "Did you have an affair with Mrs. Morris?"

"Walter's wife? Nay!" His da looked genuinely shocked. "What a ridiculous notion! Why would ye think such a thing?"

Assuming he believed his da – and he did – that narrowed the options to one. His mum had slept with Duncan or Walter Morris, and that's why Brodie was showing up as Knox's half-brother in the DNA results.

"Da?"

"What? More questions? Ye insult me, Brodie. I have done nothing to disgrace ye or yer mum. I have always done right by both of ye so much as it has been in my control to do so."

Okay, so he felt pretty sheepish about accusing his da of such a thing. Munro was a little rough around the edges, but he was his da, and he'd always been good to him.

Brodie tried to stay in control of the various emotions churning through his body. He looked at his da and squinted to read the label on the peanut butter jar. "Where did you get a jar of Skippy Super Chunk Peanut Butter? I don't recall buying any for you. I don't think they carry it at the grocery."

"I found it wedged in the hedgerow and considered it to be a gift from God."

"So it's Heather's."

"If ye want to return it to her, feel free to ring her."

"Right. After you've been eating out of the jar. Da, I doubt peanut butter is on your approved cardiac food regimen."

"It is a little sticky and hard to swallow. I think I'll wash it down with some butter."

Brodie watched as his da went to the icebox and found a stick of butter, got a hunk of it on his knife, and then dipped it in the peanut butter jar. Lord, help me, he thought. He said, "Have you looked into starting cardiac therapy like the doctor in Aberdeen said you should?"

"Nay. I get enough of a workout wrestling with cattle and chasing grunters down."

"But you're not doing any of that. I am."

"That will all change soon."

"Right," Brodie said. "When you start going to physical therapy and working out so you get your strength back."

"Ye always were a lippy lad."

"You've worked hard on the farm for decades and you still had a heart attack. That's why they want to teach you healthier ways to eat and specific exercises that will strengthen your heart."

"This peanut butter is delish, but I think the creamy variety would suit me better."

"Good grief, Da. I don't know what to do with you. I'm glad I could come and fill in the gap for you, but I can't stay here forever. I've been offered a job designing and building a bridge between Mull and the Ardnamurchan Peninsula. My dream job."

"Well dinnae let me stand in yer way. No worries. I'm sure I'll get on fine without ye."

"I have complete confidence in you getting on without me one day soon, Da. That's why I want you to get started on your cardio therapy. My job offer has a deadline, and I'd hate to miss out on the opportunity because you're not quite ready. Will you work with me on this?"

"What aboot the woman at McKnight Farms then? Are ye going to walk away from that opportunity?"

Brodie snorted. "So now you want me to hook up with her so I won't move away and leave you alone?"

"Well, she does seem like a nice enough woman. Maybe if ye'd get married and start working on giving me some grandchildren, I'd have more reason to live. I might start taking better care of myself."

"I thought you didn't like her! And it is not up to me to provide you with the will to live. That's your job."

"It would be nice to have ye nearby."

Brodie huffed. "So I can keep doing all your work."

"I've heard she's an excellent cook. Ye could do worse."

"Da. I am not going to choose a wife based on your desire to have good meals delivered to your door every day." He shook his head.

"Any word on the bull that disappeared from her pasture? Maybe if ye were married, she would look after me while ye're out gallivanting around with the bridge folk."

"Her name is Heather. And no and no. And bridge folk? You make my co-workers sound like a bunch of trolls." Brodie sighed. "I'm going to ring the doctor right now and get you set up with the cardiac therapist."

"Make sure ye ask for a woman. Maybe she'll tickle yer fancy if the McKnight woman doesnae."

"Heather McPhearson is everything I want and need in a woman, but if and when I pursue her, it will be in my own way, in my own time. Not yours!"

"Ye do what ye must." His da took another dip from the butter pot, and then the peanut butter jar. "As will I."

Chapter 12

Heather watched through the open window as Knox approached her office. What now, she wondered?

"Miss Heather?" Knox leaned against the door jamb and cocked his cowboy hat. "I just wanted to let ye know that the grunters have already gained ten percent of their body weight. They're thriving on that feed ye suggested."

"Thanks for letting me know." So she'd finally done something right.

"I trimmed down the sharp edges of the little ones' teeth just like ye told me to. There has nae been a single instance of tail biting since I did."

"Good."

"Nae sense inviting infection. We dinnae want anything to set them back at this stage. Especially since they're coming along so well."

She swallowed hard. "I appreciate your attention to detail, Knox. Good job."

"I just want to be helpful," Knox said. "The more I reflect on what I went through growing up on the farm, I become convinced that the problem was nae with the farm or the animals, but with my da. Now that he's moved away and ye're here, tending the land and the animals takes on a whole new meaning."

Her insides did a scary summersault. He was being too polite. It worried her. What was going on? She'd challenged him to be a better employee, a more productive team member. But had she somehow encouraged him personally? She hadn't meant to. Was Knox lying or being sincere? Had he had a change of heart or was he putting on an act, playing her, or harboring ill-intent?

She wished Brodie would walk through the door. He was a good judge of character, and knowing Knox since they were kids was a huge asset when it came to figuring out what he was up to. Sadly, Brodie was nowhere in sight. She felt uncomfortable and alone, and she hated that she did.

She looked up and focused her attention on Knox, who was still going on about something to do with the grunters, making himself out to be the savior of McKnight Farms. And maybe, in the end, he would be. How was she supposed to know?

The land line belonging to the farm jingled and she was thankful for the interruption – until she found out who was on the line.

The police.

She asked if they would mind giving her a second.

"If you don't mind, Knox. I need to take this call."

"Certainly." But there he stood.

"No. I mean, I'd like some privacy."

"Oh," Knox said. "Sure." He moved the other side of the room, near the door.

How obtuse was this man? She caught his eye and motioned for him to leave the room. Finally, he took the hint.

She closed the door behind Knox, sat down at her desk, and returned the telephone to her ear. "Sorry for the delay."

The policeman's voice was deep. She tried not to feel intimidated. "We were wondering it ye could come into town and visit the police station."

"Sure. Today?"

He grunted. "If ye want yer bull back."

"You found Beauty?"

"We ken who has him."

"I'll be right there. Well, I'll be there in a half hour." She still had a tiny, fuel efficient car with even tinier wheels, and even if she'd been a pro at driving on single track roads, she'd still have to go slow over the ruts in the lane.

Twenty-five minutes later – the roads might be getting worse, but she was getting better at dodging the potholes – she pulled up in front of the police station. She wished her car wasn't blue, and that she hadn't gotten custom plates. It wouldn't take long for everyone in Alford to know she was in town.

"Hello," she said to the receptionist. "Heather McPhearson."

The woman gave her a dirty look. "Oh, I ken who ye are."

Heather sighed. Everybody might think they did...

She recognized the deep voice that spoke. "Come through."

He spoke again without having the respect to tell her his name. "One of the men who works for ye has yer bull."

"What? Why? Did he take Beauty, or rescue him from whoever took him?"

"The man claims he dinnae trust ye to recognize the bull's value. He claims he believed ye would sell Beauty at auction so ye could bring in a new, younger, unproven bull."

"Why would I do that? Beauty is a great asset to our herd, and from what I can see, he's at his prime. I have no thought of replacing him. None at all."

"Ye'll have to figure the rest out for yerself. I'm nae going to get into it."

"You obviously know more than you're saying. I want to know what's going on. Are you going to press charges?"

"Just be glad ye got yer bull back."

"What – that's it? I'm just supposed to go on like it never happened?"

"It's nae my job to tell ye how to run yer uncle's business."

"I'm asking for your help. How am I supposed to make better decisions if you won't tell me what's wrong?"

"Fine." He glowered at her. "Yer staff claims that ye have nae respect for tradition and that ye intend to change everything until nothing of the old Morris Farms' customs remain."

"I have never said I would change everything. Morris Farms was on the brink of bankruptcy when William bought the property. My job, with his help, has been to examine every aspect of the operation, and improve the areas in which it was lacking. I have been very upfront about which—"

The deep voice interrupted her. "If ye cannae even maintain control of yer staff, it's doubtful ye can manage the job of restructuring the farm. I dinnae ken if it's because ye're a woman, an outsider, a goerby, or an American, but yer staff has nae confidence in ye."

She tried to keep her temper in check, but it was impossible. "I haven't even been here for a month. I was kind enough to let them keep their jobs – to give them a chance to help me make the farm better and more profitable. I've tried to pass on my excitement and enthusiasm for the success story that we can all celebrate once we get back on the right track. They need to extend the same courtesy to me. They need to give me a chance."

"All I ken is that these kinds of things ne'er happened when Walter Morris owned the farm."

Heather tried not to let her anger become visible. "Who was it? Who stole my bull?"

"I strongly suggest that ye dinnae press charges. It was a misunderstanding. Beauty will be back in his pasture by the time ye return home."

She shook her head in disbelief. "So that's why you wanted me to come into town?"

The police officer whose name she still didn't know stared at her from across the table. If she had felt intimidated before, she now felt censured, judged, and condemned.

She tried a different tack. "I can't have a person on my staff who I do not trust. If I don't know which one of my staff took the bull, I will have to fire all of them."

"That is yer choice, but ye need to ken that these men have friends and supporters throughout the area. Ye will nae have an easy time replacing them or finding a new crew."

"Was it Knox Morris?"

"Knox has a firm alibi."

That didn't mean he hadn't planted the idea that led someone else to take the bull.

She stood. "Am I free to go?"

"As long as ye're here, I'd like to ask ye a few questions aboot the murder of Duncan Morris."

"Why? I was already questioned. I know nothing about what happened."

"Ye were the last person to see the man alive, the last person to have words with him."

"Except for the murderer." God help her, she didn't mean to sound snarky, but she was innocent. Whoever had killed Duncan had certainly seen him, and very probably said a few choice words before they struck the fatal blow.

The policeman didn't even flinch. "Duncan dinnae accept the sale of his parent's land. He dinnae recognize William McKnight's acquisition of the land as legal or binding. If Duncan had continued in his quest for justice and persuaded a judge to take the case, yer assets would likely have been frozen and that would have caused problems for ye and William McKnight."

"I understand what you're saying, but neither William nor I deal with a problem like you mentioned by murdering someone."

"And perhaps ye should understand that seeing as I dinnae ken ye, I'm reluctant to accept yer word at face value." He glared at her. "Please refrain from leaving the area until our investigation is complete."

She wanted to tell him not to waste his time, but she simply said. "No worries. I'm not going anywhere." She probably sounded flip. He was lucky she didn't flip him off. Eejit.

#

Brodie wandered though the back pasture, checking on the cattle that grazed on the tall grasses near the tree line. He paused long enough to rub each one's shoulder or pat their rumps, depending on which they liked best.

He knew each of them by name, and how they liked to be treated. It had taken him a few days to get to know the newer calves and heifers. Inventory came and went on a beef farm. That was the nature of the business. He was a firm believer that each animal that was part of their farm deserved to be treated with concern, respect, and high esteem for as much or as little time they spent in the McBryde's care.

Of course, he had a special penchant for the heifers who were saved back to become breeding stock. All growers did. The ones you got to know better and better with each season that passed, the ones who birthed outstanding calf after calf, were always favorites.

He greeted the last heifer and noted she was starting to show signs of having been bred. Their bull wasn't as renowned as Beauty, but at this point he guessed any bull was better than no bull. He subconsciously looked into the McKnight's pasture while he was thinking on Beauty, and there he was.

"He's back!" He called out to the heifers, to anyone or anything within hearing distance, which was no one. He didn't care. He was just thrilled to see that Beauty was back. He reached for his mobile to ring Heather and find out what had happened. And then he remembered that he'd decided to distance himself from McKnight Farms, and most of all, Heather. Farming in the Highlands wasn't what he wanted. It was the right thing to do for both of their sakes. It would make things a lot easier when he left for the Isle of Mull.

His shoulders were slumped as he trudged back to the house. When he found his da taking a nap, he decided to spend a little time on the computer. His da wasn't very tolerant of him being online or staring at a computer screen for long periods.

He poured himself a glass of local wine, sat down on a chair, and tried to scoot it up to the kitchen table without making too much noise. Man, he missed his wheels. He glanced at his da to make sure he hadn't woken him up. His da's head was still drooped to one side.

He logged into the ancestry company to see if there were any new clues. Yes! He sucked in his breath when he saw what the most recent updates revealed, then exhaled when he realized he'd gotten all excited for nothing. The first reported that he had a possible half brother in Aberdeenshire – nothing new there. Knox was – his eyes flipped back to the screen. It wasn't Knox. He looked at a photo of a man named Finn who looked like he could be Knox's brother. He wasn't the spitting image of Duncan like Knox was, and his coloring was a little darker, but the resemblance was there. He could see a little of Walter in his eyes and chin, which could have come from Walter or Duncan. Although another half-brother certainly factored in and added some additional drama to the mess, he was no closer to solving the mystery of which man was his father.

He scanned the next clue. He could come back another time and investigate Finn, then decide if he was interested in meeting him.

His eyes almost blistered from the massive number of blinks – two sisters in Cyprus? There it was. To the best of his knowledge, Walter had never even visited Cyprus, at least not when they'd all been young. Duncan had fathered him then, along with Knox, this Finn fellow, and two girls, albeit younger than the rest of them, from Cyprus. He flicked through the data. The women both looked Cyprian, so their mother must have been a native, or Greek or Turkish at the very least.

He felt so angry that he might have murdered Duncan if he were still alive. At the same time, he could acknowledge a sense of regret that he never got the chance to talk to Duncan, or get to know him as a man, as a birth father.

There were other questions footing it through his brain. Had Duncan raped his mother and the other women with whom he fathered children, or had they been star-crossed lovers? Had Duncan been so charming, or built, or competitive, or crazy-sexy that his mother and the other women lined up to sleep with him?

It had been a different time, a different era. People had been different, especially women. The norms of the day had not been the same, nor the expectations, dreams and desires. Had free love still been a thing?

And why, he wondered, had his mother never had another child? Knox and he were both only children. He wasn't sure about Finn. Based on what he knew of his mum and da's relationship, he thought he could safely speculate that whatever had happened between his mum and Uncle Dunk had done irreparable damage to their marriage. It had to have been even harder on Walter and his wife – assuming Walter had known that Knox was Duncan's child and not his.

His da was still asleep. Again, he felt compelled to call Heather, to hear her calm, reassuring voice, and enjoy her peaceful, easy manner, and her sweet but snarky sense of humor. He reached for his mobile, and snapped his hand back just before he made contact. The last thing he needed – Heather needed – was for her to get drawn into his family situation. But in a way, she already was due to Duncan's murder. Was it possible that one of Duncan's other children, or their mothers, was responsible for his death?

At least he knew who his birth father was. Brodie had one important answer, but there were dozens of others that needed to be found. His mum wouldn't tell him anything. Neither would his da. Walter was rumored to be in Cyprus. Duncan was dead. That left Knox.

Chapter 13

Heather was eager to get home after her encounter with the police. She couldn't wait to get home. But how could she feel confident, accepted, and secure in her home now that she knew there were traitors in her midst?

One of her staff had actually stolen Beauty. How was she supposed to go on trusting the people who worked at the farm when one of them had so little respect for her that they would take a bull so valuable, taunt her with the loss, and then lie to protect themselves? She knew she had to deal with the situation immediately. Part of her wanted to run away and head for Rabbit Hill Lodge where she truly did feel loved and wanted and appreciated. But she knew she didn't have that luxury. But it was a nice thought to savor, even if only for a few minutes.

She decided to drop by the store as long as she was in town and pick up a few provisions – and maybe some of her favorite comfort foods from the grocery. What she was really hungry for was a jar of Skippy Super Chunk Peanut Butter. She could have sworn she'd brought a jar when she'd moved to Alford.

"Hello." She smiled and nodded at the clerk as she entered the store, a carry back to her summers in Minnesota where you greeted everyone. The woman didn't nod back, but that was to be expected, she supposed. Highlanders weren't the most demonstrative people. And she was new to town. The woman probably didn't know who she was – probably thought she was a tourist.

"Oh, I ken who she is awright."

Heather heard the hushed voice cutting through the even quieter grocery like a hot knife slicing cheesecake. Who were they talking about? She was halfway down the first aisle, most likely out of sight. There were not many people in the store. Was the woman speaking of her? She took a box of Mr. Kipling's Exceedingly Good Mini Battenberg Cakes off the shelf with care to be quiet.

"I can abide American tourists just fine as long as they're polite and follow our customs."

"They spend a lot of money when they're visiting." a second voice said.

"Aye. They make their mark and then they go back. All fine by me." The first voice was a wee bit louder and a lot more judgmental in tone.

Heather listened for what she feared would come next.

"It's the ones who ne'er go home that I have a problem with. Thinking they can adopt our lifestyle and become one of us just because they love hairy coo, or little lambs. Who do they think they are?"

"Aye. And then they creep in and try to take over."

"They're like the gorse, or rhododendrons. They're colorful and pretty to look at and everyone thinks it's great cause for celebration when they sprout up in yer yard. But then they spread and spread until they've choked out the native grasses and bushes and taken over everything in sight."

She heard a loud humph.

"And trying to run a farm. Not even the most level-headed Scottish woman would dare attempt such a thing."

"I've heard how she bosses the men around and makes them do her bidding."

"Serves her right, they stole her bull."

Both women laughed. She thought seriously about putting her items back, but she didn't want to give them the pleasure of knowing she'd heard what they'd said about her. Plus, she needed the items she'd grabbed and there was really only the one grocery in Alford. So she went to the front of the store, paid for her items, smiled and left.

She drove by the pasture where Beauty grazed before she turned into her drive. There he was, just like that – as predicted – looking as regal and in command as always.

The second she got home, she called a meeting. One of the groundskeepers was working in the garden. She asked him to round everyone up. He took off on a four wheeler – to do her bidding, she supposed. It was almost quitting time for most of the workers. If they came in right off, they could leave at the end of their shift and never come back if that's what they wanted. She was sick of this. It was time to make some changes, and that was exactly what she intended to do.

If you want something to change, you have to do something different. She'd heard the saying from someone she respected one summer when she was in America. It was spot on advice no matter where in the world you lived.

When they were all gathered in the courtyard – everyone but Knox – who knew where he was off to, she said, "I know one of you stole Beauty, and then put him back in the pasture while I was with your friend, the policeman, in Alford. Maybe it's better that I don't know which of you it was. What I do know is that I cannot tolerate a crew who does not share my goals and objectives for McKnight Farms. I still believe that this farm can be a place where I will be encouraged in my attempts to make the farm the best it can be.

"I don't mean to generalize – some of you have been a wonderful help to me, no matter what your motivation. But I can't keep going on this way. It's counterproductive and demoralizing. I'm going to ask each of you to look into your hearts and make a decision. If you support me and enjoy working with me, then I would be grateful if you'd stay." She paused, because she wanted her words, and the next, to sink in. "If not, get out. You're fired."

She looked each of them in the eye, and then, she walked a few feet away. Some got up immediately, uttering Gaelic curses under their breaths as they walked out the door. A few others sat for a few minutes, very likely in shock, and then left.

One came up to her and said, "I'm leaving, but I want ye to ken it was nae me who took Beauty."

"Fair enough. I wish you well."

There was only a handful left when the exodus was complete – a few from her pie production crew stayed, the lead cook included, thank God, and one of the groundskeepers, and a couple of all round handy men. She thanked them for staying. There were tears running down her face. There shouldn't have been. She was trying hard to remain strong and worthy of their respect.

"It's going to be hard for awhile. We're going to have to work double shifts and do things that aren't in our wheelhouse until I find replacements for certain positions. We'll work together to make this a more efficient operation so we can get by with fewer workers. But we will survive. We will do this, and we will do it well. And with the grumblers and troublemakers gone, perhaps we can finally do our work with an enthusiastic, optimistic outlook."

There were a million things going through her mind as the few remaining workers filed out. One stopped on the way out and told her she had done the right thing. Another said he would come early and get the production lines ready to go. She knew their output might suffer at first, but their quality would not. It might even surge, now that everyone was all in, and doing their jobs for the love of what they did and the pride they took in what they accomplished. Heather had to believe that once they got back on their feet, they would find new ways to produce more and even better pies.

Now that she didn't have enough help, she was going to have to fork hay and feed cattle and help on the production line. Hopefully, it would only be temporary. She felt a surge of anger toward William. She was dreading the conversation she needed to have with him. She would apologize, of course. But that didn't mean she wasn't frustrated with him. If he had let her round up and hire her own crew before she came to Alford like she had wanted to, she wouldn't be having these problems right now. Now, she was being put in a position where she was desperate for help, but had no time to interview people, search for positive, qualified individuals, or reorganize. She was already working twelve hours a day and it would likely be more now that half of her crew was gone. She was far away from her social connections, her family, and everything else she knew, which made it much harder to launch a personnel search. She felt a huge sense of relief, and she wanted to scream.

#

"Da!" Heather watched as a tall, fine-looking-as-always, Nathan McPhearson, strode across the garden. She met him at the door, grabbed his hand, and ushered him toward her house and into the lounge. "Mum didn't come? I wanted her to see how I fixed up the rooms. I never would have been able to make it look so nice if she hadn't taught me how to sew."

"It's beautiful. She told me to take all kinds of photos so she can see what you've done." Her da gave her a hug. "She wanted to come, but she and Lyndsie are catering a wedding this weekend at Eilean Donan Castle."

Heather smiled. "Her favorite thing to do."

"Weddings at the castle bring back a lot of good memories for both of us because of William and Lyndsie's wedding day."

Heather smiled. "So tell me about the wedding you're playing at in Alford. How did you happen to accept a job way up here?"

"The groom is a gent I taught school with in Dornie. He's marrying a girl from the Inverness area, but he grew up in Alford and they wanted to be married in the church here in town. Plus, it's a good excuse to see you." He gave her another hug.

"Are you playing on your own, or with a group?"

"A band. Their regular piper is on tour in America playing with the Red Hot Chili Pipers."

"Wow. So this is a hot band."

"Yes, and I'm hoping you'll come with me so you get to hear me play. They do a lot of old time rock and roll along with everybody's Scottish favorites and some slow, romantic oldies but goodies."

"Sounds like my kind of party."

"You'll come? Perfect!"

"I'm not sure I have anything appropriate to wear." She couldn't remember bringing any gowns, and she definitely didn't have a wedding hat.

"Your mum sent two gowns for you to choose from and a hat to match each."

"She's such a sweetie." Really, she was so blessed to have parents like Nathan and Violet. With the added bonus of William and Lyndsie watching over her and teaching her so many things – she couldn't have had a rosier childhood. She could only hope she could pass on the gift to a child or two of her own one day.

"If you want to bring a friend along to dance with, I've got permission to bring a plus one plus another."

"No. I really don't know anyone who... Not yet anyway." Her mind went to Brodie. She'd felt like they were getting close, but lately, he'd all but disappeared. She turned back to her da. "I'm so glad you came up a day early. I can't wait to show you the farm."

Two hours later they'd visited each of the fields and Heather had introduced him to the Belted Gallways, the Aberdeen Angus herd, including Beauty, and the Hairy Coos. They'd seen each of the different breeds of sheep, the chickens, the flock of turkeys she was grooming for Thanksgiving, and the new Red Duroc grunters Knox was taking care of.

"I love the color," her da said. "The red is just beautiful."

She was beaming with pride by the time they were ready to head home. Her boots were covered with muck from the fields, to which grass and dried up heather blossoms had stuck. Her face was smudged with dirt and her jeans were flecked with sticky things from grasses that she didn't know the name of. But she was happy and feeling delighted with herself. It was such an encouragement to have a fan, and that, her da certainly was.

They were driving the stretch of road where the road to McKnight Farms cut off. Right before they came to the turn-off, she saw Brodie pull into a passing place. To talk to her or let her by?

She rolled down her window and took the bull by the horns. "Hi, Brodie." She wanted to introduce him to her father and this could be her only chance. Why it was important to her, she didn't exactly know. But it was.

"Hi, Heather." Brodie eyed her father, but acted aloof. Did he think she'd met an older man, or hired a new foreman?

"Brodie, this is my da – Nathan McPhearson."

Brodie blushed, and her da gave her a knowing look.

"Nice to meet you, Brodie?"

"McBryde." They both spoke at the same time.

"He lives on the farm next to mine. I mean William's. He's been a big help to me when it's come to settling in."

"I'm here in the Highlands temporarily," Brodie said, sounding defensive. "I came home to help my da out after he had a heart attack."

Was that really the thing he wanted to be known for? Heather wondered. Was the fact that he would be leaving soon so important to him? Was getting away from her and the Highlands what defined him?

"It's nice you could come for a visit," Brodie said, acting like he couldn't wait to leave.

She pulled up so he could get by. He spun his wheels

in his rush to get away and didn't look back.

She sighed. "Sorry he wasn't more talkative." She sighed again. "He's really very nice."

Her da didn't say a word.

"We normally get on very well."

"Maybe he was in a rush to get somewhere," her da said.

"Sure. That might be it." But deep inside, she sensed something was wrong. Things had been so good, so comfortable and natural between them, and now, all of the sudden, they weren't.

"Who's going to help his da when Brodie heads back to wherever he's from?"

"I'm not sure. Brodie is an engineer. He worked on the Firth of Forth Bridges and now he's been offered a job designing and building a bridge that will connect the Isle of Mull on the Tobermory side to the Ardnamurchan Peninsula."

"What an amazing opportunity," her da said. "That area is incredibly beautiful."

"I haven't been to Tobermory in a long time." When she was little, they'd gone to visit Michael and Isabelle, friends of her mum and da, a few times. They'd stayed at Lyndsie's Aunt Rose's house. She was married to a Pastor, Ian MacCraig. They were some of the nicest people she'd ever known. "Is Pastor MacCraig still at the church in Tobermory at the top of the big hill?"

"Yes, but I think he's planning on retiring one day soon. Last I heard, he and Rose were moving out of the rectory and purchasing a home of their own near Calgary Bay on Mull."

"What about Michael and Isabelle? Do they still live in Scotland?"

"Last I heard they were back in Wisconsin taking

care of Michael's elderly mother. But they still own their home in Tobermory and I think they're planning on coming back, either permanently or for the summers."

It was funny the things you took for granted when you still lived at home. When you were gone, even if only a few hours away, but not living in the same house, things went unsaid – things that weren't worth a specific phone call, but things that you liked knowing about. She'd had a little taste of it when she'd spent her summers in Minnesota with William and Lyndsie, but because they were so close to her parents, and had the same circle of friends, she hadn't missed out on much.

She wondered if Brodie had experienced the same thing when he'd lived in Edinburgh – or if he'd even wondered what was going on at home. With his parents separated, or maybe even divorced – he'd never really said – it was possible he didn't care to know what they were up to when he was gone.

Once again, she felt a great sense of gratitude for the blessing of belonging to a close family who loved her dearly and weren't afraid to tell her so. If she ever found the right man, she would settle for nothing less than the kind of all-consuming love her mum and da shared.

Chapter 14

Brodie stood in front of the mirror at the farmhouse and adjusted the sash that matched his kilt. His da was in his bedroom sulking because Brodie was going to the wedding of a friend of his mum's. Brodie felt no obligation to attend – although he certainly wished he didn't have to, which made no sense. Jon was his mum's next door neighbour, and the music teacher at the high school. More than once, Jon and his mother had ganged up on him and tried to talk him into playing the fife or drums or even a saxophone in the school band. Brodie supposed he'd been a disappointment, but he'd always been a loner. He still enjoyed strumming his guitar and singing by a bonfire, at the seashore, or on top of a mountain. The stars, the sheep in the fields, and a grazing herd of cattle had been the perfect audience for his talents.

He'd spent all afternoon in the fields trying to get ahead of things that needed to be done before he left for Tobermory. His da didn't seem to care if some things were put off or went undone for weeks, months, or even years, but it bothered him no end. If he hadn't had a wedding to go to, he could have worked until nine that evening. The long days wouldn't last much longer, and he was eager to take advantage of every one.

He did one more visual inspection and lopped his

sporran around his waist, positioning it just so. He'd met Jon's bride to be and thought they were a good match. He was glad to be part of the wedding for that reason. They'd offered that he could join in and play his guitar with the band they'd lined up for the wedding music and reception, but he'd never really learned the songs that most musicians knew. He hadn't played for a couple of years. Most likely, it would all come rushing back to him – like the proverbial bicycle – but he preferred to find out while auditioning before his usual audience instead of a bunch of semi-famous musicians and a few hundred wedding guests.

"I'll be back in a bit," he said loudly so his da would hear him leaving even though he had the door to his bedroom closed. Brodie had spruced his truck up a bit when he'd finished his work for the day so he didn't arrive at the wedding smelling like manure.

The drive into town went quickly. He didn't meet a single vehicle until he was in Alford. Just the way he liked it.

He felt a mixture of discomfort and excitement when he arrived at the church. He was as comfortable as could be in his kilt, but the mixture of unknown things about to happen and so many strangers milling about was not to his liking. He would have been willing to escort his mum if she'd asked, but she hadn't. He suspected she already had a group of friends or even a boyfriend to sit with. No way he wanted to intrude on that.

He was milling around the narthex, trying to ease his awkwardness, when he saw Heather. Once again, he battled feelings of relief and reticence. She looked beautiful. She was alone until a man – a piper suited to the nines – approached her from the opposite side of the narthex, kissed her on the cheek, and motioned to her that she should take a seat. When the man turned, the flash of jealously he'd felt faded. It was Heather's father. Now that he saw him in his piper's attire, he remembered Heather mentioning that her da was a music teacher and quite a good bagpiper. Probably a friend of Jon's. That explained why Heather was here.

Ask her to sit with you.

I came alone because that's the way I like it.

You fool. Who in the good Lord's name would rather be alone than sitting with a beautiful woman like Heather?

He had to admit she cleaned up pretty nicely. He remembered the way she'd looked with straw in her hair and mulch clinging to her clothes and smears of mud – or who knew what – on her face and hands.

Looking at her now, all he could see were red highlights shimmering in the stained glass light that lit the room, and curves and cleavage and all kinds of things he'd never noticed before. Her dress was emerald green, with just enough flounces and frills to make her look feminine and absolutely tantalizing. She took his breath away.

Lord, help him, but she was beautiful. He was at her side before he knew what was happening. His legs – and other parts of his body – suddenly had minds of their own. It was embarrassing, but he hadn't the wherewithal to stay away from her.

She seemed just as surprised to see him as he was to find her. A few minutes later, he was escorting her down the aisle and sitting so close to her softly-shaped perfection that he felt paralyzed with joy. In fact, if anyone had asked him later to tell them about the wedding, he would not have been able to come up with a thing except the way Heather smelled – of roses and bluebells and sunshine and fresh mountain air – and the way her thigh felt, touching his in the church pew.

What a place to be having impure thoughts.

When they were dismissed from their seats in the chapel, he fully intended to make a beeline for the door and head for home. He'd fulfilled his duty to his mum and Jon. Sure, he'd said he was going to come to the reception, but from what he'd heard, it was a buffet and not a plated dinner with assigned seating. No one would notice if he didn't stay. There'd be more food for the others. His loss – the women catering the affair were known to be excellent cooks – but he had to get away from Heather. It was like she had some sort of hold on him, like a spell had been cast over him, like he was drawn to her by some powerful but invisible magnet. The proverbial phrase 'helpless to resist her charm' came to mind.

Heather wasn't saying much. It was like she was content simply to be with him, which was the last thing he needed! If she'd been yapping about this or that, or droning on about things he didn't care about or people he didn't know, or being catty or snippy, he felt sure he could have found a reason to be chafed or irritated or even bored. As it was, her simply sitting there, being beautiful and gracious and sweet and tender... She was going to be his undoing.

He didn't have the heart to leave her. At this point, everyone except the one or two individuals who may have seen them arriving separately would have assumed he was escorting Heather. If he walked out on her now, what would people think? He was trapped.

They went through the reception line and found a place to sit on the open air patio with a few younger couples that he knew. Couples. He'd always hated that word. When he and Barbara had dated, they'd kept their relationship a secret so as not to create an aura of fraternization in the workplace. Being seen sitting together at a wedding meant he and Heather would be labeled as a couple. In short order, the news that they were 'together' would be all over town – even though they weren't.

"The food is really delicious," Heather said. "I love Chicken Balmoral."

"I'm not a huge fan of haggis,' he admitted. "But I like the way the chicken and the peppercorn sauce help meld the flavours. It's very good."

They finished their meal in relative silence. A comfortable silence. He could not pretend otherwise. "So your da is very good on the pipes."

"He and Jon taught together in Dornie. I think Jon was a student teacher at the time."

The band launched into a slow, sweet rendition of *"In the Arms of an Angel."*

"Would you like to dance?" He heard his voice asking her.

"I'd love to."

And then he was holding her and her bare arms were wrapped around his neck. His hips were rubbing against hers and thank God for bumpy sporrans or she would have known exactly what he was feeling. There would have been no secrets between them.

A Sarah Mclachlan substitute was singing, *"In the arms of the Angels, fly away from here, from this dark, cold hotel room, and the endlessness that you fear. You are pulled from the wreckage of your silent reverie. You're in the arms of an Angel; may you find some comfort here."*

Oh, he was feeling comforted, all right.

And it had to stop. Right now.

The dance came to an end. The band started to play "Twist and Shout." and just like that, the mood was broken, and he was freed from the madness that had overtaken him.

"Em, I have to go." He pulled Heather from the warm embrace they were locked in and held her at arm's length. Stiff arm's length. She looked at him with a dazed expression.

"I have to get up very early tomorrow morning." It sounded lame even to him, and he was the one who said it.

"Oh. Sorry," she said.

"Nothing to be sorry about. Life on the farm. It is what it is."

"Right," she said.

"Much as I'd like to linger, I'd best be on my way or Da will be wondering what I'm up to."

"Right." Heather's dazed demeanor had switched to a pensive, cynical look, like she suspected he was off with the fairies.

And maybe he was.

It wasn't the first time he'd seen that look in a woman's eyes, but he still hated seeing it in hers.

He let go of her and made a dash for the door. Twenty minutes later, he was at home. His da was already asleep.

He poured himself a glass of well-aged whisky. It had been a gift from Uncle Dunk years earlier. His da had never imbibed as far as he knew. He'd claimed they were saving it for a special occasion.

Ah. Smooth, mellow, surprisingly decent. He savored the burn as it glided down his throat. "Here's to you, Uncle Dunk." Or maybe he should say Daddy Dunk.

He had a feeling that if Uncle Dunk, or anyone with Duncan Morris's ease with the ladies had witnessed how Brodie had put an end to his evening with Heather McPhearson tonight, he'd have rolled over in his grave and said, "He's no son o' mine."

#

How dare he? Heather stood tall and watched Brodie walk away while her insides crumpled with frustration. He'd taken an evening she hadn't even been looking forward to and transformed it into one of the best of her life. He'd taken her from bored and being polite to feeling beautiful and treasured and... loved.

And then, he'd made some flimsy excuse about why he had to go, and walked away. She felt like a fool – abandoned, rejected, unwanted. Was it something she'd said? The way she looked, smelled? Did she have some sort of irritating habit that left Brodie repelled and disgusted? She'd thought they were connecting, taking their relationship to the next level. And then, he'd walked away.

She stood by the wall and watched her da play the pipes. Nathan McPhearson was as good as it got. The haunting, melodic sound of the pipes floating across the open terrace and on to the moors reflected her mood perfectly. And then, to echo the theme of her evening, the music switched from sweetly romantic to wild and frenzied, even erotic. *'Shout'* made her want to scream. Her head pounded like a bellows, trying to figure out how a sweet dance that should have led to a tender kiss and who knew what else had led to being a wallflower at what felt like a funeral.

Her da was watching her, as though he could feel

her disappointment. It did not help.

"Might I have a go?" Oh, no. One of the groomsmen was holding his hand out to her, hoping she would dance with him.

"Sure." She tried to smile, but it was a dismal fail. She felt like grimacing.

He led her to the dance floor and took her in his arms. "Thanks. My name is Gus. And you are—?"

"Heather."

"And you're a friend of the bride or the groom?"

"Neither. My da is the bagpiper."

"Oh. He's really good."

"Thanks. I'll tell him you said so."

"So you're from America?"

"I'm from Dornie. My parents are from America, and I spent summers there growing up. I can speak Scotch if you prefer."

"You should speak whatever way makes you most comfortable."

"Thanks." She almost wished he'd been rude about it, or anti-American, or unwilling to get behind her mixed heritage. She was looking for a reason to dislike him. She was in the mood to pick a fight. If he'd given her the opportunity, she would have crossed him off her list with a flourish. And why? Because he had narrow shoulders instead of broad ones like Brodie? Because he looked soft and gentile instead of hard and brash like Brodie? Because he seemed like a nice man instead of an unpredictable, inconsistent brat like Brodie?

What was wrong with her?

Gus was still asking her questions. She couldn't concentrate. All she could think about were Brodie's biceps and Brodie's thighs, and what was under his kilt – or not. She wanted to leave the party, follow Brodie home, and humiliate herself no end. She wanted to act like a hussy, to make him want her, to get her way, to be in control instead of – whatever this was. She was a sore loser. She wanted to throw a hissy fit, to pout until she got her way. She wanted Brodie McBryde.

Thank goodness the wedding gods were smiling down on something that day, because the band was playing Auld Lang Syne. She would soon be going home to lick her wounds.

Gus said goodbye and that it had been nice to meet her. Right.

"Ready to go?" Her da had put away his pipes and was ready to take her home.

"Yup."

"Fun evening," her da said.

That was the last thing said until they got home.

She noticed the front door to her house was ajar the second the house came into view. "Oh, no! Did the door not latch behind me when I closed it?" She hadn't been in that much of a hurry. She hoped a squirrel hadn't moved in while she was away.

Her da tried to reassure her. "The wind is pretty stiff tonight. Maybe there was a wind vacuum when you tried to close the door. I've had that happen at home."

"Maybe." But her insides were screaming the scream she'd wanted to let loose ever since Brodie had left the wedding. She had a bad feeling about this.

Her da stopped the car. She leaped out and ran to the house.

"No!" Her emotions echoed through the hills, bouncing off the mountains to the west, ricocheting off the hills to the east, loud enough to wake the sheep from their sleep, so agitated that if a cow had been chewing its cud, it would have choked.

Her house has been broken into. Vandalized. Ruined. Her whole, recently organized and newly personalized house was in a shambles. One of Violet's paintings was slashed. Every piece of clothing she had was on the floor or in the shower. This wasn't a simple burglary. Whoever had done this hated her.

What was she going to do?

Chapter 15

Brodie woke up an hour before dawn to put out fresh hay, feed the livestock, and make sure the water troughs were full. He needed a break from the farm, and there was no reason he couldn't be gone for a day or even two if he bulked up on the animal's provisions. His da could top things off if the bulk of the work was done.

He returned to the house just about dawn, packed a bag in case he wasn't ready to come home by nightfall, and left his da a note.

He drove toward Fort William, where he could get on the other side of Loch Eil. It was a round about way to get to the Ardnamurchan Peninsula, but that was the whole reason a bridge was needed to span the waters, to allow better access to the Ardnamurchan Peninsula from Tobermory and the Isle of Mull. He planned to go via the Morvern Peninsula and check out the ferry that ran from Lochaline to Fishnish before he went up to Kilchoan and took the ferry into Tobermory. He wanted to be absolutely sure they'd chosen the best place for the bridge. Would more people benefit if the bridge connected the two land masses from one spot or the next? Of course, he'd have to study the water depths and currents to make sure his opinion was sound, but visually inspecting both areas was the first step.

He also wanted to have a look around both

peninsulas and see what their main industries were. He knew logging was big commerce on both peninsulas, as were farming and tourism. That was about it. If he scoped out the area, he could find out more about how many cars and lorries would use a bridge each day, and for what purpose.

On another note, he wanted to see how he felt about living in the area for a few years. He looked around as the miles clicked off and took note of the farms and estates he was driving by. He saw a few resorts and some B&Bs, high-quality restaurants and small town groceries. There were a lot of fences, grazing lands, sheep and cows. If only Heather would consider working on a farm someplace other than the Highlands. This was a beautiful area. Starting over with Heather at his side would be particularly sweet.

"Crap." He chastised himself. He was not going to fall into the trap of thinking about Heather again. He didn't care what was going on with her, or what her future might hold. They were both on a journey. Their paths may have crisscrossed for a few brief moments in time, but now, they were heading into the future on separate paths.

It was early evening by the time Brodie finished surveying the area around the Ardnamurchan Peninsula and caught the ferry to Mull. He found a restaurant that looked interesting and managed to get booked in for half seven. If he hadn't woken up so early, he'd likely have driven home after he had a bite to eat, but as it was, he was tired and ready for bed. He found a small hotel adjacent to Tobermory's golf course that had a last minute opening and booked a room. In the morning, when his mind was clear, he'd be able to do a little more reconnaissance, maybe even check on the availability of housing. He didn't want to buy, and renting could be tricky in an area so dominated by the tourism industry. When people could make two hundred pounds a night on a spare room with a private bath, what motivation did they have to rent a place by the month or year? If he didn't find what he was looking for on the Isle of Mull, then he would have to look on the Peninsula, where the prices would undoubtedly be less. The area would be much more remote and lacking in restaurants, social opportunities, and things to do in his off time. Not that he was that intent on living it up. It wasn't like he needed a certain amount of companionship to be happy, but...

His mind flew to Heather in blue jeans and an old hoodie, to Heather in emerald green silk or taffeta or whatever slippery material her gown had been made of, to Heather helping him sheer sheep and laughing and smiling and looking so happy he could hardly bear remembering.

He had to put her out of his mind. His calling was to build bridges. This place, this project needed him – his talents, his gifts, his knowledge, his passion. His time in the Highlands was a mere blip in the grand scheme of things. Part of him wished it were otherwise, and part of him was able to accept that it was what it was.

He entered the restaurant and waited to be seated. He was able to look out at the sunset while he ate. He ordered Chicken Balmoral and thought about Heather. While he was thinking about his future, it finally occurred to him that he had to think about her future, too. It was only fair of him to be honest with her – to tell her how much he appreciated her friendship and the camaraderie they'd shared, no matter how brief it was destined to be.

#

Heather watched the sun rise from the field where the Highland Coos were grazing in a pasture dotted with heather. The deep purple blossoms were spent, but there were patches of rose and peach still dotting the horizon. They shone in the backlight from the sunrise.

She hadn't slept for more than an hour, which put her in a horrible stead to deal with the aftermath of the break-in. Thank goodness her father had been there when it happened. She couldn't imagine coming home by herself, finding her home desecrated, and not having anyone to turn to. She hoped her da had been able to sleep more than she had.

She turned to the east and watched as the sun rose higher and higher in the sky, bathing the McBryde farm in dawn's early light. A few days ago, she would have called Brodie for help. She'd have been one hundred percent sure he would rush to her side. Now, she wasn't sure. In fact, she was so unsure that she didn't even intend to call him. Now that the police had been drawn in, everyone would know what had happened very soon, if they didn't already. If Brodie wanted to help her, he would come of his own accord.

In the meantime, her da had called her mum. Violet and Lyndsie were both going to drive up right after the lunch rush and help them clean up and put things back together. Her mum would bring her a new painting, and make sure everything was awright. Everything but the fact that she didn't think she would ever feel safe in that house again, ever be able to trust anyone again.

He father wandered out of the house and walked toward her rocky perch.

"Sleep much?" She tried to manage a smile.

"Not really."

"Me either."

"I'm so sorry this happened, sweetheart." Her father reached out and rubbed her shoulder. "Do you have any idea who might have…? I know the police asked you last night but I thought maybe someone had come to mind since you spoke with them."

"Knox is a possibility. It's getting a little old – suspecting him every time something goes wrong. I mean, he's been very cordial and polite and even helpful for the last week, but is it sincere? Who can tell?"

"Lyndsie seemed to think it was him straight off when I spoke to her and Violet last night."

She hesitated. "She could be right. He says he was at a pub in Alford all night. I hope the police follow up on his claim, but they're friends of his, so who knows if they can be trusted to be objective." She hadn't mentioned her concerns to the police, but she knew she could trust her da to think through the possibilities with her. "Do you think this could have anything to do with Duncan's death? This house was the Morris residence for years. Could it be that someone out there with a grudge or a score to settle with Duncan or Walter might not know that William bought the farm or that I live in the house now?"

"Or maybe they're after Walter now that they've got Duncan out of the way."

"Could be," she said. "And it could be one of the people I fired. But I just can't shake the thought that this has something to do with the Morris family, or Duncan's death."

Her father looked serious. "Didn't Duncan serve in the British Army? It's hard to imagine what anyone would have against an old farmer or a veteran. But the idea is definitely worth mentioning to the police."

"I'm not sure the police will even try to find out who did this to the house. They've not taken to me like I'd hoped they would."

"Heather. Please don't tell me that—"

"I've really tried, Da. But they haven't been very helpful on the other occasions I've spoken to them, including the day Beauty went missing. And at least one of them thinks I may have killed Duncan."

"That's ridiculous."

A few hours later, they were hauling trash out to the bin when Knox showed up.

"I heard aboot what happened."

She followed his eyes and watched his expressions as Knox peered at the heaps of broken furniture and puddles of shattered glass and mounds of twisted papers and perfectly good lingerie she just couldn't bear the thought of wearing ever again.

"What in criminy sakes went on here?"

"Maybe you can tell me." She tried to keep her voice calm and unruffled but the attempt was futile. She looked away from Knox. Her eye caught a glimpse of lavender in a pile of damaged goods to be discarded.

"Ye think I had something to do with this?" Knox' face went beet red. "After all I've done to help ye?"

No. Not her favorite lingerie.

Nathan stepped up. "Lad, no one's accusing you of anything. But we are curious to know if there is someone who hated the Morrises – Duncan or Walter or both – who might have done this. Please think carefully. A man's life has already been lost and I don't want my daughter to be the next inadvertent casualty."

"What makes ye think my da or my uncle were

involved in this mess?" Knox's face twisted into a knot. "How can ye be sure it wasnae yer daughter they wanted to hurt in the first place? She's offended many a man since she came here a few short weeks ago."

"So she's ruffled a few feathers, offended a few sensibilities, rubbed some people the wrong way." Nathan looked as serious as Heather had ever seen him. "That's no reason someone would try to murder her. No reason someone would do this to her home. There's got to be more to it. Your uncle is dead, lad. Don't you want to know who would do such a thing?"

Knox's face was wreathed in fury. "Maybe ye should ask Brodie McBryde who murdered my uncle, and why they'd want him dead. Has anyone asked Brodie if he had an alibi last night?"

Heather rushed to her father's side. Her heartbeat pounded in her head. "Brodie would never do this. He's the only one who's been kind to me. I trust him."

"So where is he now?" Knox fired back. "Why is he nae here helping ye clean up? Why is he nae trying to track down whoever did this?"

"I – I don't know."

"I'll tell ye where he is," Knox said. "He's off shagging his old girlfriend, that's where."

She knew Knox was egging her on. Even if Brodie had decided to go back to his girlfriend after sharing a romantic dance with Heather, Knox would be the last one Brodie would tell about it.

Her conscious mind knew that Knox was just trying to get her angry. And she might have taken the bait if she hadn't already been so mad at Brodie McBryde that she could spit nails.

Chapter 16

Brodie walked in the door of his house to find his da at the kitchen table eating from the peanut butter jar again. Good grief. He loved his da, but there were some things he would not miss when he moved out of the house again.

"Thought ye'd be over at McKnight's seeing to the lass."

"Why? Something going on?" Lord, he hoped Beauty hadn't gone missing again. Or the new grunters, or the turkeys, or the...

"So ye dinnae ken?"

Brodie's heart clutched inside his chest. "What's wrong?"

"Someone tore up the home place."

"Heather's house?"

"They found it when they came home from the wedding night before last."

Brodie said nothing. He ran from the house, hoisted himself into his truck, and tore up the drive to the neighbouring farm as fast as he could without killing himself on the potholes lining the track.

He rolled down the window as soon as he saw her. "Heather?" He braked hard, jumped out of the truck and ran to her side. "Are you awright?"

She glared at him and continued to sort through a

pile of what looked to be trash.

"I'm sorry I wasn't here to help. I was in Tobermory. On a business trip. I didn't hear about it until just a few minutes ago. If I had known, I would have..."

"It's not your job to protect me."

He looked down at his boots. "Of course not." He was on touchy ground and he knew it. Heather had every right to be angry with him. He'd gone from being a true friend to her, defending her and watching out for her, being there for her when she needed him, to abandoning her, leading her on and then running out on her without a word. What was wrong with him?

"I'm just fine," he heard Heather say. "We're almost done getting rid of all the things they damaged, and my mum and Lyndsie will be here soon to help me clean and put things back together."

"It was that bad?"

Nathan spoke for her. "What they did to the house – to Heather's and William's things – was deliberately cruel. It's hard to imagine that anyone would hate Heather or William enough to do this to either of them."

Brodie cringed. "The people who live here aren't like this. Having issues with a neighbour is one thing, but to do this? I can't believe anyone would carry things this far."

"I wish you would tell us what you know about Duncan, and Walter," Heather said. "We think this may have something to do with Duncan's murder. Did he have any enemies? Was there anything about the way he lived his life that would cause someone to hate him enough to do something like this?"

There it was. He'd kept the secret of his ancestry from everyone. And for good reason. He didn't want anyone – especially Knox – to know that he was Duncan

Morris' bastard son. Munro McBryde was not the perfect father, but he loved him. He liked being a McBryde. It was his identity. He had no desire for that to change. But if keeping quiet about what he'd discovered through his ancestry research meant that Duncan's killer would go free, and Heather and William might continue to be terrorized – how could he justify that?

"Can we have some privacy?" He was probably making a mistake. Knowing what he'd found out probably wouldn't make any difference to the investigation, but once he made his confession, everyone would know. He'd be viewed differently from this moment forward. One more reason to leave the Highlands forever.

He stepped into Heather's office and Nathan shut the door behind them. "I want this to stay between the three of us." He looked at Heather. She nodded. He looked at Nathan and received the same assurance.

"I just found out that Duncan Morris was my father. I'm not sure how it happened. Neither my da or my mum will talk about it, but Duncan is my biological father." He hung his head. "And if that whole scenario isn't disgusting enough, I've discovered that Knox is my half-brother. According to the DNA analysis, he was also sired by Duncan." He gulped back the bile in his throat. "I have three other half-siblings – a brother who lives in Aberdeen, and two sisters from Cyprus. I know I didn't kill Duncan, and despite my dislike of the man, I doubt Knox did it. If the sisters had wanted to kill Duncan, why come here? They could have done it in Cyprus. That leaves the missing brother from Aberdeen. Who knows what Duncan did to his mother, or any of our mothers, but it is conceivable..."

"I'm so sorry, Brodie." Nathan grabbed him around

his shoulders and gave him a side hug.

"Thanks for telling us, Brodie. I mean, it could help." Heather wouldn't meet his glance, possibly because she was mortified that he was genetically a Morris, and possibly because she was still furious with him about cutting out on her in the middle of the dance.

Nathan removed his arm from his shoulders, "Do you have any contact information on this half-brother from Aberdeen, and if so, do I have your permission to share it with the police?"

"Let me think about it." Did he have the guts to find his half-brother and talk to him himself? That would be his preference. Then again, he had no desire to meet the man or hear his story, no desire to know him in any sense of the word. If he let the police take care of it, he didn't have to be involved at all. He could go on with his life and eventually forget that Duncan Morris had ever existed.

Heather still seemed a little stiff, but she gave him a hug and whispered, "You'll get through this, Brodie. We all will."

#

Heather sat in the doctor's office in Fort William and waited for the specialist to come through. Her mum had been with her at the doctor's office in Inverness when she'd first heard the news that her pap smear showed pre-cancerous cells. Her doctor there had referred her to a fertility specialist and recommended that if she wanted to have children, she should have them soon, as she would probably have to have her uterus removed, or even undergo a complete hysterectomy before she was very old.

Thinking back, she was glad her mum had been there to buffer the shock of it. Half of her wished she'd asked her to come along today. But then, her mum had aggravated the situation, too. Heather hadn't wanted to hear things like the fact that she shouldn't be moving to the Highlands because she'd never meet anyone there, and that even an online relationship would be harder to pursue when Heather was isolated on a remote farm in the middle of nowhere in the high country.

She was glad her mum had it figured out, because Heather surely did not. She knew she was taking a risk. But really. She had to believe that the right man would come along at the right time no matter where she lived. If she really believed that God would work things out in His own good time, the only thing she had to do was to make sure she was where God wanted her to be – and that was in the Highlands.

The doctor finally came through and sat down opposite her.

"I've reviewed your test results and I'm happy to say there are still several options open to you if you would still like to have a child. Can I be so bold to ask if you're in a serious relationship?"

"No. I'm afraid not." Her mind flew to Brodie. Good grief. What was wrong with her? They'd never even been on a real date unless you called meeting up to sheer sheep a romantic adventure.

"Well, your options are essentially the same regardless." The doctor smiled reassuringly. "Your first option is to be artificially inseminated."

This time, her mind went not to Brodie, but to the grunters they'd bred just a week and a half ago. They hadn't wanted to invest in the purchase of a boar when they had such a small number of pigs. It wouldn't be cost effective – at least not until they had more litters and built up the number of gilts they had to breed. For the time being, they would either bring in a rented boar to impregnate the gilts, or have a vet or animal breeder come in and do it by injecting boar semen they'd purchased from a more established breeder.

She hated comparing herself to a grunter, but there it was. Option number one.

The doctor's voice went on. Somehow, she felt sure he hadn't been thinking about grunters. "Your second option is to find a friend or a random individual who might be a willing participant in your attempt to conceive. If you time things at the moment you're most likely to be fertile, there's every reason you could still get pregnant the old-fashioned way. Of course, it would be up to you and the sperm donor to decide what his role might be in raising the child, or if it would be a no-strings-attached arrangement."

Her mind flew back to Brodie. Would he consider being a candidate? How would he feel about it, having a father who was only a 'sperm donor' himself?

When they had first received the news of her predicament, Lyndsie had been in Scotland and they had shared a few of the details of Heather's situation. Lyndsie had promptly offered up her and William's oldest son, not for a romp in the hay, but for whacking off in a cup so their two families could officially be joined by blood as well as love.

Heather had actually felt very honored. Who knew if Ryan would actually agree to it or what he would think about being a sperm donor for a child he would hardly know and only see periodically. After growing up on a farm, he certainly knew about artificial insemination, and being a teenager, probably whacking off, too.

Lyndsie had also suggested that Rose MacCraig's son might be a genetically desirable candidate, if he was willing. Rose was Lyndsie's aunt, and her son, who she'd adopted when he was a wee lad, was actually the son of Lyndsie's brother. Once again, if he would offer his sperm, their two families would be tied together by blood. It would be sweet if such a thing worked out, but knowing Lyndsie, she had probably already asked the parties involved if they'd be interested. And since Heather hadn't heard back from her, it was likely their only tie would be to remain joined by love.

Heather thought about Lyndsie's family and wondered how a young man, who was adopted, would feel about fathering a child outside of marriage when he himself was adopted and had been given up by a father who didn't want to raise him. Rose and Ian's son couldn't be more than a few years older than she was.

The doctor cleared his throat and smiled broadly, clearly having saved the best for last. "Your third option would be to wait and hope that you meet someone you love and want to marry, then hurry up and have a child as soon as you can – while you still can."

Her mind started to fly with that possibility. And that's all it was. Would that be fair to the man? What if a man married her, thinking they could quick have a child, only to find out it was too late?

Would he feel cheated? Hoodwinked? It was a risky business for her, too. What if she decided to wait and take her chances on finding true love, and then, found it was impossible? How would that be fair to the man she fell in love with, who might never have a child of his own? And what about being fair to her? The longer she put off having surgery, the greater her chances would be of developing full-blown cancer and perhaps dying young and childless.

"There is one other option, and that would be to harvest a few of your eggs now, keep them on ice, and fertilize them with your husband's sperm – assuming you marry one day. When the time is right, we would use them to produce a test tube baby to implant in a surrogate mother's womb. The baby would be yours and his in every way except that you would not be the one to carry the child or give birth to it."

"Oh." She felt completely overwhelmed.

"It's a complicated situation," the doctor said, as if she should have had enough time to think on it now.

And it was. Heather might not mind having no children at the moment, but as she got older and all her friends had children and grandchildren as the focus of their lives, would she feel embittered when there was no one to snuggle on her lap and read bedtime stories to? When there was no one to carry on her legacy?

"Any questions or preliminary thoughts you'd like to share?" The doctor sat patiently. He smiled again, this time a polished, professional smile. "Of course, there's also adoption, which you could do at any time, without the pressures of time coming into play."

She didn't know how she felt about that. She was certainly willing to think on it. It seemed a better plan to be explored by a mother and a father, but she'd known at least one woman who had adopted a child on her own. At the very least, she owed it to herself to think about the pros and cons. It was a viable option.

The doctor cleared his throat again, presumably to make sure he had her attention. "Bottom line, if anyone but someone so young as you are had these sort of aggressive pre-cancerous cells in their womb, the oncologist would be arranging surgery for the soonest available slot – like tomorrow. Your risk level is that high. You need to make a decision as to how to proceed as soon as possible."

She took a deep breath and tried her best to think on the bright side – and quickly. The doctor was waiting patiently, but her womb was not.

If she went the artificial insemination route, at least she'd be able to handpick what genetic traits her bairn would have – musical genius and artistic talents to ensure he or she would fit into the family, things she admired in the people she knew – kindness, generosity, a hard work ethic, intelligence, a sense of humor. Last time she'd looked at an online sperm bank, she'd gotten totally creeped out, but she could make it work if it turned out that it was her best, possibly only, option.

She thought of a few more admirable traits and made a mental note to look for the perfect sperm with everything on her list. And then she realized she had just made a list of Brodie's attributes. She wiped a tear from her eye. The doctor handed her a box of tissues.

Such was her life.

Chapter 17

Brodie drove toward his mother's house in Alford as the sunbeams filtered through layers of hills and mountains to the west.

The last thing Heather had said to him was that she was worried that if Brodie went to interview – talk to – his brother by himself, he would be in danger of being the next one dead.

He understood that Heather had been though a lot lately. She was understandably nervous. But he could take care of himself.

Even if his half-brother was guilty of killing Duncan, it didn't mean that he wanted to wipe out the entire Morris family. He might have felt hated for Duncan, yet sympathy toward Brodie, Knox, and any other children Duncan had sired. After all, Brodie only knew about the ones who had signed up to have their DNA analyzed on the particular site where he had registered.

Although unlikely, the murderer could be one of his half-sisters from Cyprus. He made a mental note to investigate the possibility that one or both of them might have come to Scotland. For that matter, Walter might have come back from Cyprus and taken his brother out.

As far as Brodie was concerned, his mother was also still a suspect, or even his da, although he had pretty well crossed Munro off his list.

He thought about each one and what their motivation might be. Hatred? Resentment? Getting their hands on Duncan's money, or even the farm?

He wanted to understand Duncan's motivations for what he'd done as well. The man was his father. He wanted to believe that Duncan had loved his mother, or been proud of him when he was a bairn, or at the very least, felt some happiness at his birth and existence in the world.

Had Duncan done what he'd done to preserve his legacy? Brodie let his imagination run wild. Perhaps Duncan had been married when he was young. Maybe his wife could not have children. If it had bothered him that his wife could not bear him a child, perhaps he'd made sure that he would have children another way? Of course, Duncan could have just been one of those men who was a natural born charmer and took advantage of the skill to sink his dick into as many women as he could. Maybe Duncan had been told by a doctor that it was unlikely he would ever have children, which led him to have affairs with multiple women to try to prove the doctor wrong? Was he trying to establish his seed so he would be remembered, so his name would live on, at least genetically? There were all kinds of possibilities. Brodie thought if he opened his mind to things other than the obvious, he might get to the truth.

His mum could help him. He'd been polite about it the first time he'd tried to discuss it with her, but this time, he'd get the answers he wanted. She owed him that much.

He pulled up in front of her house. A few minutes later, he was knocking. For the first time since he was little and his mum had moved to town, he felt funny about having to wait at the door to ask if he could enter. What boy didn't walk right into his mum's house because she was his mum? Her home should have been his home, too. But it never had been. He'd always belonged with his da on the farm. Now that he knew Munro wasn't his real father, even that seemed strange to him. What woman would leave her son with a man who was not his real da?

"Good morning, Brodie." His mum had a smile on her face. Was he imagining it, or was it a wary smile? He took another look, a close look. No. it was the same smile she'd always had. But then, maybe she'd always been wary of him. She'd always been a little aloof when he'd come to visit. He'd thought it was just her way. But maybe it was him.

"What can I do for ye today, Brodie?"

Again, with the politeness. Who asked their son what they could do for them? Was that any kind of a greeting for someone you had born, flesh of their flesh?

"We have to talk about Duncan, Mum. I know he was my father."

"You might think you ken—"

"I know. I signed up to have my ancestry checked. Duncan fathered me along with Knox, a man who now lives in Aberdeen, and two women who live in Cyprus. There may be more. These are the ones I know about because of the DNA match."

His mother's face started to crumple. "I dinnae ken."

"About what? The others?"

"Aye."

He felt a surge of sympathy for his mum. Maybe even a little for Duncan. "Tell me about him. Duncan. Help me understand what made him do this."

His mum's face softened. "He was a good man."

He digested that small tidbit and waited.

"He was different than any other man I knew. Oh, he was a charmer awright. Good looking, broad-shouldered and strong. But he was also confident, a leader, a true gentleman. And he ken how to listen. He would ask me how I felt, and what I thought aboot things. And he cared enough to listen. He got to know me. We talked aboot books and classes, Shakespeare, and Robert Browning's poems. I wasnae just a woman, or a neighbour, or someone's wife to him. I was a person. He liked me as a person."

"So that was his secret." He said the words gently, and not just out of kindness to his mum. Of all the answers she might have given him, this was the one he had hoped for. For all he knew, the man might have been a serial rapist. He was glad to know Duncan Morris had been a man who truly cared about the women he bedded.

"I loved him. I wouldnae have left yer father for the love of Duncan, nor would I have broken Duncan's marriage apart. Duncan's wife was a good woman. A friend. But I did love him – so much that I could deny him nothing he asked of me." She grabbed a tissue from the table and continued. "I wanted him to make love to me. I dinnae ken if ye ken the difference between being with a woman and being with a woman who ye love and ken inside and out. Whether ye do or nae, yer time will come, and I am here to tell ye nae to settle for the one if ye can find the woman with whom ye can have it all."

He thought for a minute. It took no longer than that for him to admit to himself that with Barbara, it had only been sex. And then he thought about Heather, who intrigued him and fascinated him, and filled him with the desire to know her better, and completely, in every way.

He took his mum's hand. "But then you left Da and me anyway. Why? Did Da find out about Duncan? Did he find out that I wasn't his son? And if he did, why did he keep me and not you?"

"I am not sure I can answer ye, Brodie. I can tell ye what Duncan was thinking at the time, because he spoke to me on a regular basis, and shared his feelings with me. Yer father dinnae ever talk aboot his feelings or ask aboot mine. So all I can say aboot what happened between yer da and me is how I felt. And I felt it was better to be alone than with a man who dinnae love me. What happened between Duncan and me had nae to do with it except it taught me what it felt like to truly be loved. Once I ken what it felt like to be cherished and admired and appreciated, I couldnae settle for anything less."

His mum was a wise woman. But he still didn't understand. He looked down at her. She'd taken a seat at the table. "But if my da – Munro – was a man who couldnae express his feelings or show his love, how could ye leave me with him?"

"Oh, but he did love ye. With his whole heart. Ye were his life. He was kind and gentle to ye. He taught ye everything he ken. He read ye bedtime stories every night and taught ye to pray on yer knees at the side of yer bed. It was different with ye. He poured out his heart to ye. He loved ye. And still does in his own cantankerous way."

"Aye. I remember." And he understood – not his da, but that he was loved by his da.

His mum started to cry. He didn't want to distress her any longer. Truth be told, he was probably more like his mother when it came to communicating his feelings.

"I should go."

"I'm glad ye came round," she said.

"Thanks for talking to me."

"Thanks for taking the time to get to the truth of the matter instead of judging me."

"You'll always be my mum."

"I may have a funny way of showing it sometimes, but I do love ye, Brodie. With all my heart."

"I love you, too, Mum." He dashed out the door as soon as he'd said it, but it was a start.

#

Maybe Heather's mother was right. Violet had always said that Heather was unique – that she should just accept herself for who she was and learn to love the somewhat odd, one-of-a-kind world she'd been born into.

When she was little, she'd watched Sesame Street tapes. When they sang the song, "One of These Things is Not Like the Other," and the children had been asked to pick out a car among trucks, or a vegetable amid fruits – the one object that was different than the others. She'd always thought she was the mismatched thing.

Always the misfit, here she was again – not Scottish enough for the Scots and not American enough for the Americans. She hadn't fit in at school, at church, or any group she'd tried to be part of. While others liked big cities, she'd longed for the farm, or at least a small town. Always on the fringes, she didn't fit in anywhere. While her friends had wanted designer jeans and short shorts and skimpy dresses, she'd been happy with a new pair of boots, a cowboy hat, a pleated plaid skirt to complete her signature look. She'd never felt entirely at home, always the odd one out. She stood out like a sore thumb in both countries, in the Highlands or in the Isles. She was her own unique person – something that she felt alternately proud of and inadequate over.

And now, she was being told, this time by a specialist in his field, that she had a unique condition that meant she would probably never bear a child of her own. And that if she had any chance, it had to be soon. And that if not soon, it would never happen.

She climbed higher and higher on her route back to Alford. It seemed like she was on top of the world even as she crashed, lower and lower. She pulled the car over and there she was, atop the heather-covered mountain pass again. This time, the crest was dried up and crowned with brown blossoms, baked beyond repair by the sun, cooked dry like a pan on a burner whose water had boiled away. How could she not identify with the sorry state of those mountain top heather plants – long past their prime, just as she was. At least they had the seasons going for them. Springtime would rescue the heather from their temporary state, but once her womb had withered or been removed, nothing would bring her womanly abilities back to life. And how soon was soon? She wondered if she would last until spring, or if she had already had her last hurrah – which could only be called a piss poor climax – only to be on her way out.

She got back in her car and drove past the summit, then turned east to wind her way home on the narrow mountain roads. Had she missed a turn? Suddenly, she was lost. It made perfect sense. Her head was off with the fairies – so much to think about. Who knew where she'd gone wrong?

And then, in the distance, she saw a circle of standing stones silhouetted against the sky. Was she dreaming? Was she where she thought she was? She drove closer and closer, winding up and down, through narrow squeaks between thick hedgerows covered in fall flowers. She turned into a car park, and climbed the path to the top of the hill. From there, she could see the stone circle, the sunset, a ribbon of a river, hills folding over hills and wee villages gleaming in the distance. She could see hundreds of sheep grazing, and round bales of hay. She could see the entire world.

She looked up to the skies and saw the moon rising, the colors of the sunset growing brighter and brighter with pinks and yellows and purples and teals.

"Oh, Lord." She spoke aloud. She was alone. Why not be direct? "Please give me guidance and wisdom. Help me to know what to do, to make the right decisions going forward. Please, Lord. I'm not sure what I should do. And if Brodie is the one, please send me a sign that he's meant to be part of my future."

Chapter 18

Brodie wasn't sure why he decided to go to church the next morning. Maybe it was because his emotions had been such a jumble. Maybe he was looking for direction and guidance. He certainly didn't attend church all that often, so why now, when he'd planned to sleep in and have a relaxing morning fixing his da a healthy breakfast so he needn't feel guilty about him binging on peanut butter again – if there was any left.

He planned to slip in the back just before church started and keep to himself. His whole life was on the dodgy side right now, and the fewer people he spoke to, the less likely he was to blurt out something inappropriate or otherwise put his foot in his mouth. So he arrived at the last moment.

The pastor was singing a solo, presumably for the prelude, unless they were starting the service earlier than they used to. Their pastor stood six feet five inches tall and wore a neck to floor cape which he loved to swirl when singing. The organist was equally dramatic and also had a cape, which he was accustomed to flinging over his shoulder in dramatic moments or when deeply moved by the song he was playing.

He stopped in his tracks when he heard the words to the song the pastor was singing.

"*In His time, In His time. He makes all things*

beautiful, in His Time. Lord, please show me every day, as You're teaching me Your way, that You do just what You say, in Your time."

He heard footsteps and turned to see who was approaching. Heather.

Their eyes met. She smiled. He looked away and saw the pastor move just enough to swirl the hem of his cape before starting the second verse.

"In Your time, In Your Time. You make all things beautiful in Your time. Lord my life to you I bring, may each song I have to sing, be to You a lovely thing, In Your time."

Well, there it was. A second, chance meeting. Or was it chance?

"Would the two of ye care to have a seat?" The greeter, or usher, or whomever he was, motioned to an empty pew near the rear of the sanctuary.

He turned to Heather and she nodded. The usher guided them to their seats.

"Now that ye've heard the melody, please join me in singing *In His Time*," the pastor said.

Brodie wanted to tell God that he was a quick study and that he'd already gotten the message, but who was he to assume that there wasn't someone else in the congregation who needed to hear it again?

Heather started to sing, and he joined in. She had a beautiful voice. Her da obviously had a lot of music in his veins. No surprise that Heather would, too. He found himself wondering if Duncan had been a musician. His mum couldn't carry a tune and he'd never heard Munro sing, so he hadn't picked up his love of music from either of them. He'd have to try playing the song on his guitar next time he camped under the stars.

So, *In His Time*, eh? Was it also a chance occurrence

that the pastor had chosen such a pertinent song for that morning's prelude? He looked at Heather. There was a tear running down her cheek. What was that about? Was she upset with him?

The song ended and he stretched his arm out and slipped it over the back of the pew. He didn't exactly put his arm around her, but she must have taken it that way because she leaned into him and relaxed against his arm.

The pastor was speaking. "I intended to sing another song this morning, but right before the service was to begin, God laid it on my heart to sing *In His Time*." He made a show of looking over at the organist and clapping his hands. "I'm not sure who in the congregation needed to hear the words, but God knows."

Another tear streaked down Heather's cheek. Was it her? He reached down and took her hand in his. It had been a stressful couple of weeks for both of them. A feeling like a bolt of lightning streaked down his back. Maybe it was he who had needed to hear the song. Maybe it was both of them.

So what was it time for, and how did God intend to make something beautiful out of the mess they were in?

He didn't hear much of the rest of the service. He was too busy trying to figure out what God had planned for him. He had an idea it involved Heather.

He had his doubts. But then, that was the thing about God – he knew what was going to happen down the road a ways. And if you trusted Him, he might show you how to get there. But only when the time was right.

He wrapped his arm around Heather a little tighter.

#

Heather felt a great deal of clarity after she left the

worship service. Yes, she needed to be mindful to listen to her own body, have a baby as soon as she could, and not wait too long lest she end up with full-blown cancer. It was a conscious decision to put the baby thing on hold and concentrate on what she needed to do to fulfill her promise to herself and to William and Lyndsie – to make a success of the farm.

Sure, there had been problems, but she was living where she wanted to live and doing what she wanted to do. If she walked away and abandoned her dream now, she would likely never get another chance. No one in Scotland was interested in hiring an American woman with limited experience gained only in America to run a farm in the Highlands. She had tried. The attitudes she'd encountered were pretty identical to the ones she'd encountered at the police station and the grocery.

Likewise, no one in America would hire a Scot with summers-only experience to head up a farm. She might be lucky enough to get a job taking care of a farrowing house, or the maternity barn at a commercial hog operation, working her way up from mucking pens, or whatever she could find to do at a starting position. It would not be easy. William had worked with her and knew what she was capable of, but it would be hard to convince anyone else she was worthy of a job in management.

William and Lyndsie had three sons that they were grooming to take over his own farm when they were a wee bit older. As they shouldered more responsibility around the farm, William would have no need for her help in America.

The answer was clear – she had to make this job work, and quickly, so once she had a top-notch team assembled, she could take a brief sabbatical or rest on her laurels long enough to have a baby.

But first, she had to call William. He knew about the break in. Lyndsie had taken care of that. But he didn't know that she'd fired most of their crew, or that she was now desperately short-staffed. She'd asked Lyndsie to wait until Heather could tell him herself.

"Uncle William?" She tried to keep her voice from quavering. She hoped he would support her decision, but who knew for sure. "I'm not sure if you've heard that Beauty, our Aberdeen Angus bull, was stolen. It turned out to be one of the men, although I don't know which one. The police were not helpful, and called me into their office for questioning to give the thief the opportunity to put the bull back in the pasture."

"Well," William said. "It's a shocking turn of events, and it doesn't bode well that the police aren't being more supportive, but I'm relieved Beauty was returned. I guess all's well that ends well."

She paused to give him a chance to reconsider his words but no retraction was forthcoming. "I'm sorry, Uncle William, but I don't need staff members who play tricks on me, or steal things, or run crying to the police and the townsfolk in Alford about my policies instead of talking to me. I want a team that is supportive and enthusiastic and happy to be working with me. When I reiterated my expectations and asked them for an honest response, almost half of them quit. The rest of us are scrambling to keep the operation going. I promise you I'll find the people I need to get things back on track. When all is said and done, I think we'll be headed down a better path once I get things restructured."

She held her breath and waited to see if he concurred.

"I hope you're right."

There was an awkward silence.

Heather continued, "My only regret is that I didn't do this from the beginning. I gave them a chance. I know it didn't work out the way we hoped, and I know I'm taking a risk now, but it has to be this way. I'll get right on it, and I'm sure a few months down the road, well maybe a year from now, we'll all be glad this happened. Because things will get better."

She heard a long sigh on the other end of the line. "It's fine, Heather. Things are just a little crazy here in Minnesota at the moment, that's all."

"I hope you're all okay."

"We're just fine. It's the world around us that seems to be falling apart."

"What's wrong?" Her heart filled with dread.

"Land prices are sky high. We had hoped to expand our operation, but we had to scrap our plans to buy the neighbor's land. Beef prices are so high that people can't afford to eat beef, and it's hurting us. Of course, we appreciate the few who do buy product even though it's expensive, but little of the markup filters back to the farmer.

"Our new leaders want to do away with the old-fashioned tradition of raising animals on farms, and manufacture a plant-based product that tastes like beef in a laboratory setting to eliminate greenhouse emissions and rid the environment of methane gas."

"You're kidding." She couldn't imagine such a thing.

"Oh, you'd better believe it. Instead of helping farmers, the government is imposing one new tax and penalty after another. If they put any more obstacles in our path, it's going to be almost impossible to remain viable say nothing about making a profit, especially with fuel prices so astronomically high."

"I'm so sorry, William."

"Oh, I haven't even told you the worst of it. You know what havoc the COVID virus has caused us – well, the whole world. The latest news out of the Midwest is that more than eighty percent of the deer population in Iowa and Minnesota is infected with the virus. Now, there are instances of COVID infecting bovines. If it spreads the way they fear it will, whole herds may have to be put down, since they're not sure if the virus can be passed from bovine to human via milk or meat."

"Oh, my word." It was unsettling to think about the ramifications to the beef and dairy industries, say nothing about the loss of her favorite cows from William's farm. The thought of a contaminated food line was horrifying.

"Not to put more pressure on you, but it's important for you to make a success of the farm in Scotland," William said. "That's all I'll say."

"I'll do my best, Uncle William." She felt a renewed sense of purpose. And she felt completely and totally panicked. She'd been under the impression that McKnight Farms of Scotland was more of a hobby farm for William, a sentimental passion of his to reinforce Lyndsie's ties to Scotland.

"Well, no need to worry about my problems," William said. "Sounds like you've got enough troubles of your own."

That she did. Did that mean she was supposed to say it back to him? *No need to worry about my problems here in Scotland, Uncle William. You've got enough of your own.*

She couldn't say it. She needed him – now more than ever. Now obviously wasn't the time to whine about the issues she was having, so she just listened for a little longer and then said goodbye.

After she'd disconnected, she looked around at the cold stone walls of her office and tried to imagine the warm, nurturing environment she'd always thought she could create at McKnight Farms. She felt more alone than ever.

Chapter 19

Brodie was on the road to Aberdeen as soon as he'd finished caring for the animals. It was still too early to call the surgery to set up a cardiac therapy appointment for his da, but he had the number in his pocket so he could ring them after opening hours and put the plan in motion. He'd been able to find Finn Codona's address without too much trouble and was both looking forward to and nervous about meeting his half-brother.

He'd asked Heather to go along, mostly to set her mind at ease. She was still convinced that he was going to be in the company of a murderer. He would have enjoyed talking to her on the trip to Aberdeen and back, but she had so much work to do due to staff shortages, that she wasn't able to take a day off. If his own business hadn't been so pressing, he would have stayed and helped. But they'd both agreed that if they were going to find Duncan's murderer, Brodie needed to talk to his newly discovered half-brother as soon as possible.

He drove by Craigievar Castle as he wound his way out of the Highlands and down toward the shore. It wasn't as though he didn't take the possibility of Finn Codona being the murderer seriously, but he wanted to meet his half-brother regardless. He'd always wanted a brother or a sister, although not one like Knox. With this new meeting came the possibility of a man he might feel a kinship with, or connect with on some level. They shared a good amount of DNA, and who knew what traits. Other than his name and address, which was hopefully current, he knew nothing about the man. He was curious about what his brother would be like, and how he would act.

The neighbourhoods kept getting more and more questionable as he drove from the outskirts of Aberdeen, past the upscale city center, and down toward the docks. It was a rough-looking area with crude graffiti, buildings with boarded up windows, and the look of unkempt decay. He knew better than to leap to the conclusion that his brother was a murderer just because he lived in a bad area of town, or that he had grown up in a world that was opposite of Brodie's life in the Highlands. Still, he felt increasingly nervous as he searched for the street sign marking Finn's address and finally saw it dangling from a tall building with a crumbling façade.

He could see straight off that parking his truck was going to be a problem. When he finally found a spot in the street that was both long enough and wide enough to pull up on the sidewalk and be assured that traffic would still be able to get by, he wondered if he'd ever see his truck again. He also wished he had dressed down a bit, and not carried so much cash in his pocket. The only question was, could he run faster than whatever thugs might pursue him?

It was mid-morning when he finally rapped on the door to the apartment where Finn supposedly lived. He heard a peephole covering being pulled to the side, felt he was being observed, and then heard a voice asking who he was and why he was there.

"My name is Brodie McBryde. I'm looking for Finn Codona."

"What's he done now?" Silence.

Brodie didn't answer. He hadn't planned on a woman answering the door. Who was she to him, he wondered – girlfriend, sister, mother?

The voice behind the peephole spoke again. "I used to know a Mr. and Mrs. Munro McBryde – neighbours to the farm where I lived in the Highlands."

"My parents." Brodie heard the sound of several deadbolts being unlatched.

"Of course!"

The door opened slowly and a beautiful woman about his mother's age poked her head out. "I remember hearing that the McBrydes had a wee bairn named Brodie. Ye were born after I left the Morris' employ, but back then I had friends who kept me current on what was happening in the neighbourhood."

"Pleased to meet you." He extended his hand.

She was slow to respond, but eventually, opened the door a bit more and took his hand. She had all the telltale signs of gypsy descent – curly black hair, exotic, olive-tinted skin, and petite features. She looked both young for her years and like she'd lived a hard life.

Her smile changed to a frown. "What business do ye have with Finn?"

"I'd like to discuss that with him if he's here."

"He's not." Her face had a funny look.

"Thank you, em..." He paused, hoping she would fill in her name.

"Jaelle Codona."

"A name as beautiful as its owner." He had no idea where the words came from, or why he had spoken them aloud. He could feel his cheeks heating up, probably flaming red. Why had he said such a thing? It wasn't like him. It wasn't who he was. "If I could leave my mobile number with you, perhaps we could arrange another time to meet."

She opened the door even further. "Please come in. I'll find a pen and some paper."

He stepped inside. A small, tastefully decorated entry hall led to a lounge area. A colorful, hand-woven, folk scarf was lopped over the door between the two rooms, higher in the center and draped down each side.

She must have seen him admiring it because she said, "It is from Bucovina in Romania. It is called a scoartele. Duncan used to admire it as well." She started, as though she rued speaking his name.

It was just the opening he needed. "So you lived on the Morris Farm?"

"My mother was their housemaid and cook for years. I helped as well. I grew up there."

Had she left and moved to Aberdeen when she married? He did not want to be too forward.

"The Highlands are wonderful place to grow up," he said, hoping she would open up and share a little more.

"I had the opportunity to work for a large hotel chain here in Aberdeen. The Morrises set everything up for me and found me this apartment." She had a wistful look on her face. "I would have liked to raise my boy in the high country, but it wasnae meant to be."

"I understand." But he didn't. Not really. He tried to piece together what she wasn't saying. Had she been forced to leave the farm after Duncan got her pregnant? Had she been fired because she was an unwed mother? The Morrises wouldn't have been happy if their son had slept with a servant – probably even less so if she was a gypsy. The world was not a fair place, no more or less so in the Highlands. He wondered if Jaelle's mother had sent her off to keep her own job? Families had been eager to sweep such things under the carpet back then. He searched his mind for any memory of a gypsy housekeeper who had lived at the Morris farm, and couldn't remember anyone of the sort.

"I've done quite well for myself," she said. "I used to be up at the crack of dawn to cook breakfast and clean guest rooms, but I've been promoted to general housekeeping of the common areas and lounges, which they prefer to do in the afternoons so it's fresh for check-ins."

He took a closer look at her and the room they were standing in. The walls were covered in Old World European tapestries, paintings of days gone by, and exotic, colorful pieces that had a definite gypsy aura. Her dress was made of a sheer, Indian-looking, gauzy fabric in a tiny pattern of pinks, purples and teals. She was fascinating. He longed to ask her question after question, but he didn't want to offend her or make her nervous.

"So what brings ye here to see Finn?"

Again, he hesitated. He hadn't rehearsed this scenario. Jaelle seemed like a nice woman. She'd been very welcoming, but he didn't know so much about her that he was ready to reveal all his cards. For all he knew, she could be the murderer. Who knew what her relationship with Duncan had been like, or what promises he'd made to her, or how he'd treated her when she got pregnant. Her situation was entirely different than his mum's or Walter Morris' wife's. She could be harboring deep resentment or even hatred. Jaelle's house was neat, clean, and well-cared for, but it was located in one of the roughest neighbourhoods he'd ever encountered – even worse than in Glasgow. She certainly wouldn't live in such a hellhole unless she couldn't afford to live somewhere better, would she?

He still didn't say anything. Wouldn't it be better to tell Finn how they were related than his mother, who had noth–, everything to do with it.

He decided to be honest. "I signed up with an ancestry research company and found some unexpected results in my history. There's a DNA link between me and Finn; I came to find out what I could about how that may have happened."

He didn't mention that Duncan was dead – did she know?

He also didn't mention that it was believed that Duncan had been murdered.

He didn't mention that Heather's house – the old Morris house – had been ransacked, or that everyone thought it had something to do with Duncan's murder.

So why did he feel like he'd said too much? Maybe he should have let the police call Finn in for questioning and left the matter in their hands. What had he been thinking? He had no idea how to investigate a murder or interview suspects. He'd let his desire to have a brother guide his decisions, not his brain.

Jaelle looked frustrated – and a little scared. "Did Finn ken ye were coming?"

"No. I just took a chance that he would be home. I wanted to meet him in person."

He frantically wished that he had told Heather what Finn's name was and where he lived so that someone knew where he was. At the very least, he should have written down his password for the ancestry site so there would be a path to trace if he disappeared.

Jaelle's whole persona changed. "I was going to offer ye a cup of tea, but I just noticed the time. I need to be at work in less than an hour. Ye will need to go."

And how far away is the hotel where you work? He wanted to ask. Do you drive or is it within walking distance? Do you own a car? If not, how would she have gotten to Alford and the farm to confront and or possibly kill Duncan? There were so many questions to ask, and hopefully, be answered.

Jaelle straightened up like a jolt of electricity had zinged her. Concern clouded her face. "Is Heather a name that is special to ye?"

His senses went on high alert. "Aye. Very special."

"She is in danger. From without." Jaelle paused. Her face was etched with worry. "And from within."

Every muscle in his body tensed. "What is it you're seeing? Can you tell me more?"

"Ye must warn her aboot the threat. It is very real and it will cause her great harm. She will be hurt very deeply."

"What can I do? How can I stop—"

"I must go," Jaelle said. She turned and then turned back. "There is little ye can do except to love her."

He knew he should go, but his feet felt rooted to the ground. Jaelle knew more than she was telling him – about more than one thing. He was sure of it.

He tried to think logically, to organize the new clues he'd obtained, to sort through the information Jaelle had given him, both verbal and non-verbal. He had to figure out what kind of danger Heather was in, and how it tied into Duncan's death. But the only data his mind could process was that Heather was in danger. Fear and worries ran wild until they completely took over his mind.

He was so close! He could feel it.

And he was a million miles away. It was tearing him apart.

"I'll look forward to speaking with Finn another time, and getting to know you better, too. Thank you for your hospitality."

He stepped out and Jaelle closed the door. He could hear the clicks as she re-latched the deadbolts, one by one.

He wound down the hallways and back to the street, pumped up to run the gauntlet of possible problems between him and his truck. Thankfully, it was untouched.

There was nothing more he could do now except to get back to Heather and make sure she was okay.

#

Heather flipped through the applications on her desk and quickly jotted a few notes from the previous conversation. Her head and at least part of her heart were with Brodie in Aberdeen, but she'd had so much work to do that there was no way she could have gone, much as she would have liked.

She refocused her eyes on the papers in front of her. Most of the people she supposedly had to choose from were applicants who had been interested in job openings six to nine months ago, before William had purchased the farm. A lot of things had changed since then. Most of them had moved on and were no longer looking for a job for one reason or another.

But this one was new. The application had come in the mail about a week ago, before she'd known she'd be losing most of her staff. The applicant was from Aberdeen, so she could assume this was an intentional effort to get out of the city and relocate to the Highlands. That alone said something about the man's interest level and desire to succeed at McKnight Farms.

Which reminded her – the envelope had been addressed to Morris Farms, which was just fine as long as he didn't have anything against women or Americans.

A second later, she saw a beat up old car covered with dents and rust spots pull into the yard. When he parked, she noticed the back bumper was secured with bungee cords. So, he definitely needed the job and would be highly motivated to do excellent work.

Finn Codona walked through the door to her office with black eyes shining, dark curls hugging his shoulders, and a physique that would have looked right at home on the cover of a romance novel.

Something about him looked familiar to Heather – something about his eyes – but she couldn't place who he reminded her of or what made him so common looking to her. He didn't look like anyone she knew. Or did he? The thought crossed her mind that if he was at all musical and intelligent, and if it came down to it, he might make an excellent sperm donor.

She quickly blotted that thought out of her mind and asked him to take a seat. "Why don't we start by you telling me a little about yourself and why you want to move to the Highlands."

"My roots are here. I was born in the Highlands. I always thought I would move back here one day. Working at Morris Farms seemed like a good way to come home to the place I love."

"McKnight Farms."

He looked startled.

She explained. "My boss, William McKnight, bought the farm from Walter Morris a few months ago." She looked down at his application. "So you're from Aberdeen. Can you tell me about your current or most recent position and what you liked best and least about your last boss?"

"I'm the maintenance man at a big hotel that overlooks the harbor. I can fix anything they throw at me, and I keep the rooms in top notch condition. And I clean up after myself. My mother has been on the housekeeping staff for years and taught me well. My current boss is meticulous about organizing things from start to finish, which is very appealing to me. But a lot of my talents go to waste under his supervision. I don't exactly get treated poorly, but he definitely doesn't appreciate me or use my skills to their best advantage. What I'd really like is to be considered an invaluable part of a team – a team where I can use the things I know and my creative ideas to make the company better. I want my boss to challenge me to be the best I can be, so eventually, I can move up the ladder and take on more responsibility."

She drew in a deep breath. "Very well said." She was impressed with him. Finn was smart and fair and articulate. You could only learn so much about a man in a half hour long interview, but he seemed truly eager to get back to his country roots and highly motivated to work hard to make McKnight Farms excel. She gave him the job.

Finn shuffled his feet. "I hate to ask for favors when I haven't even started working here, but I live with my mother in Aberdeen, so if I could have two consecutive days off each week, I'd like to spend those days with her and make the drive back and forth worthwhile. I'll need a place somewhere around here to sleep when I'm working – a shepherd's hut or a tent – don't they call it glamping now? A corner of a shed would be fine if there are no rooms for let. If you have any suggestions, or places you could recommend, I'd be grateful."

Her mind went to the loft where Knox was living – if he hadn't already moved out. He'd been AWOL for two days.

"I might have something that would work for you. There's a two bedroom loft over the production facility. One bedroom is full, but the other is open. I'll talk to Knox and make sure he's open to having a roommate. When can you start?"

When she looked up, Finn had a funny look on his face. Maybe the thought of a roommate freaked him out.

But all he said was, "I'd like to give the hotel at least a week's notice. If they require two, I'll offer to help them out on my days off until they find someone else."

"Good answer. We can use you as soon as possible, but I want you to do right by them, especially since your mother works for them."

"Just so you understand," Finn said. "My father is not in the picture, so my number one responsibility is to look after my mother."

One more reason to admire the man.

"Thanks, Finn. I think we'll get along just fine. Welcome to McKnight Farms."

Chapter 20

"What the hell is wrong with that woman?" Knox leaned out the window of his truck and pounded his fist on the door, shouting at Brodie like he was facing down the devil himself.

"Why ask me?" Brodie scowled. He needed to get home to make sure Heather was safe. Had Knox already hurt her? He was the first one who had come to mind when Jaelle said Heather was in danger.

Knox was still shouting. He was upsetting the sheep in the pasture next to their vehicles. Knox upset everything and everyone he came in contact with.

"I have to get to the farm. Let me by!" Brodie said. "I have no idea what she's done to rile you up, but it's not on me. Heather's said nothing to me about why she does anything."

"She hired Finn Codona to work at the farm. She wants him to share the loft with me."

"What?" His mind tried to sort out what Knox knew. Knox must have seen their DNA results on the ancestry site or he wouldn't know who Finn Codona was and wouldn't be talking to Brodie about it. "She knows about Finn? How on earth did she—"

"It had to be ye with as tight as ye two are. How else would she ken?"

"I never mentioned his name to her. Not once. I'm

sure of it. Does she know who he is?"

Knox looked confused. "I just assumed."

Brodie's mind raced ahead of the conversation. So Knox knew who Finn was, but Heather didn't. That meant Finn had come to her asking for a job. What was he up to?

Knox seemed to have drawn the same conclusions. "So what are we going to do? We cannae stand by and let a murderer—"

"If you know that Finn killed Duncan, you need to tell me right now. You need to tell the police. And Heather! Where is she?" He fought the waves of panic that were crashing over him.

"Finn drove back to Aberdeen to take care of his affairs and get his things. He's going to start next week." For once, Knox had lost his cocky edge. He looked completely and totally flummoxed. "So ye dinnae think Heather kens who she is dealing with?"

"No. To be honest, neither do I. That's why you're going to tell me what you know. Now."

Knox sighed. "Jaelle Codona, Finn's mother, used to help her mother, who was the housemaid and head cook at Morris Farms for years. Jaelle grew up here. Gypsies, but completely trustworthy. Finn's grandma was the nicest woman ye'd ever meet. Loved me like I was her own, especially after my mum died. And the food... the woman was a genius."

This didn't sound good. "What happened?"

"Duncan seduced Jaelle and got her pregnant. My grandfather proceeded to fire her because she was an unwed mother. She had to leave the area, so she went to Aberdeen and found work at a big hotel. Mind ye, this is all heresay – I was just a kid when this happened, but I've heard Jaelle was abused by her employer and pimped out or raped numerous times after she left the farm. I mean, to send out a vulnerable, sheltered, beautiful young woman who'd been raised on a farm and expect her to live in a bad part of town and deal with big city folk in a place like Aberdeen – any eejit could have figured out what would happen."

"So Finn..."

"Jaelle raised Finn herself. Never married. Everyone believes that she truly loved Duncan and believed he loved her, too. He sent her money while Finn was young, but as soon as he became a teenager and was deemed old enough to work, Duncan cut off the payments."

"Man. All kinds of reasons for bitterness to take root." Brodie weighed Knox's words against what he had seen with his own eyes earlier that morning. It all fit. He'd been suspicious of this exact scenario. "So you think Finn killed Duncan with revenge as his motive? It had to have been hard for a boy and a young man to see his mother leading such a tough life and know that it was the Morrises who were responsible."

"It gets worse. Duncan kept visiting Jaelle in the city just often enough to keep her hopes up and lead her to believe that they might really be together one day. Maybe he really loved her. Maybe he just liked the sex—"

Brodie interrupted. "Like he wasn't getting enough elsewhere."

"Right," Knox concurred. "Here's the cincher. Somewhere along the line, probably in the throes of passion, Duncan evidently promised Jaelle that she would get part of the profits from the farm when Duncan got his inheritance so that little Finny would have a better life."

"So Jaelle worked and worked all those years, put up

with who knows how much crap from her employer, and never got ahead, believing that Duncan would take care of her and Finn and make everything better as soon as he could," Brodie said.

"Until Duncan went back to Cyprus and never came home." Knox snorted. "My mother swore Duncan was the nicest man ye'd ever ken. I always believed her, until I heard Jaelle's story."

Brodie shook his head. "She probably got sick of waiting and then when she found out Duncan was two timing her with some woman from Cyprus, she lost it and started thinking revenge."

Knox nodded. "She trusted Duncan all those years and he let her down. And little Finny watched it all happen."

Brodie added, "And the hatred kept growing stronger and stronger. Mother and son." There was a moment of silence as he sorted out the facts – or theories – Knox had shared. "Is Jaelle the murderer?"

Knox wasn't done. "Or did Finn do it? Finn is the one who opted to explore his ancestry. If he found out aboot Duncan's two daughters – our half-sisters – in Cyprus, that they live a wealthy life, knew Duncan well, and enjoyed a doting father to care for them... I dinnae ken about you, but if I'd lived Finn's life, it would make me furious. I saw a photo of the sisters on the ancestry site. The women are beautiful, dark skinned and exotic-looking like their mother. There was even a photo of them with Duncan in the ancestry clues. I think they're what pushed Finn over the edge."

"I can understand the reasons behind their righteous anger, but it's still murder." Brodie was almost shaking with worry for Heather. He looked in his rearview mirror to make sure no one else was coming. "I need to get by."

Knox evidently had nothing more to say, at least at the moment, but Brodie's mind was still chewing on things as he watched Knox's pickup fishtail down the track. Knox could be right about Finn, or he might be trying to divert attention from his own diabolic deeds by painting Finn as the guilty party.

He revved his engine and continued toward McKnight Farms as fast as he could. Only one thing was sure – Brodie was going to have to stick to Heather like glue until he figured out who was guilty and who was not.

#

Not more than a few yards later, Brodie pulled over to the side of the road once again. He recognized Finn Codona's distinctive look from his photo on the ancestry site. From the look on his face, Finn seemed to know who he was, too.

With their vehicles blocking the road, they both stepped out of their autos and faced each other down.

"Brodie McBryde." Brodie hoped his voice sounded threatening. "I don't know what you're up to, but you need to leave Heather out of it! If it's me you're trying to get at, let's have it out right now."

Finn Codona reached into his pocket and pulled out a knife. "I have no issues with you, ye eejit. All I'm doing is applying for a job. But you'll stay out of my way if you know what's good for you."

Brodie would have loved to play the hero – to wrest Finn's knife from his hand and topple him to the ground, land a hard one on that handsome Morris nose so Finn would know Brodie meant business, so he would know never to set foot on McKnight property again. But would besting his half-brother in a knife fight help things? Probably not. And to be honest, he wasn't sure he could beat him. The man was ripped.

"Is this about the money?" Brodie shifted his weight and dodged back and forth on the balls of his feet in case Finn lunged at him. "Because if your gripe is that you should have your inheritance, you need to find Walter and take it up with him. He's the one who rooked Duncan out of his half of the farm."

"What do you think I'm trying to do?" Finn leaned a little closer and brandished the knife.

"If you hadn't killed Duncan, he might have got the money from Walter and given it to you like he promised."

Finn's swarthy face blanched white as a ghost's. The blade of the knife glinted in the light, making it glow.

"Duncan is dead?"

"You didn't know?"

The knife clattered to the ground. "No."

"And your mother?"

"I'm sure she would have told me had she known."

Brodie wasn't sure if he believed that or not, but he did believe that Finn was innocent of Duncan's murder. He'd been truly shocked to learn of his death. But Jaelle. Jaelle was another story. The woman was one mystery after another. Who knew what she was capable of?

Brodie put his boot over the handle of Finn's knife so Finn couldn't reach down and pick it up except by grabbing the blade. "So if you don't want to work at the farm so you can kill off all of Duncan Morris' offspring, what are you doing here?

"I have to get my mum out of Aberdeen before she ends up dead – or worse."

#

Heather was almost finished with another batch of pie crust. She'd already put in a long day, but she wanted to have the dough ready to use first thing the next morning. Making the dough batch by batch took a little more time, but she found the consistency of the dough was better and far more uniform if she didn't get overly eager and try to make huge batches. She took a long drink of the cold Highland tap water and re-sanitized her hands, then worked in the rest of the flour and ate a pinch to make sure it tasted the way it was supposed to. She still used her great-grandmother's recipe, the one with a beaten egg, vinegar and a dash of baking soda. It was the flakiest crust she knew, and it set them apart from their competitors, whose pie pastry was often as tough and flavorless as cardboard.

As always, when she was doing some sort of fairly simple manual labor, she let her brain flood with ideas and worries and hopefully, some wisdom, too. She'd thanked the pastor for singing *In His Time* on Sunday and told him how much she'd enjoyed the reminder. The pastor had reiterated that he'd had no intention of singing it until a few minutes before the service started. Like about the time she'd walked in.

She firmly suspected that the song was a sign from God that Brodie was the one she'd been waiting for. It wasn't that she didn't trust God, but how was she supposed to know when the time was right, and which man was meant for her? Her da had made a wrong choice once upon a time – wasn't Stacey her name? He must have thought she was the right one because he'd gotten engaged to her, but it had almost ruined his life when he met the real right one, Heather's mum, Violet, and wasn't free to be with her. Of course, it all worked out in the end. But Heather knowing that she almost never came to be because Nathan hadn't been sure which woman was the right one was kind of freaky. Of course, her mum would say that Heather would know for sure when she really did meet the one God intended for her, so not to worry. And, her mum would add, just don't do anything stupid before then. Ha, ha. Didn't she wish.

Heather wrapped the pie crust in film and tucked it in the cooler. It would be ready to roll by morning when the kitchen crew arrived – crew meaning the other two now that half of her staff had walked out. Was it any surprise that Heather had a hard time believing in happily-ever-after endings, especially right now? She didn't want anyone feeling sorry for her, but knowing she would likely get cancer and be rendered barren before she was thirty had pretty much cinched her cynicism.

She was just browning some garlic honey butter in a heavy bottomed pan so she could fry her chicken when Brodie walked in.

Speak of the devil – or the one God had chosen for her. How was she supposed to know?

"Hi." Brodie was walking quickly but he stopped short of a hug when he saw that she was suited up and working with food. He looked at her with raw emotion on his face. He looked immensely relieved about something. Probably starved and hoping he could figure out a way to get a taste.

He gulped. "I hear you hired a new staff member."

"Yup. Really nice guy from Aberdeen. Great attitude. Good commitment level. He seems eager to learn and really excited about living in the Highlands and working on a farm."

"And his name is Finn Codona."

What? She turned the burner lower so it wouldn't burn while she processed her shock. "How do you know his name?" The only one she'd told about Finn was Knox, because she'd asked him if he would be willing to share the loft with a roommate.

Brodie looked frustrated. "I hate to take a pin to your balloon, but Finn is one of the half-siblings fathered by Duncan Morris I was telling you about."

What? "Did you tell him I was hiring?"

"I was in Aberdeen trying to locate him when he was here. I spoke to his mother. Knox is the one who told me you'd hired him."

She grimaced. "So Knox knows about you, and Finn, and—"

"I didn't tell him, but yeah, the whole kit and caboodle."

She tried to sort things out in her much confused mind. "Maybe Finn was here because he wants to learn more about where his father's people came from. Did that ever occur to you?"

Brodie looked like he was struggling to stay patient. "You could be right. But there's a lot of potential for bitterness in the Codona family because of the way he and Jaelle were treated, not only by Duncan, but Duncan's parents. Finn could be the killer. People have killed for lesser things."

She glared at him. "I finally find the perfect person to hire and now you're dishing him."

"Think about it, Heather. Why would he come all the way out here to a place that only holds bad memories for his family if it doesn't have something to do with Duncan?"

Perhaps because he'd seemed so nice, and so suited to working on the farm, and she needed help so badly. "Your problem is that you're so intent on getting away from the Highlands that you can't relate to someone who wants to live here." Like me, she thought.

"Just because my job is calling me away from home right now doesn't mean I don't love the Highlands. I want you to be happy here, and I want you to succeed. I want you to be safe. But I can't always be here to protect you."

"I don't need you to protect me."

"That's easy to say now when you're here in your comfort zone and I'm here to help you should anything go wrong. But what are you going to do when things start to fall apart and I'm in Ardnamurchan?"

So there it was. There was no way Brodie McBryde was the one God had chosen for her. He couldn't be. So how to say this nicely? Her summers in Minnesota had impressed upon her the importance of saying things in a way so as not to offend people, especially those you liked. But...

"Brodie, I do like having you around, and I will definitely miss you when you head back to the islands to build more bridges. But things are already falling apart even though you're here. And yes, things may go from bad to worse when you're not here to look over my shoulder and save me from myself, but I will survive, and I will be fine. I may even shine."

Brodie did not look happy with her vision of the future. "So don't listen to me. Ignore what I'm telling you about Finn. Sounds like you've got it all figured out. You obviously don't need me."

Wait. Did Brodie want her to need him? Didn't he want to walk away from the farm in the Highlands, live on an island, and get on with his life over the sea? Shouldn't her asserting her confidence that she could get along without him set his mind at ease and free him to let go and get on with his own life?

"I'm just disappointed," she said. "I need help, and I think Finn is an ideal fit. The way he dropped into my lap seems like a gift from God. The timing seems perfect. He's got a broad range of skills and is willing to learn to do whatever I need him to help with. I really think he's the answer to my problems."

"And now you've got an even bigger problem."

"I don't know what to do. I can't just call and tell him I've changed my mind, and I don't want to hire him after all. He knows I'm horribly short-staffed and how desperately I need help. I can't keep working 14 hours a day forever. I've got things – personal things – that I need to take care of. Things that I can't keep putting off. I thought God was sending me a sign. Like on Sunday – *In His Time* – that everything was finally going to work out the way it was supposed to."

Brodie got a funny look on his face. "Maybe they will. I mean, you shouldn't assume that they won't."

"I guess I'm confused by the subtleties of God's method of communicating with me. Maybe He needs to come right out and hit me over the head with it so I know for certain what He wants me to do."

Brodie would claim after the fact that he didn't know what came over him. That he'd had no intention of using his thumb and pointer finger to thunk her royally in the head. But she wondered, had God prompted him? Had God used Brodie to hit her over the head with it, whatever IT was? She still wasn't certain what God was trying to tell her. The options were as infinite as God himself. How could she be expected to figure it out? All she knew for sure was that she had one whopper of a headache for the rest of the evening.

Chapter 21

"Heather McPhearson?"

Heather looked at her mobile to see if she recognized the number of whoever was ringing her up. "Yes. May I ask who's calling?"

"This is Abigail, Dr. Jamison's nurse. Doctor asked me to call and give ye an update after the results of yer latest pap smear and blood tests came in."

Heather's heart went into a freefall. When she'd left the office in Fort William, they'd specifically told her that they would call her only if there was a problem. Otherwise, she would get the results in the mail.

"Go ahead." She grabbed the back of her office chair and braced herself, though little good it would do since it was on rollers.

"Well, doctor said that yer numbers are all a wee bit more foreboding than they were three months ago. He said to tell ye that he wants ye scheduled for a hysterectomy this time next year at the very latest." The nurse paused, presumably so the news could sink in. "If ye want to proceed with any of the options he outlined for harvesting eggs, fertilizing, and then implanting them, ye should set up yer appointment by first thing next week. He likes to say that just like the best restaurants, he is booked out quite a ways in advance."

If the insertion of humor was designed to provide a

bit of comic relief in the midst of a tense situation, Heather had to appreciate her for trying – even though it wasn't working.

"Ma'am? Are ye still there?"

"Yes. Just thinking."

The nurse's voice continued on in the same cheery manner. "Of course. There is so much to think on. Such a blessing to have so many options."

So many options. Every one except the one she wanted, which was to marry when she was ready and have as many babies as she and her husband wanted – when they wanted.

"One more thing that doctor wanted me to mention. Because of the test results, he would recommend that if ye can come to terms with nae having yer own child, but pursue a solution like adoption or using a surrogate mother at a later date, ye should schedule yer hysterectomy immediately. It would be safest for all concerned." She paused. "Doctor is concerned that because yer reproductive system is already somewhat compromised, even a planned pregnancy could end up nae being viable, which could mean risking yer life for—"

"For nothing." Heather supplied the words before the nurse could say them. For some reason, it helped to say the blunt truth herself than to hear whatever sugar coated euphemisms the nurse had been planning to use.

The nurse neither confirmed nor denied her comment. "Shall I plan a follow up for next Monday morning to hear what ye've decided?"

"I guess so." Heather could hear the quiver in her voice. A shadow fell across her face and suddenly, she felt cold as a winter's day. Had the shadow been an illusion that reflected how hopeless she felt, or had someone been listening just out of sight? Was the shadow the result of their leaving or had the sun gone under a cloud?

She was halfway to the door when the nurse said, "Shall we say aboot half nine?

Crap. Her mobile was on speaker phone. And there was not a cloud in the sky. She stepped outside the door and scanned the courtyard. No one was in sight. Had she imagined the whole shadow thing or had someone heard what the nurse had said?

She agreed to the appointment for the follow-up call. One week to decide – and the first thing that popped into her head was, how on earth was she supposed to find the time to consider her options or even think about what she should do when she had no one to cover for her and the work of four or five people to do every day? How could she take a day or two off to have an egg harvested or sperm implanted or anything else when she was so short-staffed?

She loved her job. She would do anything for William and Lyndsie and McKnight Farms. But was her commitment to them worth missing out on her one chance to have a baby of her own? Sure, it might be a long shot, but didn't she owe it to herself to try?

#

Brodie flattened himself against the outer wall of Heather's office and tried to hide behind the same partially ajar door that had enabled him to hear her conversation a few minutes earlier.

He hadn't meant to eavesdrop. He was mortified to be trapped in such a compromising situation.

He glanced to his left as much as he dared without

revealing his presence and tried to see if she had gone back inside.

His heart ached for her. But he couldn't very well take her in his arms and admit that he'd heard every word and offer to let her cry on his shoulder, could he? And now what? He was in possession of information that he had no right to know, but what he had heard was so unforgettable that he couldn't pretend he didn't know it.

In His Time, in His time. God make all things beautiful, in His time. Stop it, he wanted to yell. But the words to the song kept flitting through his memory. He wanted to scream at God for taunting him with the challenge to do something about a matter that was none of his business.

Lord, please show me every day, as You're teaching me Your way, that You do just what you say, in Your time.

He couldn't stop thinking about Heather and her desire to have a baby. Under a deadline no less. Of course, he didn't know all the details. But if Heather had told him she needed a father for her child, or that she needed to have that child somewhat immediately, like, evidently yesterday, he could have offered to help, to talk things through, to listen while she worked through the pros and cons of each of the options the nurse had mentioned. But as things were, he wasn't supposed to know. How could he swoop in now and try to help without coming across as a sneak and a liar? The very things he had accused Knox and Finn of.

His legs felt like jelly. He had to get out of here. What had possessed him to come and see Heather this morning anyway? *A feeling.* A little voice inside his head. The Holy Spirit? Was his knowing about Heather's plight a God thing, a freak, random occurrence due to his own bad timing, or just plain bad luck?

Ye could offer. The little voice again.

Offer what? A sample of his sperm in a specimen container for Heather to use or not, depending on her preferences? Stud services, like when they let Beauty out to breed heifers or cows? Here, Heather. Stand still while I mount you and get you with child before returning to my own pasture.

Ye could marry her, the small, still voice in his head said.

And then what? His mind raged. I might be falling in love with her. I might want to ask her to be my wife – eventually – when I know her better and when I've decided how I want to spend the rest of my life. I have a choice in this, right? It's not fair to saddle myself with something like this when I barely know Heather. It's not like I don't have a choice in the matter!

Aye. That ye do. But Heather has nae choice about the timing of when she might like to have a bairn because of what's happening to her body.

But that's her problem! Who Brodie was yelling at in his head, he had no idea.

Ye can yell at me all ye like, ye ken. I wrestled with Jacob and I can do the same with ye if that's what ye want this to be aboot.

So what was with the voice now? And God was suddenly Scottish? But the words were as clear as if they'd been said aloud. How could he ignore them?

I spoke to Joseph in a dream. Told him he shouldnae divorce Mary, that I wanted him to take care of my Son. He had a choice awright – to trust and obey, or to go his own way. He did what I asked.

Brodie felt like he was going to crumple. This was not the same thing. Joseph and Mary had already been already engaged and Mary had already been pregnant when Joseph was forced to decide whether to marry or divorce Mary.

Ye're missing the point. Mary and Joseph's marriage was arranged. I let their parents think they made the decision, but it was me who chose Joseph for Mary. It was all part of my plan. Oh, and aboot that. So sorry I had to move the timing of yer da's heart attack up a few months. I knew it was the only thing that would make ye come home.

The conversation felt so real that he would have spoken aloud if he'd dared. But he was still just a few feet away from Heather's office. Brodie started to shake. This couldn't be happening. God didn't just come down to earth and talk to people today like he did in the Bible.

Whatever gave ye that idea?

"I don't know," Brodie whispered.

Just think on it, son. Ye have a few days to decide what ye want to do.

Brodie thought he heard a chuckle.

But if ye're going to leave, do it now. Heather will be coming out the door in aboot fifteen seconds, and if she finds ye here, she will nae be happy.

That was it. Brodie ran. When he'd driven over, he'd done a loop and parked around the corner, out of sight, nose out. Thank you, God. He jumped into his truck and took off without having to circle back into the courtyard. It solved one problem. About the rest, he had no clue what to do.

He was halfway down Heather's lumpy, bumpy track when it occurred to him that he really was seriously toying with the idea of making love to Heather so that she could have a baby. His baby. And then a second thought imposed itself over the first one. Was what he was contemplating any different than what Duncan had done? Not really.

Look how that had turned out.

#

Heather thought she heard someone outside the door to her office. But then, she'd been hearing things all day. And she'd always been wrong. When she'd gone to the door to make sure, no one had been there.

She was trying to get on with the day's work, but her mind was still churning with the details of her conversation with Dr. Jamison's nurse. She knew she should be finishing payroll, but all she could think about were babies and sperm donors and God's timing and what a mess her life was.

What was she going to do? She had to speak to someone about everything that was on her mind. She would have liked to hear her mum and da's thoughts, but she hated to burden them with the thought that her life was in danger, or that they might never have a grandbaby who had Violet's eyes or Nathan's good looks or Violet's artistry or Nathan's musical genius or any of the above. She needed to speak to someone who wasn't so close to the situation.

Besides, she knew without a shadow of a doubt that her parents would tell her to have the hysterectomy tomorrow – that nothing was worth risking her life. Maybe that's why she didn't want to bring it up to them. They already knew the basics of the situation. They just didn't realize that the timeline had been moved up a bit. Her parents had put their friends, Rose and Pastor Ian, to praying that Heather would meet the right man very soon, have a baby, and live happily ever after. So in short, they were already doing everything they could.

She was on the prayer list. And there was none better than Pastor Ian and Rose's.

She picked up her calculator and started working on payroll.

"Hello?"

Heather stood to see who was there. A woman stepped through the door. Brodie's mother? Yes. She'd seen her at the wedding, although they hadn't been formally introduced. Brodie looked a lot like her. Should she acknowledge that she knew who the woman was? She didn't know what to call her – was she still Mrs. McBryde or would she find that offensive? She thought the woman would introduce herself, but so far, she'd said nothing.

She decided to play dumb. "What can I do to help you?"

"I believe ye ken my son."

"Oh. Yes. I thought I recognized you from somewhere. I saw you across the room at your friend Jon's wedding. My da is Nathan McPhearson. He played his pipes with the band."

"That's nay my concern. Yer relationship with my son is."

"But..." Heather's mind scrambled to figure out what Brodie's mother would know about their relationship, especially since they really didn't have one beyond a fledgling friendship. "Can I ask what you're concerned about then? Because we're really not in a relationship."

"I want ye to leave Brodie alone." Her voice was hard. Shaky around the edges, but hard and raw with anger.

What was this about? Had she done something to offend the woman? Had Brodie said something to his mother that had angered her, and if so, what on earth could it be for her to react this way?

"Brodie should nae be here." His mother's voice was still shaking. "He worked hard to make a life for himself in Edinburgh. He spent years getting his degrees. He should be using his engineering skills." She wiped her brow. "It has nothing to do with ye personally. I just think it's best that he stay away from the farm. I want him to have nothing to do with the Morrises. He is my son. There's nothing for him here but bad blood."

"I haven't asked him to give up his life in Edinburgh."

"Nay, but if ye continue to grew closer, one of two things will happen. One, ye will tether him to the Highlands. He willnae leave as long as ye are here. Two, history will repeat itself. Ye will fall in love with him, or he with ye. Or ye will get pregnant, and he will leave ye and move off to some far away island to build bridges and ye will be alone with yer broken heart, and ye will never be happy again."

Heather closed her eyes and prayed for the right words to come to her. Based on what she knew of Brodie's parentage, Duncan had a fling with Brodie's mother and got her pregnant. Had she been engaged to Brodie's da or married to him? She didn't know the details, but she imagined Duncan to have been charming and loving. Even Heather knew Munro McBryde was not exactly any of the above, although he seemed to have been a good father to Brodie.

She started to say, "You have no need to worry." But she stopped. Just yesterday, she'd considered asking Brodie to father her child. If there had been time to spare, she would never have considered anything of the sort. But the way things stood... Oh, how she hated this!

"I'm his mum," his mother said. "Please dinnae make

him give up his dreams of working as an engineer when he's worked so hard to get where he is. Please dinnae try to keep him here. Ye will only bring unhappiness and grief to all of us."

She was completely serious.

Heather cleared her throat. "I'm so sorry that's the way you feel. I haven't known Brodie for long, but I care about him very deeply and wish him nothing but the best."

"Then ye will do nothing more to draw him in. Ye will let him go." Brodie's mother turned her back on her and started to walk out the door. And then, she turned around and looked Heather full face on. "I will stop at nothing to protect my son. That means doing whatever I need to do to insure he is happy and safe – and far away from the Highlands."

Heather stood in complete and utter shock for a full five minutes, her head spinning and her feet stuck to the ground. Did this woman really mean what she was saying? If she was serious, she could have killed Duncan to keep him from telling Brodie the truth about his parentage, or for revenge for the way Duncan had treated her and Brodie. Add Mama Bear instincts to that, and who knows what the woman had done, or might still do.

A deep chill ran across Heather's shoulders. That's when she started to get mad.

What mother tried to sabotage her son's happiness by deciding what was best for him and then going behind his back to turn his friends against him?

What mother ignored what her son was thinking and feeling and tried to manipulate the courses of action that were open to him, the decisions that could shape his future? Who did she think she was – God?

Chapter 22

Brodie fiddled with his mobile and tried to decide what to say to Heather. He'd never had a problem talking to her before, or maybe he should say he'd found it very easy to talk to her when he first met her. But as of late, it was difficult to know what to say.

He finally gathered his courage and rang her up. He would have to trust God to help him find the right words.

"Heather? Just wondered if you're free for lunch today?"

There was a moment's silence. "I guess I don't have any plans, but I'm not sure I should take the time. There are a lot of things on my to-do list."

"How about I pack a picnic lunch? We can find a spot under a tree in the sheep pasture to sit down, eat, and talk for a bit without taking the time to drive all the way into town."

"I guess that would be okay," she finally said. "I do need to check on the ewes sometime today."

Don't sound too enthusiastic, he thought, but to himself. Poor girl had a lot on her mind these days. And he probably only knew the half of it.

"Great! We can both get something crossed off our lists and spend a little time together, too. I'll look forward to it."

He clicked off before she had a chance to reconsider or think of another excuse not to come.

Two and a half hours later, he'd packed a picnic basket with plates, utensils and a tablecloth to spread on the ground, been to town, and stopped at the bakery for take away mac and cheese. The soup of the day was broccoli bisque with potatoes, leeks and cheese, so he'd bought a couple of bowls, as well as two sausage rolls and millionaire bars for dessert. He might have overdone it a bit, but he wasn't sure what Heather would be in the mood for. He wanted her to have options.

He shifted into high and drove back in the direction of the farm. Then again, maybe having options was a bad thing. Maybe she just wanted someone to decide for her and be done with it.

The more he thought about Heather's dilemma, the more he wanted to help. He had a feeling his mum would strongly disapprove of what he was about to do, but that was her problem. His da would most likely tell him to go for it. His friends would think he was crazy. The only one who understood was God himself, and he was fine with that. Confusing as it sounded, he felt like he'd finally found his calling – that God wanted him to take care of Heather and be the father of her child.

He still didn't have a clue as to how he would broach the subject. All he knew was that he didn't have the leisure of sitting around and thinking about it for a week or two until the time seemed right. From the sound of it, there was not a minute to spare. If Heather agreed, he was good to go at a moment's notice.

He glanced down at his watch and tried to gauge the time he would arrive at McKnight Farms. They hadn't specified if they would meet in the pasture – it was a walk Heather enjoyed when she had the time. But if her day was as busy as she'd claimed, she might appreciate it if Brodie were there a little early, ready to whisk her off to the picnic spot without delay. He wanted to be there early regardless, so if all went as planned, he could pick her up. If she wanted to get even more fresh air than the picnic provided, she could always walk home.

There. He had made another decision for her – one less thing for her to worry about.

He glanced at his watch again. There had been a long line at the bakery and only one girl behind the counter. They'd probably been short staffed in the kitchen, too. Everyone was these days. Nothing he could do but wait his turn. He sped up a little, determined to be there to pick up Heather outside her office before she started the trek down to the sheep pasture.

He was only 5 miles away. With any luck, the soup and sausage rolls would still be warm when he got there.

He rounded a corner and slammed on the brakes the second he saw the utility truck. The basket that extended in the air held two men at the top of a pole. He looked around for a field driveway or a path. To the best of his knowledge – and he knew this particular track fairly intimately – there were no passing places anywhere. The nearest intersection was almost a mile back. Even if he backed up that far, he would have to drive an extra fifteen or twenty miles in a roundabout circle to find another way to get where he needed to go. Creeks, rivers, fields, the Craigievar Castle grounds, a large, self-contained estate, some stone fences... they all dictated where there were roads and where it was impossible to get through the maze.

What the heck was he going to do now? Where was God with His perfect timing when it mattered? Heather hadn't seemed all that excited to have lunch with him in the first place. If he was late, she probably wouldn't take time to eat with him say nothing about talking about how to get her pregnant. Well, he knew how to get her pregnant. It was more the when and where that needed to be decided.

He got out of his truck to speak to the utility men. He assumed they were men. It was hard to tell with their helmets on. Actually, one looked like she might be a woman.

"How much longer will you be blocking the road?"

"Fifteen, twenty minutes. Shorter than it would take for ye to drive around and come in from the other side."

"Aye. Thanks." It wasn't the answer he'd hoped for. He didn't have that much time. He was going to have to call Heather and try to juggle things a wee bit. And the sausage rolls and soup were definitely going to be cold.

He tried to re-ring her number from his recent contacts file. No signal. Great. There were spots all over the neighbourhood where there was no mobile reception because of the mountains and valleys surrounding their farms. Just his luck to be in one of them.

He felt like a caged animal. He hated it when he wasn't in control, when he wasn't free to do what he wanted to do or be where he wanted to be – like when his parents had forced him to go into town and spend time at his mum's house. He'd belonged on the farm. Why hadn't they just let him be? The farm had been where his heart was. His mum could have come out to see him in the country. It had driven him crazy when he was young. It still did.

He ignored the no signal issue and pressed Heather's number until he was in danger of his mobile going dead. If God could chat with him in the courtyard, he could certainly make a mobile signal go through a wee mountain, couldn't he?

Twenty-five minutes of stewing and fretting later, the linemen finally lowered themselves, folded up their truck, and unblocked the road.

Brodie had no idea what Heather would say, but he felt sure it wouldn't be good. The intimate, romantic picnic he'd planned was a shambles. He could only hope Heather would give him a second chance.

He was driving down the track, praying he would have no more delays, when a sudden thought came to him. Was this God's way of telling him today was not a good day to speak his mind to Heather and offer to father a bairn with her? Could it be that God had just saved his butt?

He took a deep breath. He sighed in relief.

For all he knew, Heather may have had a meeting that ran late, or an unexpected call, or something that had taken longer than she'd thought it would. Maybe she hadn't even noticed the time.

He saw the first sheep in the road and slammed on his brakes again. He could see the farm from where he was stopped this time, but a swarm of sheep were flooding on to the road, Great. Heather's sheep were out. They seemed fascinated with the dirt track for some reason. Why, he could not comprehend. The wee bit of grass growing between the tracks was dusty and probably coated with a film of oil as well. What was wrong with the eejit sheep? They had a perfectly fine pasture to graze in, plenty of water, and grass and wildflowers to munch on. Why would they want to leave all that was theirs in the most beautiful, lush place on earth and run away only to have to make do with the slim pickings on a hard, dirt-packed road?

Or was God sending him another clue? Who could

tell with God? He looked up, but all he saw was a few puffy clouds, some birds, and a few treetops.

The whole thing was beyond him. Women – especially women like Heather – were an unfathomable mystery. Even then, they weren't as unpredictable as God. Who knew what God was going to do next or what kind of alert he would resort to to get your attention? The thing with God was, you never knew anything for certain. Anything could happen at any moment. And it was driving Brodie nuts.

#

Heather waited in the pasture as long as she could. Brodie was over a half an hour late and there was still no sign of him. Since Brodie had promised a picnic lunch, she had nothing to eat. She hadn't brought so much as a snack or a water bottle to tide her over. She had to go to the bathroom, and she had a headache from being exposed to the sun and the wind, both of which were very intense. The wind had howled all through the night and she'd barely had any sleep. That, and Brodie's mother's words echoing through her mind had made for a fitful night. She'd tried to be patient, but she was mad as a hornet.

Guess what was swarming around her head? A hornet, or a yellow jacket, or a mud dauber. She wasn't sure which, but it was fierce and persistent and very bothersome. Could anything else go wrong?

Men.

She glanced up the hill in the direction of the road to see if she could see any sign of Brodie. What? The sheep that had been grazing contentedly just a few moments ago had disappeared. She scanned the rest of the pasture to make sure they hadn't wandered to another spot. Gone.

She stood and ran in the direction of the road. She'd known there was a slightly weak spot in the fence to the west, but it had been that way since before William bought the farm and the sheep had yet to discover it. Why today?

By the time she got to the top of the hill, she was really feeling the effects of no sleep, no food, and no water mixed with too much frustration, stress, and exertion. Sure enough, her black-nosed sheep were outside the fence, stretched down the road in both directions. The sheep dog she'd walked down to the pasture with was running in frantic circles, trying to do his job, but the sheep weren't cooperating, seemingly convinced they did not want to be in the pasture any longer. Stubborn little creatures. What was wrong with them? Grass greener on the other side of the fence? Eejit sheep.

That's when she saw Brodie's truck in the midst of the swell. Had he let them out, or was he trying to help round them up? These days, Heather didn't trust anyone, or any situation to be what it seemed. Stupid, screwed up universe!

She finally reached the fence and started yanking rocks from their perches, one by one, working to make a bigger hole in the fence. Sheep would leap over a low spot where the rocks had crumbled to escape a field, but would only stream back through a fairly wide opening. If she made a decent breach, she hoped her dog would do the rest.

"Heather?!" She heard Brodie's voice, but just barely, over the bleating of the sheep and the barking of the dog.

Then he was running to her, and miracle of miracle, the sheep were following him. She could see her dog cutting off any exit points as Brodie unknowingly led the sheep back toward the pasture. There were still two layers of rocks at the base of the hole in the fence, but she didn't dare lean down to retrieve them with a full grown man and more than a hundred sheep barreling toward her.

She quickstepped to the right and moved over to let them through. Brodie looked over his shoulder, finally realizing what was happening, leaped over the remaining rocks and wrapped his arms around her as he crash landed beside her. The lambs streamed through the opening with the dog bringing up the rear.

They lay together in a tangled pile of soft grass and wildflowers – thankfully not the prickly variety. Brodie's arms were still around her.

She was so mad at him. And she wasn't. She could feel her anger dissolving. It would probably go completely away once she had a bite or two of something to eat.

Their faces were so close their lips were almost touching. Was it her who leaned toward him or him that drew closer to her? It didn't matter. Their lips met – softly, tenderly – and Brodie McBryde kissed her. His arms were still around her so she wrapped hers around him. He kissed her again. It was all she could do not to act like some breathless, star struck teenager, but she hadn't been kissed all that often, and never by anyone whom she felt what she did for Brodie McBryde.

He dropped his arms and fell on his back, and she did, too – mostly because she felt limp as a jellyfish floating in water. They lay side by side, looking up at the sky.

Brodie turned to look at her. "You wanna make a baby?"

Her limp arms stiffened until they felt like they were going to pop out of their sockets. What a way to ruin a perfectly wonderful moment. Well, not perfect. She was still starving and thirsty and completely exhausted.

Be nice, she told herself. Isn't making a baby with Brodie exactly what she wanted to do? But not right this moment. When the time was right.

"I mean, when the time is right," Brodie said. "But soon."

Her anger flared once again. "How did you know? What do you know?"

"Well, that's a loaded question. And the answer is complicated."

She sat up. "I need food. I have time for a quick answer before I eat, but not a complicated one."

Brodie was already on his feet. Fifty yards and two minutes later she was sipping on the most delicious soup she'd ever tasted and chowing down on a sausage roll.

"Okay." She took a millionaire bar. "Are these both for me?"

"Well, I was going to – seriously? You'd think you were already eating for two." He looked slightly appalled.

"Watch it. You're on thin ice here."

Brodie's face went white. "I know you need to have a bairn as soon as possible because I overheard you having a conversation with your doctor as I was about to enter your office. Which was not my fault. You had your speaker on."

"True." She didn't know what to say. She had nothing to be embarrassed about but she still was.

Brodie's face went from white to red. "I'm offering to

be the bairn's father because God told me I should be."

She sat down on the tailgate of Brodie's truck in case she should pass out and tried to think of a response.

"So you're willing to donate sperm?" She felt a sense of relief – a vast, overwhelming sense of relief. "And be an anonymous birth father, no strings attached?"

Brodie frowned. "I never said that."

She tried to swallow and almost didn't manage it.

"I'm offering to make love with you, create a bairn the old-fashioned way, and raise the wee one as our own. Isn't that what you want?"

Thoughts of Brodie's mother's words, and her own doubts and fears and insecurities went to war in her head. "No," she said. "I'm not ready for that. I don't know you well enough. And we have different dreams for the future, and I'm not even sure I can trust…" Of course she trusted him. But she didn't trust anyone. The war went on. "There's just been so much upheaval and uncertainty in my life these last few weeks. I don't know what I want."

Brodie's face was stone cold. "I'm not willing to plant the seed unless I get to watch it grow. My own sperm donor of a father did that to me, and I won't impose the same on a child of my making."

"I'm not asking you to…" But she was. Probably. Most likely. How was she to know what the future held? "I think it would be better if I just got sperm from a sperm bank. Maybe some good old American sperm so I don't have to worry about running into the donor anywhere in Scotland."

Now, why had she said that? She'd eaten enough that she couldn't blame it on low blood sugar.

Now Brodie looked angry. "You'll probably take the bairn and move back to America one day anyway. And I already know I couldn't bear it. So, aye. It's probably for the best that I not do what God has asked of me. He must have made a mistake."

What? She wanted to scream. She tried to keep her voice calm, but it was shaky at best. "So know you're putting that on me? You disobeying God and blaming whatever fate befalls you on me?"

"Well, it won't be my fault!" Brodie glared at her, then looked away as though he couldn't bear the sight of her. "Let me ask you this. What if we do fall in love and marry one day? You'll have your bairn, and I feel sure I would love the wee one like my own. But you'd have robbed me of the chance to have my own bairn with the woman I love, flesh of our flesh." He took her arms, lifted her from the tailgate of his truck, and set her on the road. He slammed the tailgate shut and got into the cab. "That's what you'll have to live with if you will not let me make love to you now, while the iron is hot."

She moved away from the truck and shielded her eyes from the cloud of dust and dirt she was sure would follow.

Brodie bent his elbow over the window ledge and twisted his neck to look back at her. "I'll be back later this afternoon to fix your fence. Best leave your dog here to guard the opening until then."

"You don't have to do that. It's my responsibility. I'll take care of it!" She yelled after Brodie's truck. But he was already halfway up the road.

Chapter 23

Brodie eased his truck into the only parking space available at the police station, and wished the spot didn't happen to be right next to Heather's car. He'd just have to linger in the police station until after she'd left so he wasn't perceived as helping her out to her car. Heaven forbid he should try to help.

The whole situation between them was ridiculous. What woman didn't want a man who was willing to make a commitment to start a family with the woman he loved? He still couldn't believe she'd brushed him off the way she did.

He'd asked the police if they could please meet separately, but the policeman he'd spoken to had said no. Considering that the police had called Brodie and Heather into their office to question them about Duncan's murder, he had hardly been in a place to argue. Their exact words had been that "rumor had it that he and Heather were not being forthcoming regarding information critical to the murder investigation and if they did not comply, they could be charged with withholding evidence."

He caught a glimpse of a black truck that looked like the one Knox drove just as he was going through the door, but there were a lot of black trucks in Alford. Why would they invite Knox when he was a prime suspect?

He walked into the room. Knox. Heather was sitting across the table from him, looking uncomfortable. When Brodie walked in, she looked even more so.

Karl, the police chief, got right to business. "We're here on a fact finding mission – first, to find Duncan Morris' killer, and second, to determine if what happened at Heather's house is in any way related to his death."

Brodie tried to catch Heather's eye in hopes of showing his support, but she was looking down at the table and didn't even flinch. He could see Knox watching him out of the corner of his eye. He could care less what Knox thought of him. So he cared about Heather and wanted to see whoever had trashed her house caught and punished. Was that a crime?

"First, I want to make it clear that each of ye is still a suspect, and second, that if any of ye lie to me or forget to tell me something that may be important to this case, I will charge ye with withholding evidence."

Okay. He couldn't be more clear.

"We're going to channel Agatha Christie and go over the list of suspects. What I want is for ye to talk to me aboot the personality traits and motives each of the suspects had for killing Duncan, as well as past and current grievances that would have been cause for murder. And if any of ye ken other names that should be on the list, I want to hear aboot it now."

The policeman looked at Brodie, then Knox, the look on his face the same as a kid who was about to drop a stink bomb. "Let's start with Finn Codona."

"So you know about Duncan's illegitimate offspring." Brodie said what he did mostly to let the police know that he could be trusted and relied upon to tell the truth. Unfortunately, Karl didn't look either impressed or grateful.

"We found Duncan's laptop and took it into evidence. Because his computer was set to remember all of his passwords, we were able to see the results of his DNA test and trace each of his known offspring, including the two of ye, Finn Codona, and a pair of daughters from Cyprus. Of course, there may be more who havenae had their DNA tested. It would have been nice if we'd heard the truth from either of ye."

Great. So the police thought he was a liar. He could line up right behind Knox.

The police's findings also confirmed for the first time that Duncan knew he had fathered all of the children on the ancestry site.

The policeman leaned back in his swivel chair. "So let's talk aboot Finn Codona. What do ye ken aboot him and what might his motives have been?"

"I hired him to work at McKnight Farms before I knew who he was. He's supposed to start tomorrow morning. All I know about him is that he seems very excited to move home to the highlands and work on the farm." Heather gave Brodie a quick but very disgusted look.

"Motives," Knox said, "would have to include revenge for his mother's mistreatment, resentment, and a desire for restitution, since he's lived his entire life in a very poor area of Aberdeen without any money or creature comforts to speak of."

"You're assuming a lot," Brodie said. "Finn might have been raised in a bad part of town, but for all we know, he's the most loved and pampered of all Duncan's kids. From what I can tell, his mother loves him dearly and raised him right."

"Believe what ye will," Knox said. "Ye're wrong."

"Since Brodie mentioned her," Karl spoke. 'What aboot Finn's mother, Jaelle Codona?"

"I met her last week in Aberdeen." Brodie looked at Knox, who might have his theories regarding Finn and his mother, but had never met either of them. Or had he? "Lovely woman, very gracious, well-grounded. From what I can tell, she's moved on and made the best of a bad situation."

"Motives?" Karl asked. "Use yer imagination. First impressions are rarely accurate. Nobody is good all the way through."

Once again, Knox was the first to speak. "Not only did Duncan get Jaelle pregnant – he cost her everything – her home, her job, her family. She's certainly entitled to a little righteous anger on behalf of her and her son."

In Brodie's humble opinion, Knox was trying to pin it on Jaelle so he wouldn't be found guilty himself.

Heather cleared her throat. "From what I hear, Duncan made Jaelle promises and then blew her off. Blew her son off, too. That increases the likelihood that she would be bitter about what happened. If I was raising a child alone, and then had to watch while the father of my child enjoyed a cozy life in Cyprus with his beautiful, young, live-in lover and two cute, little daughters, I might decide to kill him, too."

"Ah, premeditated nonetheless," Brodie noted. He still thought they were wrong. Jaelle might have acted a little nervous, but he hadn't gotten a murderous vibe from her.

Karl coughed. "So, Heather. Ye just indicated that ye might consider murder as an option if ye felt it was justifiable. Shall we discuss yer status as a suspect next?"

Brodie clamped his jaw shut. Too bad she didn't want his help.

Heather huffed loudly. "That's ridiculous. You know that's not what I was saying."

"Motives, gentlemen?" Karl asked.

Brodie said nothing.

Knox said, "Heather has a lot at stake. Her job is to protect her boss' assets. Duncan was a threat to all they've built and invested in the property thus far."

So are you, Brodie wanted to say. Plus, you're obnoxious. If Heather or I were the type to kill someone, you're the one who would be dead.

Heather just shook her head and looked disgusted.

"What aboot ye, Brodie?" Karl's voice was quiet but firm.

"What are ye talking about? What do I think about Heather's motives or what do I think about you and Knox trying to pin this on someone who has nothing to do with Duncan?"

"I was asking ye if ye would like to tell me aboot yer motives or if ye'd like me to leave it up to Knox." Karl said.

"I'd like to tell you why I think Knox is guilty." Brodie tried to tamp down his temper.

"The motives would be much the same for both of them," Heather said. "Duncan impregnated both of their mothers and then abandoned them. They were both raised by their – I don't know what to call them. Stepfathers? I've met Brodie's mother, but I'm not sure what became of Knox's mum."

"She died when I was young," Knox said.

Heather looked shocked about Knox's mum. Brodie was shocked that Heather had met his mother. As far as Knox's mum, well, everyone in Alford remembered or knew what had happened when Knox was born, but Heather wasn't from the Highlands. Knox's mother had almost died delivering him. She was never the same from that time forward. Whether she'd been so harmed by the labor itself that she had never recovered, or whether regret and guilt had consumed her from the inside, Brodie didn't know.

Heather didn't say another word.

"Brodie, let's talk aboot yer da." The police didn't give up easily.

"What about him?"

Knox leered at him. "Munro had to hate Duncan for screwing yer mother, wrecking his marriage, and being yer real da."

Brodie clenched his fists. "Do not speak of my parents that way."

"We're here to lay our cards on the table." Knox stared at him, his eyes full of hostility. "Yer da is a curmudgeonly old crabbit. Yer mum is nae saint either."

Heather neither spoke up on his behalf nor disagreed with Knox's assessment. In fact, no one said anything.

"In my opinion, they're both capable of having killed Duncan, and have enough reason that nae one could blame them if they did," Karl added.

"Aye, but you'd still lock them up without blinking an eye." Brodie was seething under his skin.

Karl didn't even try to deny it. "Are there any other neighbours who had reason to want Duncan dead?"

Knox spoke. "Nae that we ken. Although I think my da may have promised to sell the farm to Munro McBryde until William McKnight offered him considerably more money, at which time he reneged on his promise. He may have offered it to the Browns as well. If so, they may have been mad aboot it."

"We can't forget the possibility of other children

fathered by Duncan who aren't on the ancestry site." Brodie said, reluctant to have his parent's names on everyone lips as they finished the discussion.

"Speaking of yer father, Knox. I assume he's still in Cyprus?"

"Last I knew. I dinnae speak to him as a rule."

Brodie snapped. "And there are no flights between here and there? He couldn't have come home, killed Duncan, and returned to Cyprus?"

Karl said, "Walter is nae a suspect at this time given his location, Brodie. Knox, if ye could try to contact him and double check his whereabouts, I would like to ken for certain that he's still in Cyprus."

Brodie didn't want to argue with Karl again – it was obvious it wasn't helping – but Karl leaving something so important up to Knox, who was about as reliable as a slug, seemed like a lackluster way to investigate someone suspected of murder.

Brodie stood. He was done. "Will that be all?"

"I'm finished for now. But if ye come up with any more clues or ideas, I would remind ye that ye need to report them directly to me. If I hear that ye're withholding evidence or sharing it with each other instead of being forthcoming with me, I will arrest all three of ye." Karl looked them each in the eye and started toward the door. "And Heather? I'd keep a close eye on Finn if I were ye."

And a closer eye on Knox, Brodie thought.

#

Heather locked the door to her house and walked across the courtyard to her office. It seemed ridiculous to have to batten down the hatches when she was only a few feet away most of the day, but after what she'd been through, she was afraid not to. Knowing that it could have been one of her hired hands set her on edge. So had the meeting she and Brodie and Knox had attended the night before. They never had gotten around to talking about who could have trashed her house the night of the wedding.

She tried to put her concerns out of her mind and focus on the exciting things in store. Not only was it Finn's first day at work, but they were releasing the first of their autumn pies and trucking them off to various suppliers across the Highlands and down into Aberdeen and Dornie. Thanks to Lyndsie's connections and marketing efforts, there were even some going over the sea to Skye.

They'd already previewed the first of the new pies to wet the taste of their customer's palates in hopes that they would start to trust in the McKnight Farms brand. The new logo featured the silhouette of a knight on a large horse with the hills of the Highlands layered in shades of green, blue and purple in the background. The hills were set off by a stunning sky glowing with the yellow, peach and rosy hues of sunset. They were contemporary, compelling and upbeat, and Heather was confident the pies would continue to fly off the shelves.

They'd released the more familiar flavors of their Chicken Balmoral Pie first to gain the confidence of their customers. The flavours were already well liked by most Scots, but hopefully, a wee bit more creative and delicious than anything similar that was on the market.

Today, they were releasing their seasonal fall lineup. First up was their Seasoned Pork, Pumpkin, and Parmesan Pie. Next was an absolutely incredible nod to Germany's Christmas markets with their Bavarian

Hunter Schnitzel Pie with homemade spaetzle noodles and mushrooms tucked in a wonderful cream gravy. Their final seasonal offering was their holiday themed Herb-Scented Chicken Pie with Apple Cranberry Stuffing and Sauvignon Blanc Sauce. She was completely convinced that each of the new offerings was going to be a huge hit. Lyndsie had worked hard to find upscale places to market the pies – garden centers, tea houses in castles, roadside kiosks that catered to tourists, and small, locally owned groceries. Anyone who loved pies but was looking for something a little different was going to be enchanted by the new flavours.

Heather fiddled with the last of the labels, checking to make sure the cooking instructions, list of ingredients, and nutritional information were all correct before printing them off. She had until half two to get the labels on and things sorted so they would be ready to send off in the refrigerated lorry.

She had just pressed the okay to print when Finn walked in the door, right on time.

"Good morning, fair Heather. I'm looking forward to working for McKnight Farms and am pleased to ask you what I should do to get started."

She'd already run a security check on him, a requirement for all food service workers. Everything had checked out.

She handed him two pieces of government paperwork, and said, "Welcome to McKnight Farms. These need to be turned in by the end of the day so I can file them with the inspector. If you'd like to follow me, I'll start by giving you a tour of our pie production facility, the butcher shop, and the loft where you'll be staying when you're not in Aberdeen. It's being offered on a temporary basis, until you have time to find something more permanent of your own."

"Thank you. I appreciate your trust in me and the arrangements you've made on my behalf." Finn looked and sounded completely sincere.

She desperately wanted to believe him, and to get off on the right foot with the man. She needed help, and she didn't have many options. "Finn, I'm going to be completely upfront here. It's come to my attention that your father was Duncan Morris, and that your mother worked in the Morris household when you were conceived. Not that it has any impact on your being hired, or influences the expectations I have for your employment here, but I want to be candid."

"You're wise to mention it, especially since there is an ongoing investigation into Duncan's murder. It's a complicated situation, and I can't truthfully say that it's not part of my reason for wanting to be in the Highlands, but I can assure you that you have nothing to fear from me. In fact, I heard what happened to your house, and I want you to know that I will do everything in my power to watch over you, your house and office, as well as the farm and the animals who reside here. I'm used to looking after my mum, and I've got Aberdeen street smarts that your other employees may not have. I promise you I'll do my best for you."

She smiled. Her first genuine smile in a few days. She'd heard Duncan was a charmer with a golden tongue, and Finn certainly seemed to have the same gift. What a difference from Knox's belligerent attitude.

"I'm sure we'll get on fine. It truly is a blessing to have you here." She'd heard what happened to Finn's mother and how she'd been treated when she'd gotten pregnant, and in some small way, it felt good to be able to welcome Finn in a place he should have been welcomed all along.

Finn smiled back at her, his white teeth gleaming against his smooth, olive skin. "If you don't mind, I'd like to put a few personal things in the loft, use the facilities, and wash my hands before we begin the tour."

"That's fine. You've had a long drive, and I have a phone call I need to make. Your bedroom is on the left, and the bathroom is between it and the bedroom on the right. I don't believe Knox is here, but I would make a practice of knocking or calling out as you go up the stairs to the loft to make sure you're not catching him off guard."

Finn nodded and went in the direction she pointed. The stairway was fairly open. There was a laundry room and bank of commercial freezers against the wall between her office and the common area. She made a note to tell him about the laundry room.

A second later, she heard Finn call out Knox's name. There was no reply. She hadn't expected he would be there.

Assuming all was well, she rang up the owner of the delivery service with the refrigerated lorry and confirmed that their product would be ready to pick up at half two. The driver reiterated the places where he was scheduled to stop, which included all of the spots in the Highlands, Glamis Castle, and Aberdeen. He also confirmed that he was scheduled to be back first thing in the morning to pick up the pies that were going to the west, to Dornie and Skye.

She had just clicked her mobile off when Finn reappeared at the door to her office, his face a shade or two more white than when he'd left.

Her thoughts immediately went to the worst. "Everything awright?"

"Knox isn't home. My room is perfect. Very comfortable bed. But I wondered..."

"Yes?"

"I could hear every word you said to your distributor, clear as a bell. If you already know you have no privacy when you're speaking on your mobile or meeting with people in your office, I apologize for being so forward. But in case you don't, I thought you would like to know."

Oh my. Her head felt like it was going to explode. She frantically tried to remember what she might have said and if Knox might have been upstairs when she'd said it. Why hadn't he told her? She knew there had been times when she'd spoken on her mobile or in person to Brodie or Lyndsie, William, her mum or da, or other staff members when she'd known Knox had been upstairs – and probably plenty more times when she hadn't known. Had the Morrises not thought to put insulation or sound proofing between the floor and ceiling when they remodeled the old shed and turned the loft into living quarters and the first floor into office and production facilities? Did it not occur to them that privacy was needed?

"Thank you for telling me. I was not aware the sound of my voice transferred so easily." She was absolutely mortified.

"If you like, I can check to see if there's a heat vent or a cold air return that's the culprit. If it's a flaw in the building design or materials in the ceiling, it would mean taking it down to correct the problem, which would be a lot more difficult and expensive, too."

"I appreciate your concern." She had forgotten he had been in charge of maintenance at the hotel in Aberdeen. "I can already tell you're going to be a huge asset to McKnight Farms."

Finn looked pleased, and with that, she stood and walked with him to begin the tour. She was going to have to confront Knox yet again and she was not looking forward to it.

Chapter 24

Brodie stormed into the farmhouse and stalked past his father without saying a word. Only then did he smell the aroma of slow-cooked beef and roasted potatoes wafting from the kitchen.

He turned and faced his da. "What have you done now? Killed a cow because you had a hankering for a bit of beef? I know you haven't been to the grocery."

"A friend of mine brought it over and took the time to brown it. Even added some rosemary and thyme to the pot as well as a generous serving of pepper – just the way I like it. Brought a big old bone for Ginger, too."

"And who is this friend, pray tell? Must be someone who owns beef cattle."

"She's a lady – that's all ye need to ken. And a lot younger and fairer than I deserve."

Brodie raised his eyebrows. He'd swear his da was delusional if it weren't for the smell of herb-roasted beef. "So do I get a bite or two, or is dinner only for you and your lady?"

"Ye'll have to ask her, I suppose."

"So it's someone I know?" His mind went to Heather. She and his da hadn't exactly gotten off on a good foot, but his da seemed to like her now. Maybe the feeling was mutual. Far be it from him to figure out his da or Heather McPhearson.

"Just talk to her, lad. That's all ye need to do."

"Heather?"

"She a winner, lad. And ye'd better believe it."

"I do. I offered to be the father of her bairn. I said I'd marry her. But she wouldn't take me up on the offer. In fact, that's when everything changed between us."

"Do ye love her?"

He looked at his da and wondered where that question had come from. What did his da know about love?

"I do love her. At least I'm starting to. I'm sure there's room for it to grow and get deeper."

"Then go to her, tell her ye love her, and ne'er leave her again," his father said.

Brodie gulped. "I don't know what she'll say."

"Since when have ye been afraid to take a risk?"

"There's never been so much at stake as there is now."

His da went to the oven, opened the door, and let a cloud of steam envelop the room. "I should have gone after yer mother when she left – should have forgiven her years before that and tried to save our relationship. But I let pride stand in my way. We could have had a wonderful life and children of our own. Who kens how much I lost by nae going after my dream?"

Brodie's heart skipped a beat. It sounded to him like his da was finally acknowledging that he knew Brodie was not his biological son. More importantly, he was admitting he'd played his cards wrong when he'd found out Duncan was Brodie's father.

"I thought I was doing the right things," his da said. "But I was wrong."

"Thank you for keeping me," Brodie said. "Thank you for raising me and letting me stay on the farm."

"Little good it did me when ye grew up. All ye could talk aboot was getting away from here so ye could be an engineer like Uncle Dunk."

Brodie's heart almost broke. How that must have hurt his da. He'd had no idea.

"I'm so sorry, da."

"Dinnae waste yer energy trying to make something up to me that ye couldnae have done anything aboot anyway. Ye were just a kid. Go to Heather and make things right while ye still can. I'll save ye some roast beef."

Brodie smiled. "What about you and mum?"

"Probably too late. But one of these days I may give it a go anyway." His da laughed. "Now get out of here."

#

Heather could hear light footsteps above her head as she stacked her unfinished paperwork in nicely sorted piles and filed away the projects she had finished, including another payroll. Probably Knox since it was Finn's day off. Finn was most likely back in Aberdeen with his mother by now or working a late shift at the hotel, catching up on his maintenance duties.

She looked at a graph that detailed the payroll totals for the last two months compared to income. Their revenues were down a little due to the fact that they'd missed several days' worth of production in the pie department. Another problem was that she didn't have enough help to get the animals to market when they were ready, which meant more food to keep feeding them until they could be transported. They just didn't have a big enough crew to man their own butchery. But her payroll was also down considerably since half her staff had quit. It was a conundrum she didn't feel like revisiting, at least not tonight.

It had been a long, exhausting day, and she was tired and hungry. It was well past dinnertime and she knew when she went home, she would be greeted by the smell of the rosemary infused potatoes she'd prepped to take over to Munro McBryde. She should have thought to cut off a slice or two of beef to roast for her own dinner but she'd known she would be gone for the rest of the afternoon and most of the evening. Besides, she'd wanted to make sure there was enough to feed both Munro and Brodie. She'd felt so bad that Munro and Brodie were being investigated as suspects in a murder case when she didn't believe either one of them had had anything to do with Duncan's death.

She half wished Brodie had been back from town when she'd stopped by. It was time to put an end to all the nonsense between them. He'd just caught her off guard the day in the pasture when he'd offered to father her child. First of all, it had come as a shock to find out that he knew about her dilemma. Second of all, she'd thought she'd be the one directing the action when she told him about her predicament and possibly needing a father for her child, not the other way around.

She was still thinking about Brodie as she locked the door to her office, walked across the courtyard, found the key to her house, and unlocked the door. The porch light and a vintage, climbing rose bush made the entryway warm and welcoming – exactly what she needed.

The door had just popped open when she felt a hand on her back, pushing her through the entry. She stumbled over the threshold, every muscle in her body tense and frozen. She couldn't see who was propelling her, but he or she was pushing hard and forcing her against her will.

She opened her mouth to scream just as she stumbled into the house, but a second hand grabbed her from behind and clamped her mouth shut.

She heard the door slam shut, the deadbolt slide into place. She started to shake. Was this the same person who had nearly destroyed her house? What was he going to do to her?

She felt a piece of cloth tighten around her eyes, then a second, tying her wrists behind her back. She tried to resist but he was stronger than she was, faster, and so vicious that she didn't have a chance.

"So ye need to get pregnant, aye?" The voice sounded weird, like whoever was talking was trying to camouflage the way they normally sounded. That meant it was someone she knew.

"No worries, darlin'. I've got just what ye need to solve yer problem."

She wanted to wretch. The only one who knew about her conversation was Brodie, but she knew without a doubt that it wasn't him. Unless – if Knox had been upstairs in the loft when she was on the phone, listening to every word... For the second time, she felt nauseous. It was Knox and he was going to rape her.

"So the only question is, are ye a virgin? Or have ye had sex enough times to ken how ye like it? If ye're a virgin, I'll do it the way I like."

Her mind sped like she was racing down the motorway in high gear. Should she call him out? Call him by name? Admit she knew who he was or pretend that she didn't have a clue? Challenge him? Be compliant so he wouldn't hurt or kill her?

"My sexual history is none of your business. Or

maybe it is? For all you know, I could have AIDS or syphilis or gonorrhea. Maybe that's why I have trouble conceiving. Maybe all the nasty, germ-ridden scar tissue that's built-up in my womb from my promiscuous sexual activity has made it nearly impossible for me to bear a child. Just think of the bugs you could catch. Is the risk to your good health worth it?"

"Shut up, ye eejit bitch."

"Maybe I have a physical deformity – maybe my cervix is so wide and stretched out that every time I get pregnant, my babies drop out. Nothing to hold them in. You'll feel no pleasure when you have me, you know. Not a thing." Her voice started to shake again. She wanted to sound blustery, indifferent, but she was terrified and it probably showed.

"Ye're just trying to freak me out." Whoever's voice he'd been impersonating – it stopped. This was Knox talking. "It's nae going to work. I trashed yer house – my house, and now I'm going to knock ye up and get ye with child. My child."

"Fine. Take your chances. I need to get pregnant. Doesn't matter who does it or how it happens. I'll be happy."

Knox screamed, "That's nae true!" He slapped her. "I'm nae good enough for ye and ye ken it. It's Brodie that ye want. But it's me that ye're going to get. And it's nae going to make ye happy, because it's going to hurt. For once, ye're nae going to get what ye want."

He tore at her sweater. She heard buttons popping and rolling across the wood floor and fabric tearing as he ripped her shirt open. Her back arched and then hit the floor hard as he pawed at her panties, tearing them off her body.

Please God, no. She tried to hold back the scream

that was forming deep in her throat. She tried to see through the cloth that was over her eyes. She wanted to focus on her mother's painting – something beautiful, pure, and happy.

She felt a hard, cold hand slapping her across the face, then, in the chest.

"What?" She tried not to cry. "Is your wick so limp that you have to slam me with your fist instead of it?" She didn't want to make him any angrier. Who knew what he would do to her if he was really mad? She wanted to undermine his confidence, to make him question what he was doing, and his ability to do it.

He heard grunts and moans and felt sick. His hands grazed her breast.

Her legs were not tied up. She clenched them together as tightly as she could and tried to ignore the feeling of being naked and exposed. Did Knox hate her so much? Was he that infuriated that she wanted Brodie instead of him? A woman couldn't decide who or why she was attracted to someone. It just happened. Because of God. Yes. She tried not to let her fear and repulsion overcome her. She had to think about something good. Like the fact that God had answered her prayers and brought Brodie into her life.

She felt Knox crouching over her, and parts of his body that she didn't want to think about touching places she couldn't bear to let him touch. She bucked her knees up under her and tried to kick him where it counted. She wished she could see so she could direct her aim. She shifted and kicked at him over and over as fast and as hard as she could. He screamed. She must have landed a boot somewhere tender, done some sort of damage.

That was when she heard a vehicle drive into the yard. It was faint. There shouldn't have been anyone coming to work at this time of night. Finn was probably already in Aberdeen. Had she really heard the crunch of tires against cobblestones or was it wishful thinking on her part?

Knox was still moaning, whether from her kick or whatever weird ritual he was going through to make himself hard enough to rape her.

Please, God. "Help! Help me!" She screamed as loudly as she could.

"Shut up!" Knox slapped her again. She didn't care what he did to her face as long as he left the rest of her alone.

"Help!" She screamed.

Knox laughed – almost so loudly that she didn't hear the doorknob rattling. Was someone trying to open the door? It was locked. Dead-bolted.

"Help! Help me!"

The next thing she heard was the sound of glass shattering. Sharp pieces, raining down on her. She closed her mouth against the onslaught.

It hurt, but not as bad as what Knox had been trying to do to her.

She felt another blow to her face. Her face throbbed. The lights started to go out. Was the sun setting behind the mountains? She had no concept of what time it was. She heard a voice, not Knox's, but one she didn't recognize. What was going on? It was as though her whole world was on a dimmer switch.

And then the light switched off.

Chapter 25

Brodie hummed a verse of *In His Time* as he slowly drove over the bumps on the track to Heather's house. The worst pothole was just ahead. He slowed to a complete stop and eased his truck over and down into it, then up again. The road was too narrow to dodge it. Last time, he'd hit it straight on going five or ten miles an hour and bounced so high his head had bumped the ceiling of his cab.

He could have helped her with that too, if she'd let him.

He sighed and rounded the last corner. He could see the warm glow from Heather's house shining in the distance. Just a little further on down the road and he could see two trucks in the courtyard. One was Knox's. The other was probably Finn's. He still didn't know how he felt about Finn living at the farm, but no one had asked his approval when the decision was made.

He pulled into the courtyard.

What on earth? Someone was breaking into Heather's house again, bashing her front window with a large stick. Or was it a golf club?

He opened the door and jumped out before it had even stopped moving, slamming it into park with his right hand as he exited. He ran toward the house. Was that a scream? He recognized Finn straight off and tackled him from the rear.

"Let me go, ye eejit! I'm trying to help! Heather's in trouble!" Finn twisted around and gut punched him.

"Aye, because you're breaking into her house again. She's terrified after what you did last time!"

Finn tried to grab his arms. "Let me go. Now! I am not breaking into her house. The door is locked and she's in there, screaming for help."

That got Brodie's attention. The glass was shattered, but there was no hole big enough to climb through. He punched his elbow through a maze of glass. "Tell me what you know."

"I got a half hour down the road and realized I'd left my mobile. I turned around and came back to this."

Brodie stepped closer to the shattered window and saw Heather lying half naked in a pool of broken glass. Oh, Lord, he prayed. Let her be awright. She appeared to be unconscious. What had Finn done to her? "If you did this. I'll kill you."

Finn answered in a whisper. "How could I have done it? You saw me breaking the window. She's inside with the door locked. Someone else is in there with her. Probably Knox. It's him you should be worried about."

Brodie tried to see who else was inside and couldn't. Coward was probably hiding. He snapped a few additional pieces of glass out of the window frame to make a hole big enough to climb through. "You guard the front door so he can't get away."

"Is there a back entrance?" Finn asked.

"Probably. Nothing we can do about it with only two of us." Brodie took out his mobile.

"I already dialed 999."

Brodie climbed through the window and crunched

over the broken shards of glass to Heather's side. He knelt down and checked her pulse. Relief flooded over him. She was alive.

"Thank goodness ye're here!" A very bedraggled Knox rounded the corner holding a wet cloth. I called 999 when I found her but I dinnae ken what else to do."

"You did this." Brodie started toward him and stopped when he saw that Knox had picked up a large shard of glass. "Why? She gave you a chance. She tried to help you."

"I dinnae do anything except try to help her. I was up in the loft when I thought I heard a faint scream, more like a whimper – but then I am a ways from the house. I had heard Heather leave and lock up her office just a little while earlier. I thought maybe she had a hot date."

"Like crap, Knox. Cut the bullshit and tell me the truth."

"I thought I would pretend to go walking and see what was going on. Then I heard a loud scream, like she was in pain, so I tried the door. It was open so I went through. As I did, a man in a face mask came running at me, nearly knocked me over, and left via the door. I slammed it shut and locked it so he couldn't come back and finish what he started."

Brodie brushed a couple of slivers of glass off of Heather's hand and took it gently in his.

He narrowed his eyes and pinned them on Knox. "If that's what happened, then why do you look such a mess? You look like you've been in a fight – or tried to rape someone."

"She attacked me! I reached up to check her pulse and my shirt sleeve must have grazed her breast. Whatever. She went absolutely ballistic and started kicking and screaming. Got me good, the bitch."

Brodie would have killed Knox then and there if he hadn't heard the sound of sirens wailing and seen the flashing lights reflecting against the walls and broken glass. *Let the police handle it,* a small voice told him. *Heather needs you more than you need revenge.*

Knox wasn't done. "Ye needn't make her out to be a saint. The only reason she took me on was because William dinnae give her a choice. She planned to get rid of me as soon as she had a chance."

"Even if all of that is true, she doesn't deserve to die for it."

"Why shouldn't I hate her? She has everything that should be mine."

Brodie kept his eyes on the shard of glass Brodie was wielding. The creep could be on Heather in a second, and if his aim was as good as he suspected, Knox could slit her wrist or go for her jugular.

Brodie tried to choose his words carefully. He spoke in as calm a voice as he could manage. "Think about it, Knox. Your real gripe is with Walter. He's the one who chased you off in the first place and refused to share the money from the sale of the farm with you or Duncan. Heather's just doing her job, and you were doing everything you could to undermine her efforts. Did you expect her to like it?"

"I was just trying to help her. If ye're going to try and pin this on me instead of finding out who was in the ski mask, I'll shred the lot of ye. I am innocent, and deep down, ye all ken it."

Knox inched closer to Heather's neck. Thank goodness Finn had called the police. It was taking them forever, but it would, considering how bumpy the lane was. If Brodie could stall Knox just a little longer – but what about Heather? He didn't know how seriously she was hurt. He seethed with anger at Knox. He'd either raped her, or tried to. Brodie was heartsick at the thought they may not have gotten there in time.

Brodie stared at his half brother and tried not to let hatred make him do something he would regret later. "How do I know you're not lying? Or that you won't come back later and finish what you started?"

"I guess ye'll just have to trust me." Knox rolled his eyes.

That's when he felt a presence behind him. He couldn't turn and look for fear of alerting Knox. But Finn was there, ready to help. Brodie could feel it.

Knox leaned back on his heels. The shard of glass was a few inches further away from Heather's jugular than it had been before. Brodie lifted his leg and slammed his boot into Knox's chest. The glass clattered to the floor. Finn leaped into the room and grabbed Knox by the neck. Knox yelped, either from pain or the realization that he had failed.

Finn squeezed Knox's neck a little tighter. "We could say he fell on a shard of glass. They'd never be able to prove otherwise."

"Let me go!" Knox howled. "I dinnae touch her."

Brodie wanted to cry as he watched bruises appearing on Heather's face. He took off his shirt and covered her as gently as he could.

He'd known Knox was up to no good, but he'd never expected this to happen. Finn's shard of glass idea actually sounded pretty good. He'd be tempted except that his first priority was to be there for Heather, just like God had said. Heather needed him, whether she realized it or not.

A siren sounded closer. The police, and hopefully an

ambulance.

"Brodie?" Her voice eked out in a whisper so soft he barely heard it over the approaching emergency vehicles. "Please stay with me."

"I will, sweetheart. I'm right here, and here's where I'll stay."

He went to the front door and unlocked the deadbolt, opened the door, and returned to her side. "Are you okay?"

"He scared me, but he didn't... I'm fine, Brodie."

She was hardly fine, but he hoped there would be no permanent damage to her body or her soul.

The police yelled though the door.

"The situation is under control," Finn said, still holding on to Knox.

Two paramedics rushed in and started tending to Heather, checking her vitals, asking her questions.

Two policemen took Knox away while he screamed, "I dinnae do anything to her. I ne'er touched her! I scared the assailant off. Ye should be thanking me for coming to her rescue!"

"We'll sort it all out once we get to the station," Karl said.

"I'll follow you to the police station to tell you what I know," Finn said.

"I'll follow you to hospital," Brodie told Heather.

Karl stood in the doorway and surveyed the scene. "Seamus, please secure the crime site and get back to Alford as soon as possible."

Finn said, "I know where there's a sheet of plywood we can use to patch the window."

Karl nodded. "Duncan would be proud of a couple of ye anyway."

Brodie could only wish he'd done more, and sooner.

He watched as the paramedics picked up Heather and lifted her onto a gurney. He held her hand while they loaded her into the back of the ambulance. The lights twirled with sickening clarity against the darkness as the vehicles crept away, no doubt dodging potholes as if their lives depended on it. Sore as Heather looked, hers might.

Brodie ran to his truck. The night had never seemed so black.

And then he remembered to look up. The Milky Way was shining brightly in the northern sky. There was always a bright spot – and you could see it clearly when you were in the Highlands, where the cities were spread far and wide. In the summer, the stars were always shining brightly, and in the winter, the Northern lights were there to flood the sky with color.

Why would anyone ever want to leave here? How he prayed Heather's bad memories would not deter her love for this place. How he hoped he could find a bridge to build over some mountain valley, loch or dale. He didn't know how it would work out, but he had to trust that it would.

#

"You let him go?"

Heather opened her eyes and watched as her da grilled the police officer standing in the far corner of her hospital room. Good thing it was a big room. Her mum and da were both present. Only Brodie was absent, but she knew he'd been there earlier. She just hoped he wasn't off killing Knox, who by the sound of it was a free man once again.

"He can't stay at the farm," She squinted at the

policeman through her swollen eye. "You may not believe it was Knox who tried to rape me, but I know for certain that it was."

"But, ma'am, ye said ye heard two, maybe three or four different voices.

"The first voice was Knox, trying to make his voice sound like a different person so I wouldn't know it was him. The second voice was Knox, so frustrated that he reverted back to his normal voice. The third was Finn, trying to help me, and the fourth was Brodie."

"But ye were nae nearly so specific when we interviewed ye originally, and those first comments are now part of the official record."

"I had a concussion! I was battered and bruised and scared half to death!"

"But so much time has gone by now that ye could have been prompted on what to say as to what would make yer case more convincing. Ye've had time to think aboot manufacturing incriminating testimony to get back at a person ye hold a grudge against. That's why we always use the first testimony we're given. It's the most likely to be honest."

"I am honest. Knox is the one who's lying. Think about it. Nothing I'm saying now conflicts with what I said originally. I'm just filling in the blanks for you as my memories come back to me."

Violet spoke up. "Believe me, there's nothing I'd like better than to have my daughter forget everything that happened in that house. Hard as she's trying to remember things so she can help you out, the least you could do is to listen to her!"

"Oh, he's listening. He's just not believing," Nathan said.

The policeman sighed. "Knox is holding firm to his

claim that he was there to help ye."

"Right. Help me get pregnant."

"According to him, he was helping ye fight off yer attacker."

"Knox was my attacker!" She let out an exasperated sigh.

Violet's voice was trembling. "I've always heard it's common for the man to be believed, and the woman accused of fabricating a story when there's a sexual assault. Heather is also the outsider here. If you truly believe Knox is telling the truth and she's lying, then you should be on your way."

"What am I to do?" The policeman twirled his hat nervously. "It's his word against yers. There are nae eyewitnesses as ye were blindfolded and ne'er saw your attacker. Ye feel sure ye were right aboot the voice being Knox's, but ye had a concussion. I could have charged him with sexual assault, but there was no semen, and no signs of vaginal bruising. No DNA other than what can be explained by his attempts to help ye."

"He did not try to help me! He tried to rape me and the only reason he didn't go through with it is because Finn and Brodie showed up when they did!" Heather fell back against her pillow, exhausted.

"You need to leave," Nathan said. "I understand that you've known Knox since he was a lad, and that you're friends with him. But I won't have you upsetting Heather any more than she already is."

Violet turned pleading eyes on the policeman. "All I ask is that you do as she asks and make sure Knox is not at McKnight Farms when she arrives home."

Nathan spoke up. "And that he never comes back. It is private property. We have every right to forbid him to be on McKnight land."

"I'll prepare the paperwork for a restraining order."

"We'll pack up his things and leave them at the end of the driveway," Nathan said.

"Miss McPhearson?" The doctor who had been treating her injuries poked his head through the door.

"Yes?"

"Could I have a word with ye privately?"

Heather looked at the policeman. "My mum and da are welcome to stay. We have no secrets."

The policeman left, at least having the good grace to look apologetic as he crept out the door.

The doctor shut the door tightly. "I spoke to yer gynecologist, yer oncologist, and yer fertility specialist today just to make sure I dinnae miss anything. They all agree that a trauma of this sort can cause a rapid progression of the severity of conditions like yers. Yer doctors are highly recommending that if ye want a child of yer own, ye let us harvest eggs tonight, or use artificial insemination while ye're still here in hospital. It appears that ye happen to be ovulating right now, so all systems are go. They all strongly recommend that we take advantage and give it a go. Now."

"Heather?" Her mum looked terrified.

And no wonder. The doctor's words did nothing for her own peace of mind either. "No." She gave her da a look and he went to her mum. "I've decided I'd like to go about things the old-fashioned way. It may take a day or two, but I believe things will work out the way they're meant to. I just need to find..."

"But you're so sore you can hardly walk. How on earth do you think..." Her da's face was beet red.

Heather could feel her own skin flushing, but she felt reasonably sure her bruises covered the hue. She looked up at the doctor. "There was some question that

Knox may have raped me after I fell unconscious. You're absolutely sure that there was no ejaculate anywhere in or on my body?"

"We used the rape kit and did a thorough examination. No signs at all. If ye conceive a baby, ye can be confident it's yers and the man ye choose to father it."

"Do you have someone in mind?" Her mum was as pink as her da.

She ignored her question. "When can I be released? If I'm going to make a baby tonight, I need to get on it."

"Where will you go?" Her da looked sincere. "We've done a little cleaning up at the house, but the window is still boarded up and you certainly can't expect to... It's too soon."

Even the doctor was a wee bit red at this point.

"Does this boy you have in mind have a place of his own where you could..."

"Unfortunately, no." She imagined Munro with his ear to the wall, trying to hear what was going on. Nope. Brodie's house was out.

"It's a nice warm evening," her da said.

"I think I'll be going," the doctor said. "I'll send someone over with yer dismissal papers very shortly." He smiled. "And good luck."

"It's time you do some explaining," her da said as soon as the doctor had left the room.

Chapter 26

Brodie wasn't sure who had turned the corner of his pasture into a scene from The Princess Bride or Braveheart or maybe even Outlander, but what he saw when he walked down the lane to the appointed meeting place was a hundred candles burning and reflecting against the stone fence, and a handmade quilt spread out on the grass, pretty pillows in embroidered cases and his grandpa's lantern and fairy lights strung between walking sticks and an antique shepherd's hook. There was a plate of sweets and another of meats and cheeses and a freshly baked meat pie for each of them.

The sky was clear and the moon, a sliver of a smile in the west. The stars of the Milky Way twinkled overhead. Everything was ready, even his heart.

But was Heather?

It had been his idea to do a handfast and then make love under the Milky Way. He wanted their lovemaking to be meaningful. Having a ceremony of some sort was the only way he could imagine it.

"Brodie? I'm right here, waiting for ye."

He'd only heard her speak in the Scottish brogue once or twice before. It suited her perfectly on this night of nights. A soft form, swathed in strands of pale lavender and wisps of lace appeared in the moonlight.

"Heather." He went to her, kissed her, and took her

hands. "Are we alone or are there witnesses?"

"Witnesses. Mum? Da? Ye can come out into the light." She squeezed his hand. "It was breaking their hearts nay to be here, and mine, too, truth be told."

"I'm glad they're here. I kind of invited Munro to read the handfast vows for us to repeat. If ye dinnae mind."

"It's perfect."

"He wants another round of roast beef for compensation."

"That I do," Munro said, walking toward them holding a wee book that Brodie had rigged with a clip on light.

Heather laughed and the stars twinkled down on them in a rainbow of colors. "Mum, Da. There's nae aisle to walk me down, but I'd be pleased if ye'd stand with me."

Brodie slipped his tartan sash over his head and handed it to Nathan, and Heather untied a cluster of colorful ribbons from her hair and gave them to Violet.

Munro smiled at both of them and started to read. "Brodie and Heather, please join yer hands." He took a deep breath. "Today ye are holding the hands of yer best friend, young and strong and full of love, as ye promise to love each other forever.

"These are the hands that will work alongside yers as together ye build yer future. These are the hands that will passionately love and cherish ye through the years and will comfort ye like no other.

"These are the hands that will hold ye when fear or grief fills yer mind. These are the hands that will wipe tears from yer eyes, tears of sorrow and tears of joy. These are the hands that will tenderly hold yer bairn.

"These are the hands that will help ye hold yer

family together as one. These are the hands that will give ye strength when ye need it. And these are the hands that – even when wrinkled and aged – will still be reaching for yers and expressing the same tenderness they do today with just a touch."

Brodie wasn't sure who had tuned his guitar and brought it down to the field – probably Nathan – but when it was handed to him, he cradled it in his arms and sang *In His Time*.

Heather smiled up at him, and they kissed, long and tenderly.

Brodie watched his da wipe a tear from his eyes. Nathan and Violet's eyes were shining in the glow of evening when they stepped forward and began to entwine his and Heather's hands together with the ribbons and the tartan cloth and a wee bit of twine.

When they were finished, they kissed again, and Munro said, "Just as your hands are now bound together, so too, are your lives."

And Brodie prayed, "Dear Lord, upon this day, our hands we bind, a symbol of our hearts entwined. To witness this, we ask of thee, our union forever blessed be."

"Amen."

"Amen."

"Amen." Their parents' voices echoed in the still of the night. A sheep bleated and another answered in a quiet, "Baaa."

And Heather's voice rang out, rather jubilantly if he knew her at all, "We ask yer blessing, dear Lord. Make it so."

And it was done. Violet popped the champagne cork and they each had a sip straight from the bottle. There were hugs of congratulations and finally, goodbyes.

And they were alone with the stars and flickering candles all around on an old quilt worn soft with love in the shelter of the old stone fence.

#

Heather woke up cradled in Brodie's arms. He'd been a picture of Scottish perfection in his kilt and leather-laced shirt, but she liked him even better this way.

Brodie caressed her cheek and kissed her. "We can have a church wedding later if you want to, with photos that don't include purple bruises and scabs from broken glass."

"I look that bad, huh?" She tried to frown, but it hurt.

"That's the way it is with bruises. They always look worse a day or two after it happens, when the colors have had a chance to bloom."

"At least they match my dress."

"True. But then, you're not wearing your dress at the moment."

"Aye, and I'm not posing for pictures either." The truth was she was glad they were in the wild with nary a mirror to look on herself. What she couldn't see, she could more easily forget.

Brodie wrapped his arms around her ever so gently. "Do you think it took last night or should we have another go at it, just to be sure?"

She smiled and burrowed against him under the quilts. "No sense taking a chance."

"Or missing a perfectly good opportunity to make love to my lady."

"Let's just snuggle until it's a wee bit warmer, can

we?"

"Aye. There's nothing I'd like better." Brodie settled back and started to rub her in places that warmed her all over.

"It was chilly in the night." She'd loved it when Brodie had spread his family plaid over the quilts topping their makeshift bed. A Highlander who knew what to do with his tartan – how happy she was to have Brodie in her life.

"Is that better?" Brodie snuggled up against her.

Their second attempt at making a baby was so natural, so comforting, that she felt absolutely healed, and in an odd way, completed, when it was done.

"I think we've done it this time," she said.

"I have the same feeling," he said.

They lay there for a long time. And then Brodie said. "This is about more than making a baby, you know."

"I know. I love you so much." Her voice didn't have her usual confident ring, but she'd never spoken more heartfelt words.

Brodie took her hands in his. "That's exactly what I meant to say. And that I promise to love you forever. I can't tell you exactly when or how it happened, but I know without a doubt that I truly love you with all my heart."

It had been a stressful few days. There was no denying it. There were moments when she felt so overwhelmed by everything that had happened, that might happen, and that she hoped would happen, that she wanted to cry. But that was a good thing, right? It meant her hormones were at their peak, and that hopefully meant that she was pregnant.

"Brodie, we haven't talked at all about what happens next – I mean, hopefully nine months from now, I'll have a baby, and then my surgery, and a wonderful long-term prognosis, but until then – I'm going to look into finding a room in town. I'll be fine at work, but I don't think I'll ever be able to sleep in that house again."

Brodie didn't say anything at first, he just held her. Exactly what she needed, but she still started to shake and couldn't stop.

"You can move in with me."

"I'm not sure how Munro would feel about that. I don't want him to feel like he's being kicked out of his own home."

Brodie squeezed her hand. "I think he would understand and welcome you, especially for the short term. I guess I would need to talk to him and see how he might feel about any sort of long term arrangement."

"Do you understand about the house?"

"Of course. It's important for you to be happy and at peace, especially as we embark on the journey of parenthood."

"I'll have to tell William and see how he wants to handle things. He and Lyndsie have left me several messages in the last few days, but I haven't had a chance to call them back."

"Too bad Knox lived in the loft – he's ruined that for you now, too, hasn't he?"

"Sadly, yes."

The birds in the grove of nearby trees started to chirp frantically. She completely understood when she looked up and saw a golden eagle soaring high above.

She looked at Brodie and let her eyes focus on what was in front of her instead of what was not. "Let's not mention him again. I only want to think about happy things. This is our honeymoon, right?"

"We could take a few days – go down to Fife, or over

to Skye, or up to Dornach. I know of a place called The Peat Inn that has the most delicious food ever, and I've heard their rooms are beautiful, too. It's not far from St. Andrews. There's another place near there, a manor house by Cambo Gardens. You'd love it there."

"I'm sure I would, and you're so kind to offer, but I'm still extremely short-staffed and I have so much to do, and I look like I've been in a barroom brawl."

He sighed. "And we still have a murderer on the loose, and who knows where Knox has gone to..."

"Or when he'll be back." She pulled the covers up around her neck and tried not to start shivering again.

"I'll go by and get your clothes and you'll move into my house for the time being, just until we sort things out. We should keep – you know – to make sure, in case the doctors were off a day or two – or a week – in their estimations."

"I'd like that," she smiled, but truth was, she felt like she was in a trance. She didn't want to let Knox win, but what had happened had terrified her more than anything she'd faced in her short years. She'd been blustery enough while it was happening, but now, she was left quaking in her boots every time she thought about it.

Brodie gave her a gentle caress in one of the places where she didn't hurt. It actually felt quite good.

"I wish I could make the world an entirely happy place for you, Heather. But it would seem that it's gone a bit haywire at the moment, and it's not in my power to make it better, at least not at this time."

"No worries, Brodie. Nothing makes me happier than being with you. And the rest – well, if I have to go through it, there's no one I'd rather have by my side, running interference when bad things happen, than you."

She rolled over and kissed him. It was going to be okay, it really was.

Chapter 27

Brodie looked up at the vaulted stone ceiling of the church. For whatever reason, when he got to church and tried to unwind, his brain went into high gear and started chasing around like he was on the track at a raceway. Even singing *God Will Take Care of You* hadn't helped.

It was a horrible conundrum, knowing he should trust God to flush the murderer out *In His Time*, and wanting to take matters into his own hands and sort it out now. Knowing that Heather felt threatened and afraid made it even worse.

He knew he should be listening to the pastor's message, but he couldn't seem to stop his brain from going over the list of suspects, trying to figure out who was guilty.

Based on his personal instincts alone, Finn had gone down a notch on the list. He'd had his doubts about Finn at first, but the more he'd seen of the man, the more he trusted him. In his estimation, Knox had risen to the top, although the police who had interrogated him after he'd attacked Heather swore Knox had vehemently denied murdering his Uncle Dunk. Of course, he'd also categorically denied attacking Heather and breaking into her house and trashing the place, and Brodie was convinced he'd done both. The outcome of their brief and completely ineffective investigation had not done anything to restore Brodie's confidence in the police.

He thought of his mum and felt a pang of guilt that he hadn't invited her to the handfast. Heather wouldn't divulge what had been said, but he knew the two women had had some sort of unproductive discussion. That didn't mean his mum was a killer, but it did let him know that when it came to his mum, everything wasn't always what it appeared to be.

Something the pastor said caught his ear, and he started to listen to the sermon. The pastor was preaching on the Parable of the Prodigal Son. He looked up, and for the first time, saw his mum, sitting alone, on the opposite side of the sanctuary. He stole a glance at Heather, and watched as his mum intercepted his glance and glared at him. What was with that? He pretended he hadn't seen her and looked away.

He tried his best to follow what the pastor was saying, but between being distracted by Heather's presence – in a good way, and his mum's – in a bad way, he couldn't stay focused.

His mum's narrowed eyes put him in protective mode and his mind went back to the newfound closeness and camaraderie he and Heather had just shared. He worried that she wouldn't get pregnant and not only miss her chance to have a baby with him, but that she would get cancer and die because she'd put off having a baby for too long.

Trust me. I've got this.

He sighed and told God they had to stop meeting like this.

And then God said, *We are in my house. When would ye suggest I try to talk to ye?*

That's when he really started to pay attention to the

sermon. The pastor talked about the prodigal son, and what happened when he'd come home hungry and so desperate that he was content to sleep in the barn and be treated as a servant on his father's farm. The pastor talked about the older brother – the one who had stayed behind and worked hard to tend his father's fields – and how very angry he was when his father welcomed the errant son home.

Suddenly, it all made perfect sense. What would have happened to the prodigal son when he came home if their father had already been dead? The older brother would certainly not have welcomed him home or butchered a fatted calf and thrown him a party, that's for sure.

Walter had not only stayed at home and worked the farm for years through hard times and good while Duncan was off living it up in Cyprus, he'd raised Duncan's son as his own. He'd dealt with the fallout of Duncan's affairs with his own wife, Brodie's mother, and Finn's mother, maybe even paying them off or helping to support them. And all of this while Duncan had stayed in Cyprus, sowing his wild oats and living with his young sweetheart.

Walter had essentially lost his wife to childbirth while having a baby who belonged to his brother, not him. Everyone said she'd never recovered from delivering Knox. Knox claimed she'd taken to her bed and stayed there until she passed. If that wasn't reason enough for Walter Morris to start hating his brother, Brodie didn't know what was.

Then, in spite of everything he'd done and not done, when it was time to sell the farm, Duncan had the audacity to think he deserved half of the profit. Walter had to be the murderer! It all made sense after listening to the parable of the prodigal son. Walter must have hated Uncle Dunk with a passion.

Brodie thought back to what his da had told them about the Morris farm. If he remembered correctly, there had been a verbal understanding that the farm would all go to Walter. His da had given him his word. Walter had assumed his da had met with a lawyer and formalized the agreement.

Brodie's theory was simple. Walter couldn't live with the thought that Duncan was going to benefit from all the hard work and sacrifice he'd poured into the farm. So he'd snapped and killed Duncan. It made perfect sense that the man wasn't about to give that lazy, overly-sexed, good-for nothing cheater of a brother half of the proceeds of his life's work.

"Brodie? Are you okay?" Heather's voice broke through his stupor.

"I know who killed Duncan."

Heather looked shocked, but she followed him to the rear of the sanctuary where people were shaking the pastor's hand as they left the church.

Heather touched his arm. "Your mother is about ten feet behind us."

"Just follow me."

"Sure."

"Good sermon, Pastor. Best I've ever heard." Brodie pumped the pastor's hand. "Very inspiring. Answered a lot of questions for me."

"What questions?" Heather whispered. "You don't even have a brother. Or a son."

"I have at least two brothers that I know about, possibly more. And I hope there's a wee son or daughter in the oven."

They exited the door. Brodie kept walking. He

wasn't trying to put Heather off, but he didn't want to meet up with his mother right now. Most likely she'd heard about the handfast and would have questions. Worse yet, objections.

"Why the rush?" Heather's eyes were wide and inquisitive.

"Let's go find somewhere where we can have a little privacy. I'll tell you all about it."

He could see Heather's mind working. "Why don't we go to Fraser Castle and take a walk in the gardens?"

"Sounds like a perfect place for a relaxing stroll." He kept walking.

"If talking about murder can be construed as a walk in the park." Heather took his hand.

"Ha, ha." They were almost to his truck. If the subject of their quick exit came up later, and it probably would, he'd play dumb and pretend he hadn't seen his mother.

#

Heather woke up feeling disoriented and – she tried to think of a word that described how she felt. Put out? She was used to spending summers in Minnesota, the rest of the year in Scotland, and the holidays wherever her parents decided to spend them. So why did being in Brodie's bedroom and opening her eyes to Brodie's tussled hair, a sight that should have brought her great joy, fill her not only with apprehension but an anxious feeling in the pit of her stomach?

When she'd moved to the Highlands, and into the old Morris house, she'd fixed it up just the way she wanted. It had made a lovely home for her until it was trashed. She'd gotten over it, moved on, and done some more tweaking to make it feel more like home again. She'd weathered on no matter what. Didn't that mean she'd learned the art of being flexible?

And then, she'd been attacked at the one place where she was supposed to feel safe. She was glad and relieved to be at the McBryde house. Really, she was. Brodie and his da had demonstrated the epitome of hospitality. She could hear Ginger's feet pattering about the hall outside Brodie's bedroom. She could smell sausages and mushrooms frying, and if she listened closely, she could hear the whistle of a teapot on the stove. Brodie was beside her, so she figured it was Munro, up early to fix them a breakfast fit for a honeymoon.

See, that was why she selfishly didn't want to live in someone else's house.

Brodie stirred. "Don't you wish you could walk naked to the loo, use the facilities, climb back into bed, and sleep for another hour or two?"

At least Brodie understood how she felt. "I do. But your da seems to have fixed us breakfast."

"I told him not to do anything special."

"So he fixes you a full Scottish breakfast every morning?"

"Are you kidding?" Brodie shifted. "He sometimes offers on Sunday morning, about the time I'm getting ready to go to church."

She smiled. "My da isn't much of a churchgoer either. I'm glad you are."

Brodie rolled over to face her. "Your da would be a great addition to a worship band at one of the newer churches in the city. They're full of people our age who love contemporary Christian music." He paused. "That's one of the things I miss about Edinburgh."

She swallowed, hard. "What else do you miss?"

"Oh, just a bunch of little things – a greater variety of restaurants with more upscale menus than we have around here, people-watching at outdoor cafes, dancing at a club every now and again. I don't know. I guess there's just something appealing about the hustle and bustle of the city after growing up on an isolated farm in a remote area."

Her heart clenched in her chest. Brodie could say he wanted to stay in the Highlands, but he'd always feel the allure of city life, would probably want to raise their child there because the doctors and the schools would be better, and there would be more parks and playgrounds and nice paved roads and sidewalks to ride bicycles on instead of cobblestone courtyards and narrow lanes with massive potholes.

Brodie kissed her on the nose. "Not that I'd be living in Edinburgh again anyway – more likely one of the islands or on some remote peninsula. If I was willing to leave Scotland, I could probably find a job in Scandinavia or maybe the Alps."

Was that longing she heard in his voice? She heard Ginger whimpering outside the door. She wanted to cry.

"And if it's the Alps where I want to live, then why not just stay in the Highlands?" Brodie sighed.

Um, because in the Alps, there are mountain chalets with window boxes full of geraniums, and Brown Swiss cows with alpine bells around their necks? She rolled over and tried to ignore the tinges of pain she felt as her ribs shifted. Maybe because they have Swiss fondue, Wiener schnitzel, and the best chocolate in the world?

"Who knows?" Brodie sighed again. "Maybe one day you'll decide you want to see the world, or introduce our bairn to a different part of the world, or even a different part of Scotland."

Mind your hormones, she told herself. He's just telling you what's on his mind, which is one of the things you love about him. He's a talker, just the way you like it. Just keep your cool and don't say anything.

Brodie kissed her again. "In the meantime, all I care about is that you're comfortable here. If there's anything I can do to make you feel more at home, just ask and it's yours."

How could she tell him when she didn't even know herself? She bit her lip. "I think I'm just on overload with so much happening at work and worries about everything else that's going on." She took a quick breath. "Or maybe I'm already pregnant like we're hoping and this is what expecting feels like for me. They talk about women getting this glow, but I always seem to react differently to things, My doctor says I'm very unique. Maybe instead of having that certain glow, I'll be freaked out and feel funny for the first trimester, or maybe I'll be out of sorts the entire time I'm pregnant. I have nothing to compare it too, because I've never been before." And never will be again, she thought to herself. "Or maybe I already have full blown cancer and it's waging some sort of cellular warfare on my body and the baby that I don't even know about." She burst into tears. What if her cancer was progressing so quickly that she died after giving birth and didn't even get to hold her bairn, or raise the wee one, or get to see him or her grow up?

Just breathe, she told herself. Breathing was good.

Brodie put his arms around her. "I promise you it's going to be awright." He started to sing, *"Be not dismayed whate'er betide, God will take care of you; Beneath His wings of love abide, God will take care of you.*

"God will take care of you, Through every day, o'er all

the way; He will take care of you, God will take care of you."

"Your voice is beautiful." It had a calming effect on her. Her heart swelled with love.

"Through days of toil when heart doth fail, God will take care of you; When dangers fierce your path assail, God will take care of you.

"God will take care of you, Through every day, o'er all the way; He will take care of you, God will take care of you."

He held her until she stopped sniffling. "Should we go have some breakfast?"

She nodded and found a tissue. "Brodie?"

"Yes?"

"That big house at the farm is too beautiful to just sit empty."

"Do you think you'll feel differently about living there in a week or two, or once Knox is apprehended, or if I was there with you?"

"No."

Brodie lay there thinking for a time. "Then we'll find a better long term solution. I can ask around and see if any of the neighbours have a vacant house, make sure Da wouldn't rather be in town for the winter – we'll do whatever it takes to make you feel happy and safe."

"I was thinking more along the lines of who might like to live in the house if I don't." She stirred and snuggled down in Brodie's arms like they'd been together forever. "You did say you liked Finn's mother, right?"

"Jaelle? Yes. She seemed very nice. Of course, at the time, I regarded her as a suspect, so I might have been reading things into what she said and being generally suspicious of both her and Finn."

"Well, I'd like to meet her."

Brodie looked at her like he was wondering what she was going to think of next. He didn't say anything right away. Probably a wise choice.

When he finally spoke, he said, "I think we can make that happen. Now, let's put some clothes on and go eat our breakfast before Da peeks in to see if we're awake or decides to bring us a tray and sees that we're naked."

"I love you."

Brodie pulled back the covers. "I love you more."

"I can see that." She smiled. What a way to start a day.

Chapter 28

Brodie took Heather's mop down from a hook on the wall of the broom closet, got it wet, and began to swab at the blood on the floor of her lounge while he waited for his call to the United States to connect.

Nathan and Violet had made sure the glass had been swept off the floor and the broken window had been replaced. The only evidence of what had occurred was a few gouges in the wood floor and a few stubborn blood stains where it had soaked in – which would hopefully be gone by the time he left.

"Hello? William speaking."

Brodie laid the mop down. "Hi William. This is Brodie McBryde, Heather's neighbour and well, no easy way to break the news – but her husband as of a few days ago."

There was a wee bit of silence, and he finally heard William say, "Lyndsie? Can you come to the phone? There's a call from Scotland I'd like you to be in on. A Brodie McBryde. Heather's new husband."

He heard some whoops and a jubilant cheer let out by a woman's voice.

"When did this happen? Lyndsie here. I'm so excited! Oh, William. Ye'll love Brodie. I was hoping Heather and ye would get together! Do Violet and Nathan know? Is Heather there?"

Brodie remembered meeting Lyndsie, and he knew Heather loved her like a second mother. "Heather is in her office working. Violet and Nathan were here for our handfast. Heather asked them not to tell you so she could do it herself. I'm happy to let Heather share the details when she's feeling better, but there's a lot to tell, and I thought you should know what's happened. Heather is a bit overwhelmed, so I felt like I should step in and let you know about some other things that have been going on."

He could feel the chill that fell over him, the house, and William and Lyndsie.

William's voice was wary. "I've left Heather several messages about various things and she's not responded. I can completely understand now that I know she was getting ready for a wedding. But if there are other things going on, please tell me. Us. You're on speaker phone so we can both hear."

Brodie listened to their expressions of grief, anger, and shock as he told them about the attack. He listened as they wept at the news of what Heather had gone through.

"I feel so awful that this has happened," William said. "I never would have asked Heather to come on board and manage the farm if I had known what a mess things would turn into."

Brodie tried to answer their questions and reassure them as best he could. He wasn't sure what or if Heather had told them about her cancer scare or woman's woes, so he left that part of the story for her to tell later. "I'm here because I don't feel safe leaving her alone. Even now, I'm looking out the window, watching the entrance to her office. And I should warn you that she's sworn she'll never sleep in this house again."

Lyndsie said, "I'm so glad ye stepped up to help. I feel so bad for Heather. We should have known that anything that involves the Morrises equals bad news."

William said, "I disagree. You're a Morris, and you're one of the most decent, kindest, honest, loving, giving people I know. Every bushel basket has its share of rotten fruit, and the Morrises are no exception. You can't let one bad apple spoil the whole bunch."

Brodie was glad William had stuck up for him, even unknowingly. Someday they would find out that he was really a Morris by the law of nature, although a McBryde by the rules of loving and nurturing. But that was a discussion for another day – like when they apprehended Knox, found Duncan's murderer, and zipped up all the bits and bobs.

"There's one more thing I want to ask you about." He went on to tell them about Jaelle and Finn and what sketchy details he knew of Heather's idea. "I thought it best to mention to you what Heather is thinking before the meeting actually takes place. If Jaelle and Finn do move into the big house, that would leave the two of you with only the loft to stay in when you're here to visit."

"We're open to whatever Heather deems best," William said. "I wouldn't have asked her to manage the farm operation if I didn't trust her. I do hope you understand that I can't gift Duncan's descendants with half of the farm. Making things right would be up to Walter, and hopefully, one day, he'll sort this whole mess out. I would certainly be willing to discuss a package deal with Finn and Jaelle that would include the house as partial compensation along with a good salary if they're amenable to working at McKnight Farms."

Brodie tried to reassure them once again. "No one's blaming you for any of this or expecting you to sort it.

And I truly believe Heather is going to be fine. She's just a little fragile right now. I'll be here to help her as long as she needs me."

"Dinnae Heather say ye were heading off to build a bridge in the Western Isles sometime soon? Are ye able to juggle yer start date or work remotely, or what will happen with that?" Lyndsie asked.

"I'm not sure," Brodie responded. "I guess time will tell." The question was, what time? God's time, his time, or the company's time? Brodie knew he had to make some decisions soon. He also knew what his first priority was. And he felt absolute peace about it. So why was he still dreading what was to come?

#

Heather looked at the sales figures for the new autumn meat pies and wished she had time to call Lyndsie and crow. Orders were higher than they'd been all summer, and reorders were off the charts. She couldn't have asked for a more enthusiastic response to their new lineup. Now she just needed to figure out how to up their production so they could keep up with the demand. To do that, she needed more help.

She glanced at the clock to make sure she didn't have time for a quick call to America, but it was almost time for Finn and Jaelle to arrive.

The last time she'd seen Finn was the night he'd heard her yelling for help and broken the window to come to her rescue. Maybe she should be feeling more embarrassed – he was a staff member, and he'd not only witnessed her lowest moment, he'd seen her half-naked.

But she wasn't. She couldn't explain it, except that she trusted him to handle the intimate glimpse he'd had into her life. She couldn't say that of many people. Maybe because Finn was Brodie's half-brother and family in a way?

Family made her think about Brodie's mother. She felt a complete sense of disconnect. But she was really looking forward to meeting Jaelle. She hoped she would be a bit warmer.

"Miss Heather?" Finn poked his head around the opening to her office and smiled.

She laughed and smiled back. "Come in. But you can't call me Miss Heather anymore."

A broad smile spread across Finn's face. "I hear congratulations are in order, but I am at a loss. Mrs. Heather sounds a wee bit odd."

"I agree. How about just plain Heather?"

He flashed another smile, his teeth white against his olive skin. "I'll try to remember."

A woman who was clearly Finn's mother walked into the room. She looked hesitant, even a bit nervous.

Heather went to her as quickly as she could considering how sore she still was. Thank goodness her bruises were starting to fade. She didn't look nearly as scary as she had a week ago.

"Welcome to McKnight Farms, Jaelle." Please let her feel at ease. The Morris Farm had been Jaelle's home from birth – until she'd gotten pregnant with Finn. "I'm Heather McPhearson. Um, McBryde."

Finn laughed again. "Even you're having a hard time remembering."

"Well, it all happened pretty quickly." Heather watched as Jaelle focused her eyes on Heather's belly. Had she eaten that much last night? As far as she knew, her stomach was as flat as it had been on her honeymoon night. She and Brodie had eaten out several times since the handfast, but it had only been a week.

But for some reason, Jaelle seemed mesmerized. Jaelle looked up at her, paused as if asking permission, and then, when Heather nodded at her, touched Heather's belly.

"The babies are doing well," she said. "Twins, a boy and a girl."

Heather looked up and saw Brodie standing in the doorway behind Finn.

"I have two sets of cousins who are twins. They run in my mother's family," Brodie raised his eyebrows. "Jaelle, are you saying that...?"

"Heather, yer babies are very young, but they are hard workers. They have been busy healing yer body. Their wish is to heal yer womb from the sickness that has gripped it so it will be the warm and nurturing environment they need to grow strong and healthy. They want ye to know that they will also mend yer broken heart, and that ye and Brodie will have more children together."

Tears were streaming down Heather's cheeks. "How did you...? Finn? Did you..."

"I haven't told her a thing about you except that you wanted to meet her."

"A few months ago, I was told that I have precancerous cells in my uterus, so that if I wanted to have a baby, I needed to do it immediately, and then, as soon as I gave birth, have a hysterectomy."

"Aye, but the babies will take care of it for ye so ye dinnae have need for the surgery," Jaelle said.

"She's always doing this," Finn said. "It's her gypsy blood."

Jaelle's eyes lit up. "Another thing we have in common, Heather."

"I don't understand," Heather said.

"Yer gypsy blood. That is how ye sensed that I would soon need a place to live. God is using yer instincts and intuition to provide for my needs."

"Don't look at me," Brodie said. "I haven't said a word to anyone about your plan, at least no one who lives in Scotland."

"I don't even know what she's talking about," Finn said.

Heather tried to overcome her emotions and choose her words carefully. "I invited your mum here today because I wanted to speak to you and Jaelle about moving into the main house. I was hoping that Jaelle would consider coming on as a staff member at McKnight Farms. The house would have to be part of yer compensation package, but it would save you having to pay rent somewhere else."

"And you'd have an easy commute," Brodie said. "Which is more of an asset than you know given the number of potholes in the lane."

"That's an understatement," Finn said. "And aye, it's on my list of repairs to be made as soon as possible. Mum? How do you feel about Heather's offer?"

All eyes focused on Jaelle. "This is why I believe ye have the gypsy intuition. I have nae even shared this with Finn, but the apartment building where I live in Aberdeen is going to be renovated to make room for a new hotel and high end apartment building as part of the harbor revitalization project. Some parts of the building will be torn down, and others, saved, but all the residents will have to vacate. The building has always had beautiful views – once it is renovated, it will rent for six times as much as I pay. Anything else in the area of the hotel where I work is either so overpriced that I can nae afford it, or so run down that I would be afraid to live there. But God kens what I need and is providing for me through Heather."

Heather felt a shiver running down her spine. Somehow, she believed that Jaelle and Finn would bring healing to the old Morris house just like her babies were bringing healing to her body. She reached out to Brodie and took his hand. Could he feel it, too?

"We will accept yer offer," Jaelle said, "if there is a job I can do, and if Finn agrees that this is a good solution for both of us."

"I'll draw up an official offer this evening," Heather said. "Would you like to walk through the facility and chat about which jobs you might feel comfortable with? I want you to be doing something you not only enjoy, but where we can utilize your skills to their best advantage for the company."

Jaelle's face was wreathed in smiles. "I grew up in the house. When Duncan started to court me, I was promised that one day it would be mine. That promise is now being fulfilled through ye."

Heather went to her and gave her a hug. "The important thing is that we feel a kinship. Brodie and Finn are half brothers, and Finn will be an uncle to our child – children."

"And I will be an extra grandmother. A child can ne'er have too many grandmums."

Brodie wrapped his arm around her shoulders. "See? I told you you should sign up with the ancestry company. You always say you don't know much about your mum or da's families or how they ended up in America. Maybe one of them had the gypsy blood."

Finn shook his head. "I'll give you one thing. It's interesting to know the secrets of the past. But we all know that finding out about your family's clandestine events can not only be fascinating, but a nightmare."

"This is true." Brodie looked at her and then at Finn. "And it's up to us to turn this bad dream into a happy ending."

"Aye," Jaelle said. "It has already begun. The two of ye will find justice as the secrets of the Morris family are revealed. And the truth shall set ye free."

Heather looked around the room and wiped a tear from her eye. "There have been so many unpleasant surprises since I moved to the Highlands. Finally, today, there has been an unexpected and delightful turn of events. Thank you so much for believing in us, Jaelle. Welcome to the family."

"Aye. And thank ye. I have waited almost three decades to hear those words." Jaelle's eyes shone with love as she reached out to stroke Heather's tummy one more time.

Chapter 29

Brodie made a conscious decision not to ask Jaelle what she knew about Walter's whereabouts. He had a vague suspicion that she knew something that might help them locate Walter – maybe even Knox. But he loved the way she'd warmed up to Heather and given her the encouragement she needed. He didn't want to do or say anything that would mar the magic of the moment.

Eventually, he would have to question her. His mind tried to sift through the theories floating around in his head.

Walter had told everyone he was going Cyprus, but had he really ever gone? Brodie suspected he'd been nearby – possibly in Aberdeen – the whole time. Brodie remembered seeing a man that he'd thought to be Walter the day he'd gone to visit Jaelle. He'd brushed it off at the time, but now, he believed he'd gotten a glimpse of him just as he was about to enter Jaelle's apartment building.

The question was – coincidence, or not? Had Walter been at Jaelle's flat? Did they have a relationship, or an agreement, or some sort of arrangement? Had Walter gotten back at Duncan by wooing Jaelle into his bed? Or, had Walter played the hero and paid Jaelle's rent every month when Duncan found a new family in Cyprus and stopped supporting Jaelle and Finn?

If Brodie was going to prove his suspicions about Walter, he had to place him in Aberdeenshire around the time of the murder. If Walter was smart, or if the murder had been planned, he probably would have killed Duncan immediately before he flew back to Cyprus, and then visited Duncan's lover and daughters as soon as he got there. All Walter would have had to do was to make a big deal about what he'd been doing in Cyprus for the last few days. They would have had no reason to doubt him, and would certainly have told anyone who asked that Walter was in Cyprus at the time of the murder. The only way Brodie knew to find out for sure was to check the airline records, and the police were likely the only ones who could secure that information.

Brodie waited until Heather was finished with her shower, and then told her that he was going to head out to talk to some of the neighbours about any houses in the area around the farms that might be vacant and available for rent.

"Sorry to be so much trouble," Heather said.

"No worries. I understand completely. I still plan on talking to Da about his plans for the future, so we know if staying here is feasible, but I'd like to have some other options lined up when I ask him so he doesn't feel that he has to leave to make room for us."

"Good idea. Hopefully, he'll feel less threatened if he knows our staying here is just one of several possibilities."

"I'm not sure I'll be back for lunch. Finn said he'd stick around until I'm back just to keep an eye on things."

"You mean me. Keep an eye on me." She frowned ever so slightly. "I'll find something for lunch at the office. I keep a stash of snacks in the mini-fridge."

"Remember you're eating for three," Brodie teased.

"I know. No skipping meals."

"You could always have a pie."

"I might just do that. The new ones are awesome."

"So lunch is pie. Do you want me to stop by Alford on the way home and pick up something for dinner?"

"We could have a picnic in our favorite pasture."

"I'd like that." Brodie kissed her goodbye and walked out to his truck with Ginger at his heels, clamoring for attention. He wished his da would take more walks. It would help him to get his strength back and be good for Ginger, too.

A few minutes later, he pulled into McKnight Farm's closest neighbours to the east. And a few minutes after that, he drove away. Any houses on their property were either already full or too tiny or dilapidated to be livable. Brodie didn't mind doing a little updating or a few renovations if they found a place that would work well, but Heather and he needed a place to live now, not a year down the road. And while a bothy had a quaint, romantic quality to its history, there was no way one of the original tiny homes was going to be enough space for he and Heather and two bairns.

He drove to the next farm, a short drive to the southeast. The property backed up to Craigievar Castle, which was owned by the National Trust. The views looked to be beautiful. New owners had bought the farm the same year Brodie had left for university, so he didn't know much about them. He welcomed the chance to get to know them whether or not they had a house they were interested in letting.

"Perfect timing!" Bruce Harris shook Brodie's hand and said, "We renovated an old barn on the west side of the property for my parents aboot five years ago. The barn was perfect for them until a few months ago when Mum slipped and fell and broke her hip. We really had nae choice but to move them into the extra-care housing in Alford. I work remotely some days, but other days I'm in Aberdeen, so I was nae able to give them the care they needed."

Mr. Harris waved his arm. "Let's go take a look. There's a separate lane to the barn, but we can walk over on the path since ye're already here. I've been so busy this summer that I have nae had the time to look for someone to let the place."

"How many bedrooms?"

"Three plus an office," Bruce said. "It has a beautiful kitchen, two and a half baths, and beautiful views to the west. The only disadvantage I can think of are all the potholes in the lane. I've been meaning to get them filled but haven't had the time."

"No worries." Brodie smiled. "Heather will feel right at home. Although, eventually, it would be nice to have them patched. They're not my favorite thing."

Bruce said, "If ye'd see fit to line someone up to do the job, I'd be happy to pay the bill. I'm an insurance adjustor, but I work with a whole different set of contractors in Aberdeen – wouldn't have a clue who to call around here."

"Maybe they'd give us a deal if we had them do this one and the lane to McKnight Farms at the same time."

"Great idea," Bruce said.

He seemed like a fair man. Brodie hoped the barn was as nice as it sounded.

When they rounded the last corner, Brodie finally got a glimpse of the barn through a dense stand of pine trees. The old stone work had been re-grouted and the front door was a bright Scottish blue along with three window boxes.

Bruce stopped abruptly and held out his arm to stop Brodie. "Several of the windows are open. I had the place locked up tight so no animals would move in."

"Well, someone has moved in from the looks of it. Are the utilities on?"

"Yes. I never dreamed..." Bruce hesitated. "Should I confront them now, or wait and let the police take care of it?"

"If it was me, I'd want them out of there now." Brodie realized his advice reflected the fact that he wasn't very happy with the local police at the moment. There was no good solution. He had a bad feeling about all of this, but in his opinion, it was better to get it over with. "At least there are two of us."

They crept up the remainder of the path as quietly as they could, with Bruce taking the lead.

Brodie quickened his step to keep up. He guessed the element of surprise was good, but the closer they got to the house, the greater the sense of dread he felt.

He and Bruce would probably be able to scare off someone their age or older, relocate a needy family, or deal with a destitute bum or alcoholic, but what if whomever was living here was armed, part of a gang, or a drug dealer? He'd never been one to shy away from trouble, but he had a wife to think about and two bairns on the way, and Bruce didn't look like much of a fighter.

He saw a figure pass in front of the window, and froze. Bruce must not have seen it, because he kept on walking – right up to the door, a bit stealthily, granted, but then he started pounding on the door. The guy had guts; that was certain. Brodie would have tried to see how many people were inside, and then assessed their odds of being able to overpower them before he went right up to the door and...

There was not a sound from inside the building or out. Then Bruce called out, "Anybody home?" Brodie's eyes almost popped out of his head. Did this guy have guts, or was Bruce a wee bit foolhardy?

The fact that no one answered was kind of a no brainer.

Bruce pounded on the door once more. "Landlord!"

Okay. That was real subtle. Whoever was staying here had to know they weren't paying rent. Why would they open the door to a landlord on a place they were poaching?

Brodie decided to sneak around to the back and see what he might find. He was betting he'd have more luck with his approach than Bruce would have with his, but who knew. That's when he saw a figure retreating into the woods. He started to run. The man was tall and had long legs, but his hair was grey. Brodie had the advantage of youth.

"Stop!" No sense being coy about it now. They crashed through the woods like two elephants, the man rushing to get away, and Brodie rushing to catch him.

He watched as the man ahead of him caught his foot on an exposed root, lost his footing, and crashed into a tree.

The man howled, and let out a string of explicatives.

No. It couldn't be.

"Walter?" Brodie grabbed hold of the older man's shoulders and turned him halfway around so he could see his face. "Bruce! Get over here right now. I've caught your squatter. A squatter who's wanted for murder no less." Walter's face went pale white and for a second, Brodie thought he was having a heart attack. He hadn't witnessed his da's episode, but Munro had described it in such colorful terms that his imagination had imprinted it on his mind.

"They ken it was me?" Walter didn't seem to realize he'd just incriminated himself. But then, this was no seasoned killer, was it?

Brodie's heart softened toward the man. "What happened, Walter?" The look on Walter's face said it all – remorse, regret, fear.

Walter's face crumbled and his eyes overflowed with panic. "I ken Duncan was my brother, and the old goat had a fine way to charm the ladies, but everyone's beloved Uncle Dunk was a royal ass. He nae did anything to help on the farm, and my da said from day one that Duncan had used up his whole inheritance by the time he was twenty-five. Me and da paid out such a plenty to the women he knocked up. Nearly every cent we earned went to the illegitimate bairns." Duncan looked at him sheepishly. "No offence intended."

"None taken." Brodie sighed. "But I'm supposing it did offend you when Duncan wanted half the proceeds from the sale of the farm."

"Of course it did! I worked that land and ran the farm, supervised our crews, fixed up the house, maintained the sheds, and never took an iota of salary. The place was mine, pure and simple. My da always said so, too."

"Sorry, Walter." Brodie didn't mean to excuse Walter murdering Duncan, but he truly could understand why it had happened.

"The final straw was when he started to taunt me. Said I always blamed everything on him. And that it wasnae his fault that he had a way of satisfying the women. He said if I'd had the brains to figure out how to keep my own wife happy, she'd nae have come to Duncan. Acted like it was all my doing, and that if I'd taken care of her the way a husband should, she'd nae have had such difficulty giving birth, or taken to her bed, or slowly withered away the way she did. Like he'd done nothing wrong." Walter had tears streaming down his face by this time. "I dinnae mean to kill him, but the rock was there, and it was like it had Duncan's name written on it. So I hit him. We'd been fighting since we were born – wrestling and punching and scrapping around. At the time, it dinnae seem any different from when we were kids. But then, he dinnae move, and I couldnae get him to say a word, and I ken he wasnae breathing."

"You've got to turn yerself in, Walter. Just tell the police like you just did to me, and they'll understand. You can't live your life in fear, always on the run. You have to face up to what happened and move on one way or another."

Walter looked chagrinned again. "I guess if ye can forgive me, and Knox, then..."

Brodie's fists clenched. "You've talked to Knox?"

"He's been staying here with me since the McKnight woman kicked him off the farm."

Brodie looked around frantically. Bruce still hadn't appeared. "Do you know what Knox did?"

"Well, aye – what they're saying he did. But it's all lies. That woman fabricated the whole thing so she wouldnae have to pay him the fair wage he had coming to him."

A chill ran down Brodie's spine. He resisted the urge to defend Heather and tell Walter the truth of the matter. "Where is Knox now?"

"Gone to Aberdeen to get supplies."

"Do you know where he shops?" Brodie pulled out his phone and did a search for the police in Aberdeen. If the police in Alford wouldn't arrest Knox, perhaps the ones in Aberdeen would.

"I willnae turn my son in just because some woman—"

Brodie's face turned to stone. "The woman you're referring to is my wife, and Knox came this close to raping her. She's still bruised and battered from the beating he gave her. I know you love Knox, but you also must know that there's something wrong inside of him. He's got to be dealt with."

Walter's face was so old and tired and deflated that Brodie almost started to pity him.

"Ye might try the Tesco on the west side of town."

"How long has he been gone?" If Knox was going to show up at any minute, he needed to know.

"He should just be getting there aboot right now."

Bruce appeared just as the dispatcher from Aberdeen picked up the phone. Brodie pointed at Walter and motioned that Bruce should mind him until Brodie was off the phone. Once he'd explained the situation to the Aberdeen police and given them his mobile number, he hung up and explained the situation one more time for Bruce's benefit.

"I'm going to drive Walter into town and let him tell his story to the local police." Brodie rubbed his temples. "But if you don't mind, I'd like to take a quick peak at the house as long as I'm here. But I'll warn you, if we're to let the house, we need to make sure there is no trace of Knox left here, and no record of his ever being here, or my wife won't even walk through the door. I can guarantee you that."

"I'll take care of it immediately. Maybe if I were to

call in a professional cleaning service?"

"That would be much appreciated." The day hadn't gone at all like Brodie had anticipated, but perhaps some good would come out of the whole incident now that Walter had confessed – even more so if Knox was finally brought to justice.

Fifteen minutes later, he'd had a quick look at the renovated barn, which seemed a perfect match for their needs. He was just herding Walter to the path that led back to Bruce's place, when he heard a truck coming down the drive on the other side of the house. A door slammed shut.

"Dinnae worry, Da. It's just me. I got a half hour down the road and realized I'd forgotten my wallet."

Brodie clamped his hands over Walter's mouth and pulled him behind a dense copse of trees. Bruce followed.

"Walter?" Knox's voice echoed through the woods. "Where are ye? Walter?"

#

Heather tried not to feel nervous as she prepared for her meeting with the supplier from Castle Garden Shops and Tea Houses. She had no reason to worry – the very fact that they were interested in McKnight Farms and wanted to discuss a contract to sell their meat pies in their home and garden shops was an amazing development. But for some reason, she couldn't shake the feeling that something bad was about to happen.

It was probably because she'd had to go in the house. She had completely avoided the lounge where Knox had attacked her by diverting her eyes away from the floor as she passed through. She'd just wanted to get one of her favorite sweaters and some earrings from her bedroom. But just being in the house gave her the creeps. Which was exactly why she couldn't live there anymore, and the very reason Brodie was out looking for a nearby place to rent.

Working with the animals in the pastures and making filling for the pies were messy jobs that required comfortable, easily washed clothing. That's what she'd taken to Brodie's after their handfast. If she'd realized she had nothing suitable to wear to her appointment before he left, Brodie would have been happy to collect the things she needed. But he'd been gone by the time she surveyed the few articles of clothing she'd brought to Brodie's and decided none of them was professional looking enough for the interview.

She was going to have to move out of the house soon anyway. Jaelle had given her employer at the hotel two weeks notice and was due to begin work in another week. Finn had already offered to help Brodie pack up Heather's things. If Brodie found them a place to move into, the whole process would be easier. Storing her things in boxes at Munro's house was the back-up plan, but she hoped it didn't come to that.

She glanced at her watch as she plated and garnished the samples of the pies she'd baked for the representative from Castle Gardens. She'd hope to hear from Brodie by now. Maybe his search had taken him further than he'd thought. Don't worry, she told herself. Keep calm and carry on.

She refocused her attention on her work. The crusts on her pies were a perfect golden brown. She was proud of the way they looked and tasted. The label was cute and the packaging was spot on – so why was she a bundle of nerves? She'd been unbearably anxious since the whole incident with Knox and it had to stop! It wasn't fair to Brodie, and she felt sure it was not good for her or the babies she hoped she was carrying.

Her mobile jingled. Lyndsie from America. What was she doing up? It had to be 2 or 3 a.m. in Minnesota.

"Has she been there yet? What did she decide? Did she try to negotiate the price down or did she think what we're asking is fair?"

"I'm expecting her any minute now." Heather tried to keep her voice unaffected and professional in case the company rep happened to be approaching her office.

"Sorry! I couldn't sleep thinking aboot ye. My times must be mixed up."

Heather smiled. "No worries. You can call any time – as long as you're the one who's up and awake in the middle of the night, not me."

"So while I have ye on the phone—"

"Someone's coming. Got to go." She clicked off, stood up and went to the door to welcome her guest. Shannon Williams, she said to herself. Forgetting the reps name was just what she did not need in her already rattled state.

She had a smile on her face and a skip in her step when she walked outside to the courtyard – and saw Brodie. Bloodied, bruised Brodie.

"Oh, my goodness!" She ran to his side and wailed out her anguish. "What happened?"

"I'm going to shower and change into some clean clothes in the Loft." Brodie said. "Finn won't care, will he?"

"No. I'm sure... Brodie? Who did this?"

"Knox. I found Walter. He admitted he killed Duncan. But then Knox showed up, claiming it was Walter who attacked you, and that you just thought it was Knox because their voices are so similar."

"I've never met Walter. He was already gone when I moved here."

"No, sweetheart. It was Knox. He's just trying to take down Walter so he won't be held accountable for his own sorry actions." Brodie swiped a drop of blood from his chin.

"I'm so sorry you were hurt." Her heart was pounding furiously in her chest.

"Knox didn't admit to anything – not even breaking into the house. But the police in Aberdeen will have him soon. They'll get to the bottom of it."

"He got away?"

"I tried my best. But Walter turned on me and somehow cued Knox that I was there. Bruce – I'll tell you about him later – had gone to his house to call the police. What a mess."

A car drove up as they reached the door to the loft. This time, it really did look to be the woman from Castle Gardens.

She touched his arm gingerly. "You're sure you're okay, Brodie? If you need to go to the doctor, I'll cancel my appointment and drive you into town."

"I'm fine. I just came here because I wanted to make sure you were awright. And I didn't want Da to see me this way. Probably give him another heart attack."

"Finn is somewhere nearby, keeping watch like you asked him to." Heather tried to tamp down her anxiety. "Do you really think they'll catch Knox soon?"

"Aye. They're not going to let him get away. They'll need to interview you and Finn about what happened the night of the attack. I already gave them a statement."

"You're sure you'll be okay?"

"I'm fine. Do what you need to do."

She rubbed his arm and tried to settle her mind. "I'll talk to you as soon as I'm done wowing Shannon Williams." She left Brodie to head up the stairs to the loft, pasted a smile on her face, and said a prayer that she could keep her mind on meat pies. But seriously. What next?

She tried to think positive thoughts. Shannon had told her on the telephone that she thought McKnight Farms Meat Pies were the most distinctive, delicious pies she'd had in years. Heather felt sure their companies were meant to be linked. Her biggest obstacle was going to be finding enough staff members to deliver the quantity of products Castle Gardens would need to keep their customers satisfied. But first she had to get a contract signed. Brodie had said he wanted her to carry on, and that's what she was going to do.

Chapter 30

Brodie stepped out of the shower and found a clean towel to dry himself. The loft was still full of Knox's stuff. It only made sense that he would come back here and try to retrieve his belongings. If his half-brother had a brain, he'd come in the middle of the night when no one was around. But from what he could see, Knox's mind was busier plotting hair-brained, evil deeds than coming up with logical solutions.

He still couldn't believe that Knox had tried to blame the break in and attack on Walter. Walter's and Knox's voices did sound a lot alike. Their inflections were almost identical. But Knox had claimed that it was Walter who would have had a key to the house, so it had to have been him who came in and trashed the place.

If Brodie hadn't known that there was no love lost between Knox and Walter, he might have fallen for Knox's twisted excuses. But Brodie knew for a fact that Knox had left home because he hated Walter. Knox had not come back to the farm until Walter sold it and left for that very reason. Knox might have believed that the farm was his birthright so to speak – a double one since he was intimately linked to both Duncan, who spawned him, and Walter, who raised him. But the truth was, neither brother really wanted Knox to have the farm when they were gone. It was sad, but it was the truth.

Brodie looked in the mirror and used a wet paper towel to dab at his eyebrow. Knox was famous for wearing big, chunky, obnoxious looking rings. The thing had hurt like hell when it imprinted his face.

For a second, he felt raw anger toward Knox. And then, he thought about Knox. He'd been brought up by a stepfather who resented him, not only because he was Duncan's kid, but because he'd essentially lost his wife while giving birth to his brother's child.

Brodie's own mother wasn't perfect, but his da had loved him immensely. Despite the imperfection of having a mum and da who were separated, he'd had a good childhood. His parents had supported his dreams and ambitions for the future. He had a good job, or so he hoped – and Heather – all things that Knox did not have.

None of Knox's problems justified what he's done to Heather, but it made Brodie hate him less – maybe not at all. How could Brodie love Heather and the babies fully and completely if he harbored hatred in his heart? Knox wasn't worth it.

In a flash, he remembered he'd promised to report to Mull to begin work in what, two days? There was no way he could leave Heather now, especially not with Knox on the loose and mad as a hornet. What had he been thinking? He'd meant to call Douglas and tell him he appreciated the offer, but he needed a different assignment, closer to the Highlands, less intense, not so demanding of his time. In the chaos, he'd forgotten all about placing the call. What was he going to do?

He heard a quiet knock on the door. "It's Heather. Can I come in?"

"I'm still naked."

"Works for me." Heather came through with a smile on her face.

He felt guilty and hoped it didn't show. But all he could think about was, would Heather still be smiling when he was forced to report to Mull or lose his job? If he'd notified Douglas right away like he'd planned, there might have been a different outcome. But now, if he refused to start working as they'd assumed he would, he'd leave the team in the lurch and delay the project. It wouldn't likely go well. Plus, he had Barbara to contend with. She'd been an ally when he'd landed the job, but she would quickly become an enemy when she heard he'd gotten married and wasn't coming to Mull.

Heather seemed oblivious to the tension he felt. "The meeting went extremely well. Castle Gardens ordered huge quantities of our pies for every location in their chain."

"I'm so proud of you!" He looked at Heather and his heart filled with love. After all she'd been through, to carry on with such courage, to still be so determined and enthusiastic, was not only admirable, but inspiring.

He knew he shouldn't compare, but Heather was ten times the woman Barbara would ever be. He knew without a doubt that if he went to the Isle of Mull, Barbara would expect them to get back together, even knowing he was married. She wouldn't care. His being married to Heather simply wouldn't matter to Barbara as long as he was in Tobermory with her. Just one more reason why he shouldn't go.

"You seem so far away." Heather looked at him with sadness in her eyes. Her glance roamed over his body and then settled back on his face. "Tell me what happened. How did you and Knox...?"

"Walter Morris confessed to killing Duncan because he didn't want to have to share his inheritance with his prodigal brother. He felt he deserved all the profit."

"Rightfully so," Heather said emphatically.

"Walter knew that Knox was Duncan's son, not his. Knowing that Duncan had slept with his wife gave him another reason to hate his brother. The fact that Knox's mother died from delayed complications of giving birth to Knox only made it worse."

"Can DNA prove conclusively that Knox wasn't Walter's son? The two brothers would have shared a lot of the same genes."

"Walter said, at some point, he had his own sperm count checked and the doctor said he didn't believe there was any way Walter could have fathered anyone."

"What a sad situation."

"Aye. Once Walter found out about Duncan's sexual exploits and learned how many children Duncan had, not only close to home but scattered around the globe, the more resentment Walter felt toward Duncan. Walter said that Duncan was always the popular one, the one the ladies all liked, and the one his parents doted on and treated like a golden boy. Walter said it was just assumed that Duncan would conquer the world and go on to do all kinds of great things while good, old Walter – who wasn't all that smart or blessed with any exceptional talent or good looks, would stay home and take care of the pigs and cows, chickens and geese because that was all he was capable of. Can you blame Walter for being angry enough to bop Duncan over the head with a rock?"

Heather frowned. "Of course. But that kind of attitude is an insult to every farmer in the world. Don't people know what smarts a person has to have to run a modern day farm? You have to know your animals, how to operate all kinds of technically advanced equipment, be an extraordinary businessperson and manager of resources, be well-versed in animal husbandry, and up on local and UK laws, regulations and requirements. I could go on and on."

"You're exactly right." Even Brodie had been brought up with the expectation that he would leave the farm one day and make something 'better' of himself than 'just' being a farmer. Which brought him back to his real concern. He hated the thought of not being able to use his hard-earned engineering degree to do what he loved – build bridges over large bodies of water. Could he give it all up to stay in the Highlands to run his father's farm?

#

Heather could tell something was wrong. Was it Brodie's encounter with Knox or something else?

She could understand why Knox bothered Brodie, why they'd gotten into a fight, but Brodie seemed unusually subdued and... defeated. "So Walter turned himself in. Was Knox there when he confessed or what happened next?"

"Walter was coming along peaceably, chatting on about why he'd done what he did, and being quite amiable." Brodie sighed. "We were halfway to my car when Knox showed up. We had spoken to the Aberdeen police and they were going to head him off at Tesco and bring him in for questioning. But he forgot his billfold and came back to get it."

She looked at Brodie's scrapes and bruises. "I'm sorry."

"I told Walter to tell Knox he'd been out walking so Knox would grab his wallet and go, but Walter must have signaled him that I was hiding in the woods. Knox pretended to leave, but he circled around and attacked me from behind."

"Oh, Brodie."

"I got in some good punches, too. I hope Knox feels worse than I do, but even if he doesn't, it feels good to have vented some of my anger toward the man."

"But, Brodie." She hesitated to say anything at all, but she was afraid that if she didn't, history was going to repeat itself. "Duncan ended up dead because of brotherly rivalries and resentment. Not that Knox doesn't deserve every bit of your anger, but if you let this escalate any further, one of you could end up dead, too. Or in prison. I just can't bear to watch the two of you…" She started to cry. "I just want to have our babies, do my job, and enjoy the magic of the Highlands with the man I love. This mess with Walter and Knox is not what I signed up for when I said I'd manage William's farm."

Brodie came to her and threw his arms around her. All she could think about was that this should be the happiest time of her life, and all she felt was fear and foreboding.

Then Brodie said, "I have to tell you something."

If Brodie's face was any sort of reflection of what was going on in his mind, it was something that was going to break her heart.

Brodie swallowed hard. "I never contacted Douglas, the head of the team I'm supposed to be working with to design and build the Ardnamurchan / Isle of Mull Bridge." He swallowed hard. "I meant to talk to him about my dilemma, but things have been so crazy. And I…"

So she was a dilemma. Their marriage, the babies she was carrying, were a dilemma. Heather tried to wipe her emotions from her face. "It's been pretty wild. And I know how busy you've been, helping me and caring for your da's farm." She closed her eyes as if to obscure what was so very clear. "Or maybe you didn't want to contact him. Maybe you really want to build that bridge."

Brodie hugged her even tighter.

She pushed him away. "I understand. I'll be fine. You said the police would have Knox in custody in no time."

"I don't have to go today," Brodie said. "But at this late date, I should drive down there and talk to Douglas in person. Barbara, too. She's the one who recommended me in the first place."

"Then that's what you'll do." She straightened her shoulders and stood tall. "I trust you." But she didn't. Not really. The Highlands were her passion. McKnight Farms was her dream. She couldn't expect Brodie to share her vision, or to give up his own calling. She couldn't bear it if he were to ask that of her. She had to show him the same grace.

He hugged her again, a quick hug that reeked of guilt. "Thank you for understanding. I'll make my position clear and do what I can to help them out until they find someone to take my place."

"Sounds like a plan." She tried to sound cheerful and unworried. She knew Brodie loved her. Everything would work out in the end. She couldn't live with herself if he had to give up his job for her. He'd done so much to help her. He'd been there for her when she needed him. What more could she ask?

Brodie smiled. "I'm going to help the police look for Knox. The sooner he's caught and in custody, the sooner..."

The sooner he wouldn't have to worry about her anymore. The sooner he'd be able to leave. The sooner he could get back to his old life, doing what he loved, without feeling guilty. Without her to hold him back.

Heather cleared her throat. "Not to change the subject, but Shannon Williams signed a contract for 5000 pies a month until the end of the year, when she'll reevaluate and hopefully place an even bigger order for our winter and spring pies. I couldn't be happier. Even if you were here, I'd probably be so busy I'd barely have time to say hi."

Brodie gave her another quick hug. "I'm so happy for you, Heather. I knew your hard work and creative ideas would pay off. William will be so proud of what you've accomplished – and in such a short time."

She buried her face in his neck. Such a short time. The same short time she'd known Brodie McBryde.

Chapter 31

Heather hated that she'd grown so dependant on Brodie – and in such a short time. Really. She was glad he was going to be gone for a few weeks. It would be good for both of them. It wasn't like she was going to be alone. She would still be staying at Munro's and Finn would be around the farm most days – Jaelle too, in another week. Her mum and da were only a couple of hours away, and even Lyndsie and William, a quick phone call across the Atlantic.

She wrapped her sweater around her torso a little more tightly in the hope that it would catch and trap a bit more of her body heat. The further into the fall calendar they got, the deeper the chill in the Highland mornings. She paid a handful of bills, went online and filed a quarterly report required by the government, and reviewed her latest sales projections. William would be thrilled.

When she was done, she phoned the cleaning company she'd hired to get the main house ready for Finn and Jaelle, and the loft for William and Lyndsie or her mum and da and any other guests who might need a place to stay. She confirmed the date and time they were scheduled to come. The housekeepers had been instructed to box up Knox's clothing and personal effects. How and when she got them to him was something she didn't care to think about. She'd also hired a locksmith from Alford to change the locks on the main house, the loft, and her office. She liked the security she felt when she contemplated that.

It felt good to be on the road to a fresh, new start. She'd even given thought to the idea of leasing out the loft as an Airbnb stay. It would generate more income for the company when not in use by McKnight Farms, and be a fun way to meet and make friends with travelers from around the world.

"Miss Heather?" Finn rapped on the door to her office. She thought about correcting him again, but decided that, due to developing circumstances, Miss was a fair assessment of who she was.

"Hi, Finn."

"Just wanted to let you know that I'll be in the west pasture checking on the Hairy Coos and the black faced sheep. One of the men heard there's been a fox poking around the area. I'll do a count of the lambs and inspect the fold for loose rocks."

"Good idea. Winter isn't far off, and it's far easier to make repairs now than when it's cold and windy."

"Aye." Finn tipped his hat. "I love working outdoors again but there's already a nip in the air in the mornings.

"Definitely. I wouldn't be surprised if we find frost on the heather one day soon." Heather adjusted her sweater where it had fallen open. The buttons were probably in a dumpster somewhere surrounded by pieces of glass after they'd popped off during the attack. She made a note to ask the cleaning crew to double check for buttons before they vacuumed. She was sure her mum would sew them back on for her if she could find them. She might have thrown the sweater away if it hadn't been one of her favorites. She was glad her mum had rescued it.

"Take care," Finn said. "I'll have my mobile in my pocket in case you need anything. Unless you'd rather I stick around here and leave the pasture for another day."

Heather didn't smile, although his offer was kind and born of concern. She knew Brodie had asked Finn to keep an eye out while he was gone. "Thanks, but I'm sure I'll be fine."

"If you're sure."

"I am. The animals come first."

"Well, that's not what Brodie said, but I get your meaning. I'll not neglect my duties. If I need to work a few more hours while Brodie is gone, so be it."

She waved him off and got back to her paperwork.

She was deep in the throes of payroll when her mobile rang. "Hi Brodie."

"Good morning, sweetheart."

"Where are you at?" She could hear engines idling and doors opening and closing.

"I'm on the Ardnamurchan Peninsula waiting to catch the ferry back to Tobermory. There was such a lineup of cars when I got here that I didn't make the first one."

"Sounds like it's going to be a long wait."

"Aye. If anyone's still not convinced they need a bridge connecting the peninsula to the island, I can certainly attest to the timesaver it will be."

"Well, thanks for checking in." She glanced at her computer screen and tried to figure out a polite way to say that she needed to get back to work. It wasn't that she didn't want to talk to him, but at this point, there was little to say. And she did have a lot to do.

"I just wanted to let you know that I'll be out of touch for about an hour once I begin crossing. I never have bars when I'm on the water."

"I'll be fine. Finn just poked his head in and I told him the same thing."

"Still no word on Knox?"

"Sorry. No." She wasn't sure she wanted to tell Brodie about the call from the police, but she guessed she should. "Walter was able to pay a bail undertaking, so he's been liberated. He can't leave the country, and it's been strongly suggested he stay in Alford until his trial."

She heard Brodie draw in a ragged breath. "Do you think Knox will find his way back to his da then?"

"I hope not." Her right hand started to shake. "Brodie? I really need to get back at it."

"Any new applicants that might ease your load?"

"Not a one. I'm just thankful to have Jaelle coming on board."

"Aye. She and Finn are a Godsend."

They had just said their goodbyes when her mobile rang again. After so many interruptions, she was tempted to let it ring, but she knew it would drive her crazy if she didn't pick up.

"Heather?" It was Jaelle. Her voice sounded anxious, high-pitched, almost frantic. "I have a visitor here with me who would like to talk to ye."

She heard a noise, looked up and saw Finn.

"I came back to get some of those running snares we bought last week. No lambs missing yet, but I saw plenty of suspicious paw prints on the edge of the woods, so thought I'd better get some in place."

Jaelle was still on the line. "Heather? Knox would like to speak to ye, if ye have a minute."

Heather saw what was likely a reflection of her own facial expression on Finn's face as they both grasped the fact that Knox was at Jaelle's flat. She shushed Finn and wrote *GO!* on a piece of paper. Finn raced out the door and started his truck. She hoped he would also alert the police to Knox's whereabouts.

Now, to do her part. "I'm listening," she said, trying to hide her dismay. What could Knox want with her?

"Heather?"

"Yes." She choked back the bile that rose in her throat.

"Ye need to call the police in Aberdeen right now and tell them it wasnae me who trashed yer house and attacked ye. Ye need to tell them the truth – that it was Walter."

"Walter?"

Knox faltered. "I should have told ye from the beginning, but I was trying to protect him. Our voices sound so much alike that I'm nae surprised ye were taken in."

"Okay," she said cautiously. The last thing she wanted to do was to upset him, knowing he was alone with Jaelle.

"Walter has gone in. I'm sure they'll get the truth out of him. But they willnae let up looking for me and trying to take me in as long as ye're spreading the rumor that it was me."

It was hard to keep the disgust and loathing from her voice, but she tried. Jaelle must be terrified. "Okay. I'll get hold of the police then. And tell them what you said." She paused. "You're sure it was Walter? I don't understand why he would—"

"When Walter sold the farm to William McKnight, he told me to look Mr. McKnight up, as he would need someone to run the farm for him, someone who kens the place, and could advise him. No one suspected he would bring in some woman from America who dinnae ken anything aboot the Highlands or the farm business."

"So he was angry that you didn't get the job." Heather ignored Knox's insults, took a deep breath, and resolved to carry on the farce as long as she could in hopes Finn had called the police. She prayed they were on their way.

"He was trying to scare ye off. Walter ken that if ye went running home with yer tail between yer legs, William would do what he should have done in the first place and give the job to me."

"So it's my fault I got attacked."

"Aye. If ye had left after I–he trashed yer house, the rest would nae have been necessary."

Heather's anger started to spike, but she ignored the feelings of rage boiling up inside her. She didn't want to do anything to endanger Jaelle.

"Ye've got to tell them the truth!" Knox yelled.

"I will." That, she could promise. "I promise you I will tell them everything I know."

"But nae what ye think ye ken. What I told ye."

"I understand."

"And ye'll do it?"

"I promise you I'll call them as soon as we get off the phone."

"Nay!"

Heather held her breath. The man was crazy. Poor Jaelle. She prayed that Knox wouldn't hurt her. If he did decide to try something, there was no way Finn would get there in time to save her.

"Okay, Knox. What do you want me to do? You tell me and I'll do it."

"I want ye to leave. I'll run the farm and live in the main house. It's almost impossible to find staff right now. William will be glad to have me. He should have hired me from day one."

She didn't want to lie, but an idea had occurred to her. "Knox? Has anyone told you that Brodie and I got married after you, well, left town? You may not know that his job is taking him to the Isle of Mull to build a bridge. Of course, I'm devastated that he can't find a bridge to build closer to home, because the commute to the Western Isles is just completely prohibitive. We're in the midst of trying to find a solution. I haven't said anything to William yet, but the fact is, I'm very likely going to have to resign my position so I can live with my husband."

"Ye lie. Ye love the Highlands."

"Ask Jaelle if we got married."

She could hear a muted conversation in the background and hoped Jaelle would tell him what he needed to know without going into too much depth. Jaelle certainly knew about her and Brodie's wedding, but she also knew full well that Heather had no intention of quitting her job at McKnight Farms.

Knox came back on the phone. "Ye're telling the truth?"

"I am."

"So there's hope."

"There's always hope."

"Will ye talk to William? Tell him how good I am with the animals, and how much the old staff members like me. I could get them to come back, ye ken."

"I'll tell him what you said, Knox. I promise I will."

"What time is it?" Knox's voice sounded frantic.

Jaelle called out the time.

"I need to go, Heather. I will be in touch, and I will ken whether ye've done what I asked. Make sure ye talk to the police, and spread the word around town, and speak to yer Uncle William."

She'd done her best to keep him on the line. She could only hope that Finn, or even Jaelle, had called the police, and that they got there before Knox disappeared again.

Knox disconnected the conversation. She dialed the Aberdeen police immediately to tell them of his last known location. And she prayed Jaelle was still healthy and well.

#

Brodie knocked on the door of Douglas' construction trailer and waited for an answer. He knocked again, but no one came to the door. He'd gotten up at the crack of dawn to make sure he was there to meet Douglas at the start of his day. No one had been around when he'd arrived the day before, so he'd started with measurement and depth analysis. He'd been told that Douglas would be in today. The only thing he could think to do was to camp outside the door to his office until he arrived.

He was eager to get home to Heather, and more than anything, determined to set up some sort of remote work arrangement. He couldn't solve any of those problems unless he could talk to the right people, and at the moment, that didn't seem possible.

He was doing some comparisons of the bridges Denmark had used to link their islands when his mobile rang.

Finn. "He came to my mum's flat. If he laid a finger on her, I'll kill him."

"Knox?"

"Aye! Who else? I'm on my way to Aberdeen now, but Heather called and she thinks Knox has already left. Probably knows he needs to stay ahead of the police. Jaelle isn't answering. I don't know what to think, but I'm nervous."

"Heather called? From where? What's she got to do with it? Is she okay?"

"Knox called her from Jaelle's with a long list of people she's supposed to talk to on his behalf to clear his name. Like that's going to happen. She's also supposed to talk William into hiring him to replace her as manager of McKnight Farms."

"You've got to be kidding." Brodie got up and paced the perimeter of the forest at the edge of the worksite. "But she's okay?"

"She's a bit shook up. Otherwise fine except that she's alone at the farm. I know I was supposed to stay with her but I've got to make sure Mum is okay."

"I understand," Brodie said. "And I'm also well aware that Knox could show up at the farm again at any moment."

"Well, I can't be two places at once," Finn said. "Heather told me to go."

"I'm not blaming you," Brodie answered, knowing he would if anything happened to Heather.

"Brodie? Is that you?" A man he assumed to be Douglas hollered from the drive in front of his construction trailer. "We finally meet! I am happy to have you onboard after hearing so much about you. Welcome!"

Great timing. He had all kinds of questions for Finn, but he could hardly tell Douglas he'd talk to him in ten minutes. If he ignored him and lingered on the phone, he'd be labeled as rude and disrespectful.

"Tell her she can't stay at the farm alone. Tell her to get back to my place and stay with Munro until the danger has passed." It should be he who called Heather, but he couldn't. He hoped Finn would step up. "I have to go."

He clicked off his mobile and walked over to Douglas. "Aye. I've looked forward to meeting you, too. And I do need to talk to you about some things." He reached out his hand. "Good to be here."

"Right! Barbara called me a couple of days ago all upset because she'd heard a rumor that you got married and weren't going to show up." Douglas eyed his face, which was still showing signs of his fight with Knox. "I hope your new wife didn't do that to you."

"No. Long story, but it did involve her, if defending her honor counts."

"So you did get married?"

"Aye." He didn't go into detail because the details were too complicated.

"So what does she think about you being half of Scotland's width away from her? Or will she be joining you?"

"It's complicated. We're both thankful Scotland's a small country." He gathered his courage and took the plunge. "That's what I need to talk to you about. Is there any way I could work remotely part of the week, or stay in the Highlands this winter and work on the design from home, touching bases via Zoom or whatever program you like to use?" Douglas didn't say anything. He waited and waited. Douglas didn't look happy. "Unless you'd rather be rid of me." Still nothing. "If you'd rather, I can talk to someone in Edinburgh and see if anyone's building a bridge over a deep valley in the Highlands."

This was not going well.

"You're not getting off that easy. You committed to being a part of this team. I committed to head up this project. I – we're – the entire team is relying on you. We need you and your expertise to complete the project in the time frame allotted. I can't pretend your change of circumstances doesn't matter. But at this point, it would be almost impossible to replace you, so I'm afraid we're stuck with you. This is a very demanding project. You need to be here body, mind and soul and you need to be 100 percent committed to your work." Douglas looked stern and unyielding. Brodie wasn't easily intimidated, but he also didn't want to lose his job. For starters, he was going to need the income assuming he and Heather had twins on the way.

Brodie knew he needed to stand up to his boss, but he needed to do it in such a way that he didn't anger or offend him. Was that even possible? He gathered his wits and tried to speak in a way that was confident but not arrogant. "Under normal circumstances, I would never suggest that I be granted permission to work remotely, but Heather is pregnant with twins, and she needs these babies. She's scheduled to have a hysterectomy as soon as they're born. She was also assaulted and almost raped not more than a couple of weeks ago and her attacker is still on the loose. I just can't be so far away from her right now." He hadn't meant to blurt it all out, or to play the sympathy card, but honestly, much as he wanted this job, he had to be in the Highlands right now. That's where his heart was. He loved what he did, but he loved Heather more.

"I don't see how it could work, but I'll give it some thought given the circumstances are what they are. And I'll speak to my bosses at headquarters. Depending on their response, you may have some hard decisions to make."

"That's all I can ask." Brodie hesitated. "I'm here. Do you want me to finish off the day?" But he was thinking, please send me home.

"Yes. This little stunt of yours is not only going to set us back, it's going to cost me a great deal. I'll take whatever I can get from you." Douglas turned away from him and then turned back. "Get to work."

"Aye. sir."

What was he going to do now? Please, Lord, he prayed. Let Heather be awright.

Chapter 32

"Mum?" Heather locked the door to her office from the inside and tried to decide what to tell her mum – or not. Her mum was too far away to do anything to help except listen. Heather was hoping Violet would do just that without getting all worked up. She'd thought about calling Lyndsie but decided not to involve her or William. Lyndsie was such a firecracker, and especially sensitive about the situation since she was related to the Morrises. Both she and William felt somewhat responsible for the troubles Heather had experienced since coming to the Highlands.

Her mum's voice was warm and reassuring. "So how is it living with Brodie and Munro? I hope you feel comfortable and – safe."

Her mum's voice was so compassionate it hurt.

Heather didn't want to lie, and she did feel pretty safe when she was at Brodie's. But right now, she was terrified at the thought that Knox would try to rape her again. He'd all but gotten away with it the last time. The police hadn't even filed charges. Why not give it another go if they were going to look the other way?

"Brodie is down in Tobermory right now. The bridge project I was telling you about has officially begun, and Brodie felt it would be best if he spoke to his supervisor in person about working out a schedule that wouldn't require him to be there all the time. A lot of corporations are still letting their people work remotely."

"I hope it works out the way you're hoping it will. Maybe when you get your staff back up where you need them to be, you can spend some time down on Mull with him. Rose and Ian would love to see you a little more often if you're able to swing it."

Heather felt like she was being hugged the second her mum mentioned Rose's name. Rose had been through so much, and was wiser and stronger for it – a true inspiration.

"I can't wait for Brodie to meet them. Although if he's working long hours like it appears he will be, he won't have much of a chance to socialize. And if he's back here on the weekends, he won't be able to go to Ian's church."

"Well, that's one more reason for you to drive over to Mull and spend a weekend with Brodie every so often."

"It's a good idea in theory, but I'm still working seven days a week. Maybe once Jaelle gets here, I can take a little time off every once in awhile."

"Speaking of Jaelle," her mother said. "Have you bought a pregnancy test yet? I'd love to just take the woman's word about your twins, but it would be nice to have confirmation."

"Right. I'll get one eventually. I was hoping not to have to buy it at the grocery in Alford. I'm afraid the news would be all over the Highlands by the next morning."

"I understand. It's the same way in Dornie. Small towns."

Heather sighed. "It's even worse when you're the new girl in town." She didn't say it to her mum, but she could just imagine what people would think if they caught her buying a pregnancy test. Heather knew the babies were Brodie's, not Knox's, but if she were to go and buy a kit, everyone would probably think she really had had sex with Knox. Most married couples didn't try to conceive a baby on their honeymoon night, but Heather had known more than one woman who accidentally got pregnant with one man and then quick married another to make sure everyone thought the husband was the father of the children.

Her mobile rang through with a call from Brodie. "Have to go, Mum." Violet said a quick goodbye and clicked off.

"Hi, Brodie."

"Finn called me just as I finally got a chance to speak with my supervisor. I don't have long to chat, but you have to get over to my house before there's any possibility that Knox could drive from Aberdeen to the farm. You have to stay safe. Please go now. If you wait too long, you won't even be able to safely walk across the pasture."

"I understand." She had been so rattled by Knox's call that she hadn't even thought about it. "I'll go as soon as I finish with my—"

"Go now!"

"Brodie?" An unfamiliar man's voice interrupted Brodie's words. Heather could hear him like he was in the next room. "I thought I made it clear that just being here isn't enough. Really being here means concentrating on your assignment and not making personal calls while you're on the job."

"I have to go," Brodie said. "Just finish your work quickly and go home as soon as possible. Watch your clock and make sure you're there by the earliest moment

Knox could be at the farm."

Brodie's mobile went dead. She could only imagine how frustrated he must be about his phone call being cut short. It wasn't like they'd been talking for an hour or about something trivial.

At least he'd been able to warn her. Although what he was asking her to do wasn't all that comforting. Sure, she could leave now and run back to Munro's like a scared little rabbit, but what then? Would she, Jaelle, Finn, and Munro all have to live in fear, constantly worrying about when Knox might show up?

She looked at the stack of work on her desk and decided to work for at least a few more minutes. Who knew what tomorrow would hold, and whether or not she'd feel safe even coming in to her office? Gone were the days of open doors and people dropping by at will. She hated that Knox was robbing her of her freedom.

She needed to check the sheep in the grazing grounds near the woods where the fox had been seen as soon as she finished her paperwork. If she hurried, she could do it on the walk home.

First, she needed to finish a promotional pamphlet to include with the pie orders the garden shop had placed. It shouldn't take long, although she wanted the copy to be just right – upbeat and trendy, yet homey and comforting.

She started to write as quickly as she could, hurrying to rewrite, and edit and rewrite it again, until she finally had it down. She wished Brodie or Finn was around to try it out on, but an empty room would have to do. If it sounded good to her ears, she would call Lyndsie or William and see what they thought. She polished off her most confident voice and read it aloud.

"Pies from the McKnight Farms Kitchen are a

handcrafted wonder of delicious, buttery pastry filled with fresh and tasty fillings – slow-cooked beef, tender chicken, melt-in-your-mouth pork, locally-sourced vegetables, and lamb fresh from our own Highland pastures. At McKnight Farms, we sift East Lothian milled flour and knead our pastry in small batches until it's the perfect consistency for a light, flakey bake. Our pies are glazed with eggs from our own free range layers. Easy to prepare and with the ability to freeze, our pies are ideal for home and commercial use. Already nominated for Great Taste and British Pie Awards, our new flavours will captivate your taste buds. You can now buy our pies at Castle Garden Shops and Tea Houses throughout the Highlands and beyond."

She loved it, if she did say so herself.

But when she looked down at her mobile, almost an hour had gone by.

Her hands started to shake. It had felt so good to put her problems aside for a few minutes and get something done! Accomplishing a task she'd been putting off felt even better. But – she tried to do the math in her foggy state – Knox could have left Aberdeen as early as an hour and ten minutes ago. That meant she had to get home to Munro's now.

She gathered her purse, wrapped her sweater even more tightly around her shoulders, and peeked out the door. There was so sign of anyone. She looked one more time, slipped out the door, looked both ways, and dashed across the courtyard to the pasture. It was the shortest way to the McBryde's. There was no reason anyone else would be walking cross-country between her farm and theirs. She needed to check the lambs anyway.

Her eyes were wide open as she started across the field. The fox that Finn had mentioned preyed on her mind. She steered clear of the forest and walked though the center of the pasture, winding around tall patches of grass and clumps of faded heather.

Her eye caught a glimpse of something at the edge of the woods. A shadow? She came to a complete stop. Was it the fox? Probably a tree or a big branch. She saw a limb hanging from a bigger branch, probably blown down in the last windstorm. The leaves clinging to the dangling branch were dark brown and crumpled. It had startled her. That was all.

Or... it could be Knox. It had been over an hour and a half now, close to two. Depending on how fast he'd driven, and how the traffic had been, it could be him stalking her. More likely, it was a fox. At that moment, she'd most definitely rather face down a fox than meet up with Knox again.

She shivered. The bright sunshine that had flooded the field got lost behind a cloud, turning everything in its path dark. The grass, now enrobed in shadows, looked almost black, the heather, a deep brown. She looked down to make sure she didn't step in a hole.

A foxhole. She brushed off her fears and kept walking. She was just imagining things. It was completely natural for her to be a little freaked out. But there was nothing to be afraid of except her own insecurities.

Her eye caught a bit of color in the grass. It was too late for rhododendrons and heather. What other flower would be so bright? The terrified eyes of a half-eaten little lamb, it's bright, white coat stained with blood, stared up at her. One foot was gone. A leg bone, eaten clean, stuck out from the curly wool. The fox would be back. She'd probably interrupted its meal.

Her scream stuck in her throat. She ran. She didn't

stop until she came to the stile that went over the top of the fence. A cloud of dust was the best predictor of an auto coming down the lane, and she could smell the dirt being kicked up before she saw the car.

#

Brodie's shift was fifteen minutes from being over when Finn called to update him on the situation with Knox.

"Jaelle is fine. Shook up, but she'll put it out of her mind. The scary thing is, she feels sure that Knox is heading home to Alford, and she insists you're in danger. How she arrived at that conclusion, I don't know. But you know how she is about reading into the future. Maybe it was something Knox said. They obviously had words I don't know about."

"I wish I was there."

Finn grunted. "I'm just glad she's not hurt. Knox evidently stole a key to her flat from a keychain I had when I stayed at the loft. Clever one, he. Do be on guard."

"He won't find me whilst I'm here in Tobermory. Jaelle most likely confused me with Heather. Please watch out for her until I get back."

"I promise you I will." Finn's voice was strong and reassuring.

"I can't talk much longer. My boss is looking for reasons to make me out to be an irresponsible eejit."

"One last thing. There's a fox prowling about the area, so I set some running snares in hopes that no more lambs will disappear. Now I'm told I should have gotten a permit. Are you familiar with them and do you know where I need to go to get a permit in Alford? I don't want to bother Heather about it with all that's going on."

"You'll have to go to Banchory. All I know is that you need a permit, and that once the traps are placed, they have to be checked every 24 hours. And please tell Heather where you put them. She walks across the pastures between my farm and the house to check on the sheep quite often."

"Done." Finn disconnected and Brodie went back to measuring the slope of the incline down to the sea.

In his mind, the more he could get accomplished when he was on site, the more likely it was that Douglas would soften and not be so rigid when he needed an extra day or two at home.

He tried not to feel irritated at being interrupted again. Of course, if it was Heather, he wanted to take the call. But – Knox? Every muscle in his body tensed when he saw the caller ID.

"Ah, Brodie." Knox's tone of voice was designed to irritate and ignite. "Did ye ken that ye are the last person on earth I would have chosen to be my brother?"

"It doesn't surprise me. But I don't know why. What have I ever done to make you hate me?"

Not one second passed before Knox answered. "Ye have what I want. Ye always have."

Brodie rolled his eyes in disbelief. "What? You lived in the bigger house on the larger farm. Your grades were very comparable to mine, maybe even better at times. You had more friends. You had three girlfriends before I went on my first date."

"Ye had a mother who loved ye. Mine was dead. Ye had a da who doted on ye and encouraged ye to do yer best. All I ever got from my da was criticism. I was ne'er good enough. I couldnae do anything to please Walter."

"You're a smart man, Knox. You know as well as I do

that you can't base your self-worth on what others think of you."

"But with Heather and ye telling people I trashed her house and tried to rape her, people are going to hate me. That's why I told her she needs to tell the truth – so people ken it was Walter that attacked her, nae me."

Brodie didn't want to incite Knox. He wanted Heather to be safe. But to ask Heather to lie...? "Sounds to me that this is between you and me, Knox. Let's leave Heather out of it and settle this like men, shall we?"

There was a pause and then Knox spoke. "I will settle it like a man – by making Heather my wife. The farm will be mine to run, and once I get Heather pregnant with my son, it will be Morris Farms once again. Perfect."

Brodie's heart clutched. Knox wasn't kidding around. He was dead serious. "You know it will never happen."

"I should be the one running Morris Farms, nae her. And it will be Morris Farms again. I will be in charge and run things my way. Heather will stay home with our bairn."

"You're delusional, Knox. Heather is not going to tell anyone how wonderful you are."

"She has nae done it yet, but she will." Knox's voice was cocky with assurance.

Brodie contemplated how Knox would know or not know whether Heather was spreading the word about how wonderful and helpful Knox was. The only possible explanation made him very uncomfortable. It confirmed to Brodie that Knox was either nearby the farms or Alford, and knew what Heather was doing – or not, or, that Knox had friends, spies, in high places. It was scary. But he wasn't about to tell Knox that.

What he did say to Knox, very adamantly, was, "Heather is not going to marry you."

"She will when ye're gone."

The mobile connection went dead.

Chapter 33

For three horrible days, Heather waited for Knox to appear. He did not. Brodie was still gone, but it was almost the weekend, and Heather couldn't wait for him to return. Jaelle was shaken up, but fine. Finn was back at work, and had put out more traps to try to catch the fox that had been stealing their lambs. The next day, Brodie would be home and Finn was going to go back to Aberdeen one last time to help Jaelle move out of her flat and into the big house at McKnight Farms.

By Monday, they'd be settled in and justice would be restored on at least one level. But that knowledge did nothing to calm her nerves.

Where was Knox? Scared as she was, all Heather wanted was for him to show up and be done with it. The tension and apprehension were horrible. Munro had driven her to the farm to retrieve her computer and enough work to keep her busy while she waited things out at his house, but it wasn't enough. She wanted to be free. She ran a farm, and although the things she could do on her computer were part of it, she needed to be outside, and supervising pie production and taking animals to market and buying new breeding stock, and a hundred other things.

The fox had not yet been caught and another lamb had been attacked.

The suspense was awful. Why didn't Knox just come?

"Maybe it's because he's waiting for you to meet his demands," Brodie suggested. He'd called early to avoid irritating his supervisor.

"But to do that I need to spread the word around the farm and go into town."

"You can call the police. Take Munro with you when you head into town. You must need to go to the grocery. Just try."

It went against the grain to even think about praising Knox – for anything. He'd been a disappointing employee who had undermined her at every opportunity, he'd ransacked her home, and then he had tried to rape her.

"Yes, it involves telling a few lies, but if it draws Knox out into the open, it would be worth it."

"Okay." She struggled to take a deep breath. "I'll do it. I can't keep living this way." Her biggest fear was that even if Knox was caught, the police would let him go again and the intimidation might never stop.

As soon as she'd said goodbye to Brodie, she called the police.

"I was wrong," she told the receptionist, and the officer, and the detective. "I'd be negligent if I didn't tell you that Knox is innocent. It was Walter who assaulted me. Knox was only trying to help. The reason he didn't tell you what really happened was because he didn't want to implicate his father. Knox has actually been wonderful. In fact, the more I think about things, I've come to realize that it should be him who's running the farm instead of me. Please, just ignore what I said the night of the attack. I was – you know – in a state because I was upset."

When Finn was done at work, she asked him to take her into town to go to the grocery. They stopped by the church on the way so she could brag Knox up at the Ladies Bible Study, and then, the grocery, where she casually mentioned to Finn, in a loud voice, what a huge help Knox had been to her, and what an asset he had been to McKnight Farms. She made sure to say how happy she was that the whole misunderstanding with the police had been cleared up. They stopped by the farm on the way home and spread good tidings of Knox among the remaining staff members who were still at work. She was sure they couldn't wait to tell the others.

Finn gave her a little time to gather some papers she needed to work from home the next day, and then offered to drive her to Munro's.

"I think I'd rather walk if you don't mind. I could use some fresh air."

Finn gave her an odd look. "If you don't mind me asking – what's going on? I couldn't believe my ears when we were in town. I thought when we drove home you'd tell me the truth, but you didn't say a word. I never dreamed you'd lie to your staff, so now I'm wondering what is happening. I'm worried about you."

"Would you consider walking me home through the pasture?"

"No problem. I need to check the running snares anyway, and I should show you where the new ones are set."

She didn't want to risk explaining things to Finn where someone might overhear them, and she didn't want to get tangled in a trap. It was all good. At least that's what she tried to convince herself.

The truth was that she was exhausted emotionally and physically. The combination of her already weary body, pregnancy emotions, and stress – lots and lots of stress – was taking a toll on her.

When she walked into Brodie's house and saw Munro sitting on the couch with one arm slung over the back and the other holding the remote, she lost it and started to sob. She wanted Brodie, or her da to hold her and give her hugs and just listen to her talk.

Munro must have read her mind because he said, "I'm sure ye'd rather my son or yer own da were here to comfort ye, but I'm happy to fill in if ye'll let me."

She thought back to their first meeting and cried some more at the thought of how their relationship had grown from instant dislike to a gentle understanding.

"I'm so sorry about all the trouble I've stirred up. It's not fair to you or Brodie. I keep thinking that even if Knox is arrested this time, he won't be in jail for long since he didn't actually rape me. Plus, I can't even prove for certain that it was him who attacked me."

"There's been bad blood between Knox and Brodie since they were boys. A lot of history there that has nothing to do with ye. So ye can stop feeling guilty aboot that."

She went to the couch and sank down next to Munro. "But you're supposed to be minimizing your stress levels and working to un-complicate your life. I'm sure all of this – me plopping into your home unannounced and riling up a hornet's nest – is not helping."

Ginger hopped onto the sofa and snuggled up to her. The dog wasn't supposed to be on the furniture or even inside the house, but Munro wasn't as keen on keeping her outdoors as Brodie was.

Munro squeezed her hand. "Ye have to remember I've got a fair amount of experience being a da to a son who's nae my own flesh and blood, but is a true son nonetheless. Now, ye're my daughter. That's just how it works out sometimes."

Her heart melted. "You know. Brodie never really said... How long have you known?"

"Always, in my head. Never, in my heart."

Munro's arm was still slung over her shoulders. They sat in comfortable silence for a long time as she contemplated how much Munro loved Brodie even though he knew he wasn't his real son. How did Munro find it in himself to choose joy over bitterness? More importantly, could she do the same?

It was at that moment she knew that whatever happened with Knox, and the babies she hoped she was carrying, and all the other complications in their lives, she and Brodie would be fine.

#

Brodie's longing for free time to go and do where and what he wished was far more than a regular case of the long workweek woes. It was killing Brodie not to be with Heather, first because they were still in their honeymoon period and the bond that he felt made it pure torture to be separated from her. And second, because Heather was in danger. It was his job to protect her and their babies.

He'd thought long and hard about the threats Knox had made against his own life, but he really believed it was Heather who was in danger. He had to find Knox and make sure he couldn't harm any of them. He couldn't do that when he was working in Tobermory. It had been a long week, and Brodie was beyond thrilled to be going home for 2 days. He intended to leave the second the clock said five pm.

"Sorry aboot yer plans for the weekend going awry." One of his co-workers gave him a wave from the other side of the pier. "I'm bummed, too. My daughter's third birthday is supposed to be tomorrow, and I'm going to miss it."

"What?" Brodie's hackles raised.

"I'm planning on moving the family up here as soon as I have time to look for a place on the peninsula – can't afford island living. But it's hard to even look for a place when we have to work weekends."

He had a bad feeling. "I was never told anything about working this weekend."

His co-worker was a surveyor and not an engineer. Maybe the surveyors were being required to work the weekend, but not him.

"He's right," Brodie heard Douglas' voice from behind the construction office. "We're all required to work the weekend because of the dreich weather we've had this week. We're finally going to have some sunshine tomorrow and Sunday that we can use to catch up on all the tasks we're running behind on."

Brodie lost it. "I can't work the weekend. I shouldn't even be here now, but I've stayed to fulfill my commitment to you and my job. I'll be back bright and early Monday morn, but I need to try to resolve the dangerous situation I told you about back in Alford this weekend."

His boss planted his feet against the cobblestone plaza and said, "I cannot require from one man what I do not require from all. I cannot make an exception for you."

Brodie knew he could lose his job if he refused his boss' directive, but he had to get back to Heather. He had to find Knox and make sure he was taken into custody. But he also knew that his boss needed him and would have a hard time replacing him if he were to quit.

"Can I speak to you privately?" Brodie waited until they were inside the construction trailer before he spoke again. "I committed to this project for a three year period. Three long years, during which time we'll have weeks when we're going to get behind, and weeks in which we're going to accomplish far more than you think humanly possible. My da could die during that time, your mum or da could die. A child could take seriously ill. My wife will have our babies, and very probably surgery immediately following. I have to know that I can have personal time built into the schedule."

"I've explained that we're on a tight time frame. If I gave that kind of consideration to everyone on the crew—"

"The time frame you committed to has got to include not only dreich weather, but downtime in the midst of a crisis. I already explained to you that I'm perfectly capable and more than willing to perform my duties remotely or work double time one week so I can have time off in the midst of a personal crisis."

Douglas glared at him. "It's obvious you think you're someone very important, that you think you should be granted a higher degree of consideration than myself or your co-workers."

"I'm a hard worker, and I've always produced above and beyond my supervisor's expectations. It's not like I'll just disappear or go AWOL without fulfilling my responsibilities. If we're going to work together, I have to know that you respect me enough to work with me instead of against me. You'll get the best work from me if you let me work this out my way instead of chaining me to the foot of the bridge and forcing me to do things your way. I'll not let you down if you're reasonable with me."

"I'm sorry, but that's just not the way it works around here. I understand that you feel compelled to ask, but—"

"I'm not asking. I'm telling you I will be leaving for Alford..." Brodie looked down at his watch. "Now."

Douglas' eyes blazed with hostility as Brodie turned and walked to his truck. He didn't turn back. When he got into his vehicle, he saw that Douglas was still staring in his direction. One more person hating him was not what Brodie needed, but he had to do what he had to do. He tried to compose his emotions so Heather wouldn't pick up on what had happened. When he thought his voice was steady enough, he rang her up on his mobile. There were parts of the trek where there was no reception, so he wanted to touch bases now, while he could.

But Heather already sounded upset. "I did what you said, Brodie. I bragged Knox up all over town and to the police and the McKnight Farms crew, where I'm sure he has friends. To be honest, they seemed relieved that I'm no longer trying to cause trouble for good old Knox. At least, that was the attitude I picked up on."

"Probably right. You've got good instincts. Knox has always been popular around town. Star athlete, good-looking, charmer, both pitied and admired because he had no mother yet turned out so well even though it was only Walter to raise him."

Heather's sigh sounded deep even over the mobile. "What I don't understand is, if everyone thinks Knox is so wonderful why doesn't he show himself? I've done what he asked and restored his good reputation around town. Why not come forward and see the situation resolved one way or another?"

Brodie didn't want to worry Heather, but he didn't want to keep her completely in the dark either. "Because Knox has a plan. I'm not sure what it is, but I have good reason to believe that Knox plans to hurt me. He may try to discredit me, or at least make it look as though I've betrayed you or done something terrible. He wants people to hate me and sympathize with him."

"He wants to be the hero of the story." Heather's voice was somber.

"Yes. I also believe he wants you, and the farm, too." Brodie tried to be gentle. If she were to detect the anger he felt, it would not help her or their situation.

"Well, he can't have me," Heather said. "I'm yours. Heart, soul and body."

"Thank you, sweetheart. I'm sorry to say that I'm going to be driving through a low valley with high mountains on both sides, and you know what that means."

"Drive safely," she said.

"I love you, Heather. No matter what happens, remember it well."

Chapter 34

"I'm sorry to say it, but there will be nae more deliveries from the Royal Mail until yer road is fixed. The potholes are so deep that they are causing damage to our vehicles and scaring our drivers."

Heather set her jaw and tried to defend herself. "But if you go slow—"

"Our drivers dinnae have time to drive slower than slow, up and down a lane as long as yours. Why do ye think yer wholesaler refused to deliver to ye? They have the same trouble. They feel the same way. Ye're asking too much."

"All that's needed is a little patience. I've contracted a road repair firm to haul in some fill and repave the road. They keep saying they'll come, and then they don't. It's out of my control until then."

"I'll nae budge on my decision. Until the road is repaired, ye'll have to come to town to pick up yer mail and yer wholesale orders. The grocery has offered to be a dropping point for your wholesalers."

She knew Brodie would have a fit if she went into town by herself, so she called Finn and asked if he would go with her.

And that's how she found herself in the grocery once again.

Her plan was to get in and out as fast as possible.

She had just rounded the corner to the area where the coolers were when she heard someone say, "It's hard to believe a nice guy like Brodie would get one girl pregnant and marry another, but I ken Teresa. She's definitely pregnant and she's sure Brodie is the father."

"Well, they were pretty tight in high school. It was a dream come true to see them get back together until that American woman showed up."

Heather suddenly felt lightheaded, almost nauseous. This couldn't be happening.

"I heard Teresa's having twins."

What? No! No. She didn't believe it. Tongues wagging about things they knew nothing about. That was all. Who knew? Maybe one of them had it out for Brodie for some reason.

"I cannae believe Brodie's nae going to help her financially. Not even if she has a paternity test, from what I hear. What a jerk."

Heather tried to block her ears. She would have gone if she hadn't been picking up a wholesale order of goods they needed to make more pies. The whole thing was preposterous. She'd been the source of all kinds of rumors since she came to town. None of them were true. And the people who spread them were the last people on earth she would believe. She realized Brodie had a life before he met her, and if that included physical relationships with other women, she couldn't fault him. But Brodie would never ignore the ramifications of his past actions and refuse to help support children who were his.

She tried to turn off her brain and ignore the rumors. She finished her shopping and was just ready to head back to Finn's truck when she heard the same voices in the throes of another conversation.

"Fool. If she wanted to marry a real man, she could have had Knox Morris. I hear he's got a thing for her."

"Knox is twice the man Brodie McBryde will ever be. She as much as said so the other day when she was here bragging about Knox saving her from whoever attacked her. Some women just can't see the trees for the forest. Especially American women."

"Aye. Totally clueless."

Heather resisted the urge to retaliate or at least say something scathing. She kept walking, holding her head as proudly as a person could when they had pregnancy hormones raging and felt like dissolving into tears.

Finn must have been able to read the look on her face. "Rough time in the grocery?"

"Gossipers spreading rumors about Brodie and me. Nothing new."

"They'll latch on to anything and anyone who's new. Fresh bait."

"I wonder if I'll ever be completely accepted."

Finn put his arm across the seat of the truck and gave her shoulders a quick squeeze. "May as well give them something else to gossip about."

"It can't make things worse than they already are." She tried to relax and forget the horrible things they'd said. "Finn? I just remembered I have an announcement about Brodie's and my handfast typed up and ready to drop off at the church. Pastor doesn't have internet. Do you mind if we stop so I can give it to him?"

"No worries."

Two blocks later, she jumped down from the truck and walked up to the church. She hoped Pastor would be in his office and he was. She handed him the announcement she'd printed up and assured him that she and Brodie were both doing well.

Pastor cleared his throat. "I'm assuming ye've heard aboot Teresa then. Sorry turn of affairs, but it did happen before Brodie met ye. If yer faith stays strong, it will carry ye through."

Heather could feel the blood draining from her face. "I heard what they're saying, but I don't think it's true. Brodie hasn't said a word."

The pastor frowned. "Teresa was here just yesterday asking for counseling aboot what she should do. I dinnae ken her exact due date, but she's showing. Best talk to Brodie aboot it as soon as ye can. I can only suppose, but he likely felt ye had enough on yer plate already without having to deal with this, too."

"So Brodie has spoken to you about what happened with Teresa?" Heather hadn't seen Teresa since the day she came looking for Brodie at McKnight Farms. Probably a good thing. Her heart was broken enough.

"Nay," Pastor said. "Just Teresa. That's why I recommended speaking to him aboot it. There are always two sides to a story. Hearing the truth from Brodie will hopefully bring a greater understanding to the situation."

Heather didn't know what difference hearing Brodie's version of a tale that included his old girlfriend being pregnant with his twins would make in the long run.

"Oh, I'll be talking to him awright," she promised.

Pastor's phone rang and he motioned for her to wait a moment.

"What?" Pastor sounded shocked. "No." He looked at Heather, his face registering obvious panic. "I'll be right there."

He hung up the phone. "This is aboot to be public knowledge since Teresa's mum is being transported to hospital, so I'm going to tell ye now. Brodie was just involved in an altercation at Teresa's home. It seems her mum complained aboot Brodie's refusal to help Teresa with the babies financially. There was a confrontation and Teresa's mum was injured."

Heather grabbed at the chair opposite Pastor's desk and barely sank into it before she collapsed.

"I'll walk ye to yer car on my way to hospital."

She managed to eke out, "Where is Brodie now?"

"He fled the scene. The police are searching for him now. Did ye ken he was in town?"

"No." But she'd known he would be back. She'd assumed he would come to her first. He'd had her convinced that he missed her terribly was worried for her safety. That he loved her.

She was almost back at Finn's truck after saying goodbye to the pastor when her mobile rang. It wasn't Brodie, thank goodness. She wasn't eager to speak with him. But she knew she recognized the number.

"Heather? This is Mr. Donaldson from the bank. I'm very sorry to have to tell ye this, but we've had a suspicious withdrawal and we wanted to notify ye immediately. Under normal circumstances, we may not have noticed a moderate amount like 20,000 pounds, but it came at a time when yer funds were low."

Twenty thousand pounds might seem moderate to the banker, but it was no small amount to her. She was horrified. "We haven't received payment for a large order of pies that went out two days ago, and I just had to pay in advance for my wholesale food shipment due to a delivery glitch. But I have no idea why there would be a large withdrawal."

"The money was withdrawn using your electronic password. That could mean that whoever it was is someone who has access to yer password, or, it could mean that someone hacked into yer computer. Either way, I would recommend changing all of yer passwords immediately. We're investigating the situation but all we know so far is that the transaction was notated with the initials B.M."

Brodie McBryde. Heather knew in an instant that one of two things had happened. What had Brodie said the last time he spoke to her? *"Knox may try to discredit me, or at least make it look as though I've betrayed you or done something terrible. He wants people to hate me and sympathize with him."* He'd said *"I love you, Heather. No matter what happens, remember it well."*

The question was, had Brodie said what he had because he truly believed Knox would make good on his threat to destroy him, or because he'd already betrayed her and was playing her for a fool?

#

Brodie sat at a dead stop at the west entrance to the new Corran Narrows Bridge over Loch Linnhe. He was never a fan of traffic delays, flaggers or pilot cars, but this time it was even worse because he was so close to home. His impatience grew by the minute. Not only did he want to see Heather and make sure she was safe, he was afraid he was going to be late to his meeting with Knox.

He still didn't quite understand why Knox had called him to try to work things out before they escalated any further – Knox's words – but if it meant Knox coming out of hiding so he could be apprehended, it was all good, and exactly what they all wanted. Knox being in custody was the only way he and Heather could resume their normal routines and go safely about their lives.

He'd tried to ring Heather to tell her he'd be late a couple of times, but she wasn't picking up. When Knox had called, Brodie had just been leaving Tobermory and had no reason to believe he'd be late getting back to the farm. He'd already been in line at the ferry terminal, and assured a spot. He'd checked the traffic reports to see if delays were expected along the route, and no road construction had been anticipated.

He peered as far into the distance as he could and couldn't see any indication of trouble, but it was a long bridge. Probably a car accident. That's when he noticed the design of the bridge. It was definitely not as long as the bridge he was working on, and its feet extended into a deep loch instead of spanning a fiord, but the design was not entirely dissimilar to what he was working on. He held his phone to his eye and snapped a couple of photos so he could refer to them when he was back on the job. If he was back on the job.

The minutes clicked by and finally, a long string of cars came through on the one lane that was open. And came. And came, and came, and came. When the procession finally ended, he was no less impatient. The accident must have been bad if it was taking this long to sort. He looked to the flagman for a signal that he could go but his stop sign was still held high. He tried to occupy himself with thoughts of bridge designs once again. Too bad he couldn't have been a part of the crew that built this bridge. He snapped another couple of photos. Ten or fifteen minutes later, the flagman waved him forward, and the string of cars heading east finally started to move.

The rest of the trip flew by. He'd intended to stop at the farm and see Heather before meeting Knox, but he was running so late after the delay that there was no time. He hoped the police from Aberdeen hadn't arrived before he did. First, he wanted to hear Knox's explanation aka flimsy excuses about why he'd done what he did, and second, he wanted to see his face when the police apprehended him. Knox might have the Alford police in his pocket, but the Aberdeen police knew what was what when it came to Knox Morris.

The pasture was quiet when he arrived. Knox had said to meet him where they'd found Duncan's body, probably because it was a secluded area bordered by woods. Sneaky like Knox.

Knox's truck was no where in sight. Neither was there any sign of the Aberdeen police.

Brodie got out of his truck and warily approached the pasture. There were no birds singing, no cows mooing, no sheep bleating. The whole world had gone eerily still. He walked in a circle, eyeing the perimeters of the grazing land. He straddled a low fence and crossed into the field, still looking for Knox. Were the shadows in the forest shifting ever so slightly, or was he dreaming? Was that a flash of red? He thought he saw something or someone streak from behind one tree to a second. Finn had mentioned setting out snares for foxes.

A second later, he saw a blur of activity coming from the woods. Knox ran toward him, followed by a handful of police. Finally! The timing was a little off – he wasn't going to get to have it out with Knox, but he felt a huge sense of relief that Knox was about to be nabbed and held accountable for his actions. It was about time.

He gradually became convinced that something was wrong, and was sure of it when Knox and the police got closer. The police didn't catch up with Knox, which he would have thought they would, them being trained in pursuit and theoretically in good physical shape. Then Knox veered sharply to the right, and the police kept running – not toward Knox, but him. What?

He stood tall and waited for them to stop. What reason would they have to come charging toward him? He looked again. Their faces were familiar. These police were not from Aberdeen, they were from Alford.

He started to run toward his truck, which was on the other side of Knox. Unfortunately, Knox was a gloating spectator at this point, and it didn't take him long to see what was happening. Knox tried to intercept him. Brodie stuck out his foot. Knox tripped and he kept running. He heard a yelp just as he reached his truck and jumped in. The police stopped to help Knox, who had evidently caught his foot in a snare.

Brodie started his truck and roared down the road. Who knew where the police and Knox had parked? Probably on the other side of the woods. Lucky for him, he would end up with a nice head start. But on the way to where? He had no idea where he should go, or why the police were after him, or who to go to for help. He preferred not to involve Heather, and he didn't want to give his da another heart attack.

Finn? He should be at the farm. The driveway was a one way disaster and if he drove slowly enough to navigate the potholes, he'd be giving the police enough time to catch up with him, which would leave him trapped at the farm with no way to escape.

He thought about driving straight to the police station in Aberdeen, but something told him he needed to find Finn. He was almost at the turnoff when he decided to ditch his truck and run across the pasture between he and Heather's places. It was shorter and would take a fraction of the time. He was banking on using Finn's truck to leave. He prayed he would be there.

A few minutes later, he was pounding on the door to Finn's loft. Finn's truck was in the courtyard, but it was Jaelle who answered the door.

"Jaelle! Can you help me? The Alford police are after me and I don't know why. I need to get out of here and figure out what's going on."

"Finn is in the far pasture with the Aberdeen Angus calves. Come with me." Jaelle started to run. He followed her behind the shed.

"I hope ye ken how to run this thing, because I sure dinnae," Jaelle said.

The key was in the four-wheeler, and yes, he did know how to drive it. The woman was pure dead brilliant.

She hopped on the back. After the shock wore off, he decided he would enjoy having her along for the ride. His heart was beating a little more quietly knowing he had an ally. He hoped she could tell him what was going on.

Twenty minutes later, they'd given the police the slip and found a place in a woods three farms over to hide out.

They hadn't had a chance to talk – couldn't over the roar of the engine.

"What is going on? Is Heather okay? Do you know why the police are after me?"

"I only know what Finn has told me, but I feel a great sense of evil regarding yer half-brother, Knox."

"Your instincts are good."

"Heather is fine. The babies are fine. But she kens – thinks she kens, aboot what ye have done, and the other set of twins you created with Teresa."

"What? I have not created anything with anybody

but Heather. I saw Teresa for five minutes sometime this summer and we did nothing but talk." He knew Knox was going to try and get to him. "What else have I supposedly done?"

"The police are after ye for beating up Teresa's mum after she challenged yer decision nae to help Teresa and the bairns financially. They say they have DNA that is a match to yers."

"Ridiculous." When did I supposedly do this?"

"Earlier today. Ye're a wanted man."

His mind was racing. He could account for all of his time except the hours he'd spent on the road. "And Heather believed this woman?"

"Nay. Nary a word when she heard it being discussed by the gossips at the grocery. But then she heard it from yer pastor, who seems quite convinced that Teresa and her mum are telling the truth."

Brodie wanted to scream. Did it ultimately matter if the women were lying if everyone believed they were telling the truth? The damage had already been done. Heather's trust and confidence in him had been destroyed.

"This DNA found at the site – if Knox is involved, I wonder if our DNA is similar enough to confuse the tests."

"Brother against brother. It never bodes well."

"Jaelle? I feel like I need to go to Heather. What do your instincts tell you about that?"

"She needs to hear the truth from ye. But ye will be walking into the lion's den. Knox's hatred for ye is deep, and I believe he wants ye out of the way so he can have Heather and the farm."

"If Knox impregnated Teresa and then beat up her mother – just enough to make it look bad, and compensated them with some sort of monetary reward for participating in his little scheme..."

"Or threatened them with worse if they dinnae comply – the man is evil, I tell ye."

Brodie let his mind fly through a list of scenarios. "It wouldn't have been hard for Knox to get some of my DNA from the farm – or from me directly after we fought the other day. Knox drew blood with his knuckles and got a fistful of my hair at one point."

"If Teresa demands a paternity test, the bairn could show up as a very close match if it's Knox's because ye are brothers."

"I thought that you said Teresa was pregnant with twins?"

"I believe there is only one bairn. Twins is a lie designed to make Heather more suspicious of ye."

Brodie motioned for Jaelle to get back on the four-wheeler.

Jaelle said, "I believe Knox intends to make ye look so bad that when he kills ye, everyone will think ye deserved to die because of the horrible way ye treated Teresa."

"Knox wants to be perceived as a hero for killing me."

"Whether by death or destroying yer reputation, he's setting the stage to get ye out of the picture."

"And out of Heather's life."

Chapter 35

Heather took a deep breath and tried to fight the waves of panic that were flooding over her.

She tried to think good things instead of bad. God would take care of her. He already was. Munro was an unexpected ally and she knew without a doubt that he would love her and her bairns just as unconditionally as he had Brodie. She'd been blessed with a loving set of parents who would support her through whatever lay ahead. William and Lyndsie loved her like she was their own child. She knew she could count on them no matter what transpired. Even her brother was someone who she knew would help her if the need arose. She would make it through this. She could and she would.

She heard a commotion in the yard and went to the window. Ginger sounded so distressed and frantic that her barking sounded like more like crying.

Knox? Her heart started to pound. It looked like he had a posse of police with him. Were they there to protect her from him or what was going on? No matter what Brodie had done or not done, it didn't excuse Knox's actions and assault on her.

She went to the door and opened it a crack. Ginger lunged through the opening and came to her side, ready to protect her. Munro came through from the kitchen.

"We're looking for Brodie McBryde."

"I haven't seen him all week."

"Me neither," echoed Munro.

The police ignored Munro and looked at her like she wasn't capable of telling the truth, pure disgust written all over their faces. Knox had obviously won them over. She suddenly felt a great sense of dread. Knox was just evil. Somehow, he'd twisted things to make her out to be the bad guy, and now, he was trying to destroy Brodie. This whole thing with Teresa was a ploy on his part to get rid of Brodie. And she'd almost fallen for it.

"I'm nae sure if ye're aware of the allegations that have been made against yer new husband, but if ye see or talk to him, ye need to contact us immediately."

Hadn't she once heard that people often accuse someone of doing exactly what they'd done to make themselves look innocent? That's what Knox was trying to do to Brodie. Who knew how he'd convinced Teresa and her mother to play along? He'd probably paid them off – or just charmed them into doing his bidding. Knox could be very persuasive when he wanted to be.

But none of it mattered. It wasn't going to work with her. She knew that Brodie loved her – and that he would never do what they'd accused him of.

But what to say to the police? "I'm looking for him, too," she said. "So it would seem we're in agreement about that."

She saw Knox approaching the house. Her knees went weak with repulsion at the sight of him. She could smell the cloying scent of whatever cologne he used. Oh, yes. It had been him who tried to rape her awright.

"He's here," Knox said. "He's got to be here. His truck is just down the lane and he's nae in it. If I hadnae stumbled into the snare, we'd have him already."

She cringed. She was relieved to hear that Brodie

was nearby, but Knox and his friends made her nervous. They were like a lynch mob of good old boys.

Munro flared. "She said she has nae seen him."

"She's lying. Ye ken the first thing he'd do was to run to her – to protect her from me." Knox laughed. "Besides, where else could he be?"

"I repeat," one of the policemen said, "If ye cover for yer husband, ye will be charged with aiding and abetting."

She looked at Knox, took another sickening sniff of his cologne, and felt suddenly emboldened. "He's in the root cellar," she whispered. She couldn't see Munro's face, but she hoped he would play along. Even if he didn't, and called her out, they'd believe her. They were already convinced Brodie was there.

The men grinned and looked at each other with drooling leers on their faces. "We have him now," one whispered.

She pointed to the kitchen and put a finger to her lips. "Shhh..." She tiptoed toward the sink and stood to one side when she got to the heavy wooden door that went to the root cellar.

The men started down the stairs, at first trying to be quiet, and then, realizing the futility of it. Her mind raced with what ifs as she watched them race down the stairs. If this didn't work, Knox would probably beat her to a pulp while the others watched him put the little liar in her place.

The last man crossed the threshold and started down the stairs. She could hear the men calling out, trying to find the light switch.

Her hands were trembling as she swung the heavy door shut. Munro saw what she was doing and helped her lower the wood board that latched into an old iron bracket. The door was locked, and there was no way out.

Heather was halfway to her and Brodie's bedroom to get her mobile when Brodie burst through the front door.

"Brodie!" She had never seen him move so fast.

His arms were around her waist in seconds. "You're awright?"

"For the moment. I just sent Knox and his cronies down into the root cellar to look for you."

"Oh, baby," Brodie said. "You're not only beautiful, you're genius."

"Will ye two quit mooning at each other and figure out what we're going to do?" Munro said.

Heather came out of her trance when she heard the men pounding on the door and yelling. She also saw Jaelle peeking around the corner of the front door. She didn't ask for an explanation but waved her inside.

"I called the police from Aberdeen before I left Tobermory and asked them to meet me here," Brodie said. "Any sign of them? I was late because there was an accident on the bridge."

Munro snorted. "They're nae going to be any help to ye now. Knox was in their jurisdiction when ye called them the first time, but this is different."

"Jaelle," Heather said. "This is Munro, Brodie's father."

Jaelle smiled. Heather looked at Munro. Munro had a silly grin on his face. His eyes sparkled. She'd never seen him like this. He looked like a boy again.

"Oh, I ken Munro," Jaelle said. "We were friends when we were growing up."

Munro smiled. "The years have been kind to ye, Jaelle."

Brodie said, "I hate to spoil yer little reunion, but

we're in a bit of a crisis here. We need to come up with a plan."

Intriguing, Heather thought. "Munro, Jaelle and her son, Finn, are going to be moving into the house where I was at McKnight Farms. You'll have plenty of time to get reacquainted."

"I'll look forward to it," Munro said.

"Good grief, Da," Brodie said.

"I can barely hear ye above the clatter." Munro tried to look stern and ended up sporting another silly smile.

Jaelle smiled back.

"Snap out of it," Brodie said. "They're going to bust down the door."

Munro was thinking. Heather could almost see the wheels turning. She had to give him one. It was hard to concentrate with all the screaming and cussing rising up from below.

Munro said, "The old police chief. The one who's retired. What's his name? He was friends with my da."

"Grandpa?" Brodie asked. "Do you mean his friend, David Thompson?"

"Aye."

"He must be 80."

"Aye, but he'll ken what to do. He grew up in Aberdeen. Moved here to head up the police department. He may ken people who can help."

Heather typed the name into her mobile. "Here." She dialed the number and handed the phone to Munro, who explained the situation, or what he knew of it.

"If ye could talk to someone on the Aberdeen force and tell them we need back-up as soon as they can manage it, I'd be grateful." Munro nodded. "He's on it."

"Thanks, Da." Brodie looked impressed.

Heather started to relax.

"Would ye like to go for a wee walk while we wait, Jaelle?" Munro still had a big smile on his face. "Leave these two lovebirds to get on with their reunion?"

Jaelle looked pleased. "I'd like that very much."

Heather and Brodie also went outside to wait but they sat on the front steps and watched the sun slip down behind the mountains and listened to the sheep baaing in the pasture. The sky was streaked with slivers of pink and lavender, yellow and peach. Shades of green outlined the stone fences and wildflower hedgerows to make a patchwork of the rolling hills in the foreground. The mountains were layered in blues and purples with overlapping valleys and peaks. It was the Highland reverie Heather had always wanted, and she was sitting beside the man she'd always dreamed about and finally found. Except for the curses piercing the evening air, it was nearly perfect.

They could see Munro and Jaelle walking in the distance, their silhouettes glowing where the sun backlit their forms. Why hadn't she thought of introducing them sooner? But they already knew each other. Maybe now was just their time.

The clattering from the cellar had not grown any quieter when the Aberdeen police finally arrived.

"Nay worries," the police assured them. "We'll take care of everything from here on out. Now that we have Knox on breaking and entering charges in Aberdeen, we'll be able to hold him and prosecute in our jurisdiction."

"Thank you," Heather said.

"Let's go walk in the pasture where we said our vows," Brodie suggested, reaching for her hand.

"Good idea. I don't want to see or have memories of these people being in our home." Heather linked her fingers in Brodie's.

Brodie's long legs set the pace. "We've got a few obstacles to jump over before we find a clear path to whatever it is ye want our future to look like."

"I'm going to trust that God will work it out when the time is right," Heather said. "He brought you home to the Highlands and brought me here at just the right point in time. "It's only the details that need smoothing. The basics are in place."

"Speaking about things that need smoothing, I noticed the potholes on the road have been patched."

Heather squeezed his hand. "Just yesterday. Maybe it's a sign."

"Aye. The choppy waters are behind us now. There'll be smooth sailing from here on out."

"I love you so much, Bridge Builder Brodie McBryde."

"And I love you, Highland Heather."

There was a scuffle behind them, and Heather glanced over her shoulder just long enough to see that the Aberdeen police were still in control of the situation.

Brodie kissed her hand. "And you trust me to do what needs to be done to figure out our future?"

"As long as ye'll come home to the Highlands as oft as ye can," she said.

Brodie took her hand and kissed her. "Then I think we have a plan."

She kissed him back a little more inventively. "Many are the plans in a man's heart, but it is the LORD'S purpose that prevails."

"Well, the Lord has taken pretty good care of us up until now." Brodie kissed her again. "I can live with it if you can."

"I'm so glad you're going to be the father of my

baby."

"Babies. Have a little faith."

She kissed him again. "Aren't McBryde sheep famous for twinning?"

"They are."

"Then it's a McBryde specialty. Double the pleasure, double the fun." Heather watched as the Aberdeen police drove down the lane. Joelle and Munro were walking toward them, and a few seconds later, joined them in the corner of the pasture where they'd held their handfast.

Jaelle smiled knowingly. "The twins are growing stronger with every day. And they will nae be yer only set."

"Oh, my," Heather said.

Brodie smiled. "That's what happens when a man's plans are blessed by the Lord."

Heather said, "And when a Highland lass meets a bridge builder."

"Aye," said Munro. "They have a love that spans the ages."

THE END

If you'd like to read more about Finn Codona, be on the watch for Sherrie's upcoming mystery, ALPINE MEADOW. Brodie and Heather (HIGHLAND HEATHER,) Munro and Jaelle, Nathan and Violet (SHY VIOLET,) William and Lyndsie (SWEET WILLIAM,) and all your favorites will be there waiting. Coming in 2023.

ABOUT THE AUTHOR

By day, Sherrie Hansen operates a Victorian B&B and Tea House, the Blue Belle Inn. By night, she paints, writes murder mysteries, takes photos, plays piano, and goes on European adventures. Sherrie and her husband live in Northern Iowa.

Made in the USA
Monee, IL
13 April 2022